Populazzi

Populazzi

Elise Allen

Houghton Mifflin Harcourt

Boston   New York

The text of this book is set in Adobe Garamond.

Library of Congress has cataloged the hardcover edition as follows:
Allen, Elise.
Populazzi / Elise Allen.
p. cm.
Summary: When awkward, socially inept Cara moves to a new school just before junior year,
her best friend urges her to seize the opportunity and change her life using "The Ladder"—a
concept that will allow her to climb to the top of the social order by transforming herself into
the perfect girlfriend for the most popular boy in school.
[1. Interpersonal relations—Fiction. 2. Popularity—Fiction.
3. High schools—Fiction. 4. Schools—Fiction.] I. Title.
PZ7.A42558Po 2011
[Fic]—dc22
2011008437

ISBN: 978-0-547-48153-1 hardcover
ISBN: 978-0-547-72196-5 paperback

Manufactured in the United States of America
DOC 10 9 8 7 6 5 4 3 2 1

4500367136

To Randy, Maddie, and Riley,
the loves of my life

Chapter *one*

"Don't you see, Cara? This will be the year everything changes!"

I laughed out loud.

I hated to do it. Claudia is my best friend in the universe and has been since kindergarten. Still . . .

"What?" Claudia asked, but I was already halfway under my bed, dragging out the giant plastic bin in which I keep all my journals, from my first grade Hello Kitty diaries through the leather-bound notebooks I use today. Some would say under my bed isn't the smartest place to hide my most private thoughts and observations. Surely my parents could find them there. What if they wanted to sneak in and read them?

The truth is my parents would never read my journals. Not because they're such saints, but because after sixteen years (twelve, technically, for my stepdad), they're 100 percent confident there's nothing juicy in them. This is part of my problem.

"'Deer Diary,'" I read from Hello Kitty, "'today I go to first grade! It will not be like kindergarten. It will be grate for

Claudia and me.'" I held up the page so Claudia could appreciate not only the spelling but also the adorable stick figure drawing of the two of us holding hands, massive grins on our giant bubble heads. Claudia nodded; adorableness noted.

I tossed that diary aside and grabbed a turquoise journal with cover art featuring a plume pen spouting a rainbow of sparkles. "'Dear Diary,'" I read, "'fourth grade was the same as always. It's all about fifth grade. *This* is when everything will change.'" I dropped the journal and plucked up a funky striped notebook in gradations of pink, red, and orange. "'Okay, diary,'" I read, "'tomorrow starts Junior High. *Junior High!* It's a whole new school! Seriously—this is the year everything changes.'" I looked at Claudia. "I could go on."

"Don't," Claudia said dramatically.

Claudia says everything dramatically. Her mom read Shakespeare to her insanely early, and she took the "All the world's a stage" thing to heart. Not that she's an attention hound. Unless she's playing her cello, the very idea of being in the spotlight sends her ducking for cover. She's not fake either; it's just that her real-life emotions are maybe ten times larger than other people's.

"I know what you've always said," Claudia continued, "but this year is earth-shatteringly different. You're going to an entirely new school, where nobody knows anything about you. Nor do they know about . . . The Incident."

The Incident was pretty much the inciting event in our friendship. It happened on the first day of kindergarten. Ms. Jewel lined up our class for a trek to the bathrooms—"a potty party"—first thing in the morning, but I was way too nervous to do anything but count to ten and come back out again. That meant by halfway through circle time my bladder was so full I was dying, but I was too embarrassed to raise my hand and say anything. Instead I danced in my spot on the floor, madly jouncing my crisscross-applesauced legs and squinching my face super tight. Looking back, I can't believe that Ms. Jewel didn't realize what was happening . . . or what *would* happen if she kept ignoring me.

Heather Clinger was the first to notice. She pointed and squealed from across the circle, "EWWWW! That girl peed herself!"

Immediately, the kids on either side of me leaped away screaming, while the rest of the room laughed or sneered. I didn't want to cry, but I couldn't help it. I just felt so small and embarrassed and ashamed . . .

Until a grinning little girl with super-pale skin and the same two looping black braids she's worn every day of her life cried out, "Look at me! I peed my pants, too!"

The girl was Claudia, and she was sitting right next to Heather, who screamed again. The whole room erupted into chaos. Finally, Ms. Jewel called in an assistant, who took Claudia and me out of the room, cleaned us up, and shoved us into mismatched castoffs from last year's lost and found.

"Were you embarrassed to raise your hand, too?" I asked her.

"No," she said, shaking her braids. "You just seemed sad to be the only one all wet with pee. So I did it with you!"

Just like that, I'd made a best friend for life.

Unfortunately, while our origin story formed an intense bond between Claudia and me, it permanently grossed out everyone else in the class . . . all the same people who would follow us through elementary school, junior high, and Pennsbrook High School. And while it's not like they actively held day one of kindergarten against us, it's pretty tough to kill such a vivid first impression. The Pants-wetters were never going to be allowed among the Populazzi: the most adored of the social elite.

But now Claudia was right: I wouldn't be with those people anymore. The day after sophomore year ended, my family had moved from Yardley to Malvern—about an hour and several Pennsylvania Turnpike exits away. My new classmates all went to Chrysella Prep, a charter school my parents kept telling me was "known for both the teachers' and students' creative thinking and extreme academic excellence." They'd shown me a brochure about it called "The Charter School Difference," but it didn't seem terribly different from Pennsbrook at all . . . except for the fact that every single student there was a complete stranger whom I'd meet for the very first time in just three days, fifteen hours, twenty-five minutes, and thirty-one seconds.

Not that I was freaking out about it or anything.

Claudia leaned toward me, her dark eyes intense. "You have the chance to rewrite your life story. No, not the chance . . . Reinventing yourself is your *destiny!* It's in the name of your school: Chrysella, the chrysalis from which you will emerge, no more a pupa, now a butterfly!"

Actually, the school was named after an ex-student named Chrys who'd died from some rare and hideous disease, but I couldn't tell that to Claudia. She was on a poetic roll. I was fairly certain her last phrase had been in iambic pentameter.

"You can be anything at Chrysella," Claudia continued. "You can break into their Populazzi. You can even be the *Supreme* Populazzi: The Most Popular Girl in School."

That's when I really should have laughed. The Incident notwithstanding, I have never been the Supreme Populazzi type. It's not that I don't want the title; who wouldn't? SPs never get laughed at for personal quirks like navigating the halls with their nose in a book. SPs never feel shy or insecure; they can walk into any room and know that everyone there is dying to see them. SPs never have to pine for the guys they like; those guys pursue *them*.

So I should have laughed, but I didn't. I recognized the look on Claudia's face.

"You have an idea," I said.

"I have a *plan*," she amended. She reached into her fuchsia, faux-leather shoulder bag and pulled out a huge, overstuffed yellow binder, which she thudded down in front of me. "I hereby present: the Ladder."

Sure enough, there it was on the front of the binder in black-Sharpie calligraphy: "The Ladder."

"What is this?" I asked.

"Your ticket to a new life. The Ladder is how you climb from one tier of the Popularity Tower to another."

"You *can't* climb from one tier of the Popularity Tower to another."

That was the whole point of the Popularity Tower. Claudia and I had named it and all of its tiers back in seventh grade. There were kids who were more and less popular before that, but by seventh grade everyone was cemented into a specific and universally accepted Tower position. Like it or not, you were either a Happy Hopeless, Cubby Crew, DangerZone, Penultimate Populazzi, or Supreme Populazzi. You didn't get to choose, and you didn't get to change.

"That's what we always thought," Claudia said. "But there *is* a Ladder. Its rungs are relationships. You can climb into a new Tower tier if you have a boyfriend there. You get that boyfriend by already having one in a slightly lower tier. Having a boyfriend makes you desirable."

"Okay . . . but I don't have a boyfriend." I said it like I was talking to a mental patient. It's not like she didn't know.

"Not *yet*," Claudia said. "When you get to school, you target a first boyfriend: someone who's not a total loser but is low enough on the Tower that he's easy to get. From there, you date your way up higher and higher until by the end of the year you've achieved the ultimate goal: Supreme Populazzi and the title of Junior Prom Queen. Your date for that event? The male Supreme Populazzi—the most spectacular guy in the entire junior class."

Claudia glowed with excitement. She loved this idea. I was tempted to take her temperature. And maybe check her pupils for concussion.

"Claude, I've never had a boyfriend. How am I supposed to 'target' some guy and get him to go out with me?"

"That's the beauty of a brand-new school!" Claudia said. "You can be *anyone,* including *exactly* what each guy you target thinks is the perfect girlfriend."

"So I lie to these guys, use them, and that makes me popular?"

"You don't lie. You highlight different aspects of your actual personality. And you don't use anyone. They're *guys*. Guys are psyched to have girlfriends. You'll be helping them. Just like you, they'll be more desirable when they're part of a couple. When you're ready to move on, it'll be easy for them to get someone new."

It was a lot of insight for someone with as much guy experience as I had. In other words, next to none. Claudia *had* seen a penis, but it was attached to her first cousin Rob, who's fourteen and a total dork. His idea of biting satire is to tape googly eyes and paper elephant ears on the front of his jeans, then let "the trunk" hang out of his fly.

I, on the other hand, have never in my life seen a penis. I've tried to imagine what that eventual momentous occasion might be like, and even spent a whole class period once staring at the word in my notebook, but all I pictured were other words you could make from its letters. Like SPINE. And SNIPE. And E-SNIP, which seemed like a good name for an online circumcision service.

"You have doubts," Claudia said. "You shouldn't. I've done the research." She nodded to the binder. "Open it."

I did. The book overflowed with reams of magazine articles, written notes, and Xeroxes of book and newspaper pages.

"My God, Claudia, when did you do all this?"

"You were busy packing; I had time on my hands." She scooted next to me to read over my shoulder.

"The whole book is filled with evidence," she said. "Tons of situations where the Ladder led to success. Like in the musical *Evita*—how does Eva Perón go from poor villager to First Lady of Argentina? The Ladder. Or *Cinderella*—a million different Cinderella stories from a million different places in the world and a million different points in history turn a scullery maid into royalty. How? The Ladder. And it's in real life, too! Would anyone care about Yoko Ono's art or music if it weren't for John Lennon? Would anyone care about Sharon Osbourne's opinion if she weren't married to Ozzy?"

"Since when did you play Carnegie Hall with Yo-Yo Ma?" I had just flipped to a perfectly Photoshopped picture of them on the famous stage, their heads bent over their instruments in twin concentration.

"Metaphorical Ladder," Claudia explained. "Happens in music and sports all the time. You always want to practice with people just a little better than you so they pull you up to their level."

I smiled at Claudia's implication that Yo-Yo Ma was only a little better than she was at the cello. A lack of confidence had never been one of Claudia's issues, and she seemed *extremely* confident about this Ladder idea. I had to admit it sounded intriguing. And going into Chrysella with a specific mission would certainly be less intimidating than just being myself and nervous and shy and hoping that people would see through to the real, fun, fascinating me.

Still, I had major doubts that I could pull it off. "I don't know, Claude . . ."

"You can do this, Cara," she said, leaning in close. "I know you can. And you won't be doing it just for yourself; you'll be doing it for me, too. For everyone who has ever felt like a misfit, or was ever picked on, or laughed at, or treated like they weren't good enough. You can prove we're no different than the Supreme Populazzi by becoming one of them. And you can do it with the help of the Ladder."

Claudia believed every word she was saying . . . and in that moment I almost did, too. I wanted to believe it. If I did, then maybe starting a new school didn't have to be scary at all. It could be a chance to make a statement, to show something to the world, even if Claudia and I were the only ones who ever knew about it.

But was it really possible?

As if reading my thoughts, Claudia rose and walked to my night table, where a small replica of the Liberty Bell sat next to an unopened pack of Tastykakes. She put one hand on the replica and looked into my eyes. "This will work, Cara. I swear it will work."

She was swearing on the Bell. It wasn't something we did lightly.

For just a second I let myself really imagine it: me walking down the halls of a brand-new school with a huge smile on my face, completely at ease and at home. Me: the Supreme Populazzi.

"Okay," I said. "I'll do it."

Chapter *two*

Four days later it was September 7, and I was about to walk into a school where I knew absolutely no one. I told myself it would be fine. I was strong, confident, and fearless.

I reached for the door handle . . . and panicked.

My cell phone chirped with a text from Claudia. *"Fear not, C—the Deer Friends are with you!"*

I laughed out loud. It was a reference to Shakespeare. In *Henry V,* before the battle of Agincourt, the king stirs up his troops by shouting, "Once more unto the breach, dear friends, once more." But when Claudia heard it and told me about it in second grade, she thought it was *"deer* friends," which made us think a team of ferociously loyal woodland creatures was rallying behind King Henry to power him through. We liked the image; whenever we faced a challenge, we imagined the Deer Friends were along to help us out.

I may have been in an unfamiliar place, but I wasn't alone. Claudia was with me. And we were on a mission. I pulled open the door to Chrysella Prep, found my locker, then strolled down the halls with purpose, constantly taking pictures and video clips with my phone and sending them to Claude. I had to be subtle about it: even though cell phones were allowed before and after school, I'd score major dork points if anyone noticed.

Despite its seemingly normal brochure, I expected Chrysella to feel like a strange alien planet. It didn't. I already saw familiar representatives from every tier of the Popularity Tower. It was kind of comforting.

"I feel a great disturbance in the Force."

Uh-oh. I wheeled around to see a guy with his eyes closed and his fingers to his temple, not only quoting *Star Wars* in casual conversation but doing so while dressed in a floor-length, hooded brown cloak. "You must be new," he said, extending his hand. "I'm Robert Schwarner."

Leave it to me. The first person I meet at my new school and he's a Happy Hopeless, the very basement of the Popularity Tower. Happy Hopeless are so socially out of it, they don't even know the Tower exists, so they don't notice or care about their less-than-stellar position on it.

Robert may have been a perfectly nice guy, but hanging out with him on my first morning would be instant social suicide. Claudia would be horrified. I quickly shook his hand, then excused myself and moved on. As I did, I checked out the throngs on the next Tower tier: the Cubby Crews. Little groups so into their own thing that they geek out on it, and everyone assumes that's all they're about.

Of course, not all Cubby Crews are created equal. Some barely rank above the Happy Hopeless, while others are only that little bit of cachet away from being Populazzi.

At Pennsbrook, Claudia and I were a lower-echelon Cubby Crew. Even though we were always up for hanging out with other people, everyone assumed we weren't, so they pretty much stayed away. The more they stayed away, the closer we got and the more inside jokes we had, so the harder it was for anyone else to break in. Eventually they stopped trying.

Picking out the individual Cubby Crews was easy.

The low-key guys and girls in jeans and ironic T-shirts chatting and laughing easily with the faculty? The Geniuses.

The proud eccentrics in bizarro clothes talking in goofy voices with huge full-body gestures? The Theater Geeks.

The polished fashion-forwards who reeked of cigarettes and breath mints, sipped lattes, and gave a running catty commentary on everyone around them? The Cosmopolitans.

The stringy-haired, glazed-eyed androgynes with no books who sat against the wall leaning heavily on one another? The Wasteoids.

There were other Cubby Crews, too, including ones without titles—scattered partnerships, trios, and quads that were clearly islands unto themselves. Yet all of these moved out of the way when a lone guy strode down the hall.

If they hadn't moved, I think he'd have plowed right through them without even realizing it. He was the hottest guy I'd ever seen, but I got the sense he didn't care about that kind of thing. His eyes were a million miles away, and his long black trench coat and the guitar case slung over his shoulder seemed totally out of place, like they belonged to another era. He was different, but he was no outcast. He had a force field of cool around him. People went silent when he got close, then stared and whispered after he passed.

I snapped a picture and sent it to Claudia with the text *"DZ?"*

"DZ!!!" she shot back.

DZ stood for DangerZone, the next tier on the Popularity Tower. DangerZones can pull off the "different" thing because they're so dark, troubled, and fascinating. It's tough to call DangerZones popular. They're above labels like that. They do whatever they want, and all the others—from the Happy Hopeless to the Supreme Populazzi—feel honored if a DangerZone wants to talk to them.

I turned away so the DangerZone wouldn't see me watching him . . . and was almost blinded by the glow of the uppermost tier on the Tower: the Populazzi. I saw them through a large picture window. The Populazzi lazed among the branches of a sprawling oak tree, basking in the leaf-filtered sun. It had to be the best spot on campus, and I wasn't surprised they'd claimed it. They were the Golden Ones: beautiful, confident, and admired.

I snapped a picture of them and sent it to Claudia. At Pennsbrook, she and I had criticized the Populazzi a lot. They were too cliquey, too judge-y, and way too tyrannical about keeping the rest of us stuck in our spots on the Tower . . .

. . . and I'd be lying if I didn't admit we totally wanted to be them.

Okay, maybe not them *exactly*, but we wanted to be in their position. Who wouldn't? They sat around their tree, on display for the whole school to see, yet none of them looked the slightest bit self-conscious. In fact, they radiated ease and happiness. Going through life like that . . . it would be like living a fairy tale.

Of course, the problem with all the Populazzi we'd ever known was that they'd been born into the fairy tale, so they didn't appreciate it. The people who'd make great Populazzi were people like Claudia and me. We knew the other side, so we'd recognize how good we had it and wouldn't be harsh to anyone on other tiers.

As I continued watching the Populazzi, I noticed one girl stood out more than the others. She sat on the lowest branch of the tree. Her shoulder-length chestnut hair had beautiful waves and highlights that I swear seemed to sparkle in the sun. Perfectly white teeth beamed out of her sun-bronzed face, and her cowl neck white sleeveless top and jeans looked both casually thrown together and catalog-model flawless.

I'd spent hours figuring out my own look for the first day of school and had felt really good about my mop of brown curls tucked behind a funky headband, my cute new jeans, my ballet flats, and a fun textured vest over a basic tank. But watching this girl, I felt ridiculous, like I was trying way too hard and looked dorky anyway.

I wasn't the only one looking at her. All the other Populazzi girls kept darting their eyes her way, as if checking in to make sure she approved of what they were saying, doing, and thinking. That settled it: the girl was the Supreme Populazzi. The others were Penultimates. And if she was the female Supreme Populazzi, it stood to reason that the guy next to her with his arm slung over her shoulders was her boyfriend, the male Supreme Populazzi. He wore preppy-cool clothes, and his hair was short, dark, and wavy, brushed back from his face, and . . . Uh-oh . . .

He was looking right at me.

The guy's face scrunched up. He tapped his girlfriend on the shoulder and pointed to me. She turned and squinched her face like she smelled something nasty.

Why was I still staring at them???

I dropped to my knees so I was below their sight line and

crawled away from the picture window. My phone chirped. Claudia had cropped my earlier picture so it showed just the male Supreme Populazzi. *"Say hello 2 your prom date!!!"* her text read.

"Yeah, right," I muttered, and kept crawling as the bell rang. I was almost clear of the window, when—

"Ow!"

I had crawled right into a pair of khaki-clad shins. And they were hard.

"Oh—sorry," a confused male voice said. I looked up. The khakis were attached to one of the Theater Geeks. I recognized him because he wore a gray 1920s Gatsby hat. He frowned and cocked his head as he studied me for a second, then asked, "I'm sorry, are you . . . crawling to class?"

"No, I . . ." I went for the obvious. "I lost a contact lens."

"Oooh." Gatsby Hat winced. "Been there. Let me help you." He dropped to his knees and started poring over the floor. The halls had already emptied out. We were both going to be late, but he was clearly a true Samaritan and was not going to give up until he helped me find my lens . . . which didn't exist.

I sat back on my knees. "I don't wear contacts."

Gatsby Hat peeked up at me from his position on all fours. "You don't?"

I shook my head. "I . . . I'm new here."

"I see," he said. "And at your old school you crawled everywhere?"

I sighed. How exactly was I going to explain this to him? Then I saw his sly half smile and realized I didn't need to.

"Yes," I said, "we did. It was an underground school. Literally underground. Tunnels everywhere. Very low ceilings. They said it was once part of the Underground Railroad."

"Ah," Gatsby Hat said. "Sounds very edifying."

"Very. 'Experiential Education,' they called it."

"'Experimental Experiential Education,' no doubt," he said.

"Exactly."

Gatsby Hat and I smiled, taking goofy delight in our mutual powers of alliteration. Then he sat up and held out his hand to help me.

"My name's Archer," he said, "and we're both very late for class. What do you have first period?"

"Cara." I of course responded to the question he *didn't* ask. Oops. "My *name's* Cara. First period I have . . ." I rummaged through my funkadelic brown and orange paisley messenger bag until I found my schedule. "English. Mr. Woodward. Room ten."

"Me too. We're lucky; he's the best in the school. I'll walk you there. Or we could crawl, if it makes you feel more comfortable."

"That's okay. I think I'm getting used to the standing-erect thing." Like an idiot I blushed. I waited for Archer to pounce on it.

He didn't, though he did raise an eyebrow and smirk almost imperceptibly before leading me down the hall.

Claudia had *way* too much faith in me. I could already imagine my next journal entry. "I really thought this would be the year everything changed, but even though the place is new, Cara Leonard is exactly the same."

Chapter *three*

"My reputation precedes me," Mr. Woodward boomed as Archer and I tried to sneak in. "You were afraid to enter my class. You were wise."

The room tittered as we sat, and Mr. Woodward retreated to a closet. He pulled out a two-foot-long billy club. Archer gave me a knowing look. He had told me Mr. Woodward was infamous for this: "the Bat." No one knew what the Bat was for or what horrors it could unleash, but it was legend. A chill ran down my spine and my palms started to sweat. Was he taking out the Bat because Archer and I were late?

Mr. Woodward sat at the end of the horseshoe of three long desks. He held up a book and said, "*The Love Song of J. Alfred Prufrock.*" As good, trained automatons, we all scrambled to pull out our copies, but Mr. Woodward cleared his throat and shook his head. "Watch and learn."

He held the Bat by its handle and let it rest on the desktop. He started to read.

"'Let us go then, you and I, / When the evening is spread out against the sky . . .'"

As he read, he let the Bat rise until it was almost at a ninety-degree angle to the desk.

"'Like a patient etherized upon a table.'"

He let the Bat drop back down.

He did this for several lines of the poem: let the Bat rise as the narrator got excited about his topic, then let it drop when his enthusiasm deflated. Finally, with a gleam in his eye, Mr. Woodward turned to us. "What is Eliot illustrating with his choice of words?"

It seemed pretty obvious what *Mr. Woodward* was illustrating, and while Eliot was doubtless illustrating the same thing, no one in the room wanted to say it out loud. Several people in the room snickered, but none of them tried to answer.

"Come on, kids, this is the good stuff. This is Junior English. This is T. S. Eliot. Let's dive into this! What is Eliot doing with his images? Anyone: shout it out!"

I almost giggled when I realized I could now say this twice in one hour. "Um . . ." I began, "he's making them stand erect?"

"Yes!" roared Mr. Woodward, and this time Archer didn't hide his smirk. "You've almost redeemed yourself for being late . . ."

"Cara," I said.

"Cara," he repeated. "So each time, Cara, when his images are at the peak of their 'erection,' if you will, what does Eliot do to them?"

There was only one answer, and I wished I could say it without blushing. Still, I didn't hesitate. "He lets the images go flaccid."

Mr. Woodward thrust the Bat into the air. "The woman is

correct! In just the first stanza, this is what we're learning about J. Alfred Prufrock. Metaphorically, this is a man who can't keep it up. He can't make a decision, he won't face tough choices, and though he feels the longing pull of his hopes and dreams, he's too paralyzed to do anything about them!"

Wow. The entire class was riveted. The next forty minutes flew. By the time the bell rang, several of us had gotten so involved in fervent Prufrock talk that we weren't even sitting on our chairs anymore—we'd migrated to the tops of the tables. That never would have been allowed at Pennsbrook, but I guess here it was part of the whole charter-school-teachers'-and-students'-creative-thinking thing. Whatever it was, I liked it. And although poetry had never been my thing, I was now willing to make an exception for anything by T. S. Eliot.

As we filed out of the classroom, Archer asked what I had next. "Precalc," I said.

"Ah," said Archer, "I was hoping it might be geometry. More opportunity for you to talk about verticals."

"Ooh, you're right. Bummer." I looked at my schedule. "I have art fourth period, though; I could propose we *erect* a statue on campus."

"Not bad." Archer nodded. "Or you might want to come to my seventh period theater class. We're going to do some d*irect*ing."

I winced.

"Too big a stretch?" he asked.

"Too big a stretch."

Archer glanced down at my schedule. "We both have fifth period lunch. Maybe I'll see you then. I promise I'll work on being more clever."

He gave me directions to my next class, then disappeared down the hall in the other direction.

This was great. I'd had an amazing class, I was maybe making a friend . . . things were going well. Maybe I wouldn't even need the Ladder. It's not like I *had* to be Supreme Populazzi. One or two good friends, that would do it. Two—so I wouldn't be totally lost if one was out sick. Two people to hang with between classes and at lunch. I'd be happy with that.

I took a seat in precalc and was pulling out my notebook when a breeze of fruity vanilla-jasmine made me look up. The Supreme Populazzi girl had just slipped into the desk in front of mine.

A bolt of panic surged through me as I remembered her look of disgust when she saw me through the window. I slunk down in my seat.

What was she doing in here, anyway? Was she a junior? I'd assumed she was a senior.

Whatever. It would be fine. As long as she didn't turn around, it would be fine.

"Trista!" a guy behind me called out.

She turned around and—looked right at me.

No!

But Trista's eyes passed right over me, then locked on the person who'd called her. "Hey!"

Wait . . . had she not recognized me?

Or maybe she and her boyfriend had never actually seen me. It wasn't like their tree was right next to the window. Maybe they'd been making faces at something else entirely.

Whatever it was, I'd totally dodged a bullet.

"Sweet party Saturday," the guy told her. "You rock."

"Thanks," she said.

That opened the floodgates. Now half the room piped up to tell Trista how much they'd loved her party. The other half—clearly the Happy Hopeless and Cubby Crews who hadn't made the cut—looked out the window or down at their books and pretended to ignore the conversation.

I was impressed that Trista herself didn't talk about the party at all. She let everyone else rave about it, and she was nice and thanked them, but she didn't go into it or anything. It was like she knew the other people wished they'd been invited and she didn't want to rub it in. It was cool.

I wondered what she'd do if I introduced myself. Would she say hi? If she did, what would I say back? What could I say that would be interesting to a Supreme Populazzi?

I spent the entire class trying to think of the perfect conversation starter, but since "So have you always been the most popular girl in class?" was unforgivably lame, I let it go.

After precalc I had study hall, then the whole school got a fifteen-minute break. Most people probably welcomed this, but I dreaded it. There's nothing worse than free time when you don't know anyone. I walked the halls and tried to look like I belonged—like I was alone because I *wanted* to be alone. At the same time, I tried to exude approachability.

End result? Me with a dopey smile on my face, looking hopefully at all the students who passed . . . then pretending I was smiling at some invisible person just beyond them when it became clear they weren't going to notice me.

It was exhausting and depressing.

I wished Archer was around. I could've talked to him.

I wished I could call Claudia, but she'd be in class.

I wished I was Trista, with everyone in school falling all over me to be my friend.

I wondered if she and the other Populazzi were back in that oak tree.

I went outside to take a peek, and realized what I'd seen that morning was only part of the picture. The Populazzi's tree and the flat lawn around it actually sat at the top of a steep, grassy hill. The hill sloped down away from the school, so I hadn't seen it this morning. It was dotted with more Populazzi, sprawled out and talking in clusters.

I walked closer, curious.

"Hey, loser!" a large Populazzi guy yelled.

He was looking right at me.

I stopped in my tracks.

"Yeah, you!" he said. "You a senior?"

He looked intimidating. I got nervous and words tumbled out of me.

"Um, no. I'm a junior. Cara. Cara Leonard. I'm new here. Hi."

Someone needed to smack me. How had I not shut up yet? Why was I introducing myself to this guy? He'd just called me a loser!

"Senior Slope," the guy said. "You got ten seconds. Ten . . . ! Nine . . . !"

All the other Populazzi on the hill were watching now, and they joined in on the countdown: "Eight . . . ! Seven . . . !"

If my legs didn't unlock, I'd still be on the Slope when they got to one, and I didn't want to know what would happen then. I backed away and made it to the top of the hill by three, at which point I tripped and fell on my butt.

"Nice one!" someone called. Hot shame crawled up my neck, but I turned around. Trista, her boyfriend, and all the others at the oak tree—which I now understood was the hangout for the *junior* class Populazzi—were laughing at me. For sure they'd all heard the guy call me a loser. I had the instant, hideous sensation of being five years old, soaking wet, with Heather Clinger's witchy finger pointing at me and twenty-nine high-pitched voices shrieking in my ears.

I was desperate to run away, but I knew that would only make things worse. I pretended to be unruffled, stood up, and strolled off as normally as possible, my head held high. It helped. I actually started feeling indignant, which was way better than ashamed. How was I supposed to know it was the Senior Slope? It was my first day! It's not as if they had signs posted. Now I was a loser because I couldn't read their minds?

I had the feeling Chrysella was loaded with land mines like this. I wanted no part of them. For fifth period lunch, I grabbed a Diet Coke and a Zone bar from the vending machines and retreated into my car. If this were Pennsbrook, I'd have driven off somewhere, but Chrysella's rule was that students stay on campus during the school day, even for free periods and lunch. More of the "Charter School Difference," I supposed.

I turned on the car, cranked the air conditioner and the radio, and called Claudia, hoping she'd ended up with fifth period lunch, too. The times didn't match up exactly, but she *should* be free to—

"Are you Supreme Populazzi yet?" she answered.

I groaned and told her everything.

"When you've reached the top of the Tower, you're going to look back on today and laugh so hard," she said.

"Did you not hear me? I was just officially introduced to two years' worth of Populazzi as 'Loser'!"

"It's the first day of school! You shouldn't be anywhere near the Populazzi. That's not how the Ladder works."

The Ladder. Just this morning I'd thought I might not even need it. Now I'd already had a complete social meltdown. Clearly I could not be trusted to handle high school on my own.

"What do I do?" I asked.

"Stop hiding in your car. At this moment, your cafeteria is awash in potential targets: lower-level Cubby Crew guys who would kill to have a girlfriend like you. Get in there, find one, and start going after him!"

"It's just so not me, Claude," I said.

"Are you happy right now, Cara?" she shot back.

"No."

"Does Trista seem happy?"

"Yes, but—"

"Don't you want to be as happy as she is? Don't you deserve it just as much?"

That one I had to think about a minute.

"Yeah. I do."

"Yes! You do! That smell in the air? That's not just sloppy joes; that's your future! The Ladder awaits you, Cara Leonard! Once more onto the rungs, deer friends, once more!"

I laughed and promised her I'd do my best, then hung up feeling much lighter. I walked into the "awash in potential targets" cafeteria. It was filled with eight-person tables, and most of them were full. Somewhere among them sat my perfect target . . . I just had to find him.

A voice boomed across the room. "'From the benches, black with people, there went up a muffled roar, / Like the beating of the storm-waves on a stern and distant shore. / 'Kill him! Kill the umpire!' shouted some one on the stand; / And it's likely they'd a-killed him had not Casey raised his hand.'"

Okay, that was weird. Some guy at the back of the cafeteria was standing on his chair and shouting poetry to everyone in fifth period lunch.

Wait . . . it wasn't just some guy. It was Archer. I recognized the Gatsby hat. I walked closer and I realized he was *performing* the poem, but it's not like he was trying to get people's attention. It seemed more like he was doing it for his friends, the other Theater Geeks. He was just so into it and so good that most of the cafeteria was watching. Happy Hopeless, Cubby Crews, DangerZones . . . even Trista and her Populazzi had stopped eating to check out the show.

I watched, too. It was weird. I'd spent a big chunk of the morning with Archer, but I'd been so busy making sure I didn't come off like a complete idiot, I'd never really looked at him. Now I did. His clothes were pretty traditional—so much so that they actually seemed unique. Khaki pants, blue-and-white striped oxford with the tails hanging out, abused sneakers he'd probably worn for years. I could even see the outline of undershirt sleeves on his biceps. He topped it all with the gray tweed Gatsby hat with the brim snapped down. He wore his black hair short, cut bluntly at the nape of his neck. His skin was a rich coffee color, and his brown eyes seemed impossibly huge.

How had I not noticed it before? Archer was cute. Really cute. And he was smart—I *had* noticed that. And he made me laugh. And I seemed to make *him* laugh . . .

Archer's shoulders slumped, the picture of resignation. "'Oh, somewhere in this favored land the sun is shining bright; / The band is playing somewhere, and somewhere hearts are light, / And somewhere men are laughing, and somewhere children shout; / But there is no joy in Mudville—mighty Casey has struck out.'"

Silence . . . then Trista stood and applauded. Everyone at her table and most of the cafeteria followed her lead. For the first time Archer seemed to realize the size of his audience. It didn't faze him. He took off his Gatsby hat and gave a deep, exaggerated bow, then plopped back down into his seat.

Wow. Even the Populazzi thought Archer was amazing. Claudia would definitely approve.

I started walking toward his table, getting more and more nervous with every step. I reminded myself he'd said he'd see me at lunch—it was totally normal for me to walk up and say hi. Besides, it's not like I was really risking anything. I was just playing my part in a grand social experiment.

I told myself that . . . but it didn't stop my palms from sweating.

I had found my first target.

Chapter *four*

"Hey, Archer . . . that was great," I said.

"Oh!" Archer wheeled around and his cheeks flushed red. "Cara . . ." He turned back toward his friends at the table with . . . Was that a pleading look?

Of course it was. I was just some random new girl. He'd only hung out with me this morning to be nice, and now I was bothering him in front of all his friends. I felt my cheeks start to match his.

"I'm sorry," I said. "I shouldn't have . . . It's just . . . the poem was really good. Bye."

"Wait!" Archer said. "Thanks."

"You're welcome."

Excellent. Compliment paid and accepted. That had to be a good first step, right? Only problem was I hadn't planned anything else, so Archer and I smiled and said nothing for just this side of forever.

"Hi!" said a sweet-faced girl across the table. "I'm Sue."

Sue had blond shoulder-length hair and big blue eyes and was round without being heavy. Everything about her seemed sweet and nonintimidating. I liked her immediately.

"Cara," I said.

"Right, sorry," Archer said. "Cara, this is Sue, Ember, Molly, Doug, Tom, Dinah, and Noah. Sue-Ember-Molly-Doug-Tom-Dinah-Noah, this is Cara. She's new."

I'd never in a million years remember all those names. Except maybe Sue's.

"That's great," Sue said. "Did you just move here?"

I answered her, but I was distracted by two of the other girls. They kept exchanging smiles and giving me weird looks that made me wonder if I had Zone bar stuck in my teeth. I tried to check with my tongue while still keeping up a conversation with Sue. It didn't work. I lost track of what I was saying and tripped over every other word.

I sounded like an idiot. I needed to get away before I ruined any chance I had.

"Okay, so . . ."

That was it: my whole exit line. Very memorable. I grimaced and was about to head out when Archer jumped in his seat.

"Ow!" He winced, then glared at the girl next to him. She was one of the Smilers. Archer pushed back his chair.

"Actually, I'm done," he told me. "I'll come, too. Just let me clear my tray—"

"I've got it," Smiler said.

"Thanks," Archer said through gritted teeth, then walked out with me. He limped a little on one leg.

"So . . . have you come up with anything more clever?" I asked.

"More clever?" he asked worriedly. "Oh! Actually I was going to, but I thought maybe you wouldn't come to lunch, and I didn't want to be *stood up*."

"Very nice."

"So I know you've already been here for half a day, but have you had the official tour?" he asked.

"Nope. I'm still absolutely clueless about where I'm going."

"Perfect. Walk this way." He lurched like a hunchback, then quickly stood up and gave me an abashed smile. "Stupid joke. You don't actually have to walk that way."

"*Young Frankenstein*," I said. "I love that movie."

"Which means you have excellent cinematic taste. But you still don't have to walk that way. Unless you want to," he added.

"I'll pass. Let's tour."

Archer's tour took the rest of the period. Not that there was so much to see, really, but he presented each spot with elaborate tales of its deep, rich, and completely fabricated history. Like the science lab that once burned to the ground six times in a single year in bizarre Bunsen burner accidents. Or the theater that was home to riots after the first faculty production of *Hair*, complete with full frontal nudity. Or the faculty bathrooms that were actually rigged with age-sensing alarms that triggered trapdoors whenever students entered—students that were never heard from again. At each stop, he ended with "and of course, George Washington slept here."

I groaned when the bell rang.

"Ah, the groan of disgust," Archer said. "The true sign of a perfect tour."

"No!" I laughed. "I love it. I'm sad it has to end."

"End? This was only the Chrysella Prep *Historical* Tour. You can also experience the majesty of our other offerings, like the Stars of Chrysella Tour, the Chrysella Ghost Tour, and of course, the Culinary Tour through the Chrysella kitchen, complete with tasting menu."

"Sounds absolutely hideous," I said. "I'm in."

"Excellent. I'll make a note of your reservation. See you later?"

"That'd be great."

I was still smiling halfway through French class when Madame Renault leaned on my desk and wailed, *"Que pensez-vous, Cara? Aimeriez-vous partager avec la classe?"*

"Oui, madame!" I quickly replied. *"Je pensais que j'aime beaucoup mieux cette classe que celle de mon ancienne école."*

"Merci, mademoiselle!" Madame Renault said with a proud smile and a wink. The rest of the class was glaring at me. I knew I hadn't made any friends kissing up to the teacher, but she had asked what I was thinking, and since I couldn't answer her question honestly without humiliating myself, I figured I'd make her happy and tell her how much more I liked her class than the one at my old school.

Archer and I didn't have any more classes together, and I didn't see him before I drove home. Not that I stuck around for long—I was dying to call Claudia and give her the full update.

"Brava!" she cheered. "I'm inwardly throwing roses at your feet!"

"Thank you. I'm inwardly Bactine-ing all the thorn scratches on my shins."

"Pessimist," Claudia said. "Remember, this is just the beginning. The Ladder only works if you work the Ladder."

"Pithy."

"Great truths always are. Promise me you'll hang out with him before class tomorrow."

"If I see him, I will," I said, as if I wouldn't have tried to do that anyway.

Claudia wasn't the only one happy with me that evening. My stepfather, Karl, was practically glowing as he plopped down next to me at the dinner table.

"What?" I asked. I wondered if he'd slipped away to Atlantic City for the day and hit a winning streak.

Karl had been in my life since I was four, and in all ways except the most technical, he was my dad. My actual dad was called "the Sperm Donor" by my mom—this despite the facts that they'd been married for ten years and my grandmother swore Mom had been crazy in love with him when they met. Dad now lived in Media, in the huge house he shared with the Bar Wench and their two astoundingly spoiled sons. He'd met his new wife at a bar and left Mom for her almost immediately afterward. That was back when I was three.

Now that we lived in Malvern, Dad was only a twenty-minute car ride away, but none of us imagined that would change his practically nonexistent visitation schedule.

Karl, on the other hand, was almost always around, and right now he was looking at me with a big loopy grin. I laughed. Karl was fantastic when he was happy: funny, smart, caring, insightful . . . the polar opposite of an *un*happy Karl. An unhappy Karl . . . that was something Mom and I worked really hard to avoid.

"I have good news, Cara," Karl singsonged. "I made some calls, cashed in some favors, and it turns out Mr. Stevenson Jaffe would be *thrilled* to meet you when he comes out here in April. He'll be visiting family, but he's willing to take time out and have lunch with you, just to get to know what he calls 'the Whole Cara Leonard.'"

What? I didn't get it at first, and I could see Karl's smile start to harden into a frown.

Then I realized and smiled extra-wide. "That's great!"

And it *was* great. Stevenson Jaffe was the dean of admissions at Northwestern, Karl's alma mater and my first-choice college. I'd been hearing about the place for twelve years now, and honestly couldn't imagine going anywhere else. That Stevenson Jaffe himself was willing not only to meet me but to spend a whole lunch with me was *huge* . . .

But April was a lifetime away and so not where my head was at that moment. I was busy thinking about Archer and what I'd say to him tomorrow morning. I couldn't wait to finish dinner and call Claudia to bounce ideas off her, but the Dean Jaffe thing had Karl so happy, he declared it Family Night. By the time he'd finished destroying Mom and me at Scrabble, it was past my okay-to-use-the-phone hours. I had to settle for texting.

I fell asleep counting not sheep but possible opening lines. Claudia must have done the same—I woke up to an e-mail from her with a huge list of options.

"Really, Claude? 'Good pilgrim, you do wrong your hand too much'?"

I had her on speakerphone as I drove to school. Mom and Karl didn't like me to use the phone at all when I drove, and I understood that maybe it wasn't the safest thing in the world. But what was I supposed to do, go without talking to my best friend because *they*'d decided to move away from her? I tried to use speakerphone so my hands were free, and I never *ever* texted when I drove.

"It worked for Juliet," Claudia said. "Romeo fell head over heels for her."

"You are aware that they both die at the end, yes?"

"Did you seriously just ask me that question?"

"Did I seriously ask it, or did I seriously think you didn't know they died at the end?"

"Fine. Forget Romeo and Juliet. Forget the centuries-old benchmark of true romance. How did *you* want to start?"

I took a breath, then offered up the best of my bunch. "Hey! Do you play Scrabble? 'Cause I had the *best* triple-word score last night!"

Claudia's silence was deafening. I couldn't blame her. Maybe I'd go with the good pilgrim thing after all.

As it turned out, I didn't need an opening line. The moment I got my books into my locker, I heard Archer's voice behind me.

"You are a woman of mystery," he said, and my whole body grinned as I turned to face him.

"How so?" I asked.

"You disappeared after classes yesterday. Most mysterious indeed."

So he was looking for me after classes yesterday.

"Was that when my next tour was scheduled?" I asked. "I didn't realize."

"It was." He nodded sadly. "And it was brilliant."

"Can I reschedule?"

"Depends on the tour you want. Our most popular offerings have limited availability and need to be reserved several months to a year in advance . . ."

Suddenly inspiration struck. It might not have been Shakespeare but . . .

"I know *exactly* the tour I want," I said. "What's your last name?"

"Jain," he said. "Why?"

"I want the Official Archer Jain Tour. Everything you can tell me about yourself in the next"—I checked my watch to see how much time we had before the bell rang—"ten minutes."

"Hmm," he mused, "the topic's a little broad. Help me out—ask me what you want to know."

"Okay," I said as we started down the hall, "do you have any brothers or sisters?"

"I have seventeen brothers and thirteen sisters, all younger than I."

"That is a lie."

"But it's interesting. Tours are supposed to be interesting."

"I promise I'll be just as interested in the real stuff."

Archer sighed.

"I have one sister," he said. "Older. Her name's Lila."

"How much older?"

"Five years."

"Are you close?"

"Do you watch a lot of police interrogation shows?"

"I'm interested! If it makes you feel better, you can answer my next question as ridiculously as you want."

"Yes, that makes me feel much better."

"So are you and your sister close? That's not my next question; it's the last question over again."

"We weren't," Archer said, "but now that she's in college, we talk. She likes to give me advice."

"What's the best thing she ever told you?" I asked.

"Never trust curly-haired women who inexplicably crawl on the floor."

"Nice. Your sister is very astute."

The bell rang. It was perfect timing; Archer and I were only a few feet away from Mr. Woodward's class. We slipped into seats next to each other like it was the most natural thing in the world. During class we kept looking at each other and checking in as if we'd been friends for ages.

Afterward we poured back into the hall with everyone else, but before we could go our separate ways, Archer cleared his throat. "So, um . . . lunch. Do you have a place you like to sit? Because if you don't, I'd be happy to save you a spot, you know . . . if you need one."

I felt a giddy thrill and tried to rein it in. It was just lunch; it was no big deal. Still . . .

"I'd love that, thanks."

"Great . . . you're welcome. I mean, you *will* be welcome. At lunch. I mean . . . I'll see you then."

I watched him walk off, then breezed down the halls to precalculus and spent the next three periods counting down to lunchtime.

I didn't go into the cafeteria right away. If Archer was saving me a seat, I wanted to give him the chance to do it. Unfortunately, it's not easy to kill ten minutes in a school hallway and look at all natural. I walked in slow motion from my fourth period class, searched through my locker as if it were cavernous, and became completely engrossed in the wall-posted monthly lunch menu. Finally it was time to go in.

I found Archer at the same table as yesterday, only this time two of his friends were gone, so there was space. I noticed Sue was one of the ones who wasn't there, and I was a little bummed, since she was so easy to talk to.

"Cara!" Archer rose a little until I sat down next to him. Very chivalrous. Very cute.

"Tell us about yourself, Cara." It was one of the Smilers

from yesterday. "How long have you lived here? Where did you move from? What do you like to do? Do you have any brothers or sisters? Any pets? Are you freaked out about the college thing, or is it not on your radar yet? Do you like plays? Did you ever do any at your old school? What kind of extracurriculars are you signing up for? Do you drive, or do you have to take the bus? Do you already know what you're going to be for Halloween, or do you need ideas? And how are you liking your second day at Chrysella?"

My jaw was literally hanging open.

"Ember . . ." Archer said.

"What?" she said. "Cara's new; we want to get to know her. Don't *you* want to get to know her?"

Archer blushed.

"It's okay," I said to Ember. "I kind of did the same thing to Archer this morning."

I started answering her questions, and was still at it when the bell rang. By then I sort of knew the names of all Archer's friends. They, on the other hand, knew more about my life than anyone other than Claudia, Karl, and my mom.

"We did *The Pit and the Pendulum* at drama camp last summer," Archer said as he walked me out of the cafeteria. "I'm not sure Ember got the Inquisition out of her system."

"It's fine." I laughed. "I like her. I like all of them."

"Good," Archer said. "I mean, not that you have to like my friends . . . not that you *don't* have to, but you don't . . . I mean . . ."

Archer grimaced, then took a deep breath and smiled. "What are you doing after school?" he asked. "I sometimes go to the mall to sit and do homework for a while. There's a particularly good fry place at the Plaza food court . . . insofar as 'fries' and 'food court' can come together to make 'particular goodness.'"

"See, and I'm of the culinary school of thought that says a well-made food court fry can be the epitome of gustatory satisfaction," I said.

"I had no idea that was an actual culinary school of thought."

"Clearly you have much to learn from me."

"Clearly. Should we meet at your locker after school? We can caravan."

"Perfect. See you then!"

I soared off to French class, but I knew I'd learn nothing. In just a few hours I'd be out with Archer; I couldn't think about anything else if I tried.

Chapter *five*

"Ask me where I am!" I chirped as I drove.

"Why, Cara," Claudia asked, "wherever are you?"

"I am on my first date with Archer!"

"You are?" Claudia cried. "Wait—how are you calling about the date when you're on the date? Is he right there with you?"

"No. We're caravanning." I was keeping Archer in sight but purposely staying several car lengths behind him so he couldn't see me talking on the speakerphone. Wouldn't look cool. "We're meeting at the mall."

"You're meeting at the mall."

"Yes!"

"You're in separate cars, and you're meeting at the mall. Are you stopping at home to change?"

"Why would I stop at home to change?"

"Uh-huh. Is he buying you dinner there?"

"It's four in the afternoon! No, he's not buying me dinner. We're going to get a snack at the food court and do homework."

"Cara, that's not a date."

"Of course it is! Archer *asked* me to come *out* with him to the mall. He *asked* me *out*. It's a date!"

"It's not a date! A date involves a change in habiliments; the guy providing or purchasing transportation, sustenance, and entertainment; and some form of physical contact, ideally a kiss."

Claudia had been on as many dates as I had—namely, none—so her expertise on this was in question. "Claude, you had to hear him. He wanted my phone number in case we got separated on the way to the mall, and he got all nervous when he asked. I really think it's a date."

"How about we compromise: we'll call it a date*let*. When you get the actual date with all the qualifications intact, you'll officially be on Archer's rung of the Ladder."

"The Ladder?"

"The *Ladder*. You know, your mission for the school year? The whole reason you targeted Archer to begin with?"

Oops.

Honestly, it wasn't that I had forgotten the Ladder; it's just that I'd stopped thinking about it in terms of Archer. I liked him. And maybe the Ladder had made me brave enough to go after him, but if things got to the point where he amazingly, miraculously, hopefully wanted to be my boyfriend, there was no way in the universe I'd drop him for someone on a higher rung, not even for the Supreme Populazzi.

But I couldn't tell Claudia that. She'd worked all summer on the Ladder.

Claudia and I didn't lie to each other. Years ago we had sworn on my mini Liberty Bell that we never would. But it felt like it would be even worse to let her down than to lie. Especially when right now, it didn't make a difference. Ladder or no Ladder, I was still going after Archer.

"Sorry—went through a dead spot," I said. "Got it, though: real date equals first rung of the Ladder."

"Exactly. But this is a good start. Excellent work."

"Thanks. Pulling in now."

"Call me when you're done. 'Once more unto the breach'!"

I hung up and parked my car next to Archer's. He was at my door instantly and opened it the moment I turned off the engine.

"Shall we?" he asked.

"Are you kidding? After the buildup you gave the particularly good fries, I can't wait."

We walked toward the mall side by side. Archer whistled. He seemed to look everywhere except at me. Was he uncomfortable? Did he regret asking me along?

He darted his eyes my way and smiled . . . then looked away again. The smile was good. I felt better.

I wondered if he'd hold my hand. Should I expect him to hold my hand? I tried to remember if hand-holding was on Claudia's checklist for a real date.

I realized my hands were in my pockets. He couldn't hold one even if he wanted to. Not unless he actively dug it out, which would be weird. He probably thought I was sending him a specific message *not* to hold my hand.

I took my hands out of my pockets.

The problem is I like having my hands in my pockets. It's my natural position. They felt unwieldy hanging by my sides, as if I was walking like a Neanderthal.

Why was I so bad at this?

I glanced at Archer to see if he could tell how socially inept I was.

He had his hands in his pockets.

I let it go. I wasn't going to get weirded out about hand-holding that maybe should or maybe shouldn't be happening. I *might* get weirded out about the fact that we'd now been walking through the mall for several minutes and we hadn't said anything to each other. Conversation wasn't usually an issue for us.

Of course, I was basing "usually" on just over twenty-four hours of knowing him.

I really needed to get over myself.

"Is this the food court?" I asked, though it was plainly obvious to anyone with a brain stem that we had indeed arrived at the food court. "I mean, where do we get the fries?"

Archer led me to his stall of choice and bought fries and drinks for both of us. His treat: real date behavior. Ten minutes later we had all our stuff spread out over a four-top table and munched as we bent over our homework.

At least, *I* was bent over my homework. Archer didn't seem to be. I lifted my head and saw him staring at me, slack-jawed.

"What?"

"What are you doing?" he asked.

"My homework. Precalc."

"No, with your food."

"What do you mean?" I asked. I picked up a fry and swished it through my chocolate milk shake, then took a bite. "I'm eating it. You're right, the fries are really good."

"But you're dunking them in your shake."

"Mm-hm." I held out a newly coated fry. "Want a bite?"

"You're committing a crime against food. You're lucky I don't report you to the Hague."

"Haven't you ever heard of chocolate-covered pretzels? It's the same thing: salty and sweet."

"A hot fudge pickle is salty and sweet, too. Would you eat that?"

"That's salty, *sour*, and sweet. There's a difference. I've eaten chocolate-covered bacon, though."

"That's disgusting."

"And this isn't salty and sweet, but sometimes I'll take raw oatmeal—rolled oats; it doesn't work with steel-cut—and mix it up with strawberry jelly."

"Then you cook it?"

"No," I said, pausing for another bite of milk-shake fry, "you just stir it really, really well until every piece of oatmeal is coated with the jelly, then you spoon it up and eat it. It also works with brown rice. You can mix in a little cottage cheese, too, if you want it more pudding-y. But not too much—you want it to stay pretty dense."

Archer looked like I'd poisoned his dog.

"I'm serious! It's good!"

"It's a biohazard! How can you possibly like that?"

I shrugged. "It's a textural thing. I like the feel of interesting things in my mouth."

"Really?"

"Yeah. Like Cool Whip with raisins and Grape-Nuts mixed in with a little chocolate syr—"

Archer was staring at me with one eyebrow raised. Only then did I realize what I'd just said. I felt the blush heat my face.

"I wasn't saying . . . I just mean . . ."

Archer's grin spread wider. He knew what I'd meant. He was just having fun watching me squirm.

It happened a lot with Archer. We went back to the mall every afternoon that week, and it never failed. My mouth always moved faster than my brain when I was around him, so at some point I'd end up saying something ridiculous or something I'd meant to keep to myself. Like the time he did a goofy voice that was almost exactly like one he'd used in my dream the night before. I was halfway through a long, twisted story about the two of us on this weirdo globetrotting spy mission before I realized I'd admitted I was dreaming about him. Once I got it, I was so embarrassed and flustered and worried about how he'd react that I couldn't even finish. The whole story devolved into incoherent stammers until I just gave up and changed the subject.

It drove me crazy, but Claudia didn't think it was strange at all.

"You like him," she said. "You're not thinking clearly. You're too distracted because you're secretly dying to jump his bones."

"I'm not!"

And I wasn't. I'd only known him five days; bone jumping seemed a little extreme. I just loved being around him. I looked forward to seeing him every morning. My heart gave a little leap when I saw him sitting in the hall across from my locker, waiting for me. Or when I found him at the lunch table, the seat next to him always reserved until I got there. He didn't even ask me after that first time—it was already a given we'd sit together, just like in Mr. Woodward's English class.

But it wasn't as if we were a couple. We hadn't even touched. At least, not intentionally.

Except once. Just yesterday. Archer was making fun of my chocolate-shake fries again, so I gave one an extra-thick dip and ran over to his side of the table.

"That's it! You're trying one! You'll love it!"

"No!" he'd screamed, and grabbed my wrists before I could get the fry anywhere near his mouth. We'd wrestled like that, Archer pushing me back while I'd strained to feed him the french fry. At first it was purely a battle, but as it went on, I became acutely aware of his hands touching my skin and how close our faces were as we struggled.

Archer won the fight. All the shake dripped off the fry until it was just soggy and gross and I agreed to throw it away.

I could still remember the exact feel of his hands, though.

"I'm not saying you want to *actually* jump his bones," Claudia clarified, "only that you want him. Probably as more than just a Ladder rung."

I winced. Was she upset?

"Maybe," I admitted. "Would you hate me for that?"

"Are you insane? If you really like him and he likes you, that's huge! It's bigger than the Ladder—it's *epic!* I love it!"

I felt so relieved. Even though I'd been telling her things, I'd been holding back, too, so I wouldn't hurt her feelings. Now I had a million things I wanted to ask her.

"So it's Friday," I said. "Do you think he'll ask me to do something over the weekend? And if he doesn't, is it okay if I invite *him* to do something over the weekend?"

"Absolutely not. You invite him and you look too eager. If he wants to see you, he'll do the inviting."

That made sense. When Archer and I went to the mall that day, I didn't even mention the weekend. I said neither the words "week" nor "end." I simply channeled all my concentration into the words "invite me," then shot them toward Archer in a continuous beam of psychic energy.

"Cara?" he finally asked.

Success!

"Yes?" I batted my eyes. No, really, I did.

"Are you okay? You're holding your head and your face is all scrunched up. Do you have a headache or something?"

"Oh. No. I just . . . precalc. Hard problem. I'm having tangent issues."

So much for psychic energy.

Maybe he forgot it was Friday.

Just before we got into our cars I said, "See you Monday!"

"Yep. Have a great weekend."

So he knew it was Friday, but he still didn't say anything. And yet he opened my door and waited as I drove off, just like a chivalrous prince.

Or a highly competent valet.

This was *not* a good sign.

Chapter *Six*

I called Claudia on my way home from the mall, and she tried to talk me down. While she agreed the lack of a weekend invitation wasn't ideal, she didn't think it was a disaster. She invited me to spend the next two nights at her house, where we could sift through every second of my first week with Archer and see if we could figure out ways to maybe adjust my approach and get better results. We didn't come up with anything brilliant Friday night and had just woken up Saturday morning when my phone chirped.

"Imagining your breakfast . . ." read the text from Archer. *"Cotton candy dipped in Tabasco?"*

"He texted me!" I screamed to Claudia. "He's been thinking about me!"

She and I debated far too long over my answer before I texted back, *"That's lunch. Breakfast a chocolate-chip-and-swiss omelet. Make you one?"*

We'd agonized over the last sentence, worried it was too suggestive and implied he'd be with me for breakfast because we'd spent the night before together. I wondered if maybe I *wanted* to imply it. Not that I was actually suggesting we *do* anything like that . . . but maybe it was okay to let him know I thought about him that way.

I bit my nails until Archer texted back. (:-P). A grimace face. If he'd noticed the innuendo, he didn't say anything about it. I didn't either. We spent the rest of the weekend texting more and more bizarre food items to each other—until Monday morning when I walked into school and handed him a shoebox.

"For you. I made them myself."

Archer slowly pried off the top. "Is this a fast-acting poison, or will my death be lingering and painful?"

"Lingering and painful, for sure."

He peered into the box, which I'd lined with wax paper and filled with one of my favorite delicacies.

"Is that peanut butter and . . . cream cheese?" Archer winced.

"Spread on green apple slices, then rolled in Cap'n Crunch cereal. Try one!"

He looked like he'd rather eat mud, but he lifted one of the apples to his face, cringing away from it until he closed his eyes and forced himself to bite.

He didn't want to admit it, but I could see he was hooked. He even took another bite.

"See!" I crowed. "I know what I'm doing. Two weeks, tops, and you'll be *begging* to dip your fries in my shake."

"You think?"

It took me a second before I realized I'd done it again. My mouth seriously needed a chaperone.

After school I assumed we'd head to the mall, but Archer had a different idea. "Ping-Pong," he said. "What are your thoughts on Ping-Pong?"

"As a general rule, or are we talking about something specific?"

"Do you play?"

I laughed. I may have even cackled. "'Play' is far too friendly a word for what I do at Ping-Pong. We had a table in our basement in Yardley. I am an unstoppable Ping-Pong machine."

"That is a stunning coincidence," Archer said, "because *I* am an unstoppable Ping-Pong machine. Which means one of us is going to be in for a very rude awakening this afternoon."

"You know where there's a table?" I asked.

"My house. Follow me there?"

Follow him to his house? His *house?* Wasn't this a step beyond meeting at the mall? Was Archer trying to tell me something? There was mischief in his eyes, but that could just have been his wild misconception that he could possibly beat me at my ultimate sport of choice.

I met his gaze. "You're on."

It killed me that I couldn't talk to Claudia while I drove, but I had to follow Archer closely to find his place. After about ten minutes, he pulled into the driveway of a cute brown townhouse in a row of other identically cute brown townhouses.

"Ready to meet your destruction?" he asked, opening my car door.

"I'm assuming you were asking that of your own reflection."

Despite its cookie-cutter exterior, the inside of the house was vibrant and alive, its décor a wild mix of colors and textures. A large gold statue of a many-armed woman sat in a corner, tapestries and framed canvases draped the walls, and a host of curiosities fought for space on every horizontal surface.

"It's a little messy," Archer apologized.

"No, it's beautiful!" I crossed to a quilted and beaded art piece that looked like an umbrella, but there was no way you'd ever take it out in the rain. I ran my hand over its soft golden tassels. "I love this."

"Really?" a woman's voice called from the kitchen. "I'm so glad! I got it on my last trip to see my mother in India and had to fight Lila tooth and nail to stop her from taking it back to school with her."

The woman was a little shorter than me, with thick, straight black hair that fell all the way to her rear end. She wore jeans and a white cotton shirt with a bit of embroidery at the collar. It was simple, but on her it looked lovely and breezy. She wore no makeup, but her smile and eyes sparkled as if she found the whole world endlessly amusing.

"I'm Bina, Archer's mom," she said in her slight British lilt. "You must be Cara. I can't even tell you how happy I am to meet you; we've heard so much about you!"

"You have?" I asked.

"Of course! Come." Bina took my arm. "If you like the umbrella, you'll love this tapestry—it's from the same artisan. And these little dolls were made for Archer's father, Edward, by *his* grandfather, back in the Philippines."

"Mom, Cara and I were actually going to go down to play Ping-Pong . . ."

"Of course! Of course! Go. I'll bring you some tea. Cara, do you drink Indian tea?"

"I don't know," I said. "I've never had it."

"You'll like it," Bina assured me. "If you don't, I'm sure Archer will drink it. I'll get the phone, too, so you can ring your parents and tell them you're here. Unless you've already called . . ."

I could've lied and said I had, but I already liked Bina too much to do that. Truthfully, though, I hadn't intended to call my parents at all. As long as I was home by dinnertime, Mom and Karl knew I was okay and staying out of trouble. But Bina wanted me to call, so . . .

"Hello?" my mom answered.

"Hi, Mom! It's me. I just wanted you to know I'm at my friend Archer's house—"

"Is everything okay?" Mom knew this wasn't our usual MO.

"It's fine. Bina—Archer's mom—just wanted to make sure you knew I was here."

"She did?" Mom sounded both surprised and intrigued by this idea. "Put her on for me, please."

"Really?"

"Yes! If she's looking out for my daughter, the least I can do is say hello."

"Hello" would be fine, but I had a feeling Mom would say something far more mortifying than that. It was my own fault. I should've lied.

I handed the phone to Bina. "She'd like to talk to you."

Bina beamed and slipped back to the kitchen, but we could still hear every word. "Hello! It's so good to speak with you! Your daughter is just darling . . ."

I shot Archer a pained look.

"Ping-Pong?" he asked.

"Immediately."

"Your mom's probably smart to check up on me," Archer said as we trotted down to the basement. "My reputation precedes me. Especially when I have a paddle in my hand."

"Bring it."

Archer hadn't been lying about his Ping-Pong skills. He was good . . . *almost* as good as me and just as fiercely competitive. We played for two hours straight, pushing each other with endless volleys that had us both running around the room, sweating and panting and gasping until I finally squeezed out match point on our tie-breaking third game in a row.

"You're a worthy foe, Cara Leonard," Archer said. He took my hand for a postgame shake.

"As are you, Archer Jain."

The shake was done. This would be the part where we'd let go of each other's hands.

But we didn't.

At least Archer didn't, and I wasn't going to pull away before he did.

Archer was only an inch or two taller than me, but his hand was much larger. It cradled mine. His palm felt soft against my skin.

My heart started to speed, and I hoped he couldn't feel it in my pulse. I was grateful we'd just played Ping-Pong, so my palms had a legitimate reason to be sweaty.

I smiled, but Archer didn't do the same. He looked serious. He looked . . . nervous?

Was he getting ready to kiss me? What if my breath was horrible? What had I eaten for lunch? Oh God—pork rolls with mustard. So not okay. But that was hours ago. Didn't food-breath neutralize itself after a certain period of time? And what about my lips? I hadn't put on gloss since before school ended; what if they were too dry? I could purse them to check, but then Archer might guess what I was thinking. And if he did kiss me, what would I do with my tongue? I couldn't just shove it in his mouth, but if I kept it in my own, would he think I was a prude? Would he be able to tell I didn't know what I was doing?

I wished I had a mint.

I suddenly had to pee.

Really badly.

I considered ignoring it, but then I had a horrible image of me bouncing around to hold it in while Archer tried to kiss me.

This sucked.

I looked into Archer's eyes, filled with . . . longing? Desire?

"I'll be right back," I said.

Afterward, I desperately hoped we could pick up where we left off, but the mood was broken. Archer was back on his side of the Ping-Pong table, counting how many times he could bounce the ball on his paddle.

I had never in my life been so filled with self-loathing.

"It's six," I said, glancing at my watch. "I should go."

"Okay," he said.

That was it. "Okay." Clearly, any romantic feelings he might have had for me were wiped out forever. Stupid bladder.

Archer walked me to my car and held the door as I got in. "Think maybe you could come back tomorrow?" he asked. "We were really close . . . I'd love another chance."

For a split second I stopped breathing. His voice sounded casual, like he was talking about Ping-Pong, but what if he wasn't?

"I'd like that," I said.

I called Claudia the second I was out of eyeshot.

"He was going to kiss you and you stopped to *pee?*" Claudia shouted.

"What was I supposed to do?"

"I don't know . . . hold it in?"

"Like in kindergarten?"

As always, The Incident required a moment of respectful silence.

"Your bladder seriously has it out for you, Cara."

"I know! I totally ruined everything."

"You didn't," Claudia said. "He asked you to come back tomorrow."

"To give him another chance, he said."

"Exactly. Breath mints and lip gloss. And nothing to drink after lunch."

"You really think he's going to try again?"

"He definitely will," Claudia said. "But if he doesn't, *do not* kiss him."

"If he doesn't, I'll assume it's because he's mortified. There's no way I'd try to kiss him."

"I'm sure he's not mortified. But he *would* be if you made the first move. It freaks guys out. People pretend that's not true, but it is—I know from my Ladder research. Even if it takes him a while before he tries again, you have to be patient."

"Okay. I can totally be patient."

"Didn't I tell you, Cara? This will be the year everything changes."

It was the same thing she'd said a couple weeks ago . . . except this time I believed her.

Chapter *seven*

$\mathcal{I}$ learned something about myself over the next few weeks.

I am not a patient person.

It was crazy because, seriously, I was still only just getting to know Archer. But once you're sure something good is going to happen, you want it to happen *now*. It's why waiting for chocolate chip cookies to cool is so brutally painful—and probably why I prefer eating the raw dough.

That next day, despite everything, I was positive Archer would kiss me. He had asked for another chance, right? Of course he was going to kiss me. I wore a cute outfit and armed myself with mass quantities of meltaway breath strips and pomegranate lip balm. I was so excited, I couldn't trust myself to speak to him at school. I said the bare minimum so he wouldn't think anything was up.

That afternoon I followed him home. I knew the way now, so I could stay a few cars back and talk to Claudia. She was sure he'd kiss me, too, but she reminded me to be patient if he didn't.

Specifically she reminded me "how poor are they that have not patience." I figured it was Shakespeare, since she pronounced it "*pay*-shee-*ence*" so it would scan.

Bina met us at the door with two mugs of Indian tea. It smelled delicious, but there was no chance I was drinking any. I pretended to take a few sips so I wouldn't hurt her feelings.

"Come on," Archer said. "I have a surprise for you."

There was something wicked in his voice. I followed Archer downstairs. Before I'd reached the last step, he leaned in close to my ear and said, "Close your eyes."

My heart started thumping so hard it hurt. Archer took my hand and gently led me down, then a few more steps forward. He gave my hand a little squeeze. It was coming now. The anticipation was brutal. I leaned toward him just a bit, my lips seeking his . . .

"Behold the Wall of Degradation!" Archer declared.

Huh?

"Open your eyes," he said.

I did. Archer was standing in front of a huge yellow poster board he'd mounted on the wall by the Ping-Pong table. It was indeed labeled THE WALL OF DEGRADATION, and was split into two columns: ARCHER and CARA. My name had two hash marks under it; his had one: our games from the day before. A circle of Velcro held a pen to the sign.

"At the moment it's the wall of *my* degradation," Archer said, "but you see there's plenty of room for me to redeem myself."

Part of me was still waiting for him to kiss me. It took me a minute to shift into this new reality. I'd be lying if I said I wasn't disappointed, but there was a plus side: the poster was enormous and 99 percent of it was blank. Archer was clearly expecting me to be here for many weeks of Ping-Pong.

"Let the continued degradation begin." I grinned and grabbed a paddle. Pretty soon I was so involved with the game that I wasn't thinking as much about whether or not Archer wanted to kiss me. I did hope he'd try before I went home, but when he gave me a high-five instead of a handshake, I figured it wasn't happening. I wondered if he'd lost interest overnight. But I'd promised Claudia I'd be patient, so I pushed those thoughts out of my head. I had plenty of breath strips and lip balm—I could wait.

Wednesday afternoon Archer couldn't concentrate on Ping-Pong at all. We didn't have a single volley; he missed every other shot. I was sure I knew what he was thinking. I wondered how I could get him to admit it.

"You know I love slaughtering you, but it's not fun when you don't even put up a fight," I said.

"Sorry. I just keep thinking about auditions."

Oh. Fall play auditions. Of course. Sitting with Archer and his friends at lunch every day, I'd heard all about them. The play was *Cyrano de Bergerac*. I'd never read it, but the lead was a role Archer had been dying to play for as long as he could remember. All his friends thought he was a shoo-in, but Archer himself had seemed pretty philosophical about the whole thing—until now.

"Friday after school, right?" I asked.

Archer nodded.

"Do you think you're ready?"

"I think so. We've known all summer this was going to be

the show, so it's not like I haven't been practicing, but . . . Would you listen to me do it?"

"Of course!"

"Great." He raced upstairs to grab a dog-eared copy of the text, then opened it and pointed to a section. "Right here. This is the part I'm going to do. You can follow along and make sure I have the lines right. Just . . . picture me with a really big nose."

"Big nose. Got it."

Archer stepped back a little, giving himself space, then launched in. "'Ah no, young man! That was a trifle short! . . .'"

It was a long monologue describing a million ways the "young man" could have better insulted his—Cyrano's—nose. I tried to follow along in the book, but it was impossible; I couldn't take my eyes off Archer. His lines were so funny that I was laughing out loud, but I could also sense his Cyrano was covering a layer of pain he didn't want anyone to see.

When he finished, I leaped up and cheered.

"Really?" Archer asked. "You really thought it was good?"

"Good? It was *great!* There's no way they can give this part to anyone else. You're perfect for it. If they don't give it to you, I'll boycott the theater. I'll stage a sit-in in the lobby. I'll go on a hunger strike."

"Thanks. But given your food proclivities, it might be more effective to go on an *anti*hunger strike. You could sit in front of the director and force him to watch you eat until he gives me the part. He'd make it through two chocolate-shake french fries, tops."

"You're just jealous that my palate is sophisticated enough to appreciate eclectic flavors."

"If by sophisticated you mean 'dulled' and by eclectic you mean 'disgusting,' then yes, you're absolutely right." He nodded toward the Ping-Pong table. "Ready to play?"

"Am *I* ready? I'm not the one who let a little audition pressure affect her game."

"Oooh, ow!" he cried, grabbing his heart as he staggered back to the table.

Two days later, I was sitting in my room after school, amazed by how strange it felt to be home and not at Archer's. It was audition day, and he'd stayed late with all his friends. I had no clue what to do with myself, but I eventually decided to make the most of it. I pulled on comfy sweats, mixed a treat of peanut butter stirred with chocolate syrup, and settled onto my bed to eat and dive into a novel. I'd just gotten the third book in Jasper Fforde's Thursday Next series, and I couldn't wait to read it . . . but the words kept melding into goo.

Had Archer finished his audition? I didn't want to bother him if he was still there, but I couldn't think about anything else. The part was so important to him. Should I have stayed after school with him for moral support? Maybe that would have been presumptuous—it's not as though he'd invited me. I might have just been in the way, or made him more nervous. But maybe he would have appreciated it. Maybe he'd been hoping I'd volunteer to come, whether he actually wanted me there or not. Wasn't that what good girlfriends did? Not that I was his girlfriend . . .

Whatever. I was his friend, and I was dying to find out how it went. I jumped up and grabbed my phone to text him, but it rang before I could even open it.

"Hello?"

"Cara? It's Archer!"

I could barely hear him over a chorus of voices screaming along to Madonna's "Holiday."

"Archer? Hey! How did it go?"

"Great . . . I think!" he shouted, then his voice muted a bit as he said, "You guys, come on . . ." Then I heard him more clearly. "So, um . . . how's everything going?"

"Oh, for God's sake . . ." a voice rang out.

"Hey!" a muffled Archer cried. "Give it back!"

"Cara, it's Ember. We're done with auditions, we're going mini-golfing, and we're picking you up. Give me your address and I'll put it in my GPS."

Ember? Mini-golfing? Now?

"Cara?" Her tone made it clear that obedience was my only option.

"Oh. Sorry, um . . . four-eighteen Avery Lane."

"Cool. We're five minutes away. Meet us out front."

She clicked off.

Five minutes? I looked at myself in the mirror: a shapeless blob of filthy old sweats, with sticky smears of chocolaty peanut butter glued to my face from licking the bowl. And peanut butter breath, no doubt. Disaster. I lost a full minute gaping at the horror, then raced to wash my face, brush my teeth, and change before zooming out front just as Ember's battered SUV scraped against the curb. I opened the door to the back seat and was blown backwards by the insanely loud music.

"Postaudition eighties sing-along!" Ember cried. "Get in!"

I wanted to . . . but there didn't seem to be any room. Ember was in the driver's seat, Archer in the passenger seat, and Sue, Doug, Molly, and Dinah were crammed onto the back seat. Even the cargo area was filled with Tom's massive bulk and the wiry frame of Noah.

"I, um . . . I don't think I can," I said.

"Of course you can!" Ember shouted over the music. "Just sit on Archer's lap!"

Archer turned red.

"Is that really safe?" I asked.

"No, it's *not* safe," Sue told Ember. She turned to me and smiled apologetically. "I told her it wasn't safe. Maybe another time?"

"Sure," I said. "It's good to see you, though." I really hadn't seen Sue since she'd switched lunch tables.

"Good to see you, too," she said. "Bye!"

"Come on, Cara. You'll be fine," Noah said. "Tom and I don't even have seat belts back here, and we're not worried, right?"

"Exactly," Tom said, "because Ember is an excellent driver."

Huge eruption of laughter from everyone in the car, including Ember herself. I smiled uncomfortably.

"That's okay," I said. "Thanks for thinking of me."

"No—here," Archer said, clicking off his belt. "Take my seat."

"Are you sure?" I asked.

"Yes! Excellent idea!" cried Doug. He rose and patted his seat. "Plant your tush right here, Archer. *I'll* sit on your lap."

Archer squeezed between Sue and Molly. Doug settled in on top of him. I climbed into the passenger seat and buckled in.

"Ooh, Archer!" Doug cooed as we jounced down the street. "Is that a pencil in your pocket, or have I just made your wildest fantasies come true?"

"Pencil?" Sue objected.

"Are you saying you'd know otherwise?" Doug asked.

Sue didn't answer.

"'Lovecats'!" Ember screamed. She turned the radio even louder and bounced in her seat as some eighties song I didn't know shrieked from the speakers. Everyone else sang along at the top of their lungs, completely unconcerned that Ember's seat-dancing took her mind off the car, which veered unsteadily in and out of our lane. I gripped my seat and wondered if there'd be a socially acceptable way to call a cab to get home.

By the time we got to the mini-golf course a half hour later, I was indebted to the gods of at least seven different religions, all of whom I had silently promised my immortal soul if I survived the ride.

"You okay?" Archer asked once we were safely in the parking lot.

"I'm great." At least I would be after a few more gulps of fresh air.

"Loser pays for ice cream?" Tom asked.

"Um . . . I'm not really good at mini-golf," I said.

"This is different," Archer said. "We play for style. The most unique putt that sinks a ball wins each hole."

"Oh." Somehow I didn't find that comforting.

I was right to be worried. Archer and his friends had been playing this game for years. They were experts at finding truly bizarre ways to sink a mini-golf ball. They'd putt behind their backs; they'd lie down and shoot the ball as if with a pool cue; they'd whack the ball while leaping through the air. Putter use wasn't required; at one hole Tom executed a perfect pratfall and "tripped" over the ball, which went flying into the hole. Noah did a handstand, then swatted the ball in without losing his balance. Sue, who had until now struck me as a little shy and proper, placed the ball in her cleavage, then leaned down and squeezed her breasts together so the ball popped out and rolled into the hole. She won that round.

It was easily the weirdest afternoon I'd ever spent in public. I was sure I'd die of embarrassment when a group of senior class Penultimates got caught behind us and started making cracks. Archer and his friends weren't bothered at all. They just ignored the seniors and kept doing their thing, and eventually the group jumped past us and kept playing.

Once I stopped caring what everyone around us thought, I attempted a few tricks of my own. I tried a one-handed putt; I swatted a putt backwards between my legs. I even tried to bat one in with my head, like in soccer, but that just hurt.

Still, I had no hope in this crowd. Even with their sympathy points, I lost by double digits.

"Cara pays for ice cream!" Doug crowed.

"You don't have to," Archer said.

"Of course she has to!" Sue said. "She lost; it's the rule!"

"I'm happy to pay," I said.

And I was. I'd had a lot of fun—way more than I'd thought I would. I was even okay with the ride to Friendly's, their ice cream spot of choice, as long as I could sit buckled into the passenger seat. I genuinely felt like part of their group, and even though the Ladder had nothing to do with my real reasons for being around Archer, I saw how well it could work. I'd gone from being a complete no one to a solid Cubby Crew member. Sure, it was a lower-level Cubby Crew and miles away from the Supreme Populazzi, but it was a position I could build on and work my way up.

Theoretically, I could do that. In practice, nothing sounded worse. If it meant being Archer's girlfriend, I'd embrace my inner Theater Geek forever.

Monday morning I came to school with a huge box of the peanut-butter-cream-cheese-Cap'n-Crunch apples. To me they're among the ultimate comfort foods, and Archer and his friends needed comfort. The *Cyrano* cast list was going up before the first bell rang, and each second of nervous anticipation was torture for them. Sue was pretty grossed out by the apples, but everyone else really liked them, and they all munched anxiously as they waited for Mr. Gates, the director. When they saw him, they gripped one another in a Gordian knot that included me.

Mr. Gates was brutal. As I understood it, he was pretty much the faculty advisor of the Theater Geeks and had been a huge part of their lives for the past two years. As he moved closer and closer, I saw each member of the group scan his face, searching for some kind of clue—a smile of approval, a sigh of sympathy. But he gave them nothing. He wouldn't even make eye contact.

Without releasing one another, we tiptoed close to read the list. There it was: Archer was Cyrano.

"You got it!" I screamed, and threw my arms around him.

He hugged me close and said "Thanks" softly in my ear. For a second I completely forgot we were in the middle of the school hall. We were in his basement again, all alone, and any moment he'd pull back and bring his lips to mine . . .

"Come to me, my darling!" Ember screamed. She ripped Archer away and gave him a huge kiss on the cheek. I checked the cast list. She was Roxanne, the female lead and the love of Cyrano's life. As she and Archer hugged, I noticed Sue looking at them wistfully. I knew she had also wanted the part of Roxanne and had to be disappointed, but I could have sworn there was something else in her eyes . . .

Maybe I was crazy, but I was suddenly very happy that Ember was cast as Archer's love interest and not Sue.

Rehearsals started that very afternoon and would severely impact Archer's and my Ping-Pong schedule. Archer made me promise we'd play on weekends. Of course I said yes, and we easily settled into a new routine. Saturdays we'd do things with the gang. They weren't just the Theater Geeks to me anymore; they really felt like my friends.

No matter what we did as a group on Saturdays, Archer and I would always end up at his house playing Ping-Pong. Sunday was homework day: I'd bring my books over and we'd study at his kitchen table.

More than a month went by this way. Archer and I spent an insane amount of time together, and no matter where we were or what we were doing, I'd feel his eyes on me. He always looked away when I caught him, but I knew what he was doing, because I did the same thing. I stared. I watched him as he chewed on his pencil when he pored over a history text. I watched him as we ran his lines for *Cyrano*. I watched him practice piano after he got into jazz band. I watched him, and I knew what I was thinking when I watched him, and if he was thinking the same thing when he watched me . . .

Except he never did anything about it. Not even when we were alone in my room, with the whole house to ourselves.

I hadn't arranged it that way. Mom and Karl had a wedding to go to one Saturday, the same day a guy was supposed to come fix our washing machine, so Mom asked if I'd stay home and wait.

"You can even have Archer over to keep you company," she added. It was the parental equivalent of a nudge and a wink. After Mom and Bina's first phone chat they'd exchanged numbers, and now Mom was Archer's biggest fan. Had it been at all possible, I'd have stopped liking him on principle alone.

I did have him over, and since we couldn't play Ping-Pong, we made Saturday our study day. We started out very productive, but then I brought out snacks, which led to a debate over whether or not Frosted Mini-Wheats without milk qualified as a snack. I said it did, but Archer maintained that breakfast cereal by definition was meant to be enjoyed at breakfast time only. This led me to wonder aloud about his intense need to categorize foods by meal and if it might be a deep psychological issue from his childhood. Somehow that reminded Archer of his mom's and Lila's obsession with DailyPuppy.com and how Bina would call him to the computer every morning to share an adorable puppy picture or video. He said it with a scoff, but I'd never heard of DailyPuppy.com, and it sounded like the cutest thing in the universe. I had to see it immediately and raced upstairs to my computer. He followed me.

As I plopped down at my desk and typed in the URL, Archer noticed the Tastykakes on my night table.

"You gave me Mini-Wheats when you have Tastykakes?" He picked up the package from its spot next to the mini Liberty Bell replica.

"Don't open that!" I shouted.

"Wow. Okay." He replaced the Tastykakes and backed away from it, his hands up.

"Sorry, it's just . . . you don't want to eat that."

"Because it's far too normal a food to have in your house?"

"Because it's about five years old."

Archer scrunched his face. "Tell me you're lying."

"I'm lying."

"Tell me you're lying without lying."

"Lying about lying? Or lying about the Tastykakes?"

He opened his mouth to speak, then paused. "I'm not sure. I'm confused now. Why would you have a five-year-old Tastykakes on your night table?"

"It's kind of a shrine," I admitted.

"A shrine to prepackaged snack cakes?"

"It's from a trip we took downtown when I was in sixth grade," I said. "I got to bring Claudia, and we did the whole Independence Hall/Liberty Bell thing, then Mom and Karl wanted to go on a walking tour. We begged until they said we could hang at the Bourse, as long as we held on to one of their cell phones. It was a huge deal because my parents had *never* been okay with me out in the world without a grownup."

"Sixth grade?" Archer asked.

"They were a little overprotective. They got better."

"So what did you do with your taste of freedom?" Archer asked. "Wait, I know. You and Claudia got matching tattoos. Liberty Bell tattoos. Rebellious and patriotic at the same time."

I was wearing shorts and a tank top, so I stretched out my arms and legs. "Do you see a Liberty Bell tattoo?"

Archer wiggled his eyebrows and looked me up and down. I gasped as if scandalized.

"No! No tattoos. We got soft pretzels and ice cream. Then we went to a cheesy gift shop where I bought the Tastykakes and the mini Liberty Bell, both of which I swore

I'd always keep on my night table, like a symbol of my independence."

"Wow . . . the Liberty Bell as a symbol of independence. I'm amazed no one else ever thought of that."

"I didn't say it was original."

Archer sat on my bed and plucked up the Tastykakes again. "I actually don't think these go bad."

"You wouldn't—"

"They're Peanut Butter Kandy Kakes. I love Peanut Butter Kandy Kakes."

"I'll buy you Peanut Butter Kandy Kakes."

"But these are right here. And you've only offered me dry Mini-Wheats. No jury would convict me."

"Archer . . ."

Archer held the package to his nose. "Mmm. Peanut buttery."

"Archer!"

"Want to split them?" he asked, and crinkled the package as if he were about to rip it open.

"Archer!" I leaped onto the bed and grabbed for the Tastykakes, but he leaned back, holding it just out of my reach. I lunged for it, but he quickly rolled off the other side of the bed. I pounced after him and raced around the room to catch him before he could open the package. I finally tackled him back onto the bed, pinning him down with my body so I could snatch the package away.

"HA!" I cried. I rolled onto my back and brandished the Tastykakes in triumph.

"Well done," Archer said, but when I looked over to rub in my victory, I froze.

He had propped himself up on one elbow and was gazing down at me. Our faces were inches away from each other, and I recognized something in his eyes: a look I saw when he read his lines as Cyrano, opening his heart to Roxanne.

I couldn't move. I made my breath shallow. I didn't want to do anything the least bit jarring. I didn't want to break the mood and stop what I knew was about to happen.

Only it didn't.

We stayed like that, lying side by side on my bed, all alone in the house, our eyes locked together . . .

Then the doorbell rang, and the spell was broken.

The repair guy.

We ran downstairs to open the door, then Archer and I went back to our books like nothing had happened.

I didn't want to tell Claudia about it. I'd actually stopped calling her lately, or only called when I knew I'd have to get off the phone in a second. I let her calls go to voice mail, and I answered her texts and e-mails as vaguely as possible.

I knew it was wrong. It wasn't that I didn't want to talk to her, but I didn't want to hear what I knew she'd say. It had already been a couple weeks since her texts changed from urging patience to pressing me for details on why Archer still hadn't made a move. I could only imagine her reaction to this. Better not to mention it. After all, I told myself, I'd only known him six weeks total. What was six weeks? It was nothing.

Sunday, after a day of Ping-Pong at Archer's house, I drove home for dinner to find Claudia's car parked in front of my house and a familiar braided figure sitting on our front stoop. There was no way I could keep driving. She'd already seen me, and I knew she would stay there all night if she had to. I parked my car and painted on a smile.

"Claude! It's so great to see you!"

I tried to hug her, but she held up her palm and gave me a steely glare.

"This is not a visit, Cara. This is an intervention."

Chapter *eight*

"I'm not saying he *is* gay, Cara. I'm just saying you have to consider the possibility that he *might* be gay."

I didn't even know how to respond to that, but apparently my face said it all. Claudia rolled her eyes and threw up her hands.

"Honestly, Cara, don't tell me you've never thought about it! You and Archer have been completely in each other's space for ages now. If he were really into you, wouldn't you have been . . . in each other's *space?*"

"Claudia!"

"What? I'm just saying most guys would have made some kind of move by now."

I blushed, thinking about the move he specifically *hadn't* made the day before. Claudia misunderstood. "He *did* make a move! How could you not tell me?"

"He didn't . . ."

I explained everything.

"But that doesn't mean he's gay!" I finished.

"No, it doesn't. It could just mean he's not interested."

"Thanks. That's great."

"*Or* that he's really shy. You said he's never had a girlfriend, right? So maybe he's like the forty-year-old virgin."

"Nice. Way to make him sound completely undesirable."

"Other options: gay or not into you."

"Okay, forty-year-old virgin. But it's not like *I've* ever had a boyfriend, and I'm not too shy to do something!"

"Then do it," Claudia said. She folded her arms like the conversation was over.

"Do . . . what?" I asked. "Make the first move? The thing you told me *not* to do because it would scare him away?"

"I was wrong," Claudia said.

"How do you know? What happened to patience? What happened to 'even if it takes him a while'?"

"A while, yes. This is an epoch! New species have mutated into existence since you and Archer first started flirting!"

"It's only been six weeks!"

"Cara, you stopped the Ladder for this guy!"

"Oh! So this is about the Ladder!"

"This is about *you*," Claudia said. "If Archer really likes you, I don't care about the Ladder. But if he doesn't, you're wasting an amazing opportunity and you're torturing yourself waiting for something that won't happen!"

I was all energized to respond. I really was. Except she was right. I honestly didn't think Archer was gay. If he was, he was very closeted, and he didn't need to be—not in his Cubby Crew. Doug wasn't. But it was possible. And it was a lot better than thinking that even though to me we seemed like the perfect couple, he really didn't think of me that way. The very idea made my stomach hurt.

Then again, maybe Archer *wanted* me to make the first move. Maybe he really *was* just crazy shy and needed a little encouragement. Maybe the second I leaned over and kissed him, he'd throw himself on me, kissing me, holding me close, inching his hand slowly underneath my shirt . . .

I was starting to sweat.

"So . . ." I asked Claudia, "did your Ladder research tell you anything about *how* to make the first move?"

I hate horror movies. Really, truly hate them. Would never in a million years go out of my way to see one. I even know that Archer hates horror movies, too.

This did not for one second stop me from adding *Saw* to my parents' Netflix queue. It came two days later, and I told Archer I really wanted to watch it. Friday night. At his house.

The timing was very specific. Saturday would be huge at Chrysella Prep. During the day was the Homecoming football game. This meant less than nothing to me, except for the fact that in the name of school spirit, Archer didn't have play rehearsal Friday night. In theory, this was so cast members could attend pep rallies, but neither Archer nor I were pep rally types.

Saturday *night* was the school's Halloween dance. Aside from the casting of *Cyrano,* this was the biggest event on the fall schedule for Archer and his friends. They started planning their costumes over the summer and coordinated to make a massive group statement. I'd seen pictures of the eight of them freshman year as the Muppets and sophomore year as the Eight Wonders of the Ancient World. Technically, there are *seven* wonders of the ancient world, but everyone agreed that Wonder Woman qualified as the eighth.

This year they were going as Greek gods and goddesses. They'd invited me to join them, but I had no confidence that I could pull off a costume as ornate as theirs, even after Sue promised to help me with the sewing. Besides, I had a kitty cat costume from last year that made me look *very* cute, so I figured I'd wear that.

My grand plan was for Archer and me to seal the deal and become a couple on Friday, making Saturday's Halloween dance our first official date. And who doesn't want to spend her first date all dressed up and dancing the night away with her brand-new boyfriend?

On Monday I told him my cinematic plans.

"Really?" Archer grimaced. "*Saw?* I thought you weren't into horror movies."

"People say if you're going to watch one, this is the one to watch," I said. I walked away enigmatically to avoid any questions I couldn't answer. At least, I tried for enigmatically, but I tripped over the outstretched feet of a Wasteoid and went sprawling. So much for mystique.

For once I was glad Archer was so busy with rehearsals. It was hard even to be around him that week. My head was too swimmy with what I knew I was planning and all the wonderful and horrific ways it could turn out. It played a constant fantasy loop that ranged from an insane makeout session on the Ping-Pong table to Archer racing from the room screaming, arms flailing as he ran to disinfect himself from the full-body assault.

I didn't go right to Archer's after school Friday. First I met

Claudia at my house, and we spent no less than four hours figuring out what I should wear, how I should do my hair, and how I should smell. Thankfully, Mom and Karl had their own Halloween party that night. They were so busy getting ready and out the door, they didn't notice the intensity of my preparation. Not that Mom would have objected. Had she known my plan, she probably would have jumped for joy and helped Claudia get me ready. Check that—first she would have called Bina, then they'd *both* have jumped in to help. Gross.

The first snag Claudia and I hit was underwear. Claudia insisted that my underwear had to be matching, clean, and cute. I figured clean was a given, but I couldn't imagine any scenario in which I'd be modeling my cute, matching underwear for Archer.

"That's not the point," Claudia said. "Articles of clothing could get moved around. Things could come off. You never know what he's going to see. Everything has to look good just in case. Besides, women are more confident when they have on sexy underwear. It's a documented fact."

Claudia knew her documented facts. I didn't question it. Unfortunately, I'd never bought underwear for any purpose beyond wearing it *under* things, so I didn't exactly have anything that worked as a smashing ensemble. And I certainly didn't have anything sexy.

Eventually, we settled on a basic white silky bra and white cotton bikini panties with a little lacy trim at the top. I stood in front of the mirror and we both studied my reflection. It wasn't anything we hadn't seen before; Claudia and I lived in bikinis over the summer. But this felt different.

"I don't know . . ." I said. "Do I look good?"

"You're slouching a little. Stand up straighter," Claudia advised.

I did. She nodded. "Perkier. Better."

"You think?" I turned to the side to get another view. "You don't think the waistband makes my stomach pook out a little? You don't think I need a fancier bra?"

"No pookage," Claudia said. "And you don't *have* a fancier bra. It's okay, though. If Archer actually gets to the bra, he won't want to judge it. He'll want to get *around* it, *beyond* it, and get you *out* of it."

Was it bad that the idea made me smile? Of course, if he got me out of it, I would be half naked with Archer. Half *naked*. Nobody had seen me naked since I was a kid. I didn't even let my mom see me naked. *I* didn't even like to look at me naked. But Archer might see me naked.

Not that it was likely. This would be our first time fooling around, and I was fairly certain neither one of us was an expert at getting people naked . . . but it wasn't out of the question. Naked was at least a possibility.

I might see *Archer* naked. Did I want to see Archer naked? The question was ridiculous; it made me think of him standing in front of an art class, throwing off a robe, and striking a pose. If naked happened, it wouldn't be a formal thing. We'd be attacking each other: kissing and unbuttoning and feeling and touching and . . .

I giggled as a shiver ran through me. Yeah, I wanted this. Badly. I quickly pulled on the rest of the outfit Claudia and I had picked: a skirt, which was both cute and more accessible than jeans; a thin long-sleeve shirt; and boots with heels. I tamed my hair with product and let the curls hang loose, and put on just enough makeup that I looked better than usual but not so much that I'd arouse suspicion right off the bat. We went fruity with the perfume: alluring without screaming "jump me" and in a small enough dose that he wouldn't smell me the minute my car pulled up out front. I grinned at the end result in the mirror. I looked good.

"You look *great*," Claudia amended. I swear she could read my thoughts. "Do you feel seductive?"

"I kind of do."

The drive to Archer's was all but impossible; I was concentrating so hard on my breathing, I forgot little things like headlights and turn signals. I took limited solace in the fact that if I died in a car wreck, I'd be wearing not just clean but cute, matching underwear.

As I parked and walked to Archer's door, I had to keep wiping my sweaty palms on my skirt. This was crazy! I'd been here a million times before! Why was I freaking out like a complete loser?

But of course I knew exactly why, and it made me blush the moment Archer opened the door.

"Wow . . . you look great," Archer said with more than a hint of surprise. Was it bad that me looking great surprised him?

I held up the DVD. "Ready to see *Saw*?"

"Seesaw? I've always been more of a monkey bars man myself, but sure."

We said hi to Archer's parents. Bina took in my outfit with a look that made me immensely grateful my mom and Karl were out. If they weren't, I had no doubt Bina would be on the phone with my mom immediately. I put the thought out of my mind and vowed not to think about Bina and Edward being right upstairs while Archer and I did whatever we were about to do. We grabbed two enormous cups of soda—not that I'd be touching mine—and a huge bowl of popcorn, then disappeared into the basement and put in the DVD.

I honestly can't tell you what happened in the movie. For me it was all about finding moments nerve-racking enough to lurch into Archer's arms and cower close. Luckily, there were a lot of those moments. Within the first fifteen minutes, Archer and I were locked together, gripping each other for dear life. My eyes were technically on the screen, but I saw nothing. I was completely tuned in to my other senses: the smell of Archer's skin, the feel of his body pressing against mine, the sound of his quickening heartbeat thudding against my ear.

In my head, I pored over Archer's every move. Was he holding me because of the movie or because he really wanted to hold me? His hand was moving on my arm . . . was he caressing me or was it just a distracted motion? Was he breathing harder because he was frightened or because we were closer than we had ever been? The few glimpses of the movie that actually sank in were gruesome, hideous, and everything I despised. It was disgusting . . . and I wanted it to go on forever.

Then it ended, and suddenly we had no excuse: we were just two people tangled in each other's arms. We shifted apart awkwardly. I knew what I had to do next—but I was terrified. And thrilled. My heart beat triple time. I felt like I was being chased by wolves.

Archer licked his lips and smiled. Did he know what I was thinking? Was he thinking the same thing?

He picked up his soda and took a sip. "So . . . what did you think?" he asked. His voice sounded higher than usual. Could he be nervous? Could he be secretly dying to kiss me but too afraid to do it? If so, it really was up to me. It had to be now. I'd never find a better time.

I shut my eyes for just a second and took a huge breath. This was it. I dove forward to close the gap between my lips and his—

"Want more popcorn?" he yelled, and leaped back and away so fast that the entire couch toppled over backwards. His soda poured all over us.

"*Ow!*" I screamed as my head thudded onto the floor.

"Oh God! Are you okay?" Archer leaped up and held out his hand to help me, but physical contact with him was now the last thing I wanted.

"I'm fine! I'm fine!" The soda plastered my thin shirt to my body. When I stood, the sticky liquid drained down my legs and into my boots. Then I felt the soda seep into my underwear. Perfect.

"You're soaked. I'm so sorry. Here, I . . ." Archer grabbed a bunch of napkins and reached out as if he was going to dab me dry, but he just waved the napkins in front of my drenched skirt and shirt, clearly too mortified to dream of actually touching me.

He didn't have to worry; he had nothing on me in the mortification department. "It's fine," I said, taking the napkins and uselessly blotting the mess.

"Cara, I—"

I couldn't bear an explanation.

"No, stop," I said. "Please. I'm okay. I just . . . I need to go."

I grabbed my purse and raced up the stairs, but he stopped me halfway.

"Cara, wait!"

I winced. I swear I didn't want to hear how much he hoped

we could still be friends. Reluctantly I turned and looked at him. The soda had spilled all over him, too. He looked wet and miserable. Of course he was miserable. The idea of my lips touching his had repelled him so much that he chose to risk concussion rather than let it happen. I could see it in his eyes: he thought I was pitiful.

"Cara . . ."

I was going to cry. If I had to hear him try to make it better, I was going to cry, and crying in front of him was the one thing that would make this even worse. I gripped the railing, curled in my lips, and bit down on them, fighting back the tears.

"You're, um, forgetting the movie," Archer said. The tone of his voice had changed. It was flatter. Good. He must have decided not to explain. There was a chance I could survive. I realized he was holding out the DVD and I snatched it, making sure our hands didn't touch.

"GreatThanksBye," I said. I raced upstairs, out of the house, and into my car. I got there just before the tears started rolling down my cheeks. I was such an idiot.

Back home in my room, I peeled out of my wet clothes, put on my thickest pajamas, and crawled into bed. My skin was still sticky from the soda, but I didn't even care. I just wanted to get under the covers, close my eyes, and forget the day had ever happened.

It was nice in bed. With the covers pulled close around me, I could tune out everything else. I felt warm and safe. I guess there's a reason they call it a comforter.

I determined to stay right there for the rest of my natural life.

Chapter nine

Whatever happened to taking to one's bed? Virginia Woolf once took to her bed for eight weeks. I barely got eight hours before Karl was banging on my door.

"Cara, wake up! Family constitutional!"

"Idonwannafamlyconstooshnl." I tried to sound incoherent and ill, just this side of my deathbed.

"You love a family constitutional. Come on!"

How did Karl speak deathbed? I tried another tack. "I'm tired!"

"You were home before us, and we're wide awake!"

Oh, that was a great way to make me feel better. Remind me my parents have a better social life than I do.

"I'm staying in bed!"

That did it. I heard the heavy tread of Karl's feet moving down the hall. Good. Now I could go back to sleep and dream I was someone with an easier life than mine. Like a leper.

Two minutes later I heard the return of Karl's heavy tread. "Make sure you're decent!" he called.

Oh God, really? Was he really going to come in here? I willed myself to lie perfectly still so he'd think I was asleep.

He opened the door. I could hear him at the side of my bed. He was waiting for me to move and blow my cover. Wouldn't happen.

"You leave me no choice, Cara," he said.

He gently poured a Dixie cup of water on my head.

"*KARL!*" I screamed, bolting upright. "Are you mental?"

When I was *six*, the Dixie cup of water on my head had been funny. At sixteen? Not funny. And after last night's drenching? *Especially* not funny.

Karl didn't seem concerned. "Ah, so you *are* awake! Come on, get out of bed. Family constitutional time. We're leaving in twenty minutes."

He walked out of the room, shutting the door behind him. Infuriating. But he won. I took a quick shower, pulled on some clothes, and twenty minutes later I was out the door for a family constitutional. It was really just a *walk,* but Karl liked the more proper sound of "constitutional."

It was nice, actually. Karl was in a good mood. He and Mom had lots of funny stories from their party. It was warm for October, and the air smelled like freshly mown grass. For maybe five minutes I could almost forget last night's disaster.

Then we got home and my cell phone was beeping and of course it was Claudia and of course I told her everything.

"So what do you think?" I finished. "Think our parents will mind if I move in with you and go back to Pennsbrook?"

Claudia sighed. "We already asked, remember? They turned us down flat. So barring that, the next best move is clear: you rise like the phoenix from the ashes—or like the kitty cat from the ashes—and you go to tonight's Halloween dance."

"Oh, Claudia, there's no way."

"You have to show him this didn't break you. 'The robb'd that smiles steals something from the thief; / He robs himself that spends a bootless grief.'"

"I know that one. *Othello*. It's a tragedy. Everyone dies at the end."

"Not the duke, and he's the one who said it," Claudia noted. "You don't have to go for long. Just put in an appearance. The cat costume looks amazing on you. Archer will *wish* he'd wanted you. At the very least he'll see you're not pining over him. And if you really put your mind to it, you might even find your next rung on the Ladder."

I didn't even want to think about the Ladder, but I did like the idea of Archer seeing me in the cat costume and maybe regretting his decision. And I *really* liked the idea of him knowing I had better things to do than pine over him.

So I went to the dance. I went late. I wanted Archer to be there already, and I knew he and his friends liked to make an entrance. Plus I wanted extra time to make sure I looked hot—which I did. The costume was basically a sleek black leotard over densely woven fishnet stockings. The neckline was just low enough to show a little cleavage and trimmed in fuzzy black fur. With a thin black ribbon choker around my neck, the headband ears pulling back my curls, the tail pinned to my butt, a little bit of eyeliner to make my blue eyes pop . . . I looked really good. If I had turned myself down the night before, I'd see me walk in and know I had made a horrible mistake. I pulled on a pair of heels, promised Mom and Karl I'd be back before my midnight curfew, and took off for Chrysella.

The dance was in the gym, and I could feel the deep bass thrum of the music from my car as I pulled up. I fully intended to do just what Claudia had said: strut in, show my stuff, make a round, maybe dance one song just to pound home the fact that I was well beyond okay, then leave. I honestly don't know what changed my mind—a small voice of self-preservation?

I did strut—but only to the nearest doorway. Then I stopped. Safely hidden in its shadow, I peeked in.

The gym was packed, but all I could see were the Populazzi. With all four grades at the dance, there were a lot of them, and they lit up the party, especially the Populazzi girls. They ruled the center of the room, dancing and laughing and having more fun than anyone else.

The junior class Populazzi in particular jumped out at me . . . mainly because they were wearing my same costume. Let me clarify: they were dressed as cats, just like me . . . but they were cats in heat. "We're the Pussy Posse!" I heard one of them squeal.

Their costumes were two-pieces. The tops were black bustier halters with red velvet bra cups and plunging décolletage. The red velvet skirts flared out in black ruffles that fell only to their upper thighs. Like me they wore fishnets, but theirs were topped off with rhinestone-studded garters. Their choker collars were also rhinestone-studded, their cat ears were lined in more red velvet, and their tails were wispy . . . as opposed to the rat tail hanging off my rear end.

There was no way I could go into the dance now. The Pussy Posse were feline supermodels. Next to them I'd look like a mangy alley cat fresh from the dumpster. I should have turned around and left immediately, but I couldn't take my eyes off them, especially Trista. She was constantly engaged. I saw her lean in close and share things with the senior class Populazzi, with the younger classes, with her Penultimates. Everyone glowed brighter when she turned her spotlight on them—though no one glowed as brightly as Trista herself.

A slow song came on, and Trista gave a hopeful look to her boyfriend, Brett. The hopeful part was just to be cute; she must have known he'd come to her. When he did, it was like a scene in a romantic movie. He looked at her as if she was the most dazzling girl he'd ever seen. As he pulled her close and she rested her head on his chest, I almost cried. It surprised me, but then I realized why.

It was exactly the moment I thought I'd have tonight with Archer.

Where was Archer? I hadn't even looked for him. I clung even more tightly to the shadows as I scanned the room.

My breath caught in my throat. He was . . . a Greek god. As Poseidon, Lord of the Sea, he wore a flowing aquamarine toga festooned with seashells. A long dark wig braided with more seashells curled past his shoulders, a huge shell-crown sat on his head, and he carried a large trident. Every bit of his costume, hair, and face had been brushed with glitter, so his whole body glistened like it was under water.

He looked magnificent. Worse, he looked happy. The Theater Geeks might not have been in the center of the room like the Populazzi, but they'd carved out their own corner, and within it they sparkled. Their costumes were a million times more ornate than anyone else's, and while that seemed to draw more sneers than awestruck stares, they didn't care. They danced and laughed and struck poses of godlike glory.

Archer wasn't missing me at all. Why would he? He was in his element, having the time of his life with all his closest friends. I had to be the furthest thing from his mind.

As I kept staring, one of the other Theater Geeks walked up to him, and it took me a minute to realize it was Sue. She was Aphrodite, Goddess of Love, à la *Venus on the Half Shell*. She wore a glittering skin-tone unitard, perfectly adjusted to push her every curve into its ideal position. Her long blond wig cascaded to the floor, clinging strategically to her body as it fell.

She was absolutely breathtaking.

Archer leaned close to whisper something in her ear. She laughed and put her hand on his arm.

I tasted bile.

I suddenly remembered that in Greek mythology, Poseidon had been one of Aphrodite's lovers. Did Sue know that? Did Archer?

Sue placed her hands on Archer's shoulder and pulled herself up on tiptoe to whisper back to him. I saw the curve of her breast press against his arm, and anxiety sped up my heart. I felt the blood pulse in my head with almost unbearable pressure, and I gripped the doorjamb to keep from falling. I wasn't sure how much longer I could watch and still survive.

The DJ saved me. I don't even know what he played, but it was loud and it was fast and it made Ember squeal and dive between Archer and Sue to rally them for a huge group flail-fest.

Eventually, my heartbeat went back to normal and I started breathing again, but I felt exhausted, as if I'd just gotten over a long illness. I knew I needed to leave and recuperate, but ripping myself away from the door was like peeling back Velcro.

"'I've been waiting for you,' Cara Leonard," said a voice from the shadows as I trudged back to my car. "'We meet again at last. The circle is now complete. When I left you, I was but the learner; now *I* am the master.'"

I had to smile. I knew only one person who opened conversations with *Star Wars* quotes, and he was the very first person I'd met at Chrysella. Claudia would kill me, but what the hell. I turned to face him.

"'Only a master of evil,' Robert Schwarner," I continued the quote.

"Nice," he said. Robert sat on the grass between the parking lot and the gym. In the lotus position. He swayed to the music. "How was the dance?" he asked.

"I didn't really go in." I walked over and plopped down next to him. "You?"

"Nah. I don't really like dances. But I like Halloween. And I like music. So I dress in costume and come sit out here."

I checked out his outfit. "Aren't you wearing the same cloak you wear to school every day?"

"It only looks the same. This is Throck Medvale's winter cloak from *BeastSlayer II*. It's for costume purposes only. My daily cloak is from the first *BeastSlayer*."

"I see." I studied him, then asked, "Robert, are you happy at Chrysella?"

Robert thought a minute, then shrugged. "It's high school. One day it'll all be over."

He went back to swaying. I watched him a moment, then headed to my car.

"Good night, Robert."

"Night. Oh, and Cara—you look really hot."

I laughed. "Thanks."

I drove home thinking about what Robert had said about being happy. He was right. High school was just high school. One day it would all be over. The key wasn't to try to make it amazing, but just to get through. And from now on, that's exactly what I'd do. I'd keep my head down, study, and work like crazy so there was no doubt I'd get into Northwestern.

That's when everything would change: college. I was done with the social scene at Chrysella, I was done with banging my head against the wall, and despite what Claudia wanted, I was *definitely* done with the Ladder.

Chapter *ten*

Claudia wasn't happy when I told her I had no intention of ever getting back on the Ladder again. I drove to her house to let the bomb drop, then watched her do a ten-minute dumb show of frustration. She threw her arms in the air and stormed away just far enough that it seemed she was leaving me forever— despite the fact that I was in her house and sitting on her bed, so that clearly wasn't an option—then turned her head to me and stared daggers. She stalked back and eyed me appraisingly, twitching her braided loops in a way that should have been physically impossible. She reached her arms to the sky, imploring the Lord Above to help her, help her save this lost and confused soul. She paced in front of me, arms clasped behind her back, and discussed me as if to a jury.

"I ask you," she asked no one, "what am I supposed to do with this woman? How do you help someone who has no idea what's truly good for her? What more can I do?"

I piped up and entered into evidence one fact I hadn't mentioned: that I'd managed to strike up what could conceivably be called a friendship with a member of the Happy Hopeless.

Claudia fell to her knees in shock.

All told, she reveled in her outrage for about a half hour. Then she brought out the Uno cards. After she beat me, I borrowed her mom's old bike and we made the several-mile trek out to Core Creek Park, where we cooled off with an easy cruise by the lake before turning around and cranking it back to Claude's. The fall air was just crisp enough to burn my lungs each time I strained uphill, standing in the saddle and fighting to keep my momentum. I wasn't the most coordinated rider—I had to look straight ahead or I'd veer off in whatever direction my gaze wandered. Still, I couldn't help letting my eyes roam the trees that lined the streets. Every leaf had exploded into color—huge, beautiful flakes of red, orange, and yellow. With each gust of wind, they burst off their branches and rained down on us. It felt like riding through confetti.

That was Sunday, and Sunday was fantastic.

Monday, however, was a misery. I knew I'd have to see Archer. I considered playing sick, but that would only postpone the agony. I reminded myself school was a job, not a social opportunity, and it was time to go to work.

The whole drive there, I fantasized about getting into a car crash. It couldn't be my fault, of course, and I wouldn't want to get hurt in a life- or long-term-quality-of-life-threatening way, but if the crash put me into a coma until after graduation, that would be good.

They say people can hear things in a coma, and I had faith that my mom would read textbooks to me so I'd stay up to date on schoolwork. By the time I woke up, I could ace a GED and go right on to college. Northwestern would go crazy for me. The "I Spent Junior and Senior Years in a Coma" story would make a great application essay. Karl would burst with pride. Maybe I'd even end up on *The Today Show*. Then I could land a motivational speaking tour and make so much money I wouldn't even need college. I'd still go, of course, but money wouldn't be an issue. I'd even give Karl a monthly allowance so he could hit the blackjack tables guilt-free.

Unfortunately, by now I was pulling into school, and since I was decidedly *not* in a coma, I had to deal.

I saw Archer within two seconds of walking in, but he wasn't waiting for me at my locker. He was back by his old window seat with Ember, Sue, Dinah, and the rest of the gang. He stood in the middle of their group, making them all laugh, but he froze when he saw me.

Of course he did. He had thought it was perfectly clear we were just friends, and I'd thrown myself on him like an unhinged nymphomaniac. I was sure the coma-till-graduation option would have been fantastic for him, too.

That's when I realized something. While I couldn't actually disappear, I *could* make what had happened disappear. I'd just act like it had never occurred, and I'd stay far enough away from Archer that we'd never have to deal with it. Ever.

Uh-oh. He was walking toward me. He looked nervous. He was probably worried I was going to do something stupid like collapse into tears or profess my undying love right there in the hall.

"Cara, hey!" he said. "I, um . . . didn't see you at the Halloween dance. I would have called, but . . ."

I laughed, as if the idea of him calling was the most preposterous thing in the universe. "I didn't go," I said with a shrug. "A little under the weather, no biggie. Talk to you later!" I turned and strode toward my locker, but he followed right along.

"I, um . . ." He took a deep breath, then lowered his voice. "I kind of thought maybe we should talk."

"About what?" I asked. And here was the impressive part: I stopped walking and turned to face him with a perplexed look on my face, like I genuinely had no idea what he was talking about.

"About . . . you know . . ."

I gave him nothing. I shrugged my shoulders again and looked at him curiously.

The standoff continued for maybe a minute, and I had no idea how to get out of it gracefully. Then inspiration struck. "Ooh, it's my aunt's birthday! I want to text her before class starts. I'll see you later, okay?"

"Okay," he replied, but I was already zipping out a side door to deliver my pretend text.

Wow. That kind of worked. It wasn't fun, but it worked. I could handle being in the same universe as Archer without falling apart. I could.

When I walked into English, I saw Archer had saved my usual spot next to him. I walked right past it and settled in across the room, sitting between a Happy Hopeless and a Cubby Crew. I don't know how Archer reacted. I didn't let myself look.

Lunch was a little more challenging. Finding a whole new group to sit with was way too daunting to handle. Happily, the vending machines still had Diet Cokes and Zone bars. I could've eaten in my car, but it felt conspicuous. I might be a loser, but I didn't have to look like one. I wandered around the main building until I found a small cement stairwell that led to some kind of basement door. The stairwell was littered with dried leaves—not surprising, since the whole area was half hidden by trees. The door itself was padlocked. I could only imagine what was in there—storage, I supposed. Whatever it was, it looked as though it hadn't been disturbed in ages. No one would see me down here, and it offered a bit of shelter from the cold. It was the perfect place to curl up with my lunch, hang out, and read until it was time for my afternoon classes. After school I drove home as quickly as possible.

This became my daily schedule. At first Archer tried to catch my attention and make conversation. I wasn't surprised. He was a nice person; I'm sure he felt obligated. I was always smiley, friendly, and very, very busy, so he soon realized he didn't have to make the effort.

It was perfect. Sure, I was more isolated than I'd have liked, and I did worry a little that someone might catch me in my lunchtime hideaway and mistake me for a homeless person, but I wasn't in pain on a daily basis, and that seemed like a totally reasonable tradeoff. As the weeks rolled by, I even decided the hermit life suited me. Oh, sure, there were some things I missed. I couldn't bring myself to go see Archer in *Cyrano,* for example, even though I knew he'd be brilliant. I'd spent so many weeks running lines with him and imagining he was thinking about *me* when he said each romantic word . . . To hear them now would be torture.

I still might have tried if I hadn't already experimented with the previous week's jazz band concert. It was awful. Seeing Archer play piano reminded me of when I used to watch him practice at his house. It hurt too much. I tried to focus on the rest of the band and concentrate on the music, but it didn't help. I sneaked out in the middle of the show.

On the plus side, I threw myself into classes and studying, and easily pulled Karl from his newspaper every night at dinner with deep discussions about U.S. history, physics, and what could have possibly driven the otherwise brilliant T. S. Eliot to write *Old Possum's Book of Practical Cats*. I had been a great student all year, but now I was Super Scholar, more knowledgeable than a speeding megacomputer, able to read tall textbooks in a single sitting.

With so much on my plate, time flew, and soon it was Thanksgiving break. It started out perfectly. My report card came in the mail, and it whisked me into Chrysella's honor roll stratosphere. Karl practically had a party for me when he saw it. He faxed the report card right to Stevenson Jaffe. If I got really lucky, I figured Dean Jaffe would be so blown away that he'd suggest I skip the rest of junior and senior years and get my butt to Northwestern immediately.

I spent Thanksgiving morning with my parents—or technically with Mom, since Karl's Thanksgiving was all about the NFL. Mom made the bird, the stuffing, and the pumpkin pie and set the table. I handled the green bean and sweet potato casseroles, and the rolls. I was also the official cranberry sauce musher. I took great pride in crushing away every last vestige of metal can lines. My aunt and uncle came in from Connecticut with my two little cousins and their super-mellow corgi mix, Lulu, and I forgot everything in the happy flurry of family chaos.

That night Karl fell asleep in front of the TV while Mom and I cleaned up. It took forever, but then we settled in at the kitchen table for late-night coffee and pie.

"Did you have fun today?" Mom asked.

I nodded, my mouth full. "I'm totally getting a dog like Lulu when I have my own place."

"She's a sweetie." Mom took her last bite of pie and a swig of coffee, then said, "So I spoke to Bina the other day . . ."

I froze. I looked at Mom, but she was concentrating on running her finger over her plate to sweep up scrapes of pumpkin. She wasn't giving me her Face of Ultimate Sympathy. That meant she might not know.

"Really?" I asked. "How is she?"

"She's good. She mentioned she hadn't seen you in a while, and I said I'd noticed the same thing, that you and Archer didn't seem to be spending time together. Is everything okay?"

"Everything's great," I said. "We just both got busy, that's all. But if you talk to Bina again, tell her I say hi. I really like her."

Mom smiled, satisfied. "I will. I like her, too."

"Want to play backgammon?"

"We haven't played in ages. I don't even know where the board is."

"I do. I'll get it."

I raced upstairs, pausing for just a moment in the bathroom to splash cold water on my face and shock back the giant lump of emotion threatening to push its way out. I stared at myself in the mirror and took two deep breaths. I was strong. I was fine.

I smiled at my reflection and trotted off to grab the backgammon board.

Friday morning I drove out to Claudia's for the weekend. As always, it made me wish I'd never moved away or that she could go with me to Chrysella. It was just so easy with Claudia. There was no pressure of wondering if this person or that person liked me and wanted me around. There was no second-guessing everything I said and worrying that I was messing up a potential friendship. There was no new-school/new-friends angst. I could just be myself.

I'd promised my parents I'd be home by dinner Sunday so I could "get a good night's sleep" before school, but as I knelt on Claude's bedroom floor rolling up my sleeping bag, something huge and heavy slammed down in front of me. It was the giant yellow binder with THE LADDER written on the front.

"It's time," Claudia said. She sat cross-legged on her bed like a guru.

"Seriously? Haven't we had this discussion? Didn't we determine I was done with the Ladder forever?"

"In a fit of pique, you made a grandiose statement you didn't really mean. I shan't hold it against you."

"Oh, shan't you?"

"You fail to realize it, but you have already had tremendous success with the Ladder," she said.

There was no clever retort to that; it was so beyond the realm of sanity, I couldn't do anything but gape at her for several seconds. She was unmoved. Was she really going to make me spell this out again?

"Here were Archer's choices," I said. "A: endure a single kiss from a reasonably attractive girl, or B: risk severe head trauma to both himself and said houseguest, who could conceivably then sue his family for everything they have. Guess which one he chose?"

"That means nothing. We've established that he's probably gay, remember? If a gay man doesn't want to kiss you, it only means you're not masculine enough for him. To me, that's a compliment."

It was an argument she had used before, and it wasn't entirely wrong—*if* Archer was gay. Which I doubted.

"Even if he's not gay," Claudia continued, "even if he's just ridiculous and stupid and not interested, there is no denying that by being his close friend, you officially earned a spot on the Popularity Tower. Am I right?"

Of course she was right. I'd noticed it myself when I started hanging out with Archer's friends. Even though I couldn't act to save my life, for a while I'd been an honorary member of the Theater Geek Cubby Crew.

But that was *before*. Now I didn't see them at all. I reminded Claudia of that little factoid.

"Doesn't matter," she said. "It's been, what, a few weeks? That's a blip. Nonexistent. You'll pick up right where you left off the minute you restart your friendship with Archer."

Restart my friendship with Archer?

I wished I'd been middrink so I could give her comment the spit-take it deserved.

"No way," I said. "Can't do it. If I do, he'll think I want him again, and he'll get that sad look on his face because he'll feel like he has to let me down gently and I swear, Claudia, I would rather drink hot glue."

"So the drama!" Claudia raised the back of one hand to her forehead, then grinned and leaned down to me. "He *won't* think you want him, because of the beauty of the Ladder! The minute you hook back up with Archer, you ask for his help getting you someone on the next tier of the Popularity Tower: a DangerZone. Instant fix: immediately Archer knows for a fact you're no longer interested."

"But I *am* still interested," I said.

"Of course you are. But what's the best way to get you *not* interested? A distraction. Actively working to get someone new, exciting, and incredible—not to mention someone who's actually into *you*. Now think about it: Are there any DangerZones you like? Any Archer could help you get?"

I thought about it. I thought about everyone in Archer's circle. They were all Theater Geek Cubby Crew. There were lots of other people who knew and liked Archer from a distance, I supposed. There was everyone who'd watched him perform that poem the first day of school, all the people who'd raved about him in *Cyrano,* and everyone who'd gone crazy over the jazz band concert . . .

The jazz band concert. There was a guitarist in the jazz band. Nate Wetherill. I remembered seeing him my very first day, stalking down the halls with his guitar case on his back, wafting DangerZone hotness with every step. I'd seen him a few times after that. He and Archer always said hi in the halls. Or Archer said hi. Nate always gave a moody upward nod, which was still a million times more attention than he gave most people in the school. Even then, when I thought Archer and I were basically together, Nate made me stop and stare. But it was the way a hot celebrity would make me stop and stare. It was fantasy. Nate was way out of my league. He wasn't even an option. I had to laugh.

Claudia pounced. "You thought of someone! Who?"

"Nate Wetherill," I admitted. "And he's Archer's friend . . . ish."

"That's perfect!"

"It's ridiculous. Nate would *never* be interested in someone like me."

"You're forgetting the rules of the Ladder. There is no 'someone like' you. You find out the kind of girl Nate wants, you *become* that girl, then you burst out of your Chrysella chrysalis transformed and blow him away! You'll get together, you'll move to his tier on the Popularity Tower, and most important, you'll be so completely distracted that you'll finally get over Archer."

Getting over Archer sounded great—exactly what I needed to make Chrysella bearable again. Getting over Archer by hanging out with him and getting his help with the Ladder? That sounded like the craziest kind of reverse psychology ever, which is what I told Claudia.

Claudia climbed down from her bed and sat in front of me. She took my hands and looked me in the eye. "Archer does not want to be your boyfriend," she said mercilessly.

I cursed myself for feeling tears spring to my eyes.

"Know it," she continued. "Believe it. Be cool with it. If you can do that, not only will you get to be with someone who *does* want to be your boyfriend, but you'll also get back a guy who had become a really close friend. Don't you want that?"

The tears dried up before they ever spilled over. Once again, Claudia knew exactly what to say. I did want that. I wanted it badly.

"Okay," I finally agreed, "tomorrow morning I climb back onto the Ladder."

Chapter *eleven*

I left Claudia's house feeling strong and decisive. She was right—climbing back onto the Ladder was my key to getting over Archer. After all, I tried to convince myself, it's not as though I was in love with him or anything. How could I be? We were never even together. So it couldn't be heartbreak that had my stomach in knots at the very idea of being around him again. It had to be simple embarrassment. Yet if I stepped back and looked at the big picture, was what happened between us *that* hideous? No, not terribly. It could even be funny one day, months and months from now, when I was happy with someone new.

But that would come later. If Archer and I were going to be friends again right now—something I really did want—there was only one way to make it work.

I let my car idle in the school parking lot and listened to the drum of the downpour outside. I concentrated on the sound and took deep breaths, letting the noise drown out every negative thought in my head. I knew exactly how I wanted this to play out, and I didn't want anything to throw me.

Finally I raced inside, ditched my coat in my locker, grabbed my books, and zipped into English class less than a minute after the bell rang.

"The Hyacinth Girl!" boomed Mr. Woodward as I walked in. He pointed the Bat at me, stopping me in my tracks, then fixed me with a knowing glare. "Do you know *why* I'm calling you the Hyacinth Girl, Cara?"

"Because I'm late, my arms are full, and my hair is wet?" I said, remembering the passage from T. S. Eliot's *The Waste Land*.

Mr. Woodward smiled. "I see the tryptophan didn't stop *someone* from doing her reading over vacation. Well done."

He lowered the Bat and let me pass. I walked straight to my old spot next to Archer as if the past several weeks had never happened, and I reclaimed my old perch on top of the table.

"A continental shift," Mr. Woodward noted, then continued with the class. Archer, however, sat in his chair with his jaw hanging open. He looked up at me as if for an explanation, but I didn't give him one. I didn't ignore him, though. Not even remotely. I smiled down at him every time Mr. Woodward or someone else in the class made us all laugh. I rolled my eyes to him whenever someone said something ridiculous. I made sure he was one of the people I looked at whenever I spoke up to make a point.

I expected it to be harder than it was. But any time I looked at Archer and felt a pang, I heard Claudia's voice saying, "Archer does not want to be your boyfriend." It wasn't fun hearing it over and over in my head, but it was effective. And while I didn't exactly get over him in that English class, I started to feel like maybe one day soon I could. Plus I had a new incentive: just interacting with him the littlest bit in class reminded me how much I missed hanging out together. Getting that back without all the pain was totally worth a few harsh reality checks.

But I knew I couldn't really be around Archer without some ground rules, so when class ended, I fell into step next to him.

"Cara, I—" he started, but I held up a palm and silenced him.

"Just answer me one question: do you want to be friends again?"

"I never wanted to stop being friends. Look, can't we—"

"Please-please-please, just say yes or no. Do you want to be friends again?"

I could tell he was struggling not to say everything he wanted. I appreciated the effort.

"Yes," he said. "Of course I want to be friends again. I just—"

"Please!" I begged. "I do, too. But first I need you to promise me something."

"Okay . . . what?"

"We never speak of it again." I said it very clearly, with no emotion.

Archer looked confused. "But Cara—"

"No. That's the deal. It's like it never happened. Can you be cool with that?"

Archer opened his mouth to speak . . . but he didn't. He looked frustrated, concerned, even angry. Finally he sighed and shook his head.

"Fine," he said.

I felt a rush of relief so huge, I almost wanted to hug him— then I let Claudia's words scream out in my head again.

"Is there still a seat next to you at lunch?"

I was suddenly sure he'd say no, that Sue now sat next to him every day. It was a land mine I hadn't thought of until now.

"There's a seat. I'll save it for you."

"Great! See you then!"

I walked off to precalc feeling lighter than I had in weeks. This was going to work. There'd be rough patches, but it would work.

Dealing with Archer's friends turned out to be one of the rough patches. For once Claudia was wrong—they weren't happy to pick up where we'd left off. They were nice enough; they were just distant.

The lunch seating had changed, too. Sue and Doug were back at the table; Noah and Molly were gone. I got the feeling it was a keep-your-enemies-close thing for Sue. By now I was pretty sure she had a crush on Archer. I think she wanted to keep me off her turf. If I had been feeling more charitable, I could have told her she had nothing to worry about. I was actually surprised she didn't already know. Maybe Archer hadn't told them everything that had happened between us.

Things with Archer himself went fairly smoothly. We'd been such good friends, it was impossible not to fall back into our easy rapport. It wasn't long before we were grabbing fries together at the mall, and soon after that we even started playing Ping-Pong again. I was happy to see he had never taken down the giant wall chart, even though it gave me a romantic pang I had to quash.

In the meantime, I dedicated myself to the Ladder and filling my mind with Nate Wetherill. It was a little weird. I had gone after Archer because I really liked him. I was attracted to Nate—anyone would be attracted to Nate—but I knew nothing about him. I had to *work* at liking him, as if he were a school assignment. Sometimes it bothered me that I was being so calculating, but then Claudia would remind me of the alternative—permanent Archer obsession—and I'd get over it.

So I studied Nate. And I looked for things to like.

Nate was very broody. He frowned like he was constantly tortured with deep, troubling thoughts. That wasn't really my thing.

He didn't seem to have a lot of friends. Any, really. Also not my thing.

He did have the attention of the Populazzi. I saw it when I was in the halls between classes. Just like everyone else, Trista Camello stepped aside and stared when Nate walked by. Even the Senior Populazzi noticed him. If I were his girlfriend, part of that mystique couldn't help but rub off on me.

It was cool to think about, but it still wasn't enough to make me like him.

Then one day I was late coming in to lunch, and I saw him. He sat outside on a rock, strumming his guitar and singing softly.

I stopped to listen, then moved closer, staying behind him and far enough away that he wouldn't see me.

He was incredible.

I didn't recognize the song he played, but it was beautiful. I wondered if he'd written it himself. His broodiness seemed melodramatic when he walked through the halls, but it was perfect for the song. Just watching him, I could tell how serious he was about his music. He seemed to pour his entire soul into what he played, and seeing it happen right in front of me . . . I was awed. I wanted to sit at his feet and listen all day.

Talent and passion: *those* were my thing. Those I could fall for.

From that moment, I tried to watch Nate as often as possible while he was playing guitar. It wasn't that challenging: any spare moment he had, he used it to play. I just had to slip outside or look through the right window and I'd get to see the show.

Nate was hot no matter what, but when he played, his hotness went off the charts. His spiked hair fell across his left eye as he bent over his guitar. Shadows played over the sharp angles of his face. His eyes, which were so distant normally, filled with emotion.

The more I watched Nate play, the more fascinated I became not just with his music but with him. I followed his fingers moving over the guitar strings, and I imagined running my thumb over their calluses. I listened to his songs and imagined he was singing them to me. I imagined the two of us cuddled together on a couch somewhere, Nate strumming chords and making up lyrics to try to put into words everything deep and wonderful he felt about me.

I was a good student. I was totally falling for Nate Wetherill.

Eventually Archer noticed. We'd be talking and I'd see Nate out of the corner of my eye and lapse into fantasyland, losing track of our conversation entirely. Sometimes Nate would look our way and nod or even give a sly half smile. I'd melt a little, imagining the look was for me . . . but of course it was meant for Archer. Archer always caught me when I got dazey like that, and he'd scrunch his face at me, but I'd snap out of it pretty quickly. I didn't want to let him in on my plan until our friendship was rock solid again.

It took about two weeks.

"Archer," I said as we split a massive sundae at Friendly's, "we're friends, right?"

"Only if you let me have the peanut butter cup," he said.

"Done."

He plucked it out and took a bite.

"And friends help each other," I said.

"I believe that is indeed part of the *Webster's* definition, yes," he said after another bite of the candy—which looked really, really good.

"You're totally giving me the last bite of that, right?"

He pondered a moment, then handed it over. I popped it in my mouth, looked around to make sure no one from school was in earshot, then leaned across the table. "I want you to help me go out with Nate Wetherill."

Archer grimaced like I'd just told a bad joke. "What! Since when do you like Nate?"

"Shhh!" I looked around again to make sure no undercover gossip hounds were texting this information to the entire school. "I just do," I said, my voice barely above a whisper. "He's . . . you know . . . hot. Like . . . rock-star hot." Yeesh, that sounded lame when I said it out loud.

Archer thought so, too. "'Rock-star hot'?"

"Whatever. I like him."

"So, what, you want me to tell him or something?" Archer asked, digging back into the sundae.

"No! You *can't* tell him. Not until I'm ready."

"Ready? Ready how?"

Ugh, how was I going to explain this? I couldn't tell him about the Ladder. There was no way he'd ever understand.

"You spend time with Nate in jazz band," I said. "You know him. You know what he likes to talk about, where he likes to go, what he likes to do . . . maybe even the kinds of girls he's into."

"Yeah. Not girls like you."

"Ouch. Blunt much?"

"You asked."

"I did. For a reason. That's why I need your help. I want to know everything about Nate. Everything he likes—especially everything he likes in a girl. Then once I know it, I can become it."

"Kind of *Fatal Attraction* meets *The Talented Mr. Ripley*. Classy."

"Archer . . ."

"What? You don't turn yourself into someone else to get a boyfriend. If it's the right person, it's supposed to just happen naturally. You meet, you click, you hang out . . ."

Did he not realize what he was saying? That's what had happened with us, and it had ended in disaster.

"I know, but I can't let it happen naturally with Nate. You said yourself that wouldn't work."

"Because you're not right for each other."

"Haven't you heard of 'opposites attract'?"

"Yes, but they attract as opposites, not because one changes for the other one. What do you even like about Nate? Aside from his 'rock-star hotness'?"

"I don't know yet! I don't know him! Maybe when I do, I won't like him, but I can't even *get* to know him if I seem like . . . you know . . . me."

"I think it's a dumb idea," Archer said.

This was going nowhere. Obviously, Claudia thought I had far better recruiting skills than I actually did.

But did I need recruiting skills for the Ladder? Sure, it would be easier to go after Nate with Archer's help, but I could conceivably do it on my own, right? The main reason I was telling Archer in the first place was so he'd know I was totally over him. That mission *had* to have been accomplished.

"Fine," I said. "You don't have to help me. I just thought it would be more fun that way."

"Fun? How would this possibly be fun for me?"

"It would be fun because it's a project, and we'd work on it together. Like"—I suddenly thought of exactly how I could make him understand—"like a musical! Think of it as *My Fair Lady*. You'd be Henry Higgins; I'd be Eliza Doolittle."

Archer thought for a moment. "How well do you know *My Fair Lady*?"

"I know Henry succeeds; he turns Eliza from a flower girl into a lady. You could do the same thing. It's a Cinderella story; you could be my fairy godmother."

"I do look good in a hoop skirt and wings."

"You see? You're thinking about it. You know it would be fun . . ."

"I know you have a twisted sense of fun."

"Come on. Let's do this together. You said you're my friend. You want me to be happy, right?"

Archer looked at me skeptically. "And you think Nate will make you happy?"

"I told you, I have no idea! But getting the chance to find out will make me very happy. Especially if I get to do it with you."

Archer thought a second, then he burst out in a perfect upper-crust British dialect. "'I'll take it! I'll make a duchess of this draggle-tailed gutter-snipe.'"

"You're quoting, yes?"

"Yes." Archer looked me in the eye. "Let's get to work."

Chapter *twelve*

"NateGate" was the name of our plan. We gave ourselves three weeks to make my transformation: the last week of school before Christmas break plus the break itself. After vacation I'd return to school as the new me and take Nate by storm.

Studying to become Nate's girlfriend took far more effort than studying for any other test I had ever taken, including the PSAT. Even the reading material was more intense, or at least there was more of it, most in graphic novel form. I had to read *Watchmen,* which Nate had told Archer was pretty much his bible. I also had to read a slew of other graphic novels, none of which involved Spiderman, Batman, or any other superhero I had ever heard of. While some of Nate's favorite books had become movies, I was strictly forbidden by Archer to watch them. Or if I had seen them, I was warned to either forget them or simply feel unclean from the sullying experience.

Then there was music. Music was not surprisingly the most important thing in Nate's life, and he would pretty much discount any girl who was into music that he considered pop and shallow. Music pointed to character. I told Archer I was neither pop nor shallow, and I thought my music choices reflected that just fine.

Archer pressed a preset button on my car radio. An old Britney Spears song blared, and I sang along to every word, bopping in my seat. Archer just looked at me.

"Oh, come on!" I said. "Who doesn't sing along to Britney?"

Archer changed my presets, but radio stations are fickle, and since he didn't want me listening to anything objectionable, he recommended I avoid the radio entirely. Instead he reprogrammed my iPod. Nate's particular passion was emo punk, which included some bands I actually knew from their big hits, like Paramore and My Chemical Romance; and a bunch that I had never heard of, like Jawbreaker, Braid, and Sunny Day Real Estate. Some I liked, some I didn't, but I made my new iPod mix my constant soundtrack, and even read up on the bands so I could speak intelligently about them.

What would be more challenging than changing my interests would be changing *me*. I was way too happy, well adjusted, and goofy for Nate, Archer assured me, and to prove it, we secretly tailed three of Nate's ex-girlfriends. Honestly, we could have saved time and just tailed one. Archer hadn't lied. Nate had a type, and it wasn't me. While my mane of curls burst out of my head in every direction, Nate's girls had poker-straight hair, with bangs that hung low over one eye. The hair could be dark, blond, or a streak-dyed combination of jet black and green, but the style remained the same.

They also seemed to dress in uniform. They all wore tight jeans with black belts that were sometimes chunky and ornamented. Over that they wore close-fitted tees: concert shirts of bands I knew from my new and improved iPod. All three wore snug zip-up hoodies that looked vintage seventies. One wore black boots, the others flats. Their makeup had some minor variations, but all three of them seemed to use an entire stick of black eyeliner around each eye. Several bangles adorned their wrists, and their nails were painted black.

Then there was the attitude. None of the girls seemed particularly happy. Not that they were actively crying or moaning, but I tend to think if someone saw me going about my daily business, they'd get the idea that I was probably a pretty happy person. Not so much with these girls. Even when they were hanging in the halls with their friends, even when they were *laughing* with their friends, they had this air of despair, like the moment was just a blip in an otherwise endless sea of malaise.

Could I really pull that off?

"Okay," I told Archer a few days later, "I've got the music, I've got the graphic novels, I've got the look and the attitude . . . or at least, I know what the look and the attitude are supposed to be. Do I need anything else?"

"A full brain transplant?" Archer suggested.

I threw a pillow at him. I was sitting on his bed as he packed. Christmas break had begun, and he and his parents were leaving in the morning for a trip to Chicago. Archer wouldn't be back until the night before classes started up again, so the rest of my training would be more of a correspondence course.

As it turned out, this was for the best. The biggest thing I needed to concentrate on now was my physical transformation. That meant tons of shopping, tiny dressing rooms, and honest opinions on whether this or that outfit pooched out my flab in horribly unflattering ways. For that, Claudia was far more helpful than Archer ever could have been.

Two days after he left town, she and I spent an entire day at the mall. We nailed a ton at Hot Topic: skinny jeans in several shades of black, some with added zippers, some pre-ripped, and one with skull designs that made me feel like a particularly ridiculous pirate. We also chose a few short black skirts with several different pairs of leggings. We got creative with the leggings: in addition to all varieties of black, we also found bright purple fishnets and a fuchsia zebra stripe. For shoes we went with one pair of boots, one pair of flats. We grabbed hoodies, tees, bangle bracelets, necklaces, earrings, arm warmers, and wrist warmers. The last two were important for the emo-chick mystique because, even if you've never considered cutting, it's apparently good to look like you have.

The day was insanely fun. It was like Claudia and I were playing dress-up. We'd both try on what were for us the most bizarre outfits imaginable, and even though we'd send several to the counter to be held, I didn't really comprehend that these would be my new wardrobe. Nor did I have any concept about how much I'd actually be spending—until I was rung up and I felt my head go swimmy. Claudia later told me that I grew so pasty white that I drew jealous sneers from several of the vampire wannabes in the store. Claudia slipped an arm around me to keep me upright.

"It's okay," she whispered in my ear. "You *never* use your credit card. Spread this over the past two and a half years and it's inconsequential."

She did have a point. My parents had given me a credit card on the first day of high school, and it was a matter of pride that I could count on one hand the number of times I'd actually used it. Still . . .

"We should just go," I said.

"What the hell! Are you kidding me?" asked the goth-faced girl behind the counter, who'd just spent an eternity ringing up my massive pile of merchandise.

"Give us a second," Claudia said. She pulled me a few feet away. I shook my head, completely overwhelmed by the absurd futility of what we were trying to do.

"We shouldn't be doing this. It's crazy. It's never, ever, ever going to work. It doesn't matter what I'm wearing; a guy like Nate Wetherill would never go for someone like me. He's totally out of my league."

"You mean he's better than you?" Claudia asked.

It sounded stupid when she said it out loud, but yeah, kind of, that's how it felt. I mean, I knew Big Life Picture he wasn't, but I didn't live in Big Life Picture. I lived in high school, and high school had a hierarchy that couldn't be ignored.

"Cara, ask me how things are going at Pennsbrook," Claudia said out of nowhere.

"Okay . . . how are things going at Pennsbrook?"

"'Hell is empty, / And all the devils are there,'" she quoted.

I shook my head. "I don't know that one."

"That's okay. It's *The Tempest,* and I changed a word, but you get the idea. Pennsbrook is hell, Cara. I'm a Cubby Crew of one, with no chance to reinvent myself because I'm surrounded by zombieheads who made up their minds about who I was before *I* even knew. I would give anything to have the opportunity you have now. I'm just as interesting a person as the Supreme Populazzi—so are you—but *I'll* never have the chance to prove it."

Claudia's eyes bore into me, finishing her thought without saying it. I *did* have that chance. After ten years I was finally away from everyone who had labeled and categorized me and put me in a cubby—and now I was doing the same thing to myself.

"Pretty fancy speech just to get someone to dress like the undead," I said.

"Did it work?"

I walked back to the girl at the counter and handed her my credit card. "We're ready now."

Of course, Hot Topic was only our first stop in the day's transformational odyssey. From there we went to Sephora and grabbed several soft black eyeliners, thick black mascaras, smoky-colored eye shadows, and black nail polish. This time I didn't hesitate. I presented my credit card with a smile.

The next stop was more difficult. After we pulled into the parking lot, I had to close my eyes and breathe deeply to still my pounding heart. Claudia put her hand on mine. "You don't have to do this part, you know. It's okay if you can't."

I took another long, deep breath, then opened my eyes. "No," I said. "I want to."

We walked inside the shop. I strode the three steps to the front desk and smiled at the perfectly coiffed and painted woman behind the counter.

"Hi. I'm Cara Leonard, and I have an appointment for a hair relaxing."

I couldn't imagine myself without curls. From the time I was three years old, they'd been my trademark feature. I could wear them up, I could wear them down, I could tuck them behind a headband, but they were always there. People I hadn't seen in years would recognize me on the street because of my hair. My curls defined me; even my personality was curly, bouncy, springy, and playfully twisted.

But the look I wanted didn't include curls, and a simple blow-out wouldn't get me the style I needed. If I was going to go for it, I had to really go for it. Claudia had done tons of research on the best curl relaxers in Philadelphia and found Yumiko, the guru of the field. She used only a special relaxer from Japan that wouldn't damage the hair and wore out after two to three months.

I must have looked terrified when I sat in Yumiko's chair, because after she ran her hands through my curls, she looked at me in the mirror and gave me a big hug. "I promise you," she said, "you'll love it."

I had absolutely no reason to believe her, but I did. I took a deep breath, smiled, closed my eyes . . . and didn't open them again until she was completely finished.

"Cara," I heard Claudia say, "it's over."

I didn't want to open my eyes, but I did . . . and found a complete stranger staring at me in the mirror. She had the same wide, amazed expression I knew I was wearing, but otherwise she was totally alien to me.

Claudia bent down next to my face and looked that strange reflection in the eye.

"Claudia?"

She shook her head, then a smile broke across her face. "I love it. It's a whole new you."

Chapter *thirteen*

$\mathscr{I}$ couldn't stop staring at myself in the mirror.

This wasn't ideal, since I was driving to school and almost caused a slew of accidents, but it was unavoidable.

I still wasn't over the hair. I'd had three days to get used to it, and it still shocked me every time I saw it. It was *straight*. Totally straight, not at all frizzy. It was layered for body, much thicker on the top than on the bottom, and hung down past my shoulders. The color had changed from a chocolate brown to an inky black—a fact I couldn't forget because it was constantly in my face. I had long bangs now, and they swept over my right eye and cheekbone. I could wear them long and broody, or I could tuck them behind my right ear if I wanted to do something wild and crazy like, oh, see.

I loved it. I felt like I had entered the witness protection program and was embarking on a whole new life as someone I didn't yet entirely know. It was absolutely thrilling.

My parents were far less thrilled, but they hadn't freaked out anywhere near as much as I'd thought they would, mainly because Claudia and I had decided to spare them the full effect. We hid all my shopping bags in my room while Mom was making dinner and Karl was locked away in his home office, then revealed the haircut as a little something new I tried on a lark—a very temporary lark that would reverse itself within three months. Karl quickly did the math and realized I'd be back to my normal self in plenty of time for my April lunch with Dean Jaffe, so he was fine with it.

I got off easy because Karl was still on a high from my last report card. Also, my PSAT scores had come in over Christmas break. I'd landed in the ninety-sixth percentile, and qualified to enter the National Merit Scholarship Program—news that Karl had immediately broadcast to anyone even remotely connected to the Northwestern University admissions process. At that moment Karl loved me unconditionally, no matter what temporary insanity had made me straighten and color my hair.

Mom was worried. She kept asking if the hair change was my way of acting out on deep, hidden anxieties about the move and the new school. I assured her again and again that it wasn't.

Karl stuck up for me. "Her performance says it all, Lo-Lo."

Claudia and I smiled. Nothing ended an argument like Karl calling Mom Lo-Lo. It was Karl's response to her claiming she didn't like it when he screamed "Helloooo" for her across the house. Instead of changing, he just made the call into a pet name. Mom hated it, and as she laid into Karl for the zillionth time, I knew I was off the hook—at least until the credit card bill came.

Now, three days later, I was ready to reveal my new look at school. I'd started the day in my usual Gap finery, said an early goodbye to Karl and Mom, and driven straight to Wegmans. My mom loved Wegmans because it was the best supermarket in the area. It was huge, pristine, and filled with fresh, amazing food. I liked that, too, but today what I *really* liked about it was that it had an enormous ladies' room. I locked myself into the massive handicapped stall and changed for school: a black patterned T-shirt over super-skinny black jeans with a black stud-and-stone embossed belt, black flats, and a tight-fitting black and white zebra-striped hoodie.

I emerged from the stall and gave thanks to the gods of Wegmans that they'd decided to build a long glass shelf above the sinks: the perfect staging area for my makeup. I slathered on the eyeliner, shadow, and mascara, and topped off the look with a touch of pale lipstick. I stood back to get as much of my body as possible; the only strike against Wegmans was no full-length mirror. I brushed my hands through my chunky-fabulous hair, mussing it up to perfection.

I looked nothing like myself. I looked deep. I looked interesting.

I looked like a DangerZone.

Awesome.

I ran out of Wegmans and smashed the speed limit to get to school in time. It was only as I was about to race into the building that I had a panic attack.

If I had even dreamed of showing up at Pennsbrook looking like this, I'd have been laughed out of the building within seconds. Was there a chance that would happen here? Claudia had said no. She said I was still too new. I had only one true friend at Chrysella, and he was in on the new me. No one else knew the old me well enough to judge. The other Theater Geeks sort of did, but if Archer didn't act like it was a big deal, they wouldn't either. For all the rest of the school knew, this was my preferred way to dress. Or I could be one of those girls who just likes morphing her look.

Whatever. Claudia had said the key was owning it. As long as I owned it, no one would question.

Okay, then. I'd own it.

I ran in just as the bell rang, threw my books in my locker, dashed into English class . . . and directly into the crosshairs of the one person who would never let my new look go unquestioned.

"Trick or treat," Mr. Woodman said as I took my regular top-of-the-table perch. I pressed my lips together in a grimace and hoped he was finished.

He wasn't. "How appropriate that you dressed up for *The Crucible*. I can only imagine what you'll wear when we start *Moby-Dick*. Any thoughts?"

I knew he wanted me to do my usual thing. It wouldn't have been hard: he'd set me up with a giant white sperm whale. But I didn't like that he was calling me out for the way I looked. It wasn't cool.

"No thoughts," I murmured.

Mr. Woodward's eyebrows shot up in surprise. "Oooh. 'Are you a good witch or a bad witch?'"

Great. Now he was quoting *The Wizard of Oz*. I didn't respond. I just slinked off the table and into my chair.

I could feel Archer staring at me. The whole time he was away, I'd texted him everything about my ongoing transformation, but I guess seeing it was pretty jarring. I was dying to talk to him about it, but I had to wait.

"Hey," he said in the hall after class, "you have a little something on your face." He reached out as if he was going to brush something away with his thumb, then said, "Oh, wait, that's just a *ridiculously insane* amount of makeup."

"You say that like you didn't help engineer the look, Professor Higgins."

"Maybe I'm having second thoughts."

"*Now* you're having second thoughts?"

"Look at yourself. You don't even look like you."

I grinned. "I know. It's kind of cool, right?"

"No!"

"Why not?"

"Because!" He took a deep breath and calmed down, then added, "'I've grown accustomed to your face.'"

He looked at me pointedly, like that was supposed to mean something beyond the words themselves. It didn't.

"My face is still here," I said. "It's just slathered with stuff."

He didn't answer.

"Archer, come on! This isn't a big deal! We talked about it. The look is a tool so I can get to know a really interesting guy. Is that so horrible?"

"Is what so horrible: the theory or the actual look?"

"Either! Just . . . are you still going to help me or not?"

"I'll help you," he said. "Meet me here at the start of fifth period."

He slouched off, and I happily let my mind wander to the next phase of NateGate. Nate had lunch fifth period, just like Archer and I. Yet as I'd discovered, Nate preferred sitting outside and playing guitar to actually eating.

Archer's plan was that he'd go to Nate with some trumped-up excuse to chat. I'd come along, Archer would introduce me, and ideally something approaching a conversation would ensue.

Archer was under absolute orders not to leave Nate and me alone. He had to stick around and make sure I didn't do anything to embarrass myself and ruin everything. He was fine with that, but it meant the conversation had to be quick. Halfway through fifth period, Archer was due to meet the rest of the Theater Geeks and run lines for that afternoon's spring musical auditions. The show was *Little Shop of Horrors,* and Archer was going for the role of Seymour, the male lead. *Little Shop* was one of the few musicals I knew really well. The movie version was one of Karl's favorites, so he'd had us all watch it together a zillion times. I knew Archer would be perfect for Seymour, but I also understood he'd be way too nervous to function if he didn't get in this last practice.

One minute into fifth period, Archer and I crunched over the partly frozen grass, on our way to Nate's favorite rock. We could already see him, strumming, lost in his music. His back was to us. As we got closer, I felt a hot crawl of nerves race over my scalp. I stopped in my tracks.

Archer wasn't the only one having second thoughts.

I'd spent the past three weeks so involved in the excitement of becoming someone new, I'd kind of lost track of the reason. Now here it was: this complete stranger was in front of us, and I was supposed to make him my boyfriend. Did I even want him for my boyfriend? I knew nothing about him. The things I did know were all superficial: the clothes and the music he liked. And if anything, learning all that stuff had brought me closer not to Nate but to *Archer,* since he's the one who'd taught me.

I stopped myself. That was a dangerous train of thought. And it wasn't like I really knew *nothing* about Nate. I knew he was talented, and passionate, and . . . well . . . really hot. If I got to know him better, I'd probably find tons of other things I liked about him. I just needed to give it a chance.

"Are you okay?" Archer asked.

"Yeah . . . how do I look?"

Archer raised an eyebrow. I rolled my eyes.

"Aside from the obvious, how do I look?"

"You look cold. Are you sure you won't wear my jacket?"

He had an incredibly cozy-looking wool trench coat, but it was nowhere near as cool as my close-fitting hoodie. Right now "cool" trumped "cold" in a huge way. I shook my head.

Archer shrugged, and we closed the distance between us and Nate.

"Hey, Nate," Archer said.

Nate looked up, but he didn't stop playing. He gave Archer a half smile that wiped out all my second thoughts. Then he turned to me.

Wow.

It sounds crazy, but I swear, the way he turned, it was clear he'd just meant to note who was with Archer, then turn right back again. Then he saw me, and it was as if his eyes stuck. He didn't smile, didn't stop playing his guitar, but he *focused.* On *me.* Oh. My. God.

"I'm Nate," he said.

I almost blew it right there. It was a sheer act of will that stopped me from bursting into giggles and babbling, "Of *course* you're Nate! I've only been studying you for several weeks and using every bit of my energy to plot and plan for this very moment, and now you think there's even the slightest chance I wouldn't know who you are?"

Thankfully, I did none of this. I remembered what Claudia had said. This was the new me. I had to own it. The new me didn't giggle and gush. I didn't even smile. I simply raised my chin in acknowledgment and responded with a single word: "Cara."

It was my turn to get Nate's half smile. Oh, wow. Now I understood why you couldn't look directly at an eclipse. The head-on effect had to be like this: completely dizzying and disorienting.

Archer jumped in, taking Nate's attention long enough for me to catch my breath. "I checked out those Brubeck sessions online. Great stuff."

"Yeah," Nate said. "Cool, right?"

He bent back over his guitar. Archer looked at me. He had said what he'd come to say; I'd been introduced. Were we done?

Were we? I'd kind of imagined something more, although if I listened to my imagination, I'd expect Nate to leap off his rock at the first sight of me, pull me into his arms, and swear he'd never met anyone as enthralling as me in his entire life.

I had a very vivid imagination.

Archer and I had already turned to leave when I realized something: I knew the song Nate was strumming. It was on my reprogrammed iPod. I knew it . . . and I loved it. It was actually one of my favorites.

"Hey," I said, nodding to Nate's guitar. "I know that song. 'Disenchanted,' right? My Chemical Romance."

Nate didn't stop playing, but he rewarded me with another gaze from those eyes, which I was beginning to believe had their own gravitational pull.

"Yeah," he said.

"Except your version's a little different from Ray's."

He looked me up and down. I bit my cheeks to stop from smiling.

"I tweaked it a little," he said. "You like it?"

He was asking my opinion. I was having a conversation with Nate Wetherill. A DangerZone, a guy far too hot to actually exist in high school, cared what I thought. How cool was that?

"I do like it," I said. "A lot."

Nate smiled—a wide, open smile this time. "I saw them in concert a couple years ago. *Black Parade* tour."

"I read about that," I said. "They brought Gerard out on a gurney, right?"

"Yeah." Nate nodded. "Very, very cool."

Uh-oh. Nate was still looking at me, but I was out of things to say. I quickly scoured my brain, but before I hit on anything, he turned back to Archer. "Thanks for letting me know about Brubeck. See you at jazz band?"

Clearly we were being dismissed.

"See you," Archer said. He turned to walk off. I fell into step next to him, but before I'd gone two steps—

"Cara," Nate said. "Got a minute? I want to play something for you."

Inside I jumped, screamed, and did a wild touchdown dance. Outside I shrugged. "Sure," I said. I gave Archer a silent, thrilled scream before I turned and walked back to Nate.

Nate moved over and tilted his head to indicate the spot next to him. I took it. I noticed Archer still hadn't left. He just stood there, watching Nate and me for a beat. I was sure he didn't approve of what I was doing, but at the same time he'd been a huge part of it. He could disapprove only so much without being completely hypocritical.

Eventually Archer left. He had to; it was almost time for him to meet his friends. I knew I wouldn't see him again before his audition, and I felt bad that I didn't get to give him a final "break a leg," but I knew he'd understand.

I stayed with Nate the rest of the period. He wanted me to hear some other tweaks on songs I knew from my iPod list. To be perfectly honest, I was sitting so close to him it was hard to concentrate, but I did my best to look like I was carefully considering every note.

When the bell rang, I stopped the Pavlovian urge to leap to my feet. I had a feeling Nate wouldn't think that was cool. Instead we both sat there a moment, looking at each other. He gave me another body-melting smile.

"This was good," he said, rising from the rock. "I'll see you, Cara."

"See you," I said.

As he walked away, my head spun with a zillion questions. *When* would I see him? Did he *want* to see me? Was that an invitation to *try* to see him?

"I'll be here tomorrow," Nate called back.

I watched him until he disappeared. The moment he was out of eyeshot, I ran into the building as fast as I could go. I was late, but that wasn't why I ran. I ran because I was bubbling over with excited energy and if I didn't do something to let it out I'd explode.

Nate Wetherill wanted me to meet him tomorrow. It was practically a date!

Chapter *fourteen*

The next four days were unreal. It's not like I saw a lot of Nate. We only hung out at lunchtime on his rock. I always took my time to get there. Those were Claudia's orders—never be there before him, let him wonder if I'd show. It seemed to work. He always looked a little surprised when I arrived, in a good way. It worked for me, too. Since I was skipping lunch every day, the late arrival gave me time to scarf down the Zone bar and Diet Coke I now bought every morning during my Wegmans change-a-thon.

Nate liked playing for me, and he seemed to honestly respect my opinions. He'd try out new variations on songs we both liked, or he'd play and sing something I'd request. By our third lunch together he even played me an original song.

It felt surreal: I sat two inches away from a guy performing a song he'd written himself. And it was really good. I asked if he had a recording of it so I could play it on my iPod. He furrowed his brows like he thought I might be messing with him, but he let me enter my e-mail address in his cell phone, and when I checked the next morning, he'd sent me the MP3. I wondered if I was the only person other than Nate to have it. I downloaded it immediately and listened to it nonstop.

I couldn't stop talking and texting to Claudia about Nate. It wasn't like we were going out—we were barely even *hanging* out—but I felt special around him. Nate was a DangerZone. He stood alone. He didn't have friends. He didn't need them. He had his music. He didn't want anything more.

Except now he wanted me.

I don't mean he *wanted* me, but he wanted me around. Every time we left the rock he'd say the same thing: "I'll be here tomorrow." And every time I showed up, he brightened just the littlest bit.

I wasn't the only one who noticed.

The Populazzi did, too.

I was surprised they caught on so quickly. Even though Nate's rock was in full view of the Populazzi Oak and the Senior Slope, January was too cold for the Populazzi. They'd retreated to their indoor haunts. I didn't see them during my fifth periods with Nate, so I thought they didn't see me.

But they're the Populazzi. They see everything.

In precalc Thursday morning, the day I got Nate's MP3, I was getting ready for class when I caught a strong whiff of fruity vanilla-jasmine. I looked up. Trista had spun around in her seat.

"Hey," she said, smiling.

She was looking right at me, but I was sure she was talking to someone else. If I smiled or responded in any way, I'd just call attention to myself and look like a complete loser. So I tried to make myself invisible. I went stone-faced and returned to my notebook.

In my peripheral vision, I noticed Trista kept looking my way. Then she turned back around.

Only then did I realize she'd been saying hi to *me*. Four months I'd been sitting behind Trista, and now today she'd acknowledged my existence.

I felt a moment of panic when I realized I'd just blown off a Supreme Populazzi. Then I realized it was perfect. I was supposed to be a dark and mysterious DangerZone. If I'd reacted like my normal self, it would have broken the mystique.

For the first time ever, my insecurity had served me well.

I texted Claudia the first second I could. Trista's attention could only be because of Nate. The Ladder was already working.

"Did you know Nate writes his own songs?" I asked Archer. "He played one for me yesterday." We were in his basement playing Ping-Pong. Now that we didn't eat lunch together, after school was the main time we hung out—*after* I stopped at Wegmans to wash my face and change back into my regular clothes. No way could Bina see me in my full emo-gear. She'd be on the phone to my mom immediately.

"Of course I know he writes his own songs. *I'm* the one who knows him, remember?"

He slammed a shot to the far corner of the table. I had to dive to try to get it. I missed.

"Nice one." I picked up the ball and blew the long bangs off my eye, but they flopped right back. "You think Bina has a barrette around? I can't see with these stupid bangs in my face."

"That's what you get for mutilating your head," he muttered.

"You really think it's that awful? I like it." I served the ball. "Nate likes it."

"Oh, well, if Nate likes it, it has to be great."

What was with him? "You're very pissy today, Professor Higgins."

"Don't call me that."

"How about Doctor Frankenstein? Either way, you should be proud. Your creation is a huge success!" I slammed the ball with a little topspin and won the point. "Yes!"

"It is *not* my creation," Archer said. "What you're doing is all your idea."

"But you were my enabler. I couldn't have pulled it off without you. That makes you just as responsible."

I thought I was being light and playful, but Archer turned serious.

"Okay," he said. "If I'm responsible, then I have a say. I say you stop."

"Stop . . . what?"

"Stop everything! Stop the clothes. Stop the hair. Stop hanging out with Nate. Just . . . stop!"

I couldn't believe we were having this conversation. "Are you seriously telling me who I can and can't hang out with?"

Archer thought about it for a second, then crossed his arms and glared at me defiantly.

"Yes, I am," he said. "I'm telling you I don't want you hanging out with Nate."

I felt angry tears burning behind my eyes. Archer had already made it absolutely clear he didn't want to go out with me. That still hurt so much, but I'd made myself cool with it so we could be friends again. Now I was finally starting to get over him—which was still hard—and he was acting like a jealous boyfriend? No. That was completely unfair.

I was shaking, and I fought to keep my voice steady. "We're not going out, Archer. You don't get to tell me stuff like that."

He didn't say anything for a long time.

"I have to do homework," he finally said. "You should go."

"Yeah, I should."

I got out as fast as I could and cursed myself for letting him get to me again. A couple tears slipped out, but I wiped them away. I cranked Nate's song on my iPod full blast and screamed along with the lyrics as I drove home.

The next day was Friday. I sat in my usual spot in English, but I didn't even look at Archer. I don't know if he was trying to look at me. I wouldn't let myself pay attention.

I was still so upset about what had happened that I was distracted all through fifth period with Nate. Didn't really matter. He was never up for talking much. He just wanted me to listen while he played.

When the bell rang, I assumed he'd do the same thing as always and tell me he'd be around the next day. Or in this case, Monday. Instead, he asked if I ever checked out the music scene at any of the clubs in Philly.

I quickly calculated my answer: I might look like a loser if I said no, but if I lied and said yes, he'd start asking questions and I'd be caught.

"No." I realized my perfect out. "We just moved here, so . . ."

I let the sentence dangle. I hoped he wouldn't ask me from where I'd moved, since it was just another suburb of Philadelphia. He didn't.

"The Ruse is playing at the Works tonight. Want to come?"

Was Nate asking me out on a date?

I was glad I'd been distracted. It stopped me from doing anything stupid like jumping up and squealing. I let the question sit before I answered. "Sure."

"Cool. Give me your address. I'll pick you up at seven."

"Cool."

Wait. It was *not* cool. My parents would never let me out of the house dressed for a Nate Wetherill date.

"Actually . . . no."

"Okay," Nate said, walking away.

"No!" I'd shown more emotion in that one word than I had in a whole week hanging out. I had to bring it back down. "I mean, no, don't pick me up at my house. My parents, they're freaks. Can I meet you at your place?"

"Sure. I'll e-mail you the address."

The second he walked out of eyeshot, I texted madly to Claudia. *"911! Date w Nate 2nite! Must plan! Call!!!!"*

The plan Claudia and I mapped out that afternoon was simple. I couldn't just ask my parents to let me stay at Claude's place for the weekend. There was a chance they'd say no. Instead, I'd tell them Claudia had just had a terrible fight with a friend and desperately needed a full weekend of my support. They'd never deny her that—and they didn't. Mom even considered whipping up a batch of Claudia's favorite snickerdoodles to make her feel better, but I said there wasn't enough time.

Mom and Karl never even considered the idea that I might be lying. They trusted me so completely that I felt guilty. Not guilty enough to tell them the truth or skip my date with Nate, but guilty. At least it wasn't a total lie. I would go to Claudia's eventually—just much, much, much later than my parents imagined.

I left the house and drove right to Wegmans. It was a nice change seeing the evening shift. The morning shift had begun to recognize me and my quick-change act. One of the cashiers had taken to calling out, "Hey, Clark!" as I came in and marking my exit with "It's a bird, it's a plane, it's SuperGoth!" This was not only tiresome but inaccurate. There's a *huge* difference between goth and emo, but I never had the time or energy to give a tutorial.

I changed into my dressiest outfit: black lace-up boots with chunky heels, the bright purple fishnets, a short black pleated skirt accented with studs and chains, and a black lace-and-velour corset top with hook and eye closures climbing up the front. I threw on a pair of black fishnet arm warmers, which I was fairly certain wouldn't keep my arms warm at all. A few minutes piling on the makeup and I was on my way.

I punched Nate's address into my GPS and it led me to . . . Really?

It was a mansion. Other than my dad's place, it was the biggest house I'd ever seen. Not that I could see it well; it had no outdoor lights at all. Was this the right address? I picked my way across the lawn to the front door and used the light from my phone to look for numbers, but there weren't any. Should I just ring the bell? If I did, would I be disturbing some random serial killer waiting for easy prey? I was about to e-mail Nate to double-check the directions when he opened the front door.

"Hey." He half smiled.

"Hi."

"Come on. I'll drive."

He slipped out and I followed him to the driveway. I wondered if his parents were out. Even if he didn't want to introduce me, it seemed weird that he didn't say goodbye to them. Maybe he'd done that before he answered the door.

We slid into his car, and in the moment before he closed his door and the lights went out, he looked me up and down. "You look good."

"Thanks." I gave him my own version of the half smile. "You, too."

It was the biggest understatement I'd ever made. Nate looked *amazing*. He wore dark jeans, Converse sneakers, and a plain black T-shirt. Couldn't have been simpler. But on him it hung perfectly. He looked long and lanky, and he had gelled back his hair in mussed-up spikes that showed off his chiseled cheeks and jaw. I thought I'd be disappointed when he shut the door and the lights went out, but he looked even hotter in the dim glow from the dashboard.

Nate didn't want to talk. He played the Ruse's CD to prep us for the show. It was perfect for me: I knew nothing about the band. I didn't exactly fall in love with them on the drive, but I loved watching Nate listen to their music. He tapped the beat with one hand and drove with the other, and sometimes he'd unconsciously work the guitar fingerings. There was an intensity to it all, like he wasn't just listening to the music but inhabiting it. I was positive he was the most passionate person I had ever met.

The Works was an all-ages club, and packed with people. We maneuvered ourselves to a good spot, then Nate leaned close so I could hear him over the roar of the crowd. "Want a beer?"

"What?" I shouted. Clearly I'd heard him wrong. I thought he'd asked if I wanted a beer.

"A beer!" he repeated. He leaned his head back and mimed tipping a bottle into his mouth. "Want one?"

Ah. So I hadn't heard him wrong. But we were only sixteen. At least I was only sixteen. Maybe he was older than me. Still, no way was he twenty-one. "How?"

Nate rolled his eyes. "Do you want one?"

I'd never had a beer. With the exception of four sips of Manischewitz at last year's Passover Seder, I'd never touched a drop of alcohol. Okay, there was the time Claudia and I were twelve and tried to get smashed on a box of amaretto cordials we'd found deep in the back of her freezer, but I'm pretty sure the all-night giggle fest that followed was more of a sugar rush than anything else.

What if we got caught and arrested for underage drinking? Isn't that the kind of thing that lands on your transcript and keeps you out of college? Nate didn't look worried about that, but maybe Nate wasn't interested in college. Nate *did* look a little impatient, which meant that I really should answer and soon. *Did* I want to have a beer?

Big Picture, this seemed to land in the "don't look a gift horse in the mouth" category. After all, I didn't have to actually *drink* the beer.

"Sure!" I said.

Nate gestured for me to wait where I was. I wanted to pull out my phone and text Claudia, but I thought it would look really lame if he came back before I was done.

I shouldn't have worried. It took him a half hour. By the time he got back, the show was about to start.

"Long line." He handed me a bottle with a lime stuffed in the neck. "Corona okay?"

"My favorite." *My favorite?* What was I saying? And how did he get the beer? Did he have a fake ID? Did they not card at the bar? Did he have someone else buy it for him? Had anyone else noticed? Were we about to get busted?

Nate pushed his lime all the way into the beer bottle and took a big swig.

What else could I do? I followed suit. I pushed in the lime, tipped the beer into my mouth . . .

. . . and nearly snarfed it out my nose.

I didn't realize it would be so bubbly! People don't warn you about these things!

I somehow held back the snarfing reflex, but to avoid a coughing fit, I needed liquid. And the only liquid I had?

I took another sip.

I didn't love the taste. It was a little bitter. But it wasn't awful. It was cold, though, and that felt great; the club was stifling.

I drank some more.

The lights went down and the Ruse took the stage. Nate chugged the rest of his bottle and cheered wildly. As the Ruse started playing and the whole room reverberated with sound, I took another long drink. The stuff wasn't bad once you had enough of it.

Was the room supposed to be swimmy? It wasn't unpleasant or anything, just . . . swimmy. And a little fuzzy. And a little . . .

Wait a minute . . . was that Robert Schwarner?

I saw him off in a corner several feet ahead and to the side of me. He was wearing that *BeastSlayer* cloak and nodding to the music. He turned and saw me with my beer, then lifted his chin and raised his Coke can in a toast.

I closed my eyes and shook my head to clear it. When I opened my eyes the crowd had shifted and Robert was gone.

If he had even been there. Maybe the beer was giving me hallucinations. Could beer do that? I didn't think so, but maybe . . .

I took another long swig. I felt really good. Who cared if everything was swimmy and fuzzy and hallucinatory? I was happy. I was really happy—until I tried to dance. I tripped sideways into a short girl in a low-cut, fitted tank top, and spilled the last of my beer right down her cleavage.

She was not pleased.

"What the *hell?*" she screamed. "Are you insane?"

"I'm so sorry!"

"Not good enough! This top is new! It's *silk!*"

The swimminess ended. Everything came into sharp focus as Silk Tank Top grabbed a huge handful of my hair and yanked it—hard. Was she on steroids or something? She was *strong!* And she wouldn't stop. She just kept pulling and yanking me in crazy-fierce tugs.

"Ow! I'll buy you a new shirt! Just stop!"

Either she didn't hear me or she didn't like the offer, because she kept pulling. She'd buried her other hand in my hair now, too. I was doubled over, staggering through the crowd as I tried to claw her off me.

Finally a bouncer came over. "Hey—break it up or you're both out of here."

The girl finally let go. She flipped me off, then disappeared back into the crowd.

I tenderly put my hand to the back of my head, convinced it would be gushing blood. It wasn't, but I had an unbelievable headache. Each beat of the music made me feel like I was being yanked across the room all over again.

Where was Nate? I didn't see him anywhere. Panic rose in my chest as I struggled to work through the ocean of dancers.

"Nate! *Nate!*" I cried. It was no use. Unless he was right in front of me, he'd never hear me. Oh God. I'd lost him. I was alone. I had no ride. I'd have to call my parents. How could I call my parents? I'd had alcohol; they'd smell it on my breath. And look at what I was wearing! And look at where I *was!* I was supposed to be at Claudia's! I couldn't call my parents. I was on my own.

"Nate!" I screamed.

"Hey!" he said.

He was right in front of me. I'd somehow stumbled back to where I'd started.

"Great show, right?" he shouted over the music, then turned back to the stage.

Great show? Did he not know I'd just been wrestled across the room and nearly scalped by a midget with biceps as big as her boobs?

No. Nate had no idea what had happened to me. He was only interested in the music. I may as well not even be here, as far as he was concerned. I felt like an idiot. I never should have come. Nate didn't care about me at all. I should just call a cab and take it to Claudia's. It couldn't cost that much money, could it? Maybe a cab would take a credit card . . .

I was halfway through approximating the cost of a cab ride from Philadelphia to Yardley when the Ruse swung into their first ballad of the night: a cover of My Chemical Romance's "Disenchanted." Three notes in, Nate sidled behind me, wrapped his arms around me, and leaned his head next to mine.

"It's our song," he murmured into my ear.

Then he kissed my neck.

My brain melted into nothingness.

Chapter *fifteen*

Oh. My. God.

Every time Nate kissed my neck, I felt chills in parts of my body I didn't know I had.

And he didn't stop.

He held me the whole song, rocking me in his arms and singing the words softly into my ear.

I don't know what I thought. I couldn't think. I didn't want to think. I could just feel . . . and it felt incredible.

When the song ended, he gave my earlobe the tiniest bite, and I almost lost consciousness. I wanted to fall back into his arms and stay there forever, but the Ruse had already swung into their next song. It rocked hard, and Nate immediately moved away to give himself room to pound his fist and dance.

I wondered if the band took requests and if I could ask them to play "Disenchanted" another thirty or forty times in a row.

Turns out I didn't need that particular song. Any ballad was good. Each time they played one, Nate curled his arms around me again, rocking me, kissing my neck, and doing that crazy nibbling thing that made my knees buckle.

During the band's final encore—a power ballad that was fast becoming my favorite song ever—Nate let his fingers creep ever so slowly toward my chest. Part of me froze in terror at the idea of him actually touching my breasts, especially in the middle of a crowd of people. But I didn't stop him.

The song ended before it could happen. Nate immediately released me to cheer and scream like crazy. I joined in—it seemed like the thing to do—but really I was obsessing about what would happen next with Nate.

I hoped he would kiss me. I wanted him to kiss me. I *really* wanted him to kiss me. But the near-public boob touch made me nervous that for him kissing would just be the start. If he tried more and I asked him to stop . . . would he be cool with that? Would he think I was a loser? Would he even listen?

When the lights went on, Nate looked at me in a way that both thrilled and scared me. "Let's go," he said. He led me through the crowd to the car, holding my hand the whole way.

I liked that. It felt like he was taking care of me.

He didn't kiss me before we got into the car or once we were inside. He just drove, blaring the Ruse's CD so we could "keep the concert mood." *My* mood was 100 percent eager anticipation. I spent the whole ride imagining every possible way Nate might give me a good-night kiss.

We pulled into his driveway and he turned off the car.

My insides felt fluttery. I was most likely less than one minute from having my first real kiss ever.

"Want to come in?" Nate asked.

"In . . . the house?"

"Yeah. Come on." He got out and started walking toward the front door.

I followed him. I couldn't stay in his car by myself. It was weird, though. It was eleven. Were Nate's parents really okay with me coming in at eleven? Were we sneaking in behind their backs? And if we were, what did that mean?

I got nervous all over again. If Nate just wanted to kiss me, he could do that in the driveway. Inside seemed like a place to do more. I was pretty sure Nate wasn't a virgin. Did he expect us to have sex? I was *not* ready to have sex.

I mentally shook myself. Why was I imagining the worst? Nate might be totally fine with just kissing. Going inside didn't have to mean sex—it could just mean more than one kiss. And if I liked real kissing as much as I liked him kissing my neck, I'd *want* more than one kiss. Plus, inside we could be comfortable, like on a couch. What could be bad about that?

The foyer of the house was dark but glowed from ambient light in other rooms. Nate wrapped his arms around my waist.

"You look incredibly hot," he said. He pushed me gently backwards until my back was against the wall. Then he leaned in and kissed me.

I had always wondered why people closed their eyes when they kissed. Now I knew: they can't help it. The feeling is too overwhelming: the taste, the touch, the smell, even the sound. The sense of sight had to be excluded, or it wouldn't be possible to function.

I wondered if Nate could tell I'd never kissed before, but I quickly stopped caring. His lips were moving on mine, his tongue was deliciously inside my mouth, his hands were running over my back, my hair, my—

Suddenly he pulled away. I fought to catch my breath.

"Let's smoke," he said.

"What?" I gasped, but he was already walking into the next room. I followed, trying not to stagger.

We wound up in some kind of media room, with two huge couches, two overstuffed armchair rockers, a coffee table, a massive tower of endless electronic equipment, and a giant flat-screen plasma TV. Every piece of furniture was high-end expensive—the kind of thing my mom cut out of *Sunset* magazine and put on Karl's night table when he was having a good run at blackjack—but the place was disgusting. The hardwood floors were stained and sticky with spilled who-knows-what, and the upholstery on the couches and loungers was filthy. Take-out bags and boxes lay everywhere, and the room smelled like an odd combination of old food and something else pungent that I couldn't really place.

Nate and I weren't alone. A tweener boy sat in one of the loungers playing a Wii game that involved Pikachu and I think Sonic the Hedgehog battling for dear life.

"Dude, you've got to see this!" the kid said to Nate as we entered. Then he saw me. "Hey."

"Hey," I said.

Shouldn't he be in bed?

"That's Thackery, my little brother," Nate said as he rummaged through one of the coffee table drawers.

"Great," I said. I couldn't help asking what seemed like the obvious question. "Um . . . are your parents around?"

Thackery snorted. Nate shot him a look, then turned to me. "Not so much. Mom's in a coma and Dad's out with his girlfriend."

I shook my head. I felt completely disoriented. "What? Your mom's in a . . ."

"Coma," Thackery finished. "It's okay; you can say it. It's been five years. Yes! Pikachu is going down!" He jumped onto the cushion of the rocker and did a little victory dance.

"Car accident," Nate said, completely matter-of-fact. "Drunk driver. The other guy, not her."

"Oh my God, that's horrible," I said. "And your dad . . ."

"Got a new girlfriend about a year ago. I think he feels guilty about it, so he mostly stays at her place. There's a house-keeper who comes in and cooks for us and stuff." Nate must have caught me looking around at the squalor in the room, because he laughed. "She won't even touch this room. Says it's too far gone for her. The rest of the place is nice, though. Really. Aha!"

He grinned and pulled out a baggie of small tapered paper rolls and a lighter. "You smoke?"

I froze. Nate was asking if I smoked pot. Nate was holding a baggie of pot, and he was asking if I smoked pot like he would ask if I drank water. "Surely you drink water, ma'am, do you not?" "Why of course I drink water! Who doesn't?"

Except I didn't smoke pot. I had never *seen* pot except in the movies, and I had never smoked anything in my life.

Nate read the answer in my face. "You don't, do you?"

Did he look disappointed?

"No," I said. "I mean, I never have or anything . . ."

"It's cool. You don't have to. It's just that, uh"—he glanced at his brother, who was back into another round of the video game—"certain . . . *things* are really, really good when you're high."

Certain *"things"*? Did Nate want me to take drugs and have sex? I didn't care if leaving would make me look like a dork; this was getting insane. I had to get out.

"I don't . . . think I'm ready for . . . certain things. I don't know, maybe I should just go."

"No, no, I'm not talking about . . . I just mean . . ." Nate seemed embarrassed to have to spell it out, especially within earshot of Thackery, but he did. "Making out is really good when you're stoned. It's more intense."

More intense? If kissing Nate got any more intense, *I'd* be the one slipping into a coma. Ouch—I winced at my own thought. Way inappropriate.

"Not that you have to do it," Nate said. "At all."

He meant it. I could tell. I liked that. And I really didn't have any desire to try . . . mostly. Except for the part of me that was a little curious. Especially since for Nate it seemed to be a prelude to really good making out.

"What's it like?" I asked.

"Really cool," he said. "It's not scary or weird or anything. It's just mellow and . . . nice."

I reached out, and Nate handed me the baggie. I took out one of the joints. It had an odor to it. I recognized it as the pungent smell in the room I couldn't place before.

"Nice, right?" Nate asked. "Do you want to try?"

There was no pressure in the question; I could see that. I could also see that Nate was kind of hoping I'd try.

And I *was* curious.

And it's not like I was alone. Nate was with me, and he knew all about this stuff.

And it's not like a couple puffs would hurt me, right?

"I'll try it."

Nate rewarded me with a smile. "You'll love it. We can go upstairs to my room; it's more comfortable there."

"Your room? Nate, I—"

"Nothing will happen you don't want to happen. It's just . . . quieter there." He glared toward Thackery, and I understood.

We went up to his room. Nate hadn't lied: the rest of the house was much nicer than the media room. I wondered if he even spent any time up here. It was immaculate. Like a hotel room.

As Nate got everything ready, he explained how big a deal pot was to him and how seriously he took the honor of introducing it to someone for the first time. Clearly we had hit on another of his passions. The only other time he spoke this much was when he was talking about music.

Nate seemed dedicated to giving me the perfect pot experience. He set up lots of pillows on his bed so it would be extra comfortable, then went to his Mac and played an iTunes party shuffle he had created specifically for times like this. Music, he said, totally made the experience. His computer had surround-sound speakers, so the whole room would reverberate. Visually, he said, it was important to have something interesting but not too complicated to look at, so he turned the flat-screen TV/monitor on his wall to a multicolored lightning-bolt screen saver.

Nate darted downstairs to get some water and snacks in case I got thirsty or hungry afterward. He wasn't gone long—just enough for me to look around and confirm my first impression. It was like a hotel room: no pictures, no books, no random personal things like my Tastykakes and mini Liberty Bell.

When Nate came back, he turned down the lights and sat next to me on the bed. "I'll get it started," he said, "then I'll pass it to you."

I nodded.

He lit one of the joints, then sucked in several times as the now-familiar acrid smell filled the air. Then he took in a big breath. He explained what he was doing, and I tried not to laugh. He was working so hard to keep in his breath while he spoke, he sounded like he was on helium.

"You breathe it in, then you hold the smoke in your lungs for a bit before . . ."

With a whoosh he blew it out.

"Now your turn." He handed it over. "You might cough but try not to. Try to keep it in."

I did what he said. I sucked in deeply and almost fell into a coughing fit, but I didn't. The smoke burned in my lungs. It hurt. I held in the smoke as long as I could, then let it go in a rush. There, I was done. I handed the joint back to Nate.

"Okay, I tried it," I said. "Now do we get to the really-good-making-out part?"

"A couple more hits," he said. "Just to make sure you get the full experience."

I thought I'd already had the full experience, and I didn't like it at all, but maybe I needed to give it more of a chance. If Nate loved it so much, there had to be something else there. And if not, if this really was the only time I'd ever smoke pot, I figured I should at least do it the right way.

I took the joint back from Nate and sucked in again, long and deep, then suffered through one more round passing it back and forth.

"Are we good now?" I asked.

Nate took another long pull, held it in, then let it out. "Yeah."

He leaned down to kiss me, and for a minute it felt amazing all over again . . .

But then I couldn't kiss him back.

It was weird. I wanted to. I was kind of dying to. Or at least I had been. But now I pulled out of his arms entirely. Now I just really wanted to lean back, shut my eyes, and listen to the music.

And grin.

It felt like I had a huge goofy grin on my face. I had no control over it. None whatsoever. And I couldn't control my body. I couldn't move. Not my arms, not my legs, not my head, not at all. I couldn't talk either.

It wasn't pleasant. It was terrifying. I was lying in a strange guy's bed! He could do anything, and I couldn't stop him. My heart started racing as I envisioned all the horrible things that could happen to me in this strange house with no parents and no rules and no one to care if I screamed, which I couldn't, even if I wanted to.

Nate's voice came to me as if through ten feet of water.

"Cara? Cara?"

Inside my head I screamed for help, but my body wouldn't respond.

I heard a chuckle through the ten feet of water. "Wow . . . you are *so* high." He tucked the comforter of the bed around me and leaned down to whisper in my ear. "Enjoy it," he said.

I felt him lean back on the pillows, and heard him open a bag. The smell was intense: potato chips. I felt very alone, stuck inside my head next to him. But then he reached over to gently pet my forehead and hair, over and over.

It was nice.

It made me feel a lot better.

I completely zoned out.

When I regained consciousness, the room was pitch black. My mouth felt like a big fluffy guinea pig had died inside it. Nate was next to me, fast asleep.

We were both fully dressed. This was good.

Something was beeping. I followed the sound to my purse and opened it to find my phone.

Its clock said 4:30 a.m.

Oh no.

The beep meant I had messages.

I had a *lot* of messages.

First, texts from Claudia wondering where I was. Then voice mails that grew more and more frantic until the most recent one of the bunch.

"Cara, it's Claude. It's after four in the morning. Where the hell are you? I'm freaking out! Why didn't you give me Nate's number? Was there an accident? Did something happen at the club? I can't find anything on the Net. I don't know where you are, I don't know what you're doing, but it's crazy late and I'm . . ."

I had never heard Claudia like this. She sounded awful, like she was on the verge of a complete breakdown. I couldn't believe I'd done this to her.

". . . I'm ready to call your parents, I swear it," her message continued. "I'm really scared, Cara. Just . . . if you get this, just call me, okay?"

My parents? She was going to call my *parents?*

Panic ran through me. I checked when she'd called. Ten minutes ago. Oh my God. Had she actually called my parents?

I was glad I had Claudia on speed dial. My hands were shaking so hard, there was no way I could have handled ten digits.

Please don't let her have called my parents. I know I deserve it if she did, but please-please-please don't let her have called my parents, pleeeeease . . .

Chapter *sixteen*

𝒮he hadn't called my parents—but that's only because I had miraculously beeped in before she'd dialed the last two numbers.

"Cara, where are you? Are you in the hospital? Tell me which hospital you're in. Were you in a car accident? Are you still on the side of the road? Do I need to call nine-one-one? Were you abducted? Did you just now escape? Are you bleeding? Are you dressed? Did Nate . . . did he survive? Let me come and get you. I'll come get you and I'll call the police."

Claudia was sobbing. I couldn't blame her, given the horrific scenarios she'd built.

"Claudia, it's okay," I assured her. I whispered so I wouldn't wake up Nate. "I'm fine. Nate's fine. There was no accident and no abduction. I'm at Nate's house and I'm fine."

"You're at his . . . Tell me you didn't have sex with him. If you scared me like this to have sex with him, I'm going to slaughter you. No, first I'm going to make you tell me every single detail, then I'm going to slaughter you."

"I didn't have sex with him. Let me just come to your house. Does your mom think I'm there?"

"Depends how many Sominex she took. She'd have to believe you were in severe gastric distress and unable to come out of the bathroom for about five hours."

"How many Sominex do you think she took?"

"Double dose, with her Xanax. She believes it. Just know if you were a guy, I'd be castrating you."

"My balls are yours. I'm so sorry, Claude. I'll be right there."

I hung up. I was seriously thirsty. I found the water bottles Nate had brought up last night, but they were empty. I'd have to wait until I got to Claudia's. No way was I going to try to navigate this place.

I grabbed my bag, then looked over at Nate, still fast asleep on the bed. Even rumpled and unconscious, he was beautiful. I wondered what would have happened if I hadn't lost the ability to move last night. I wondered what would happen if I crawled in next to him right now . . . woke him up by kissing him on his neck, nibbling his ear like he'd done to me . . .

But I knew what would happen. Claudia would hunt me down and skin me alive. I had to leave. Should I wake him up and say goodbye? Give him a kiss on the cheek? What's the protocol for ducking out on your kinda-sorta-boyfriend in the wee hours of the morning after you went catatonic on your first date? Would he be worried if he woke up and I was gone?

I looked for a pen and paper, but I'd already seen that nothing was around. How was that possible? Did he not do homework? My room was covered in notebooks, pens, and pencils.

I opened his desk—and found a pile of pictures. Nate couldn't have been more than eleven in the one on top. He wore a baseball uniform, and his short but scruffy dark hair peeked out from under the hat's brim. With his freckles and huge gap-toothed grin, he was the poster child for All-American Boy. He faced the camera, but he was looking up at a woman behind him who had to be his mom. She was blond and beautiful, with freckles that matched her son's, eyes that gleamed with life, and a huge smile. She had her arms wrapped around Nate, and her head rested on his.

If Nate was eleven here, it had to be, what, months before the accident? Weeks?

I looked again at the grinning boy in the picture, then at the tortured DangerZone sprawled out on the bed. I wondered how different he would have been if the accident hadn't happened.

My heart broke for Nate. Of course he was tortured. Of course he smoked pot all the time and lost himself in music. How else could he deal with everything? I imagined my own mom in the hospital for five years, Karl off with some girlfriend and never around. That would be different, though, wouldn't it? Would Karl even get custody of me if that happened, or would I have to live with my dad? Either way, it was too awful to even think about. I felt so bad, I almost did jump into bed next to Nate and wrap my arms around him, not to start making out again, but just so he knew I cared.

I realized I could make a huge difference in Nate's life. We were together now. I could be his rock, the one person he could open up to about everything. I couldn't change what had happened, but if I tried hard enough, maybe I could change *him*. Get him a little closer to the guy that kid in the picture would have been by his junior year in high school.

It felt incredibly special that, of all the girls at Chrysella, I was the one Nate had chosen to let in. I would be there for him. I would help.

My phone chirped. It was Claudia. "Even as I speak, I'm training a cobra to find you at Nate's house and kill you."

"I'm leaving now. I swear."

I took a second to send Nate a text saying I had an amazing time, I had to take off, and he should call me later. I gave his cheek the softest kiss, then tiptoed out of the room and down the stairs. I didn't need to be so quiet. As I opened the door to slip out, I heard wild beeping from the media room and Thackery's sleep-deprived croak. "Starscream will bring you down, Autobots!"

So sad. I shook my head as I left, and drove to Claudia's as fast as I could.

She was waiting for me, of course. She stood on the porch and leaned on the rail, wearing a long-sleeved, high-necked, white flowy nightgown that billowed to her feet. It was a piece I knew for a fact she had never once slept in but that made her look incredibly dramatic, especially with her long black hair hanging loosely down her back. If she could have conjured up wind and a rainstorm to amplify the suffering she'd lived through by my hand, I knew she would have.

"Claudia, I am so, so sorry. I will never freak you out like that again."

"That's all you've got?"

"Pretty much. Except for the beer, the pot, the crazy making out, the *Lord of the Flies* mansion, the coma-mom—"

"That's it. Inside. Immediately. I need to hear everything."

We went into the living room and flopped onto the couch, each automatically pulling a quilt onto our lap. Claudia's mom was an artist, and one of her favorite projects was creating huge super-cozy quilts. Uniquely disturbing, super-cozy quilts. Claudia's featured scenes from Hieronymus Bosch's *Hell* paintings; mine was a Warhol-esque four-panel image of Charles Manson.

I told Claudia everything, though my mouth was still so dry that I couldn't get anything out before going to the kitchen to grab a giant glass of water and a box of Lucky Charms that Claudia and I now munched by the handful. I was almost done with the story when we heard Claude's mom pad downstairs. Claudia stared at me with alarm.

It took me a second, but then I remembered. I was still dressed and made up like the reaper's bride, a fact Lenore—not Claudia's mom's real name; she'd adopted it because she liked the Poe reference—would absolutely feel the need to share with my parents. I quickly ducked my entire head and body under the multicolored Manson blankie and wondered how I was going to pull this off.

"Morning, girls," Lenore said. I felt her move close to me. "Poor thing. Is your stomach still bothering you, Cara?"

Claudia kicked me under the covers. I remembered I'd spent the night in "gastric distress."

"Ohhhhh," I moaned.

Claudia's barely stifled snicker told me I was nowhere near the actress she was, but Lenore seemed satisfied.

"Think we have any Pepto?" Claudia asked her. "I bet it would help her a lot."

"Hmm. Somewhere we must," Lenore said. "I'll look."

Claudia was a genius. It could take forever for Lenore to dig up the medicine. I heard Lenore head upstairs. I raced into the bathroom and scoured my face, then Claudia slipped me pajamas she'd grabbed from my duffle bag so I could change.

Disaster averted. And since Mom and Karl knew I'd be with Claudia all weekend, I'd have the freedom to zip off and see Nate whenever he called.

Except he didn't call. Even though we'd spent most of the night practically locked together and I'd specifically asked him to call in my text. Did he not get my text? But even if he hadn't, wouldn't he have woken up and wondered where I was? And if he'd assumed I'd gone home, wouldn't he have wanted to make sure I was okay?

I wanted to call him, but Claudia wouldn't let me. She dragged me into her room, sat me at her desk, and placed the familiar yellow binder in front of me.

"Please open your text to page one hundred and two," she said.

"I don't know what's more disturbing: that you put together more than a hundred pages or that you actually went through and numbered all of them." I got to the page she wanted. "It's a collage of men in combat."

"Flip forward at your leisure."

I did. More collages spread across the next several pages: men playing football, basketball, hockey, soccer; men wrestling; men boxing; men lifting disturbingly heavy weights at the gym; men at Coney Island scarfing hot dogs as a crowd cheered them on.

"You may cease flipping," Claudia said. Clearly she felt her point had been made, but I had no idea what it was. My blank expression must have said that loud and clear.

"A challenge," Claudia said. "Men love a challenge. You have to play hard to get. It's the only way you'll hold on to Nate long enough to get to the next rung of the Ladder."

Or long enough to help him, I thought. I kept that plan to myself. I had a feeling Claudia wouldn't appreciate me altering her masterwork.

Claudia did have a point. If Nate didn't seem that anxious to talk, I shouldn't be either. I'd let it go. I'd wait until Monday.

Chapter *seventeen*

It really wasn't fair how long it took Monday to come around. Staying up most of Sunday night to find a Nate-friendly outfit that screamed "How Can You Not Want More of This?" didn't help any, but it was at least productive. I went hot-casual: a black and white striped shirt with a scooped neckline and a chain-trimmed pocket on the chest, plus tight black jeans ripped along the sides in irregular circles.

I left the house as early as I could without filling Mom's and Karl's heads with questions, hit Wegmans, and made it to school right after the doors opened. Remembering Claudia's gladiator images, I did my best to look for Nate without seeming like I wanted anything to do with him whatsoever.

I had no luck, and there was only so long I could wander the halls looking detached and disillusioned. When I heard a high keening squeal, I had to go check it out.

The cast list for the spring musical had just been posted, and Archer, Tom, Dinah, Sue, Molly, Ember, Doug, and Noah were all gathered around it. The falsetto screech had been from Doug, and his exuberant vertical leaps would have made him a shoo-in for either the varsity basketball team or the Miss America pageant.

Archer himself had a huge grin on his face. Despite the fight we'd had last week, I was excited for him. I knew what it had to mean.

"Did you get Seymour?" I asked.

Archer wheeled at the sound of my voice. He looked surprised but not angry.

"Yep," he said with a little bow. "Seymour Krelborn, at your service."

"That's great!"

"Yeah, thanks."

"And what role are *you* playing?" Ember asked, looking me up and down.

Archer blushed. He didn't look at Ember, just put his hands in his pockets and shuffled a second before he asked me, "Um . . . can we talk a little bit?"

"Sure," I said.

We walked a few feet away and stood by the wall. I noticed some of the Theater Geeks shooting me dirty looks. Not Sue, actually, but Ember and Tom for sure.

"I was a jerk," Archer said. "I'm really sorry."

I almost said, "It's okay." It was reflex, at least for me. People say they're sorry, I want to make them feel better.

But what he'd said wasn't okay. It had hurt. That didn't mean I was going to hold it against him—already I wanted to forget it had ever happened and be cool with each other again—but "it's okay" wasn't quite right.

"Thanks," I said.

"And you didn't mutilate your head. Your hair looks good . . . kind of."

I laughed. "Don't worry—you don't have to like it. A couple months and it'll be totally back to normal." Unless I needed to keep it this way for Nate, of course—but I didn't say that part out loud.

"Up for Ping-Pong?" Archer asked.

"Bring it. How about this afternoon?"

"Oooh, can't. First rehearsal. How about over the weekend?"

If things went well, I'd be with Nate over the weekend.

"Maybe. I'll e-mail you; we'll figure it out."

"Great."

We stood there a moment, smiling—but without anything else to really say.

A high-pitched, breathy voice squealed from down the hall. "Seymour! Seymour! We need you!"

"Sue got Audrey." Archer explained the voice.

Of course. The female lead opposite Archer. Sue must have been over the moon. I felt a pang of jealousy, but I told myself that if Archer were really into Sue, they'd be together already.

"You guys'll be great. I know it. Congratulations."

I wrapped my arms around him for a hug.

Bad idea.

Hugging Archer felt really good. Not like hugging Nate. A hug from Nate was an electrifying prelude to everything daring and sexy and exciting. Hugging Archer just felt *right*. I still wanted so badly for him to feel the same way, but I knew he didn't. I was suddenly a giant, hollow ache.

If I stayed in his arms, I'd start to cry.

I needed an escape. *Now*.

I saw one stalking the halls in a *BeastSlayer* cloak. Perfect.

"Oh! Gotta run," I told Archer. "See you in English!"

I trotted over to Robert, who seemed very busy pretending to be part of a SWAT team. He slinked between classrooms, then leaped into each doorway, shooting invisible energy jets from the ends of his outstretched hands.

At least that's what it looked like. I'd say it was odd, but this was Robert Schwarner.

"Robert, wait up!"

"'I take orders from just one person! Me!'"

"*Star Wars?*"

"*A New Hope*. Han Solo."

He stalked down to another classroom and jumped into the doorway, shooting more invisible bolts. I followed.

"Come on, stop for just a second. I want to ask you something."

Robert turned to me, folding his hands into the long sleeves of his cloak.

"Okay, this might be a weird question," I said, "but . . . were you at the Works in Philly on Friday?"

"Do gerbils juggle in your retainer case?" he asked.

Okay, now he'd lost me. "What?"

"*That's* a weird question. Yours wasn't at all. I *was* at the Works. I saw a great show. And the Ruse was good, too."

He grinned, but a second later his co-*BeastSlayer*-cloak-wearing friend, Gabe Friedman, leaped from a classroom with a wild howl and zoomed out of the building. Robert scrambled after him, leaving me stunned.

Did Robert Schwarner just give me crap?

I was pretty sure he did—and I had to admit I was kind of impressed.

The bell rang, which meant I wouldn't see Nate until lunch. The hours until then? With the exception of seeing Archer in English, I figured they'd pretty much be a wash.

I was wrong.

As I walked out of precalculus, Trista Camello fell into step next to me.

Just like that.

"So I'm taking a poll," she said. "Is it ruder to tell Mr. Scheller we know he wears a bad toupee or to let him go on wearing it when we're all secretly laughing about it?"

"Mr. Scheller wears a toupee?"

"You haven't noticed? The top and front of his hair are jet black. The sides are completely gray."

I'd never really paid attention to our precalc teacher's hair before, but now that she mentioned it . . .

I laughed.

"You're totally right—he does wear a toupee!"

"Yes! A bad one! So what do you think: ruder to tell or not to tell?"

"It has to be ruder to tell, right?"

"I don't think so," Trista said. "It's like when someone has lipstick on her teeth. Wouldn't you want to know if you had lipstick on your teeth?"

I suddenly wondered if I *did* have lipstick on my teeth. I stopped smiling, just in case.

That reminded me that I'd *been* smiling. And laughing. All of which had been very un-DangerZone of me. I made a conscious effort to be more disaffected, but it was hard around Trista. Her energy was irresistible.

She bent her head closer to mine and spoke in a conspiratorial whisper. "So . . . you and Nate Wetherill."

She let the statement hang between us.

"Yeah?" I asked.

"Are you together?"

Trista Camello, Supreme Populazzi, had just asked me the very same question I'd been struggling with all weekend.

It struck me that Trista would know better than I would if Nate and I were together. She'd probably been in and out of relationships since prepubescence. She was being so friendly, maybe I could just spill everything and get her expert take.

I wanted to do it, but if she decided Nate and I weren't really together, I was sure her interest in me would end. Plus spilling would be way too non-DangerZone.

"Whatever," I said.

I channeled Nate's way of walking and kept my eyes straight ahead and my expression blank. I could tell Trista was still looking at me, seeking more.

Then she gave up. "Got it. See you."

She quickened her pace until she could link arms and fall into step with a Senior Penultimate down the hall.

So I was on the Populazzi's radar. Very, very cool. Claudia would love this. I called her at the start of lunch, once I'd settled into my car, turned it on, cranked the heat, and busted into my daily Zone bar and Diet Coke. That was one of the many beauties of the new me: I no longer needed to eat in my cement-stairs bunker. I wasn't hiding anymore. I was a Danger-Zone now, and DangerZones were entitled to weird behavior like hunkering down in an idling car to scarf a meal. Besides, it had gotten way too cold to sit outside and eat.

"Work the Ladder and the Ladder works!" Claudia crowed after I'd told her about my Trista conversation. "How's the new coat?"

"You cannot seriously be connecting the word 'new' to this coat."

The coat was a purchase Claudia forced me into over the weekend, after I asked if it was possible to get frostbite on one's rear end. After a week of sitting on Nate's increasingly frozen rock wrapped in nothing warmer than jeans and a hoodie, it seemed as if the answer was yes. Not that I was against it—if I did get frostbite of the buttocks, I imagined the doctors would have to shave off the frozen portion and reshape the rest, perhaps leaving my tush smaller and sleeker—a cheerier posterior.

Claudia, however, didn't see this as the same happy outcome I did. She thought I needed a coat, but one that fit into my DangerZone style. She dragged me to her mom's favorite thrift store, an unsavory hole in the wall where Lenore liked to pick up ragged old clothes and repurpose them as quilting materials. I'd never liked it there. The place reeked of musty despair, which—Claudia reminded me—is the exact cologne in which a true emo girl would ache to bathe herself.

She found it immediately: an old black men's wool pea coat, frayed and tattered in places and worn to shapelessness. Blotches of odd discolorations from God-knows-what Rorschached its surface. Claudia thought it had character. I just hoped it didn't have lice. The very idea of throwing this behemoth over my new outfits seemed like a crime, but Claudia was positive it would enhance my mystique. Plus it was January, and the temperature was due to take another nosedive. We might even get snow.

I'd kept the coat in my car all morning, but I'd promised her I'd wear it to Nate's rock. So after she and I clicked off, I tugged the eyesore around me and trudged to the main building. The icy wind tortured my face . . . but the rest of me was cozy. I really should've known by now not to question Claudia's genius.

"Nice coat," Nate said as I perched next to him. He had barely looked up from his guitar, but a sly smile played on his face. I was still trying to figure out if he was being genuine or sarcastic, when in a single motion he slid the guitar to his side, wrapped his arms around me, and pulled me in for a kiss.

Did I say "a kiss"? That didn't do it justice. Our lips seemed to melt together, and his tongue rolled over mine in a way that made me dizzy.

A beautiful eternity later the kiss ended, but Nate still held me and my blanket of a coat tucked close under one arm. "I had a great time Friday," he said.

"Me too."

Do not ask why he didn't call, I screamed inside my head. *Don't do it. Do* not *ask why he didn't call.*

"I was kind of surprised you didn't call, though," I said.

WHY? Why did I say it? No good could come of that statement!

"Whatever," Nate said.

He peeled his arm off me, spun his guitar back around, and started playing.

"Not that I would have answered if you had," I said, trying to dig my way out. That sounded mean, though, so I added, "Not that I wouldn't *want* to talk to you—it's just that I was away from home and I forgot to pack my phone cord, so I couldn't charge it up after it ran out of power, which it did pretty much right after I saw you . . ."

What it really came down to was that I couldn't be trusted to function on my own as anything close to a normal human being. Nate hadn't moved since I'd started babbling, but I could feel him pulling further and further away. I thought about Claudia's football players and hot dog eaters and realized I had only one hope to save this encounter.

I let the silence take over for a few minutes as Nate strummed, then casually stepped away from the rock.

"I'm gonna take off," I said. "See you around."

Nate stopped playing. "Why?"

I shrugged, lifted my hand in a bored farewell, and turned back toward the school.

"Wait. Stay," Nate said. "I want to play you something. I wrote it Saturday. I was thinking about you."

Hold up—he wrote a song because he was thinking about me? This was huge! I couldn't show it, though. I folded my arms and silently dared him to impress me.

"I don't have the words yet," he said. "It's just a melody."

He started playing.

It was the most beautiful song I'd ever heard. Of course it was—it was the first song I'd ever had written for me. And writing a song wasn't a quick thing, was it? If he had been thinking of me when he'd written it, he must have been thinking about me a lot. I imagined him sitting in his room, strumming his guitar as he replayed every second of our evening together.

"Did you like it?" he asked.

"It's beautiful," I told him. I sat next to him on the rock again. "Thank you."

"I meant getting high," he said. "I could tell you really liked it. That's what I was thinking about when I wrote the song: your trip. I've never seen anyone get so high that they couldn't move. You must have some kind of super-sensitivity. It was incredible, right?"

"It was . . . you know." That was the best I could do. Terrifying, horrifying, the-closest-thing-to-being-buried-alive-I-ever-want-to-experience were all more accurate, but I was pretty sure they weren't what Nate wanted to hear.

"Yeah, I know." He smiled.

He started playing again, and I felt so sad for him, because I got it. Of course being so overcome by pot that you couldn't function sounded like heaven. Look what he had to deal with when he functioned. This was the perfect time to start helping him, to talk about everything he was masking with his Danger-Zone persona.

I put an understanding hand on his thigh. "You know," I said gently, "I've been thinking about your mo—"

"Shhh," he said. "This is my favorite part."

Nate shushed me. I had never been shushed by anyone but Karl. Was he shushing me because he knew what I was going to say, or was he really just that into his song?

I wasn't sure, but I shushed. When he finished the song, the bell rang.

"I'll be here tomorrow," he said. It was his usual line, but I thought I picked up something else in it this time. Like he knew he'd see me tomorrow and was looking forward to it.

"Actually," I said, "I thought maybe we could study together after school. You know, with finals next week and all."

This was off-script. I had a feeling it might be a little aggressive for Claudia's taste, but I couldn't help it. If Nate and I were going to be together, I wanted more of him. I wanted to get to that easy place I'd had with . . . well, with Archer. Except it would be better with Nate, because Nate was attracted to me. He and I would have something deeper than Archer and I ever could.

"Sure," Nate said. "You know the place. Come by after school."

I was a little worried when I called Claudia on the way to Nate's place. She wasn't one to hold back when she disapproved. She surprised me, though: she didn't seem bothered by the plan.

"It's so beautiful," she said, sniffing back fake tears. "Baby's First Booty Call."

"Shut up! I'm going there to study!"

I was not going there to study. I had all my studying props: texts, notebooks, a six-pack of Diet Coke, and my iPod with the noise-canceling headphones. With a stash like that, I could spend a whole night studying.

But I wouldn't.

I pictured Nate and me in his room, all our books and papers spread out in front of us. Nate would sneak looks at me while we pored over the books. I'd feel his eyes on me and smile up at him with a coy "What?"

Then he'd pounce. And though there was something cinematic about us rolling around on all our books and notes, I did still need them to study, so maybe we'd push them out of the way first. We wouldn't go crazy far. We'd just make out until at some point we'd get tired or need a break to breathe. Then I'd lie in Nate's arms, he'd play with my hair . . . and he'd start talking.

He'd open up about what he was really feeling: his anger, his hurt, his fear—he had to be terrified all the time. What if his dad left for good? What if his mom never woke up? What if she did but she wasn't the same? What if she didn't recognize him or Thackery—and what if his dad left for good *then?*

By the time I pulled up to the mansion, I was practically in tears; I was so full with Nate's pain. I almost expected him to read it on my face and dive into my arms, crying tears of relief and joy because someone finally understood.

Instead he opened the door and blew a cloud of smoke in my face.

"Sorry. I was gonna wait for you, but you know . . ." As his voice trailed off, he gestured to my overstuffed messenger bag. "What's that?"

I was still blinking my way out of the smoky haze. "Books, soda, music: study stuff."

"Right. Study stuff. Let's leave that right here." He eased the bag off my shoulder, then leaned his body against mine and kissed me, long and deep. I didn't like the taste of the smoke clinging to his mouth, and I almost pulled away, but then I felt a bulge in his jeans pressing into my hips.

Whoa.

It actually took me a second to realize what it was. I mean, I knew that's what happens when guys get excited, but only in an intellectual way, not an is-that-a-Maglite-in-your-pocket-or-are-you-just-glad-to-see-me way.

The bulge was flattering, right? It meant he really liked me. I just worried that it was poking me with an expectation I wouldn't be able to fulfill.

Then Nate kissed my neck . . . and my ear . . . and then came back to my lips, and I stopped worrying. I wrapped my arms around his neck and pressed my body into his and knew I'd be blissfully happy if we never moved from this spot and just stood here making out, not two inches from the front door.

Nate pulled his lips from mine and stared into my eyes. "I want to introduce you to someone," he said.

I froze. Was it his dad? Was his dad right there in the next room while Nate and I devoured each other in the doorway?

But wait—Nate had been smoking when he'd answered the door. Was his dad okay with that? Maybe he was. Maybe a man who cheated on his comatose wife and pretty much abandoned his kids didn't live by a whole lot of rules.

Nate took my hand and led me to a long table. On it sat a large, beautiful, light purple glass tube.

"Tonight we blaze with Purple Haze," he said. "Watch and learn."

Ah. "Purple Haze" was a bong—a bong with a name. I watched as he lit it, then sucked on the top of the tube. The water inside gurgled. The whole thing looked and sounded ridiculous, but I wouldn't let myself laugh.

With his eyes closed, Nate gently pulled away from the bong, held his breath . . . then slowly blew another plume of smoke into my face. "Sweet," he said. He offered me the bong. "It's easy."

I didn't doubt it was easy, but it wasn't tempting. Not after Friday night's paralysis party.

"I'm gonna pass," I said.

"Why?"

"No reason. I'm just . . . not that into it."

"But Cara, you get *so* high. That's a gift. Wasting that, that's like . . . like Superman saying he doesn't want to fly."

"Sorry."

I worried this would be the end of the date, but Nate shrugged it off.

"Come on," he said.

He grabbed the bong and led the way to his room. He plopped on his bed, turned on the music and the screen saver, and gently placed Purple Haze on his night table. "We'll leave her here in case you change your mind."

I made a mental note to tell Claudia the bong had both a name *and* a gender.

Nate pulled me down next to him and kissed me, then pulled away, laughing.

Laughing?

"What? What did I do?"

"Nothing," he said. "I was just remembering you from last time. You just . . . stopped. And your face: total perma-grin. You really couldn't move at all?"

Seriously? Were we seriously still talking about this? Did we seriously stop *kissing* to talk about this?

"No," I said. "I couldn't move at all."

"A baked coma," he said dreamily.

Coma? Did he say "coma"? My next words were vital. I wanted him to know I understood what he meant, that he could tell me even more and I'd be there for him. But I had a feeling that if I pushed, he'd stop talking.

"Yeah," I said, trying to echo his dreaminess. "Maybe if that's what it's like, it's not so bad."

It was a ridiculous thing to say, especially since the coma experience for me had been hell on earth. But I figured it would make sense to Nate, and maybe give him a little comfort.

"Cooooh . . . ma," Nate singsonged. "Koooooh . . . na. Cooooh . . . la." He laughed, then rolled to face me and look me up and down. "Nice pocket," he said, his fingers reaching out to touch the chain trim on my shirt. "Can I try it?"

I wanted to steer the conversation back to his mom, but the next second he had slipped two fingers into the pocket and I gasped. Nate smiled and pulled me in for another kiss. This time he didn't laugh.

"Oh my God, Claudia—I think I'm a nymphomaniac!" It was an hour later and I was in the car, incinerating the speed limit to hit Wegmans and still get home in time for dinner.

"Don't you have to 'nymph' before you can be maniacal about it?"

"Define 'nymph,'" I hedged.

"You had sex with him?"

"Nooooo," I said, clearly implying more to the story.

"Were you naked?"

"Not *entirely* . . ."

"You whoreson trollop!" Claudia crowed.

"I know! I know! It's crazy! He just looks at me in this way . . . this 'You Are the Most Gorgeous Creature Alive and I Want to Devour You' way . . . and my brain melts. Gone. Completely. Claude, if I hadn't had to get home, he could've gone further. I don't think I would've stopped him."

"You wouldn't have had sex with him." It was a statement, not a question.

"No!" I said. "I mean, unless maybe he had something . . . you know, like a condom . . ."

"*Cara!*" Claudia cried.

"I know! And it's not like I'm in love with him! What is wrong with me?"

Chapter *eighteen*

$\mathcal{I}$f something *was* wrong with me, it didn't take me long to stop caring. Nate and I "studied" every afternoon that week. After the first time, I didn't bother bringing my books—although maybe I could have used them to fan away the giant cloud of smoke that engulfed me every time I walked in.

That was really the only problem; Nate hadn't given up on making me a pothead. He talked constantly about my "gift" and what a crime it was to deny myself a high that some could only dream of achieving.

"And you're just a noob," he'd say. "That means it'll get even deeper."

If my high got any deeper, I was pretty sure I'd end up dead. Nate didn't get that. He hoped a good contact high would rope me in—hence the cloud of smoke when I entered.

Part of me was flattered. Sadly for Nate, getting high was life's peak experience. I figured he had to care about me a lot to want to share it with me so badly.

Still, he never let up, and I was tired of finding new ways to say no. Plus to me the "sweet perfume" of pot smoke smelled more like a combination of wet grass and cat pee.

By Wednesday I dreaded going into the house. Then I spent the first half hour there fighting with myself about whether to leave and never come back.

But then Nate would kiss me, and it felt so good that within seconds I wouldn't even notice the pot on his breath.

Claudia always snapped up her phone on the first ring when I called her from the car each evening on my way to Wegmans.

"Sex Addicts Anonymous, this is your sponsor speaking," she answered on Thursday.

"We have not had sex!"

"Right, but you're hitting practically a base a day, which means by my calculations you'll have done the deed by this time next week."

"Okay—in baseball? Three bases. Four, with home plate."

"Whatever. So what happened today?"

The second she asked, I had a physical flashback and felt a shivery jolt. It was so unexpected, I actually let out a scream.

"What?" Claudia wailed. "Is he there? Tell me he isn't there. That's just weird. And aren't you driving?"

"No, he's not here! I was just remembering. It was kind of . . . big today."

"*It* was big?"

"That's not what I mean. I mean, it *was* big. I think. Not that I've *seen* it . . . Even if I *had* seen it, I have no basis for comparison, so I still wouldn't know, really—"

"I'm going to start playing 'Mary Had a Little Lamb' on the phone keys unless you tell me *exactly* what happened *right now*."

"Okay, so you know how I said I was going to wear that stretchy skirt today?"

"Easy access," she confirmed.

"Right. Well . . . he accessed."

"OH MY GOD!" Claudia screeched. A loud beep screamed in my ear.

"Ow! What was that?"

"That was my jaw hitting the floor. Or in this case, the pound key," Claudia said. "So was it . . . you know . . . good?"

"Yeah . . ."

"But?"

"No, it was good. It was. It was just really . . . *intimate,* you know? Almost too intimate. But I didn't think that until it was over. And then I just kind of wanted to cuddle up and wrap the comforter all around me."

Neither one of us said anything for a minute.

"Cair, are you okay?"

"Yeah! I mean, it felt incredible. Honestly, he didn't do anything I didn't *really* want him to."

"Swear on the Bell?"

"Swear on the Bell. Sorry, Claude, gotta run—Wegmans. I'll call you back after."

I thought about it while I did my quick-change act and decided I was making a big deal out of nothing. It wasn't like I was twelve. I was sixteen. Lots of sixteen-year-olds had actual sex. The fact that I'd maybe gone a little further than I might have imagined I would was seriously no big deal. And I hadn't been lying to Claudia: It had felt amazing. Really amazing. And I'd wanted it in a huge way.

So there we were. I was fine. I was better than fine. I was great.

Except that night I couldn't sleep at all.

It wasn't what we'd done that bothered me. It was Nate, and the way I was with Nate. We never talked. At all. Okay, yes, we talked about music, and we talked about pot, and we talked about how much he wanted me to hear his music and smoke his pot, but we didn't talk about anything real. And that was cool when we were just hanging out, but now we'd had this really deep, intense physical experience. But without the other stuff it felt kind of . . . empty.

I desperately needed to know how Nate felt about me, but even the idea of asking made me burn with embarrassment. Too lame and sad-little-puppy. And I was sure anything Nate did feel would evaporate the minute I asked.

If I wanted to know Nate's feelings, I had to test them.

Since I wasn't Claudia, my test wasn't baroque. The next day, Friday, I simply didn't go out to the rock at lunchtime. Not right away and not after my usual lag time. I forced myself to stay in my car and eat my Zone bar with teeny, tiny bites, chewing thirty times before I swallowed. It was meditative, actually, and gave me something to concentrate on other than how Nate might—or might not—be reacting to my absence.

With five minutes left to the period, I hunkered down in my beast of a pea coat and made my way to the rock. My heart pounded. I glued my eyes to each skeletally leafless tree I passed, stretching time before I'd see what I wasn't sure I wanted to know: whether or not Nate had cared enough to leave the rock and look for me.

My insides deflated when I saw him, same as always, playing his guitar without a care in the world. I had another physical flashback to last night, but this time I didn't feel a shivery jolt. I felt stupid and embarrassed.

I was close enough now for Nate to notice. He smiled up at me. "Hey."

Normally, this was when he'd pull me close for a kiss, but I purposely stood out of his reach. He beckoned for me to come closer, but I didn't move. For the first time with Nate, I didn't have to concentrate on squelching my normal curly-haired energy. I had never felt less curly and bouncy than I did now.

"You don't look worried." I tried to sound nonchalant, but even I could hear the bitterness in my words. Not cool, but I couldn't help it.

"About what?"

"I always meet you during fifth period. Today I didn't."

He looked at me pointedly, clearly noting that I was indeed right there in front of him during fifth period. The fact that he was right didn't make me any less upset.

"Okay, I'm here *now*, but didn't you wonder where I was? What if I'd been sick, or hurt?"

"You weren't," Nate said.

"Yeah, but I could have been!" I screeched just as the bell rang. Without a word, Nate rose and strode toward the building. Halfway there he turned and looked back at me.

"I'm around later if you want to come over and study," he said, then kept walking.

I was floored. Seriously, I couldn't have been more offended if he'd asked if I wanted to go drown puppies. He didn't get it! Like I would actually want to go wade through pot smoke and get half-naked with him when he didn't care about me at all!

My shock didn't wear off. I spent the rest of the afternoon with my mouth hanging open. Our whole situation— our whole relationship, if that's what you could call it, which clearly you couldn't—was exactly what I'd feared. No matter how close we were physically, emotionally I meant absolutely nothing to Nate. But did that matter to him? Did that stop him? No. Nate Wetherill was evil. Pure, unadulterated evil. By the end of seventh-period AP U.S. history I had proof. Know what you get when you rearrange the letters in Nate Wetherill? HATE WILL ENTER.

Halfway through eighth-period physics, I had transformed my pencil and some paper clips into an excellent Nate Wetherill voodoo doll and was mercilessly grinding another paper clip into its groin. The whole enterprise felt immensely satisfying.

"Cara Leonard!" called Mr. Feinhorn. "Why does that not disprove Einstein's theory of relativity?"

Uh-oh. Apparently we were in the middle of a lecture, but I hadn't heard a single word of it. I palmed the voodoo doll and racked my brain for any information that didn't have to do with my undying animosity toward Nate. I found none.

"Um, because . . . because . . ." I scrunched my whole face as if struggling for the answer. I practically broke a sweat.

Mr. Feinhorn wasn't impressed. He sighed, then called on Seth Minkoff, who dutifully responded, "Because it was an invalid test."

"Yes," said Mr. Feinhorn. "*That* is the answer, Cara. It was an invalid test."

Mr. Feinhorn looked me in the eye as he said it, and suddenly I understood. Not the Einstein stuff—I had absolutely no idea what he was talking about there. But the invalid test—*that* made sense. Nate had failed an invalid test. He and I hadn't made specific plans to meet at the rock today, so it's not like I'd actually missed a set appointment. Sure, I usually met him there, but I had the freedom to show or not show as I pleased.

Nate wasn't possessive that way. That was a good thing, wasn't it? And even when I laid into him, it's not like he'd dumped me or said he didn't want to see me. He told me I should come over and study. When I looked at it that way, Nate actually came closer to *passing* my test than failing.

Maybe testing Nate wasn't the best way to find out if he really cared about me. I still thought asking it outright was awful and lame and worthy of the kind of *are u mad @ me?* notes friends passed around in seventh grade. But maybe there was a subtler option. Maybe I could just ask about him, about his mom, about his dad or his brother or his life. Then he'd ask about me, and we'd talk and I'd know there was actually something real between us, and I wouldn't feel so hollow about everything else we were doing.

So after school I went to his place to study.

"Hi," I said, and before Nate could even try to offer me a smoke, I added, "I was hoping today we could talk."

"About what?"

"I don't know . . . anything. About you. Maybe about your mom."

Nate grimaced like he smelled a skunk. "Ouch. Buzzkill."

"Well, yeah, but—"

Nate was no longer listening. Instead he was lighting up.

Okay, Mom was too painful. I could respect that.

"How about *you* decide what we talk about," I said. "It doesn't even have to be about you. You can ask *me* something. Anything. Anything you want."

Nate smiled and put his hands on my waist, slipping his fingers under my shirt.

"Anything I want?" he said.

His fingers traced up my body toward my breasts, both of which had clearly turned treasonous on me, because they were screaming for Nate's hands to keep climbing.

I stepped back.

"I'm serious," I said. "I don't want to fool around. I want to talk. It's important to me."

Nate opened his eyes wide, tilted his head back, and made a groaning sound like a giant garbage truck stuck between gears.

What was he doing? Had I pressed his self-destruct button? Who made noises like that?

Finally Nate pulled himself back from whatever brink he was on. He smiled and nodded, like he'd just solved a mystery.

"Ooh," he said. "I get it."

He took my hand and pulled me close. He kissed my neck, then whispered in my ear. "You're raggin' it. It's cool; it doesn't freak me out. I have my red badge of courage."

That was it.

"I gotta go," I said. I pulled away and darted to the door, already dialing Claudia on my cell.

"Beast with Two Backs Hotline," she answered. "You're calling early."

"I just broke up with Nate," I said.

Claudia's voice screamed into my ear with the impact of a major collision. "You *WHAT?*"

Chapter *nineteen*

As I drove, I told Claudia everything. When I was done, she took a huge dramatic breath and slowly let it out. "Do not scare me like that again, Cara. I was afraid you actually broke up with Nate."

"I did."

"You walked out on him," she clarified. "Neither the word 'break' nor 'up' was ever specifically stated. Hence your place on the Ladder remains secure."

"Very nice. So even though I now feel completely horrible when I fool around with Nate, I'm supposed to keep doing it so I don't lose my place on the Ladder."

"Yes, Cara, I'm pimping you out," Claudia said. "No! Don't fool around with him at all! Just don't break up with him. Not until you've found a Penultimate for your next target."

"I can't *not* fool around with him. It's what he expects us to do."

"Gee, Battered Wife, I guess if he expects it, then it's what you have to do."

"I'm just saying, I doubt *he'll* want to stay together if we're not fooling around anymore."

"Not forever, no. But we're talking about a few days—enough time for you to find a target and focus in. And the timing's perfect. You have finals next week, right? So it's totally normal that you'd be too busy studying to go 'study.'"

"Okay, but what about at school? What if I'm hanging out with him on the rock and he wants to fool around?"

"Tell him you have a cold! Tell him you have a sty! Tell him you have herpes! No, wait, don't tell him you have herpes. That'd get around the school and ruin everything."

"Oh, good, thanks for clarifying. Because I was totally ready to go with the herpes thing."

"Just try, Cara. Do not let everything you've already done be in vain. Look at how hard you've worked to get to this spot on the Ladder. Look at all the success you've had! You snagged a DangerZone! Trista Camello, Supreme Populazzi, knows who you are! You cannot give up now. You *can't*. Do I have to invoke the Deer Friends? Because if I have to, I will."

I took a deep breath. I didn't want to stay with Nate. It didn't feel right. But I also didn't want to fight with Claudia, and it wasn't like I could do anything about Nate until Monday anyway. I wasn't going to go see him over the weekend, and breaking up over the phone or by e-mail wasn't at all okay.

"I won't do anything now," I said. "I'll figure it out on Monday."

She seemed satisfied with that.

I didn't leave the house all weekend. I vaguely remembered Archer and me talking about maybe playing Ping-Pong, but I texted him that I couldn't. Claudia had been right: after my week of "studying," I really did need to study if I was going to have a prayer of nailing finals, keeping up my average, getting into Northwestern, and avoiding the gutter that would certainly otherwise be my fate.

I spread out on the kitchen table surrounded by books, notes, and Diet Cokes and tuned out the world with my iPod and noise-canceling headphones. Karl even let me read during meals, which was unheard of. He and Mom were so impressed with my academic discipline that they took turns acting as my cut man, rubbing my shoulders and offering snacks and encouragement.

Come Monday, I woke up ready to attack two goals: acing my French exam and breaking up with Nate. I'd had plenty of time to prepare for both. At Chrysella, the finals schedule was totally different from the schedule for normal school days. Every day was broken into two two-hour exam periods, with lunch in the middle. We didn't even have to show up at school unless we had a scheduled exam. French was in my Monday afternoon slot, but I wanted to go a little early and squeeze in a lunchtime breakup at Nate's rock.

As I stopped at Wegmans to change, I was spotted by my nemesis cashier. He was in the parking lot gathering carts. He perked up at the sight of me and started singing to the galloping tune of the "William Tell Overture," "SuperGoth Super-Goth SuperGoth-Goth-Goth . . ."

I wondered how long after Nate and I broke up I'd have to keep changing at Wegmans. It had been fun and exciting at first, but now it was tedious. I figured I'd have to phase it out gradually. I'd probably be done by the winter formal, about a month away.

Of course, first I had to find Nate and break up with him. For most couples, this would be a nonissue, since they would know each other's schedules. I had no clue about Nate's schedule. I had no idea when he had any of his exams—I wasn't even 100 percent positive about all the classes he took. I could only show up at the rock and hope.

For her part, Claudia had called and texted pretty much constantly, from the time she woke up to the time she got to school in the morning, trying to convince me not to jeopardize my position on the Ladder. It hadn't worked. Her fallback was to hope Nate's and my schedules would mismatch all week long, giving me time to find and go after a Penultimate while securely ensconced in a DangerZone relationship.

I didn't bother to tell Claudia she was delusional if she thought I could land a new boyfriend—a *Penultimate* boyfriend—in a matter of days. It had happened that way with Nate, sure, but I'd had Archer help with the introduction. This time I was on my own.

I got to school just as lunch was starting . . . but I had trouble getting out of the car. I'd never broken up with anyone. I wondered how Nate would react. Though if I was honest with myself, I knew. He would deal with the breakup like he dealt with everything else between us: with pure, unbridled apathy.

It wouldn't exactly be an ego boost.

Eventually I bundled up and trudged outside to seek Nate, Rock, and Guitar: my Holy Trinity of these past weeks. I was in luck; they were all there. It was fascinating watching Nate as I approached. He was still gorgeous. He was still passionate, talented, deep, and brooding . . . but there was no full-body frizzle at the sight of him. I was over it.

"Hey," I said when I reached his side.

"Hey."

The last time I'd seen him, I was rushing angrily out of his house. A small part of me wondered if he'd ask about that, or at least look a little concerned when he saw me. He didn't. He glanced up from his guitar, just like always, then scooted over so I could sit next to him. I considered it, but it didn't seem right. I tried standing, but that felt too strident. Instead I sat on a patch of grass. From this angle, I had a far better view of Nate's crotch than his face, and the frosted grass was seeping through both my ratty pea coat and my jeans, leaving me with a cold, wet butt. Not a good call.

"Hey!" said a voice.

I recognized the guy, even though I didn't know him. His name was Eddie Riegert, and he was a Penultimate. He wore jeans and a T-shirt featuring a glasses-wearing, book-reading dinosaur labeled THE-SAURUS. He was muscular without being buff and had wavy, reddish-brown hair. He looked cold; he clearly didn't intend to be outside very long.

Nate looked up at Eddie but said nothing. I didn't either—Eddie was looking at Nate, not me.

After several moments, Eddie seemed to realize Nate's stare was all the acknowledgment he was going to get. He laughed. "Cool, okay. Look, I'm having a party at my house Saturday. Punch in your e-mail. I'll send you the stuff."

Eddie held his cell to Nate, but Nate didn't take it. He just looked at it and kept strumming his guitar.

"Dude, if you don't want to come, that's cool, but say it," Eddie said. "Don't leave me hanging. I'm freezing my ass off out here."

Nate took the phone and punched in his information, then handed it back. He still hadn't said a word.

Eddie gave a sarcastic bow. "Thanks."

He started trotting back to the building. I felt bad for him. He was just being nice; he didn't deserve to be ignored.

"Thanks to you, too!" I called after him, and immediately blushed at my own idiocy. *Thanks to you, too?* It sounded either desperately dorky or completely sarcastic and rude, neither of which I'd intended. Nate scrunched his face at me, and Eddie stopped in his tracks to stare, like I was some alien life-form. He trotted back and handed me his cell.

"Here," he said. "Punch in your e-mail, too."

Really?

I did what he asked, then tried to salvage some dignity by giving him my best DangerZone emo-girl stare as I handed back the phone.

Eddie laughed out loud. "Thanks"—he looked down at his screen—"Cara. I'll e-mail you guys."

He darted back to the warmth of the building.

Amazing. I had just been invited to a Populazzi party. A *Populazzi* party! Or at least I was invited to be invited to a Populazzi party.

Wait—was Eddie actually inviting *me,* or was he inviting Nate-and-Cara: DangerZone couple? Because in about two minutes, that couple wouldn't exist.

"Nate . . ." I began.

The bell rang.

"Gotta take a final." Nate scowled. "I'm here tomorrow. Or you can come study later."

He gave me one of his half smiles, then strode to the building.

"Nate, wait!" I tried to get up and follow him, but my butt had gone completely numb from the cold and wet, and I immediately fell back down. By the time I got up, Nate was inside, and I had to run to make my French exam.

I called Claudia on the way home. "Do you have any idea how close you came to complete Armageddon?" she asked.

I didn't answer. I had a pretty strong feeling she'd tell me soon enough.

"This party is *exactly* the steppingstone you need to make the transition from DangerZone to Penultimate! You can't possibly break up with Nate until it's over!"

"Claude, I can't stay with him just to go to a party."

"A *Populazzi* party."

"Even a Populazzi party." I parked my car at Wegmans and strode across the lot. "Believe me, I want to go. I *really* want to go. I mean, seriously, this is the kind of thing you and I have been talking about since long before the Ladder. But I can't stay with Nate to do it. I don't feel good about myself anymore when I'm with him. And—"

"CARA?"

The scream took me by surprise.

Especially since it had come from my mother.

Chapter *twenty*

Oh God. OhGodOhGodOhGod.

This was not supposed to happen. My mom does *not* shop at Wegmans on Monday afternoons. She has a very specific shopping schedule she picked up from some self-help organize-your-life website, and she follows it religiously. Sunday night is for clipping coupons, planning the week's menus, and writing up the shopping list. Monday night after dinner is for shopping. By that time in the evening, most people are long since done running errands, and she can get in and out with ease. My mom is very proud of this schedule and its efficacy, and she would never dream of messing it up by doing something wild and crazy like shopping between the hours of four and seven— *prime shopping hours* for people on their way from work or school.

And yet here she was.

I had no idea how I was going to explain the way I looked. None. Every synapse in my brain was tap-dancing, but I was coming up completely blank.

This was so, so bad.

"Hi, Mom," I said with a weak smile.

She smiled back.

Wait—she smiled back?

"Cara, you surprised me! What are you wearing? Is this for your French final?"

I couldn't believe it. It was just like in old cartoons. The sky opened up, the sun shone its light on me, and a choir of angels sang "Hallelujah." My mother—my wonderful, loving, trusting, incredibly perfect mother—had given me a way out. She was getting the best Mother's Day present ever this year.

I released all my tension into a laugh, hoping it didn't sound too maniacal.

"Oral presentation," I said. "French pop culture. There's this whole 'emo' movement going on there. It's here, too, but bigger over there." I gave a sweeping gesture to indicate my raccoon-makeup eyes, my clingy tee and hoodie, my black skirt, my fuchsia zebra-striped leggings, my boots, and my wrist warmers. My abused blanket of a coat was back in the car. "I figured I'd add visual aids."

"I hope you got a good grade, because you look ridiculous. What would someone think if they saw you?"

"That I obviously had some kind of school project?" I offered.

Mom laughed. "Come on, let's go home. You'll want to wash up before Karl sees you." She started pushing her cart, then remembered I'd been headed inside. "Did you need to get something?"

"Just a snack."

"Don't bother. I got all your favorite things." As I accompanied her to her car and helped her load the bags into the trunk,

Mom explained the inexplicable. "Shelley got a twofer coupon to P.F. Chang's, so we made a day out of it. Manis and pedis, then lunch. Very decadent. I knew I wouldn't want to come back out later, so I decided to suck it up and shop a little early. It really was nowhere near as bad as I thought it would be."

For me either, I almost chirped. Somehow I refrained.

I cranked the radio on the ride home, singing and dancing along in a state of sheer euphoria. Claudia didn't answer her phone, but I left a giddy voice mail. I swore Karl should take me to Atlantic City immediately and pass me off as twenty-one, because I was clearly the luckiest human being in the world.

I pulled into the driveway right behind my mom and grabbed two grocery bags to take in. I could've carried thirty—to me they were light as air. We walked into the house laughing about some ridiculous story Shelley had told Mom about the cockatiel Shelley's husband was trying to get to speak, but the moment we stepped over the threshold, Karl boomed from upstairs.

"Harriet?"

A cold shower of fear washed over me, and my laughter dried up in my throat.

Karl *never* called my mother Harriet. He *loathed* the name. That's one of the main reasons he jumped at the "Helloooo/Lo-Lo" thing. He so actively disliked my mother's name that he couldn't say it with any kind of affection whatsoever. If Karl was calling Mom Harriet, things were about to get very ugly.

Mom and I exchanged a worried glance, then she called up as brightly as possible, "Yes?"

"Please tell me when your daughter gets home," he said.

The wave of fear became a tsunami, and I suddenly couldn't breathe.

He'd referred to me as "your daughter." My mom's daughter. Not his. And in that moment I knew exactly what had happened. It was so stupid. I knew it was out there—a time bomb waiting to explode in my face—but I'd been so wrapped up in the drama and excitement of Archer and Nate and the Ladder that I honestly hadn't even thought about it.

Karl had opened the credit card bill.

Mom looked confused. She turned to me. I must have looked as nauseous as I felt, because her eyes narrowed suspiciously. "She's already here," Mom called.

My outfit. My makeup. OhGodNo—Karl could *not* see me like this. I had to wash my face. I had to change. I had to *move*. I staggered toward the bathroom. "I'm just going to—"

"Stay right there," Mom warned.

Karl's footsteps thundered downstairs. I could see the credit card bill in his hand. He stopped halfway down the steps, his piercing eyes taking me in. Then they shifted to my mother.

"How long have you known?" he spat.

"Known what?" Mom said. "Cara told me she got dressed up for an oral presentation as part of her French exam."

Karl walked down the rest of the staircase with me fixed in his glare. "So you lied to your mother. Very nice," he said.

I could never be a criminal. The torture of waiting for Karl's revelation and everything that would come next was unbearable. Karl handed Mom the bill and watched my face as she read it.

"I don't understand . . ." Mom began.

"Of course you don't," Karl said. "Luckily, I'm smarter than the both of you, so I do. The biggest bill is the hair, which we knew about but which you never told us cost anywhere near this much. I'd expect more responsibility from you, Cara. At least I *used to* expect more responsibility from you."

"Karl, I'm sorry. I—"

He held up a finger. "Did I say I was done? Now, the second highest bill is from a store called Hot Topic. It's not one I frequent, so I used something called 'the Internet' and looked it up. Turns out the store has some very cute clothes. That made me think, 'If Cara bought some very cute clothes—even if she spent a little too much money on them—why wouldn't she show them to her mother and me? After all, she always shows us when she buys something she's excited about.' So I poked around the store's website a little more, and I realized that in addition to some very cute clothes, they also sell some very inappropriate clothes. Could Cara have bought these inappropriate clothes—a very sizable amount of these inappropriate clothes—and hidden the purchase from us?"

My mom's eyes were wide now. "Cara?"

Karl shook his head. "Not yet, Harriet."

He turned back to me. "So I went through your room. And sure enough, tucked away behind other things in your drawers and your closet was a whole other wardrobe of clothing. Clothing not dissimilar to what you're wearing now. Of course, not all of it was put away. Quite a bit of the clothing was balled up in your closet—dirty, one would imagine, from being worn. Now, until this moment, *I* haven't seen you wearing any of this clothing. Harriet, have you?"

"No," my mom said, looking at me with a terrible mix of anger and brutal disappointment.

"Which can only lead me to believe that you've been fooling us, wearing one set of clothes when we've seen you and another when you get somewhere else. Presumably to school. Would that be correct?"

There was no point in saying otherwise. "Yes," I admitted.

Karl smiled, triumphant. Mom looked like I had punched her in the stomach.

"So our whole conversation . . . you were lying to me? To my face?" she asked.

I couldn't answer out loud. I just nodded.

"Excellent." Karl beamed at the confession. "So here's what I've done so far: I've confiscated all your clothing and all your makeup."

"You . . . *what?*"

"When you want to get dressed in the morning, you will ask your mother to pick you out an outfit. If you want makeup, your mother can apply it for you."

"Karl—" Mom said, but Karl shut her up with a glare.

"Since you have proven you can't be trusted with privacy, you'll notice your room no longer has a door," Karl said. "Your bathroom *does* have a door, but that door no longer can lock. Both rooms are subject to spot checks at my discretion, and I reserve the right to confiscate whatever I see fit. For example, the pile of diaries under your bed is now mine, and I look forward to perusing them at my leisure."

"You took my journals?"

"I don't see that I had a choice," Karl said. "I have a stranger in my house. That's a dangerous situation for me. The only way I can protect myself is to find out everything about her that I can."

"*Dangerous?* Karl, you've known me since I was four."

Karl shook his head sadly, but his voice remained impassive. "The girl I knew—the girl I was willing to take on as my daughter—would never betray me the way you did. I've been breaking my back to try to get you into Northwestern. You think your teachers will recommend you now?"

"The way I dress shouldn't matter to them," I said.

"But it does. You think they'll want you on a college campus looking like that?"

We were having the wrong conversation. I wasn't a real emo girl. I would never dress like this at college. But no explanation I could offer would make things any better.

"Maybe," I said. "Colleges love diversity."

"Do they love drug addicts, Cara?" Karl asked. "Do they love alcoholics? Do they love teen pregnancies?"

What?

"Karl, that's not what I—"

"How do I know? I don't know who you are anymore. I don't know what you're doing. I don't know what you've *done*. How long have you been sneaking around behind our backs, Cara? What else have you been lying about?"

"Nothing! I'm sorry—I made a terrible mistake. I shouldn't have lied to you, and I shouldn't have gone behind your backs. But I swear, I'm not leading some secret double life. I'm the same person I always was."

"I don't believe you," Karl said. "But if—*if*—you're going to continue to live under my roof, here's what you will do: you will go to school, you will come home, you will do your homework. You will *not* have a credit card, a car, a phone, a television, a computer, or any life whatsoever outside of school. When you *are* in my house, I don't want to see you except for meals. You are to remain in your room and out of my sight."

I couldn't believe this was happening. Had Karl really said *"if"* I continue to live under his roof? Had I really messed things up *that* badly?

"For how long?" I asked.

"Lucky for me, you'll be out of the house in a year and a half, right? Now please go up to your room. *After* you give me your cell phone."

My insides felt shredded, but Karl looked just fine. He almost seemed happy. A smug smile played on his face. I stared at him, then handed over my cell phone and went up to my room.

My doorless, journal-less, computer-less, TV-less room. I wanted to change out of my emo-garb, but oh yeah: no clothes. Every drawer and my closet had been emptied.

What could I do? I lay back on my bed and listened to Mom and Karl scream at each other downstairs. Or to be more accurate, I listened to Mom scream, plead, and cry while Karl gave her the same disinterested attitude he had given me. At one point he even turned on the TV.

They both seemed to agree that I was horrible. It was the degree of horribleness and the extent of the consequences that had them banging heads. Mom thought stripping away every bit of choice in my life was a touch extreme. Karl thought it was the only sensible way to deal with a stranger in the house. Mom thought the demotion from "daughter" to "stranger" was also a touch extreme. Karl said if "Harriet" didn't like it, then she and "her daughter" could go live in someone else's house and leave him alone.

It went on for a really long time. At a certain point I crawled under the comforter, pulled it over my head so their voices were muffled, and cried myself to sleep.

I woke up at two. Mom was sitting on the bed next to me, rubbing my arm. Her face was puffy from crying, but she laughed when I sat up to look at her.

"You really need to wash your face. Go take a shower. We'll talk afterward."

I felt even fuzzier and drunker than when I'd had the beer with Nate, but I managed to get up and stagger into the hall. On the way, I noticed my computer was back on my desk, all my clothes were stacked on my dressers, and my door—while not reattached—was now leaning in the hallway next to the jamb. I cast my eyes under my bed and saw with relief that my giant plastic bin of journals was back in place. At least at first glance, they looked beautifully untouched.

I winced against the light in the bathroom as I peeked at my face. No wonder Mom had laughed: I looked like a badly beaten mime.

I took a long hot shower, then pulled on my favorite furry white robe that seemed to have magically reappeared on its usual hook. Mom wasn't in my room anymore, but I smelled something in the kitchen, so I padded down to find two spots set at the table: one with hot tea and one with warm milk and cinnamon, my favorite childhood drink when I couldn't sleep. I sat and sipped it gratefully.

"You missed dinner," Mom said. "Can I make you some eggs?"

I nodded, and a few minutes later Mom and I both had big plates of scrambled eggs. It was time to talk.

"He really doesn't want to see me anymore?" I asked, looking down at my eggs.

Mom sighed. "Karl . . ." she began, then thought about it another moment and frowned. "I want you to know that I'm not giving you a pass for what you did. Especially lying to my face. That hurts me a lot, and I'm going to have a very hard time getting over it and trusting you again."

I knew that, and it killed me. I wanted to tell her how awful I felt, that I'd do anything to turn back time and make it all go away, but it was hard enough just meeting her eyes.

Mom's face softened, and she sipped her tea. "Karl, though . . . you know how he gets. He doesn't react well when he feels unappreciated."

"Unappreciated?" I asked.

"Karl does a lot for you," Mom said. "For both of us. And you repaid him by lying. You had a whole life we didn't know about: different clothes, different makeup, maybe different friends, maybe dangerous friends—"

"It's not like that. I swear, it's not as if I was skipping school and running around Philly flashing gang signs."

"That may be, but when you lie to us, we don't know. And it makes Karl wonder if everything else he knows about you is a lie and you're just showing him what he wants to see so you can get what you want out of him. It's not a good feeling, Cara."

I had a headache. My brain must have been swelling, because I couldn't hold my head upright. I rested it on my hands. "Okay . . . so what can I do to make it better?"

"Karl needs time. You really hurt him. I haven't seen him this upset since . . ."

She didn't say it, and she didn't have to. I knew exactly when he'd been this upset. I was maybe eight years old and I'd been invited to Dad's for Christmas. Mom, Dad, and I are Jewish, but the Bar Wench is Christian, and they do up the holiday big-time. The house was practically ablaze with lights and decorations, including a giant singing and dancing Frosty the Snowman on the lawn. Inside, things were even crazier, but the centerpiece was a thick, full Christmas tree, nearly twenty feet tall.

I'm no fan of the Bar Wench, but she really did try to make me a part of the celebration. Even though I showed up on Christmas Eve, she had saved a whole swath of bare tree for me to decorate, and there was a stocking stitched with my name hanging from the mantelpiece. Since I clearly didn't believe in Santa Claus, she let me stay up after her boys had gone to bed and help her "prove" Santa existed. She and I shared his milk and cookies, we wrapped and put out the gifts from him, and she let me help her press rubber boots into the fireplace ashes: Santa's footprints.

In the morning, Santa had left gifts under the tree for me, too. And my stocking was as full as the boys'. All my presents that year were perfect. Dad and the Bar Wench—and Santa—had given me everything I wanted, including the gift I'd been *dying* for: a super-plussed-out Spin Art kit. The whole trip was magical. It was the only time I ever felt like I was actually a part of my dad's new family.

When I got back to Mom and Karl's on the twenty-sixth, I couldn't stop talking about the amazing visit, all the fun I had with Dad's really-cool-once-you-got-to-know-them family, and of course my incredible new Spin Art kit.

The more I raved, the quieter and angrier Karl got. He didn't want to hear it, and he did *not* want me to open the Spin Art kit. He said it was too messy. It had to go back to the store. I threw a fit; he screamed at me to stop or else; I screamed back, coming up with what I thought was a very clever line: He wasn't just a stepfather, he was a step*down*father.

He responded by opening the Spin Art kit and smashing it to pieces in front of me, then gathering up all the gifts I'd gotten from Dad, the Bar Wench, and Santa that year and throwing them in the trash. When he was done, he kicked a hole in the hall closet door. It's still there.

That was the last time he'd disowned me. He eventually got over it, but it seriously took a year before things were normal again.

My headache was getting worse.

Mom put a comforting hand on my arm. "If you really want to make it better," she said, "prove that he's wrong. Be the best daughter you can possibly be. Lie low and don't force yourself on him; he's angry. But when you do see him, be nice. Ask him about his day. See if he needs anything. Let him know how much you love him. He might not respond right away, but he'll come around. He always does, right?"

"Yeah . . . he does."

Mom nodded, then took a sip of her tea. When she finished, she sighed and studied my face.

"What?" I asked.

"I still don't understand, Cara . . . why did you do it? Did you get in with a bad crowd? Were you trying to express something you felt you couldn't talk about? Were you . . ." She looked achingly concerned as she turned my hands palm-up and carefully scanned my wrists.

"Mom, no. I wasn't cutting. At all. I'm fine. I'm happy. I'm not in with any kind of bad crowd. It's so much littler and stupider than any of that."

"Then, what?" I could see she really wanted to understand, to break through and talk about my inner turmoil, whatever it might be.

"It was for a guy," I said. "He only likes girls with that look. That's all. I promise."

"What kind of a boy only likes girls who dress up in costume every day?"

"It's not a costume to the people who are into it. And the guy . . . he's a friend of Archer's. That's how I know him."

I knew this would give Mom pause. She loved Archer; could any friend of his really be that bad?

She shook her head. "I'm surprised. But you should know any boy who's worthwhile will like you for *you*. Not the way you dress."

"I do know, Mom. I told you, it was stupid."

"And if he does only like you for your clothes, he's going to be sorely disappointed. I didn't put everything back in your room. Some things we're giving to Goodwill."

I had an image of a large group of homeless people clad in fuchsia zebra-striped leggings and chain-embossed tees and laughed out loud.

"I'm absolutely fine with that," I said. "I'd already planned to break up with the guy tomorrow."

"Good, I'm glad," Mom said with a smile—then a moment later she burst into tears.

Chapter *twenty-one*

The whole time Mom and I were talking, I'd assumed Karl was asleep in his room. He wasn't. After he'd fought with Mom, he was so disgusted that he stormed out of the house, promising her that since she was choosing me over him, the next time she heard from him would be through a lawyer.

Mom was devastated. She loved Karl. And if he divorced her, that was it. At forty, she was sure she was past anyone falling for her. Then there was the house: without Karl's income, we couldn't afford it. We'd have to get an apartment somewhere, Mom would have to go back to work . . .

"I'm so sorry," she sobbed. "I don't mean to put all this on you. You're my little girl, and I know you didn't realize you'd be doing this to us."

I couldn't speak, but I couldn't close my mouth. My mom, my world, my life was falling to pieces in front of me. *Because* of me.

Then Karl came home. True to his word, he didn't acknowledge my existence, no matter how charmingly I smiled and apologized. He did talk to Mom. He'd gone down the shore to think, and in the middle of the most unbelievable shoe he'd ever played, he'd had an epiphany. Having given birth to me, Mom couldn't help her irrational devotion. It was like a handicap, and you can't hold a handicap against someone. He had therefore decided to remain married to her but with the caveat that my care now fell to her alone. He was washing his hands of me.

Mom said she understood. Then she asked what had made the shoe so unbelievable, and within minutes they were chatting happily and practically skipping upstairs to count his winnings.

I was still at the kitchen table. No one had bothered to say good night.

I managed to clean my plate, get it in the dishwasher, and get all the way to bed before the tears started again, but once they did, I couldn't stop them. I sobbed—breathlessly wrenching convulsions from deep inside my body that Mom and Karl must have heard, but no one came to see if I was okay.

At some point I fell asleep.

A few hours later, for the first time since before Christmas break, I went to school looking almost like myself. "Almost" not just because my hair was still straight, but because my features looked more foreign to me now than they ever did with layers and layers of dark makeup. Hours of crying had left my whole face flat and immobile, like it had been infused with Botox. My skin was puffy and even too blotchy for concealer, not that I had any in my now sorely limited makeup kit. And while my eyes were usually my best feature, today they were barely visible pinpricks, wrung free of all moisture and life.

I was also exhausted.

"I feel like I ran a marathon on my face," I told Claudia as I drove to school. Mom had returned my phone as I left, "for emergencies," but any rational human being could see the current state of my life was itself an emergency. At least I wouldn't be on the phone for long. My face had so little elasticity that it hurt to enunciate.

Once I was inside the building, I found a corner, sat against a wall, and waited for the bell to ring. I had my English exam this morning, and I was ready, but at the moment my mind was completely empty. I had no idea how long I sat before a booming singing voice caught my attention.

> *"When I was younger, just a bad little kid*
> *My mama noticed funny things I did . . ."*

I recognized the song: "Dentist" from *Little Shop of Horrors.* Tom was playing the character in Chrysella's version, and he was the one singing. Ember, Sue, Doug, and Archer were fanned out behind him, all grinning as they sang backup. I guessed the rest of their group wasn't around because they didn't have a morning exam today.

I should have kept my head down, but I didn't. I looked up—and straight into the eyes of Archer. He did an actual double take at the sight of me. I knew I should smile so he could see everything was fine, but I didn't have the energy. I just stared blankly.

Archer broke from the group and knelt beside me. "Cara? What happened?"

"Archer, come on!" Ember called.

"Yes, Seymour, *please!*" Sue called in her Audrey voice, heaving out her chest for effect.

"You go ahead; I'll catch up," he told them.

Archer's friends scowled, but Tom had a song to finish, and they were soon on their way.

Archer was plopped on the floor in front of me, even though it put him in the middle of traffic. "Cara . . ." he said again, and bent to catch my eyes as I tried to look away.

"Cara, I'm serious. Is this . . . was it Nate? Did something happen with Nate?"

His voice was strained, and I had the sudden and horrible realization that he was thinking date rape, which only proved that I was now able to mess up without even opening my mouth.

"No. Archer, honestly, no." And since I didn't want to leave him with any doubt on this one, I told him everything, despite the fact that he'd now realize I was so evil and selfish that I had in effect set off a thermonuclear device in the middle of my family.

He stared at me when I was done. I waited for him to walk away in disgust.

"So wait," Archer said, "Karl's *disowning* you because you made a mistake?"

"Because I lied to him and went behind his back, so he can't trust me anymore," I muttered, wondering if this was what it felt like for people who rehashed their sins every week at confession. It felt crappy.

"Yeah, I get that. But *disowning* you?"

"Washing his hands of me," I said, "because I'm a stranger to him now."

"And your mom says you need to be really good to win him back?"

I nodded. "It worked before. It's just hard because he won't even look at me. I think he's staying with my mom, though, so that's good. I just have to make sure I don't do anything to set him off, or he could leave and we'd lose the house, and then . . ." I thought of Mom breaking down in front of me the night before and shuddered.

Archer leaned in closer. "Cara, listen to me. Your parents are crazy. Your mom's been with Karl for, what, twelve years?"

I nodded.

"So he's your dad. He doesn't get to stop being your dad because he's mad at you. And the whole thing about you having to save their marriage and keep the family together? That's not your responsibility. That stuff is supposed to be a given. I can't even imagine my parents saying the kinds of things yours did."

"But your dad has *always* been your dad. He doesn't need you to convince him he's appreciated. Besides, you're the poster child for Good Kid. Your parents would never get this mad at you."

"Granted. But what about Lila?"

"Lila, your sister in college who's your mom's best friend?"

"Lila, who *before* college spent four years in and out of house arrest. Ask me how many times she was disowned."

"A lot?"

"No, Cara. *Never.*"

"Okay, but unless Ed and Bina want to adopt me, that doesn't really help."

"I believe my mom would love to adopt you, so let's not discount that as an option."

I almost mentioned that it would be a particularly viable option since we'd already established incest wouldn't be an issue, but why ruin a good conversation?

"I'm just saying," Archer continued, "I don't think Harriet and Karl are being fair. At all. You messed up. You lied and you snuck around, and your parents have a right to be really, really mad and give out consequences, but they're punishing you for something you didn't do. You didn't make Karl feel so insecure that he thinks he has to disown you and threaten to leave your mom. You didn't make your mom so scared of being alone that she'd do anything to avoid it. *They* did that. So they have to undo it, not you."

I looked at Archer and was suddenly both incredibly grateful for and incredibly angry at Claudia and the Ladder.

My gratitude was simple: Without the Ladder, I might never have had the guts to get close to Archer. And without the Ladder as a crutch, there was no way I'd have ever been able to be friends with him again after That Night—which would have been a horrible waste, since it was so clear that outside of Claudia, I had never had a friend as good as Archer Jain.

My anger came from the realization that I was more tragically in love with Archer than ever, and in about four hours I'd no longer have any other boyfriend distracting me from that pain.

My numb features clearly weren't broadcasting any of this, because Archer looked at me worriedly.

"Cara?" he asked. "Is everything okay? I'm sorry. I wasn't trying to be harsh. They're your parents. I just—"

I threw my arms around him, wrapping him in a huge hug that toppled us both onto the floor as the bell rang.

"Well, this is *much* more exciting than giving a final," Mr. Woodward said. "If only I could grade you on your floorshow rather than the exam. I'd so love to see what happens next."

Archer and I both blushed, but I took a second to give him a quick peck on the cheek and whisper "thank you" in his ear before I rolled off, sprang to my feet, and raced to the exam room, beating both Archer and Mr. Woodward inside.

What Archer had said changed everything. He was right. I was responsible for what I'd done. I'd own up to it and accept the consequences. I was not responsible for other people's irrational reactions to what I'd done, even if those people were my parents. I would *not* keep eviscerating myself to try to make them feel better.

I'd concentrate on my own issues now. First and foremost: breaking up with Nate. This time I wouldn't let anything get in my way. Right after the English exam, I found him at his rock, planted myself in front of him, and said, "We need to talk."

Nate glanced up from his guitar to look me up and down. "What are you wearing?" he asked. "And what's up with your face?"

"This is what I look like," I said. "This is how I dress. I think it's kind of obvious . . . we're not right for each other. I don't think we should be together anymore."

"Hold up," Nate said, pausing his song. "Are you breaking up with me?"

Had I not been clear? I thought I'd been clear.

"Yes," I said. Then, just to be extra clear, I added, "I'm breaking up with you."

"Huh," Nate said. He didn't move, he didn't say anything more, but his eyes bore into me, studying my face and my clothes. I wasn't surprised. It was no secret that the real me was pretty much the opposite of anything Nate would ever want.

Yet no matter how much I knew Nate wouldn't be into me without my costumes and makeup, I could take only so much of his Silent Stare of Disgust. After a full minute of it, I was starting to feel like a fetal pig midway through its dissection.

"Okay," I said. "So . . . I guess I'll, you know . . . see you around."

No response. More staring.

I flashed him a friendly smile.

Nothing.

So much for closure.

"Right, then. Bye!"

English was my only exam that day, so I went right to my car and called Claudia. "'I have done the deed,'" I said.

"You sure you want to go with the Scottish play on this one?" Claudia asked. "Things didn't go so well for him after that little proclamation."

Claudia had a point, but Macbeth had disturbed the natural order, while I'd just restored it. And even though Claudia kept reminding me that my choice would make the climb up the Ladder much more difficult, I still felt great about it. Not even Karl could spoil my mood. With Archer's voice ringing in my ears, I followed the letter of my punishment. I went right home, remained downstairs only for my lunch, then ran up to my room, where I stayed until dinner.

Unsurprisingly, Karl ignored me during the meal. He remained buried behind his newspaper, lowering it only to ask my mom to pass him condiments that were right in front of me, including the salt I was actively using at the time. When I handed it across to him with a friendly "Here it is, Karl," he just continued staring at my mother. "Lo-Lo? The salt?"

I knew from the plaintive looks Mom kept shooting me that I wasn't doing my job. I was supposed to be extra solicitous to Karl, apologize several more times for my awful behavior, and wax rhapsodic about what an amazing dad he was to me and how much I owed and loved him. As of this morning, that had in fact been my plan. But Archer was right: making amends for my mistake was my responsibility; fixing my parents' psyches was not.

After dinner I zipped back to my room without being asked. It wasn't such a bad deal, really, especially since Mom had given me back my computer. Even without it I had plenty to do: my AP U.S. history final was the next afternoon, and I could use the parental-distraction-free study time. At one point I heard Karl and Mom rumbling about me downstairs, but Mom had also returned my noise-canceling headphones.

Bliss.

The next day I kept studying until the last possible second, so I didn't get to school until right before the exam. I planned to quickly drop my bag in my locker on the way there, but what I saw stopped me in my tracks.

Strung through the hoop of my combination lock was a single wilted red rose. A sheet of lined notebook paper was attached to it. Scrawled across the top of the page were the words "WHY CARA LEONARD IS SATAN," followed by a long list of exactly why I was indeed the Dark Lord.

The list wasn't easy to read. It had been scratched onto the paper with no regard for the lines on the page. Some words were huge, others tiny. Sentences curved up or curved down. Letters were randomly capitalized or lowercase. It looked like the mad rant of a psychopath.

Adding to the confusion was the fact that the dead rose had been speared through the paper, obliterating several of the words. Among the items I could actually make out were "Because she ripped out my still-beating heart and stepped on it," "Because she vomited derision on the musical proclamations of my soul," and "Because she seared my sweet, searching spirit with the satanic spit of her sneering scorn."

This was weird.

I didn't have time to think about it, though, because the bell rang and I was late for my exam. It took effort to push Nate Wetherill's Unabomber Manifesto out of my mind and concentrate on U.S. history, but I thought I did okay.

I would have loved to see Archer and get his opinion on the missive, but I knew he had rehearsal. Besides, I had rules: I had to get home the minute school was over. So I called Claudia from the car and nearly hit several pedestrians as I squinted through Nate's scrawls at forty miles an hour.

"'The course of true love never did run smooth,'" Claudia said.

"Since when did Nate and I have true love? We didn't even have *untrue* love."

"Maybe he felt more deeply than he let on. Maybe all the heartache with his parents forced him to build a protective veneer of indifference, under which boiled the soul of a poet."

I quoted him: "'She seared my sweet, searching spirit with the satanic spit of her sneering scorn'?"

"I didn't say he was a very *good* poet."

"What he wrote doesn't even make any sense! How did I 'vomit derision on the musical proclamations' of his soul? I loved his music! I listened to him play every day! I downloaded his song onto my iPod!"

"I won't deny that it's strange," Claudia said, "but I don't think you'll know what it's really about unless you ask him."

I tried asking him. I called, texted, and e-mailed, but he didn't answer and he didn't write back.

While going incommunicado wasn't exactly strange for him, it made me wonder: *Did* he have deeper feelings that he hadn't been able to show? It seemed impossible, but so did Nate putting dead roses on my locker. I guess I'd been pretty cavalier about the breakup, but that was only because I was sure he wouldn't care.

The next day was Thursday. I had my physics final in the morning and my precalc final in the afternoon. I didn't know Nate's schedule, but I hoped he'd be around for lunch so I could find him at the rock and talk.

Instead, I found him right away at my locker. He was covering it with pink construction paper hearts that had been crumpled and ripped into pieces. They looked like old, trashed valentines.

This was very, very weird.

He didn't see me at first, so I approached him gently. "Hey, Nate," I said in my sweetest voice, "I got your note yesterday. And now these . . . I swear, I had no idea you felt like this. I was hoping maybe we could talk and—"

"Right," he scoffed, cutting me off. His eyes were red-rimmed. "Act like nothing happened. *So* Cara."

"Um . . . actually, I was just *talking* about what happened. I was saying we should—"

"What do you want me to do, Cara?" Nate screamed, leaning back in agony and gripping his hair with his fists.

Everyone in the hall stopped to stare. I wondered if Claudia would be happy that the whole school now couldn't help but know my name. "You want me to run my heart through a meat grinder and watch you dance flamenco on the pulp as it struggles to keep beating?"

It took me a second to stop gaping like a fish at that one, but eventually I managed.

"Um, not particularly, no. I was more thinking we could get together at lunch and—"

"She breaks my heart again!" Nate howled to the universe, which now encompassed even more of the student body, including Populazzi from every grade.

The bell rang, and I seriously considered kissing it. I strode at hyperspeed to the physics lab and pretended people weren't staring at me the whole way.

For two hours I threw myself with reckless abandon into the principles of matter moving through space-time, yet after I'd finished the exam I still had a massive physics problem on my hands. In a confined space like Chrysella, is it possible for one object to successfully avoid another? After the scene at my locker, I knew Nate wouldn't let anything as petty as reality come between him and his epic heartbreak. If I didn't want to keep performing in the world's most twisted soap opera, I had to stay far away from him.

Moving like a master of espionage, I made it from the physics lab to the vending machines to my car without being spotted and settled in for lunch. Claudia's phone was off, so I texted her the latest, turned on my car radio, and sang along to all the shallow pop music I could find. I darted into my precalc exam at the last possible second. When I finished ten minutes early, I was ecstatic. I could have taken the time to go over any problems I wasn't totally confident about, but far better to take a risk on a couple of iffy answers than deal with further fallout from Nate's insanity. I turned in the test, grabbed my stuff from my locker, and slipped back out to my car as fast as I could.

"'Like a thief in the night'!" Claudia crowed when I got her on the phone. "Very dramatic. I approve wholeheartedly."

"Appreciated," I said. "Except I slipped out to *avoid* drama. Those were my last exams—now I can stay away from everything Chrysella until Monday. Maybe by then Nate will get over himself."

"You mean until Saturday."

"What? What's happening Saturday?"

"Hello! Have you also forgotten your address? Your shoe size? Your own name?"

"I promise you, Claudia, I have no idea what you're talking about."

"Saturday is only the biggest night of your life thus far, Cara: the night of your first Populazzi party."

Chapter *twenty-two*

Claudia was my best friend in the universe. I loved, admired, and respected her for a million different reasons.

And I now knew she was seriously mentally ill.

"Is this, like, alterna-Claudia from another dimension? Did you forget I'm grounded for life?"

"You also had your clothing, makeup, computer, cell phone, and bedroom door surgically removed," said Claudia, "and yet they've all been reattached."

"This is different. Everything I got back, I need for school. You're talking about a party. You really think Karl would let me go to a party?"

"Of course not. You don't ask Karl. Ask your mom. How did you do on finals?"

"Great. Nailed 'em."

"Tell her! Have her call your teachers! Prove how trustworthy you are. Even when you were sneaking around, you remained steadfast to your core values of industry and erudition!"

Claudia knew my mom well. I couldn't deny this tack had a good shot at working. But there was still one problem.

"Eddie didn't invite *me* to this party. He invited emo-girl Cara, half of the DangerZone Nate-and-Cara two-pack."

"Did Eddie *say* he only wanted you there in emo-garb? Did he *say* you had to show up with Nate?"

"Did he have any *clue* I was only playing dress-up and about to break up with Nate? No. So he wouldn't have specified. The prerequisites were implied."

"You think he's going to turn you away at the door?"

"He might! And it doesn't matter, because I'm not going by myself to a Populazzi party. Period."

"Of course not," Claudia said. "I'm going with you."

"You're . . . what?"

But I was already sold. Claudia and I had dreamed about getting invited to a Populazzi party since *forever*. Actually going to one with her? Getting to show her all the Chrysella people she'd only heard about and seen in pictures? The two of us hanging out and laughing about the Penultimates and Supreme Populazzi, even as we were embraced and accepted by them?

"You really would go with me?" I asked.

"Sure! It would be fun. Plus then I get to pick out your next Ladder target in person. Much better way to choose."

"Done! If you go, I'll go. I'll talk to my mom tonight."

I said it like it would be the easiest thing in the world, but even finding face time for the conversation wasn't simple. I was required to go to my room the minute I got home, but Mom was downstairs prepping for dinner. If I called to her, Karl would know something was up and thwart it. I could toss her a note if she passed by, but again, the Karl Factor. If he picked it up, the cause would be lost from the start.

Luckily, Karl's bowels helped me out. A half hour after dinner ended, he disappeared into the upstairs bathroom with the newspaper. I had at least a good fifteen minutes to make my case. I slipped down to the kitchen. Mom was finishing up the last of the dishes.

"You're supposed to be up in your room," she said.

"I know. I just have to talk to you about something."

I had to make an argument that was both unassailable and concise. I started by taking full responsibility for my mistake. I had lied, I had sneaked, I had betrayed her and Karl's trust, and that was wrong. Consequently, I had accepted my punishment without complaint. If I wasn't at school, I was at home. If I was at home and it wasn't mealtime, I was in my room. I told Mom I recognized she had already done a great deal to make the punishment more reasonable, and I very much appreciated it.

Then I tiptoed toward the dicey stuff.

"I'm totally fine staying with the punishment as long as you and Karl see fit," I began, "with ideally one exception."

Now Mom was suspicious. "Oh?"

I took a deep breath and explained that a guy named Eddie Riegert was throwing a big school postfinals party on Saturday . . .

The word "party" was too much for Mom. "No, Cara," she said. "After what you did, I hardly think you've earned a party."

I wouldn't let myself smile, but she'd given me the perfect opening.

"I get that. To earn a party now, I'd have to do something totally over the top—like ace all my exams and get straight As."

"I don't know if even that would do it, Cara."

"Really? But you said your biggest problem with me sneaking around is that you can't trust me. Even when I say I was doing it for a guy and I wasn't getting into trouble, you don't think you can believe me because I proved I'm a liar, right?"

"Exactly."

"Okay—but there's no way I could have straight As for the whole term if I'd been busy getting in trouble. If I'd done the stuff you're afraid of, it would show in my grades."

Mom pondered this. "I guess we'll see when we get your report card," she said.

"Yes, but that will be too late for the party. And Claudia was planning to come with me on Saturday, which would make it pretty special."

The addition of Claudia didn't sway Mom at all. She was *not* going to reward good grades on my word alone.

I heard the toilet flush. I was out of time. "Call my teachers tomorrow, that's all I ask. See what they say, then let's talk again. Please." I raced to my room and leaped onto my bed just as I heard Karl open his bathroom door.

Out of the next twenty-four hours, I spent twenty-one of them in my room. Normally a Friday without school would be amazing, but under this punishment, nonschool days were torture. I kept listening to hear if Mom was going to call my teachers, but I couldn't tell.

After dinner, though, I heard Mom and Karl talking in their room. The door was closed, so all I could make out were voices. Mom's was calm; Karl's was angry.

When the conversation ended, Mom came into my room and told me the news. My teachers—whom I now loved—had apparently raved about me. They'd noticed my temporary change in style but said it hadn't affected my work at all. Though Mr. Woodward of course had to tell her my "snitty quotient" rose proportionally with the amount of makeup on my face.

Madame Renault and Mr. Woodward were the only ones who'd already marked their exams, but each had given me an A for both the test and the term. As for physics, AP U.S. history, and precalc, my teachers had told Mom that unless I tanked the exams entirely, which they doubted, I'd have As in their classes, too.

"None of this changes how disappointed I am in your behavior," Mom said. "But you're right: it proves you kept your priorities straight. Karl, of course, doesn't agree with me. He doesn't even believe I spoke to your teachers."

"But you did. So can I go to the party?"

"Yes—provided you agree to some conditions . . ."

The conditions didn't start out so terrible. I had to be home by eleven—early, but fine. I had to stay home and in my room *until* the party; Claudia could meet me and we'd leave from here. Also fine. The minute Claudia and I got to the party, we had to call Mom. Easy.

"From a landline," Mom said, "so I can see the caller ID and know where you are. You said the boy who's having the party is named Eddie Riegert?"

She had a good memory. "Yeah. But what if his caller ID is blocked?"

"Dial star eighty-two first; that unblocks it. And I want to speak with an adult."

An adult? Like one of Eddie's parents? Would they even be there? Even if they were, I was sure they wouldn't be hanging out around the kids. I'd have to ask Eddie to get one to chat with my mom on the phone. I would be the biggest dork in history. Awesome way to start my first and most certainly *last* Populazzi party.

"Cara? Those are my conditions. Yes or no?"

What could I say? I agreed.

The next day I had nothing but time before eight o'clock, when Claudia would arrive, and nowhere to be but my bedroom and bathroom. The answer? A day of beauty. I must have spent two hours in the bathtub with my new literary obsession, an Elizabeth George mystery. I drained a little of the tub every time it got tepid, then refilled it with steaming hot water. I gave myself a manicure and pedicure, I did an exfoliating body scrub and a face mask, and I devoted hours to figuring out the grand puzzle of my hair. While the relaxed locks fell perfectly for the emo look, without the makeup and clothes to match, I just looked mullet-y. I couldn't wait for my curl to come back, but I still had up to two months. A curling iron might have helped, but I didn't own one, and neither did my mom.

After massive wrestling, pulling several muscles in my arms, and desperately wishing I were double-jointed, I somehow managed to work my thicker top layers into braids that came together in the back and spilled downward. It looked pretty, actually. Kind of girlie but sophisticated.

My wardrobe had been severely limited by Mom and Karl's culling, but I scrounged together a pair of black ballet flats, dark jeans, and a super-cute purple V-necked top with ruffle pintucks around the neckline. Very casual, very flattering, very *normal* so I wouldn't have trouble getting out of the house. A little makeup and I was ready—just as Claudia rang the doorbell.

Mom answered it. I, of course, remained quarantined upstairs until we actually left.

"*Claudia!*" my mom gushed. "Look at you! You look

gorgeous! I can't even believe it! Not that you don't always look beautiful, of course, but . . ."

Interesting. In eleven years of friendship I'd never heard my mom sound so shocked over Claudia's looks. I was dying to peek, but I wouldn't do anything that might get Mom to even consider changing her mind about the party.

I didn't have to wait long before Claudia struck a pose in my bedroom doorway. "Ready for a Populazzi party?" she asked.

"Claudia!" I screamed, and immediately understood why my mom had freaked. First of all, Claudia's hair was unbraided. It cascaded in gorgeous waves halfway down her back and framed her face, magnifying her delicate features.

Then there was her outfit. On top she wore a little charcoal-colored wool pleated jacket with ruffled trim along its front. It was beautiful, and as I squealed my approval, she took off the jacket and spun around to show me the rest: a short-sleeved gray babydoll dress, the bodice a few shades darker than the skirt. Its scoop neck showed off a simple silver chain with an angel wing charm.

The effect was subtle, sophisticated—and completely un-like anything I had seen her wear in the last decade. Claudia shunned fashion. It was too standardized for her. She chose unique outfits based on the emotional reactions they inspired in her. Denim jumpers made her look about five years old, es-pecially with her braids. But they made her *feel* playful and adventurous, so they were a regular part of her wardrobe. They rotated in with vintage floor-length dresses, flouncy skirts with ruffled tops, and her favorite camouflage capri pants that she swore paired perfectly with anything.

I always thought Claudia looked great. What she didn't look like was anyone else.

Tonight she could have stepped out of a fashion magazine. I was amazed.

"You went shopping!" I cried.

"I thought the occasion warranted it. What do you think?"

"How does it make you feel?"

Claudia grinned. "Popular."

There it was. That's what this evening would be for us. For one night we'd rewrite history and be the girls we always should have been—the girls we'd have been if The Incident had never happened.

I couldn't wait.

We ran downstairs, both of us calling out goodbyes to Karl. He had barricaded himself behind his bedroom door in a show of dissent.

"Remember, call me from a landline the minute you get there," Mom said, "and I need to speak to an adult. Back by eleven!"

"Got it," I said. "Bye!"

"You know we can't ask for this guy's parents," Claudia said once we were in the car.

"I know, but I have to do what she says. I get caught in a lie tonight and I'm dead."

"I could pretend to be his mother," Claudia said. "I could do a fake voice."

She proceeded to try out several fake voices, all of which sounded exactly like Claudia putting on a fake voice.

We were doomed.

We pulled up to Eddie's car-lined street and found a spot about four houses away. Our time was running out. If mom didn't get her phone call soon, she'd get suspicious.

"One other option," Claudia said. "We call your mom and say we're coming back because there's no adult supervision. We miss the party, but it's better than admitting the truth to the Populazzi. *And* it makes you look astoundingly responsible."

I heard her, but I wasn't really paying attention. I was distracted by the two guys racing around the front yard next to us.

Two guys in *BeastSlayer* cloaks.

"Cara?" Claudia said. "What do you think? Should we call your mom?"

"Not yet. I might have an idea."

I got out of the car and beelined for the guys, who had unsheathed giant swords and were now in the heat of battle.

"Hey," I said, then screamed and leaped away as the follow-through from a parry nearly gutted me.

"Are you crazy?" Gabe Friedman screamed, throwing back the hood of his cloak. "I could have killed you! These are real broadswords!"

"They're fairly dulled," Robert Schwarner said, "but at the right angle and velocity, they could still offer a decent disemboweling. I have another if you'd care to join. Or perhaps you and your fellow damsel might prefer the quarterstaff." He turned to Claudia. "My lady?"

"Hi," Claudia said. "Cara, can I talk to you?"

She pulled me several feet away and whisper-hissed, "Two words: Happy Hopeless."

"I'm aware. But this particular Happy Hopeless also has a deep voice my mom won't recognize."

"So you want to bring an uninvited Happy Hopeless to a Populazzi party, then ask for the phone so he can call your mom? What are you trying to do, *immolate* the Ladder?"

A high-pitched growly voice piped up from behind Claudia. "Help you I can. Yes! Mmmmm!"

I blushed bright red. Yes, Robert was a Happy Hopeless, but I would never call him that to his face. I liked him. But with the stealth of a true BeastSlayer, he had crept into earshot of our conversation and was now answering us as Yoda.

"Robert, oh my God—I am *so* sorry. You weren't supposed to hear that. I know, that sounds even worse. You have every right to be angry—"

"Anger leads to hate. Hate leads to suffering." Robert looked me in the eye. "I sense much fear in you."

I gaped. For not the first time, I wondered if Robert was my own personal Dalai Lama.

Claudia didn't share my curiosity. "We need to leave," she said.

"You don't," Robert said in his regular voice. "Eddie and I used to be friends. I know the house. We can go in the side door, I'll use the laundry room phone to call your mom, then you go join the party and I'll slip out. No one will know I was there with you."

"Are you kidding?" Gabe said. "Why would you do anything to help them? They're users!"

Robert ignored him. "I'll be right back."

"Fine," Gabe retorted. "You're only giving me a chance to perfect my technique. When you return, you'll eat cold steel!"

But we were already crossing the street toward Eddie's house. I still felt guilty.

"You're not horribly insulted by what we said?" I asked Robert.

"Why?" he replied.

I couldn't answer without insulting him even more, so I didn't bother.

Robert, Claudia, and I kept to the shadows. No one saw us approaching Eddie's side door. It was locked, but Robert knew the extra key was hidden behind the bushes, in the casing for an outdoor electrical outlet. We went right into the laundry room. Sure enough, there was a phone on the wall.

Robert said the Riegerts didn't block caller ID, so I gave him the number and he dialed. I worried a little that someone might hear us, but music blared so loudly from the other room that we had to be okay.

"Hello, Mrs. Leonard?" Robert asked.

"Ralston." I hissed Karl's last name at the same time my mom must have.

"Ralston, of course—I'm sorry. This is Brad Riegert. Your daughter, Cara, asked me to call you and let you know she arrived safely . . . Yes, my wife and I are here for the night . . . Not at all. I appreciate your concern . . . Of course. Take care now."

Robert handed me the phone. Apparently Mom wanted to talk to me. I hoped it was something quick. I was in awe that Robert had managed to say so much without once invoking *Star Wars*—I didn't want to push my luck.

"Hi, Mom."

"I'm proud of you, Cara," Mom said. "Thank you. Have a great time."

"Thanks, Mom. We will."

I hung up and turned to thank Robert, but he was already out the door. I turned to Claudia and smiled.

"Should we go in?"

Chapter *twenty-three*

$\mathcal{P}$opping into the party from the laundry room seemed risky. Probably no one would notice, but if someone did, it would be tough to explain. Instead, we slid out the side door and walked to the front, making sure no one saw us lurking in the shadows.

"Wait," Claudia said as I was about to open the door. "We stick together tonight, right?"

Claudia shifted uncomfortably, tugging on her hem and adjusting her jacket. Was she nervous?

"We totally stick together."

Claudia nodded. I opened the door, and we walked into our first Populazzi party.

Despite the title, not all the guests were Populazzi. They were there in force: all the juniors, a few seniors, a bunch of sophomores, even a couple freshman Populazzi had made the cut. But the house was full, and a lot of the partiers were plucked from upper-level Cubby Crews, like the Cosmopolitans, the Jocks, the Alts, the Cheer-Girls (Cheer-Boys were so *not* upper-level), and the Scenesters.

Claude and I did a recon loop. The living room was all about people playing and watching Wii on a big-screen TV. The kitchen was packed with people, food, and drinks—including a keg of beer. The dining room was the heart of the party. All the furniture had been pushed against the wall, and a docked iPod blared old-school funk for everyone on the crowded floor.

Trista Camello danced in the absolute center of the room, surrounded by friends and admirers. She wore a black strapless, lacy sheath of a dress with an impossibly high hemline. No one else at Chrysella could pull off that look. On her it looked perfectly natural.

"Behold the Supreme Populazzi," I whispered to Claudia.

"You think?" Claudia whispered back. "I can already feel myself falling into orbit."

That was exactly it. Trista was the sun. The whole party rotated around her gravitational center. She dazzled with heat and light. The closer you were to her, the hotter and brighter you glowed, too.

I was so grateful Claudia was there. On my own I'd have felt awkward and out of place. With her by my side, the party felt like a grand sociological experiment arranged just for us. We'd love every second.

I was about to point out the rest of the guest highlights when I felt someone sidle behind us. A low voice said, "Hey . . . you don't go to Chrysella, do you?"

It was Marsh Kinsey, a junior class Penultimate. He was meltworthy . . . and he was staring at Claudia like she was a work of art.

"I don't," she said simply.

Claudia never said anything simply.

Then she smiled shyly.

Shyly?

"I didn't think so," Marsh said. "If I'd seen you around, we'd definitely have been hanging."

That was his line? I tried to catch Claudia's eye, but she was all about Marsh.

"I'm Claudia," she said.

"You're beautiful," he replied. "You like dancing?"

"I love it," Claudia said—*which was a total lie!*

Marsh took her hand and led her closer to the sun. Of course they looked beautiful together, dancing in Trista's glow. Marsh's eyes seemed glued to Claudia, but when he finally glanced away, she looked at me and mouthed, *OH MY GOD!*

Wait—didn't Marsh have a girlfriend? I'd always seen him in the halls with Ree-Ree Wenderoth, another junior class Pen-ultimate. I looked around, but Ree-Ree wasn't in the room. Had I seen her in the living room or kitchen? I couldn't re-member for sure, but I didn't think so. Was she sick? Was Marsh fooling around on her? I doubted it. Ree-Ree was one of Trista's girls. If Marsh was fooling around on her, Trista would have to say something or at least look unhappy about it, right?

Marsh and Ree-Ree must have broken up. And Claudia was his rebound girl. Awesome.

I was psyched for Claudia, but I was also exactly where I didn't want to be: alone at a Populazzi party. I was very aware of standing by myself, watching the Populazzi dance. If people noticed me, they'd think I was pathetic. I had to move.

I wandered back to the living room. Eddie Riegert and another guy were having a Wii Sports Resort sword duel. I wondered how they'd react if they knew they were playing pretty much the exact same game as the two Happy Hopeless across the street. Then again, Robert had said he and Eddie used to be friends, so maybe it wasn't that big a coincidence after all.

I scanned the crowd for friendly faces and found none, so I kept moving. The kitchen was packed with groups of twos, threes, and fours, all midconversation. If I were Trista, I could hop into any of these groups with the perfect anecdote and instantly hold everyone in thrall.

But I was me. I had no clue what to say.

I strode to the snack table, a girl on a mission. A fake mission, but no one else had to know that. I filled five large paper cups with potato chips, pretzels, and M&M's—enough food to share with the whole group of fictitious friends waiting for me in the other room.

It was good to have something specific to do. I wanted it to last. I pored through a cooler, comparing every can of Diet Coke so I could choose one that had reached exactly the right temperature. I started off, then doubled back with a fake look of recognition, as if I'd just remembered the snack request of one more friend. I filled a sixth cup with corn chips.

I couldn't stretch my one-woman show any longer, but it had already been a while. Maybe Claudia was done dancing.

I balanced my snacks and walked into the dining room. Claudia and Marsh weren't there. I found them in the living room, curled together on a love seat. Claudia was speaking passionately about something, which was good—it meant she was back to being herself. Even better was the fact that Marsh looked totally into it . . . and totally into her.

Things were going well, and there was no way I was going to interrupt. Unfortunately, that left me with nothing to do. If

I'd been alone, I'd have slipped out and gone home, but I couldn't leave Claudia. That left me stuck in a sea of social elites who at any moment would realize that A) I clearly didn't belong here, and B) I had an absurdly large appetite.

I made sure no one was watching, then headed back toward the laundry room. I wondered how long I could hide out back there without anyone noticing. I wondered if Robert really did have an extra broadsword.

I was almost out of the living room when the front door opened, and the last person in the world I expected to see at a Populazzi party arrived.

Nate Wetherill.

I didn't think Nate *ever* came to things like this.

He looked pained and wild-eyed. He staggered in a few steps, then wailed, "Has anyone seen Cara Leonard?"

Oh. My. God.

I quickly crept into the shadows of the hallway.

"Please," Nate cried again, even louder this time. "Has anyone seen Cara Leonard?"

He had everyone's attention now. Several voices buzzed that they'd seen me around somewhere, which was almost gratifying enough to negate the far greater number of voices asking, "Who?"

"I want to play you all a song I wrote about Cara Leonard," Nate said, "the woman who corroded my heart away in an acid bath of antipathy. Cara, if you're listening, this is for you. It's called . . . 'Succubus.'"

He started playing, and I knew the tune immediately. It was the song he'd written for me. He had said before it was about my first experience with pot but he hadn't come up with the right words to describe it. Words didn't seem to be an issue anymore.

"Of this one thing I am sure
Cara Leonard is a whore
Or at least that's how she acted in my bed . . ."

I thought of Claudia sitting on the love seat. It was a crime that I couldn't see her face from my hiding spot.

"Sucked my soul and spirit dry
Ripped my heart out, let it fry
Then danced naked in my entrails while I bled."

Nate looked my way. I ducked farther back into the shadows just in time. I was still way too close. I slid into the laundry room as he launched into his hard-rocking chorus.

"Suc-suc-succubus
My rotting heart is covered in pus.
Suc-suc-succubus
The putrid corpse of the two of us."

I wondered which death would be less painful: running myself through the washer or the dryer.

"That guy is megatalented. How often do you hear the word 'putrid' in a song?"

It was Eddie Riegert. I wanted to disappear.

"You're not going to tell him I'm in here, are you?" I asked.

"Are you kidding? He's got the whole crowd with him. You think I'm gonna get in the way of that?"

Sure enough, all the party guests were singing along now. *"Suc-suc-succubus / My rotting heart is covered in pus . . ."*

"I swear, he wasn't even interested in me when we were together," I told Eddie. "I don't get it."

"He's *e-mo*," Eddie said, dragging out the word. "For *emotional*. He feels things *deeper* than the rest of us." Then he looked at me and smirked. "But you know all about that, right? That's your scene."

From the way he said it, I had a feeling he already knew the truth.

"It's not really my scene," I admitted. I waited for him to start asking questions, but he didn't. He hopped up to sit on the washing machine.

"So tell me about yourself, Cara Leonard." He eyed the six cups of snacks I'd put on the dryer. "Hungry?"

I blushed and shook my head, so Eddie started snacking on the chips. He watched me, apparently waiting for me to start talking.

It was funny: I'd spent the past couple weeks dying for a guy to show even the slightest curiosity about who I really was. Now I was sitting with a Penultimate who was asking me to talk . . . and I had no idea what to say.

"Um . . . maybe we could take turns. You could tell me about yourself, too."

"Sure. You first."

"Ummm . . ."

Why were only the most random and bizarre things popping into my head?

"Okay . . . I won't eat Hershey's Miniatures because I met the walk-around ones at Hersheypark when I was little and can't stand to see them hunted for food."

"That's . . . weird."

What I really needed was the human version of an electric dog collar. Whenever I was about to say something stupid, it could shock me into silence.

"Your turn," I said.

"I regularly scarf Hershey's Miniatures. By the handful."

"Oh."

"That was a joke, Cara," he said.

"Oh. Sorry." I forced a laugh.

"Okay, it wasn't like a laugh-out-loud joke. Are you always this nervous?"

"I'm not nervous," I said.

"Whatever. How about we make it easier. You said you want to know about me?"

I nodded.

"Okay, grab a cup of snacks and settle in. Here goes."

Eddie told me his whole story. He was the youngest of four, and his sister and brothers were all at least fifteen years older than him. He was the accident.

"When I was nine, my parents sat me down and said, 'Eddie, honey, we love you, but we're old. We're tired of parenting. You keep your grades above a C, you don't get any girls pregnant, we die happy. Everything else, you do what you want.'"

"They said that to you? Were you devastated?"

"Why? I thought they were pretty simple rules to live by."

"You didn't feel like they were rejecting you?"

Eddie squinched his face at me. The conversation had gone much better when I'd stayed out of it. Maybe I'd invent that human electric dog collar myself.

"Tell me more," I said.

He did. He said he played varsity football, basketball, and

baseball and really wanted to get a sports scholarship to college. None of his siblings had gotten any financial aid for their education, and he wanted to give his parents a break.

"Oh, and I've already been married," he said.

"You . . . what?"

It was his sister Suzanne's idea. It had happened when Eddie was three and Suzanne was eighteen. Suzanne's best friend had a little sister Eddie's age, and the two older kids thought it would be fun to throw a wedding. They arranged a huge ceremony and reception. Suzanne and her friends catered, decorated, hired a band . . . More than a hundred guests came, including Eddie's other siblings, who flew in for the occasion. Eddie wore a tux, the bride a gown, and the ceremony was performed by Eddie's uncle, a true ordained minister.

"Everyone played it up. My mom cried; the girl and I fed each other cake; people made toasts. The party went on till way after my bedtime. I seriously thought I was legally married until I was twelve."

"That's crazy! Were you mad when you found out the truth?"

"Why would I be mad? It was funny."

I laughed. He may have been a Populazzi, but Eddie was really easy to talk to. Listen to, really. He had all kinds of stories, and we sat in his laundry room for ages as he told them to me. I was surprised when my cell alarm beeped—I'd been having so much fun, I hadn't even realized how much time had passed.

"My time's up?" Eddie asked.

"No, it's . . ." I hated to say it out loud. "I have to get back for curfew."

"No problem. I haven't heard any singing for a while, so I bet you're safe." He peeked into the living room. "Yeah, Nate's gone. You're cool."

"You practically spent your whole party hiding out with me," I said as we left the laundry room. "I'm so sorry."

"Why?"

I had no good answer for that.

"Besides," he said, "it's not the whole party. This thing's going on all night."

I wasn't sure if that was supposed to make me feel better or worse. I couldn't linger on it, though, because right in front of me was the most incredible thing I'd ever seen.

Claudia was still cuddled up on the love seat with Marsh— only now they were completely making out.

This was huge. This was huger than huge.

This was also a problem. We had to leave *now,* but there was no way in the universe I'd interrupt the biggest moment in Claudia's life.

Eddie understood. "I got it," he said. He walked over and punched Marsh on the arm. "Dude, she's gotta go."

Marsh and Claudia reluctantly pulled apart. "I'll walk you out," he told her. He took her hand and the four of us walked to my car. Neither Claudia nor I said anything, but we kept sneaking glances at each other, asking a million silent questions.

We split at the car, Eddie walking to the driver's side with me while Claudia and Marsh kissed.

"Thanks for keeping me company," I said.

"No worries. It was fun."

"For me, too. Thanks." I had just said thanks about two seconds ago. Maybe what I really needed was a thesaurus implanted in my brain. I climbed into the car as a breathless

Claudia collapsed into the seat next to me. I was about to drive off when Eddie signaled for me to roll down the window.

"What's up?" I asked.

"See you at school Monday," he said—then leaned in and kissed me. On the lips. Nothing major, nothing wild, but a kiss. What did it mean?

Claudia grinned as we pulled away from the curb. "Looks like your next target on the Ladder has chosen you . . . succubus."

"Okay, Miss I-Hook-Up-with-Populazzi! Tell me!"

"'This bud of love, by summer's ripening breath, / May prove a beauteous flower when next we meet.'" Claudia sighed.

"Nope. Won't cut it. I need details."

For the first time ever, Claudia couldn't find words. She tried—she opened her mouth like she was going to say something—but all that finally came out was a scream of delight.

"Tell me!"

"I know Marsh and I go to different schools and we don't live close to each other, but in a way I think that's perfect. It's so much more romantic. We have to pine for each other. And it keeps me a challenge: he'll work to win me over again every time we meet. *Especially* since he's competing against my ex-boyfriend Paris, who's dying to get back together."

"You named your fake ex-boyfriend Paris?"

"It felt appropriate."

"What would you have done if he knew *Romeo and Juliet*?"

"Chalked the name up to an incredible coincidence. And gone back to kissing him. Immediately."

"Okay," I said, "keep in mind this is crazy because I have no idea if Eddie's even into me . . . but what if you started going out with Marsh and I started going out with Eddie? They're friends—the four of us would hang out together all the time."

"I love it! We'll be like the four lovers at the end of *Midsummer Night's Dream*. Can I be Hermia? I always wanted to be Hermia."

"You could come down every weekend and stay with me. We'd all go out Saturday nights, hang together on Sundays—"

"You have to stop. You're getting my hopes up and I don't want to be disappointed."

"Marsh'll hit me up in the halls for the inside scoop on all your favorite things so he can surprise you—"

"I'm serious, Cara, stop. I'll end up writing songs like Nate Wetherill."

"We could all go to prom together!"

"SUC-SUC-SUCCUBUS," Claudia sang, *"MY ROTTING HEART IS COVERED IN PUS . . ."*

I had to admit the song was catchy. I joined in.

"SUC-SUC-SUCCUBUS," we sang at the top of our lungs, *"THE PUTRID CORPSE OF THE TWO OF US."*

The night could not possibly have been any better.

Chapter *twenty-four*

$\mathcal{I}$t was fun to fantasize, but I didn't really think there was anything going on between Eddie and me. Sure, he'd kissed me, but it hadn't been a *real* kiss. We hadn't made out like Claudia and Marsh.

Not that I was against Eddie as my next Ladder target. I liked him. I just had absolutely no idea how to go after him. We didn't have classes together or hang with the same people. Other than in Claudia's and my double-date fantasies, our coupledom seemed impossible.

And of course there was the fact that my reputation as a soul-sucking succubus now preceded me wherever I went.

"Cara!"

I was on my way to my locker Monday morning when I heard Archer's voice. He was jogging to catch up to me. Far behind him, I saw Sue, Tom, and Doug. They looked annoyed. I didn't care. I was happy to see him.

"Hey!"

"Hey. How are things with your parents?" Between the weird finals schedule and my grounding, Archer and I hadn't seen each other since the last time we'd spoken.

"You pretty much saved my life. I mean, they're still crazy, but I'm dealing with it a lot bett—"

"Cara! I was looking for you."

It was Eddie Riegert, sporting what seemed to be his go-to outfit of choice, jeans and a T-shirt. Today's said WHAT THE SMURF?! just under one of the little blue creatures.

"You were?" I asked. I wondered if I had left something behind at his party, like a lip gloss that melted on his dryer and made a horrible mess that got him in trouble. I already felt guilty.

"Yeah. Come on."

He took my hand and led me down the hall.

"Wait," I said. "I was talking to—"

But even as I turned back toward Archer, I saw Sue grabbing *his* hand and pulling him in the other direction. Apparently neither one of us was in control of our social agenda. I gave him a helpless smile, then turned to see where Eddie was taking me. *Why* he was taking me, I didn't want to imagine—I was sure I'd get it wrong.

And yet . . . he was holding my hand.

And he'd kissed me at his party.

But still . . .

I almost stopped in my tracks as I realized where Eddie and I were headed. It was a room at the end of the building called "The Heap."

It was an apt description. When the school had been built in the 1950s, the room had been a vision of wholesome teenage bliss. Photos on the walls showed it filled with straight-backed chairs and game tables outfitted for cards, backgammon, chess, checkers, dominoes, and even tiddlywinks.

Decades later, the gaming accessories were long gone, and somewhere along the way the school had given in to students' desires to immortalize themselves. The administrators had turned the other way as class after class added their own graffiti to the tables and chairs. It was actually a cool tradition. At Homecoming, the place swarmed with alumni looking for the marks they'd left ages ago.

In the fall The Heap had entertained a revolving door of different Cubby Crews, DangerZones, and even Happy Hopeless. In the winter the junior class Populazzi retreated inside from their oak tree and claimed The Heap as their own. Once they did, no one from another Tower tier dared venture inside. It was like the change in weather triggered a force field on the doorway and anyone who didn't belong would be vaporized on entry.

But now I was going in on the arm of a Populazzi. Did that mean I belonged? Could it really be that easy?

I was excited—but terrified. Eddie's party had been one thing; I'd gone in with Claudia, and there'd been enough people around that I could disappear when I'd needed to. The Heap was filled with *only* the Populazzi. I'd be under a microscope. If I messed up and embarrassed myself, the damage would be huge and permanent.

I was also nervous about Trista. I had gotten on her radar as a DangerZone. Would she accept me as a potential Populazzi? Eddie had pretty much called me on not being myself with Nate, but it didn't seem to bother him. Would it bother Trista? Would she think I was a total fake? If she did, would Eddie not be interested anymore? Did she have that kind of power?

I held my breath a little as I followed Eddie into The Heap.

"Cara!" Trista cried. She was on the floor leaning back against Brett Seward's legs, but she jumped up to hug me.

Hug me.

She took my hand and led me to a chair, pulling me away from Eddie. He looked amused.

"I have been *dying* to talk to you," Trista said. "How does it feel to have the most dramatic social life in the whole school?"

Was she being sarcastic? No, I didn't think she was. She seemed genuine. And given the way Nate had been acting and whatever was suddenly going on with Eddie, it wasn't like she was exaggerating.

"Yeah, tell us. How does it feel to have saved Eddie from the priesthood?"

That came from Gemma Palano. She was sitting across the room and gave me a pointed stare that made my brain whimper.

Gemma was the most intimidating person at Chrysella, far more intimidating than even Trista. She looked like an exotic supermodel and could easily have been Supreme Populazzi, except high school wasn't her thing. She played on the pro tennis circuit and spent most of her time traveling the world for tournaments. Rumor had it she'd never gone out with anyone at school, but had tons of older men outside of Chrysella, and had dated her twenty-year-old trainer when she was only twelve.

Gemma never smiled. Unlike, oh, *me*—who automatically grinned like an idiot to all the people I met in the hopes that they'd like me. Gemma didn't care about that. She demanded other people prove they were worthy of *her*. I respected that . . . but it also made me feel very small and inferior.

"*I'm* the one who saved him, Gems," Trista said. "It was my idea to have Eddie invite Cara and Nate to the party."

"It was?" I asked.

"Mm-hm. I had no idea you'd be in the middle of the biggest breakup ever. Or that I'd be hooking you up with Eddie."

"Did you know you'd be hooking *Marsh* up?" asked Ree-Ree Wenderoth. She straddled a backwards chair and glared out from behind her long dirty-blond locks.

The hairs on the back of my neck rose. She was talking about Claudia. I looked to Marsh to see what he'd say, but he was only shaking his head in what seemed like disbelief.

"Oh, Ree-Ree, Marsh did that all by himself."

That was Kristie Place. She was sitting perfectly upright in her chair. Her makeup was impeccable, and there wasn't a single stray wisp on her sleek blond cap of hair. She held hands with a guy I recognized as a Jock, not a Populazzi. I was pretty sure his name was Eric.

"You think?" Ree-Ree challenged Kristie. "*Someone* had to bring the girl to the party."

Ree-Ree glared at me as she said it, and I reflexively shied back. The word on Ree-Ree was that she was real-deal crazy. I'd even heard a rumor that she'd been suspended a whole month freshman year for getting into a fight on a school bus and literally almost scratching another girl's eyes out. I had no desire to be on her bad side.

"Whatever, Rees," Eddie said. "It's not Cara's fault."

"It's not my fault either!" cried Marsh. "This girl *threw* herself at me! *After* you broke up with me and walked out of the party. So now, what, you're a little jealous?"

"I don't get jealous," she said. "I get even and I get gone."

"You wouldn't," Marsh said.

"Why not?"

"Come here."

Ree-Ree made her eyes slits, but she obeyed. When she was still a foot away, Marsh pulled her to him and kissed her. She struggled so fiercely against him that I looked at Trista, alarmed. Trista rolled her eyes. Sure enough, within seconds Ree-Ree stopped struggling, threw her arms around Marsh's neck, and attacked his throat with her tongue.

"Promise she wasn't as pretty as me," Ree-Ree said when she came up for air.

"She was hideous," Marsh said. "Deathly pale skin, big spooky eyes . . . it was like making out with a corpse."

"Ew!" Ree-Ree squealed. Then she turned to me. "Is she really that awful?"

The whole room turned to face me. I knew I needed to lacerate them with the truth: that Claudia was not at all awful; that she was in fact much prettier than anyone in this room, especially since she wasn't ugly enough to use someone and then drag her through the dirt just to make someone else jealous.

"Come on, tell me about her," Ree-Ree prodded. "She's your friend, right? So you're friends with someone who steals other girls' men?"

This was about me now? I glanced at Eddie, but he looked as interested as all the others. I had to fix this on my own.

"She doesn't steal girls' men. She didn't know Marsh was taken."

"Right, because guys who look like Marsh are *always* single," Ree-Ree said. Marsh liked that. He stood up a little taller.

Everyone was still looking at me. I felt like I was being tested. I needed to stick up for Claudia, but I couldn't really come down on Marsh or Ree-Ree. I decided to be honest.

"Claudia doesn't have a lot of experience with guys. She thought if Marsh wanted to kiss her, it had to be something special."

"Because she's, like, nine years old?" Ree-Ree asked.

I blushed, embarrassed as much for myself as for Claudia. "Because Marsh was her first kiss."

The room erupted into a riot of "Whoa," "No way," and "Are you *serious?*"

"Dude, it's like you took her mouth cherry," Brett said.

"*'Mouth cherry'?*" Trista repeated. "Oh my God, what are you?"

"See, now I'm just sad," Gemma said.

"I know . . . I feel so sorry for her," Kristie agreed.

"Hello! That's even worse!" Ree-Ree said. "Miss Purity probably thought she was getting forever with *my man!* Right?"

Her eyes pinned me to the wall. "Maybe a little, but—"

The bell rang before I could say anything else. Marsh pulled Ree-Ree back into his arms.

"Let it go, baby. We're back together now, right?"

"Better believe it," she said, and gave him another long kiss.

"Aw, see, I love happy endings," Eddie said. Everyone laughed as we poured into the hall to walk to class. Gemma walked solo, but the rest of us broke into couples: Kristie and Eric, Brett and Trista, Marsh and Ree-Ree . . . and Eddie and I. We walked as a pack, everyone talking and laughing, but I only vaguely heard what they said. I kept playing back the conversation in The Heap. I hadn't done anything except tell the truth, but I still felt like I'd betrayed my best friend.

It bothered me a lot, but I soon became distracted by what was going on around me.

People were staring.

Everyone, even the ones who tried not to stare, the ones who wanted to seem like the Popularity Tower didn't matter to them, they still snuck glances our way.

I had arrived. I had no idea how it had happened, but it seemed like it was true. I pushed the conversation in The Heap out of my head. No, Claudia wouldn't want the Populazzi to know how behind she was, but it's not like these were people she'd ever need to see again. And it wasn't as if she was losing anything with Marsh. He clearly didn't care about her, and she deserved a lot better. I'd tell her that. She wouldn't like it, but she'd agree she was better off without him.

Besides, this was all her doing. This was what she'd wanted from day one: for me to be a member of the Populazzi.

Now I was on my way.

Chapter *twenty-five*

$\mathcal{J}$'d planned to call Claudia at lunch, but I didn't get the chance. I finished my fourth period art class and was on my way to hit the vending machines and duck out to my car when a high, clear voice called out, "Cara!"

I heard the quick clip-clop of heels as Kristie jogged to catch up.

"I'm glad I saw you," she said, slipping her arm through mine. "You're sitting with us at lunch, right?"

"Is there room?" I asked.

"Of course! Right next to Eddie. Technically you're taking Eric's seat, but that's okay."

"Your boyfriend? Oh, Kristie, I don't want to—"

"It's fine. Before you got to The Heap, the guys were giving him a really hard time, so he doesn't want to sit with us anyway. Eric doesn't get it—the guys are protective that way. It's sweet. They say anyone worth my while will man up and deal until he's part of the group."

"Okay . . . but if Eric wants his seat back tomorrow—"

"Then we'll all squeeze in. It's like an extra excuse to cuddle, right?"

"Sure." I giggled.

This was weird, because while I've been many things in my life—and many more during this school year—I have *never* been a giggler. There was something about Kristie. She was so completely sweet and girlie—it was infectious. I felt girlier and gigglier just being around her.

Kristie and I stayed arm-in-arm as we strode into the cafeteria. As we passed a Happy Hopeless table, I noticed Gabe Friedman's jealous scowl and Robert Schwarner's appraising nod. Then we passed the Theater Geeks, and I swore I heard jaws hitting the table. Even Archer looked surprised. I slipped him a quick smile so he could see I knew exactly how cool this was and totally appreciated it.

At the Populazzi table, Eddie was already deep in conversation with Brett and Marsh, but he gave me a smile as I slipped in next to him. Kristie was on my other side, with Trista, Ree-Ree, and Gemma rounding out what seemed to be the girls' half of the table. I wondered why Trista and Ree-Ree weren't sitting with their boyfriends, but the answer became clear as they and Gemma leaned in to get as close to me as possible.

"So tell us," Trista whispered. "What's Nate Wetherill like in bed?"

A hot flush crawled up my cheeks.

"Trista!" Kristie objected. "Eddie's right here!"

"Whatever." Trista waved her off. "He's not paying attention."

It was true; he wasn't. The guys were concerned with exactly how much butt the Philadelphia Eagles would kick in the upcoming Super Bowl. The team's appearance in the game was apparently only a slightly bigger deal than the Second Coming. Karl would have loved the conversation. To me it was gibberish.

"You look offended," Kristie said. "Are you offended?"

"She can't be offended," Gemma said. "You do the deed, you own the deed."

"My guess is he's *highly* sensual," Ree-Ree said. She looked like she was already imagining the specifics.

"Spill it, Cara," Trista said. "We want to hear everything."

"There isn't that much to tell," I said.

Gemma snorted. Trista just looked at me and sang, "'*Of this one thing I am sure / Cara Leonard is a whore / Or at least that's how she acted in my bed . . .'*"

I blushed harder. Somehow the song was less amusing in Trista's mouth than in Claudia's.

"He may have exaggerated a bit," I said.

"You didn't sleep with him?" Ree-Ree was obviously not pleased. Even Kristie looked a little disappointed.

I had to turn this around quickly, but I couldn't totally change my story or they'd know I was lying.

Then it hit me.

"I *didn't* sleep with him," I whispered, looking around, then leaning in, "because he *couldn't.*"

Ree-Ree laughed. "For you he couldn't. I bet I'd get it up just fine."

"He's a pothead," Gemma told her. "Potheads can't always get it up."

"Exactly!" I cried. "And Nate's not just a pothead; he's *the* pothead." I launched into a vivid description of Nate's obsession with the stuff, including his bong-friend Purple Haze, who even had her own gender.

"He actually introduced it to you as his 'friend'?" Trista asked.

"Yes! I'm telling you his whole house was a freak scene . . ."

I started telling them about the place, and immediately I knew it was the right story. The Populazzi hung on every word, all four of them gasping and laughing and oh-my-Godding as I wove the tale.

So I made it even better.

I didn't lie, really. I just leaned heavily on the more gasp-worthy details. I spoke vividly about the brothers living like savages in layers of squalor and Thackery maniacally playing Wii all night long. The girls seemed to like the pot stories best, so I went back to those and enhanced them a little, giving Purple Haze a cast of cohorts and making Nate's obsession with them even crazier.

Sure, the details might have been exaggerated, but the spirit of what I said was dead-on accurate. It was just that I told a cartoon version of the truth, without the deeper things like Nate's comatose mom, his indifferent dad, how sweet it kind of was that he wanted to share what meant so much to him—or the fact that I actually liked and felt sorry for him.

That stuff would have bored the Populazzi. I wanted to captivate them. And I did.

"It's all so gothic," Ree-Ree said. "Is it weird that it makes me totally want to bed him?"

At the same time, Kristie said yes and Gemma said no.

"I bet the little brother will grow up to be a serial killer," Trista said. "You're lucky you escaped with your life."

"Did he really name all his"—Kristie lowered her voice—"paraphernalia? And talk to them? And make them talk back to him?"

"All the time!" I said. "I swear, sometimes I think he was flirting with them!"

"Hot *and* crazy." Ree-Ree smiled.

"If he wasn't getting it up for you, I wonder if he was getting it up for them," Gemma said.

"So, so wrong, Gems." Trista laughed. "Was he?"

"I never *saw* it happen," I said, "but he *would* disappear into the bathroom with one of his 'friends' for way too long to smoke or pee. And sometimes when he came out he'd ask if the others were jealous."

"And were they?" Gemma asked.

"*I* was!" I retorted.

That got all four girls laughing so hard that the guys stopped their conversation to ask what we were talking about.

"Dudes, you will not *believe,*" Gemma said, then turned to me. "Lay it on them."

Uh-oh.

It was one thing to let the story run away with me, but to purposely lay it out the same way again . . . that seemed like more of a lie. But I couldn't change it up now. And besides, the Populazzi *never* hung out with Nate, so what did it matter?

I told the story again.

The guys loved it even more than the girls. Of course they did; I'd had a rehearsal. I knew how to sell it. Marsh and Brett roared. Eddie smiled, but he was quieter than the other guys. I couldn't figure out why until I finished and Brett pounded Eddie on the back.

"Dude, you gotta watch your ass with this one," he said. "She'll tell it *all*."

"Yeah," Eddie said. "I can see that now."

I was still smiling from my storytelling triumph, but now my smile felt stale. Had I completely messed things up with Eddie? No matter how much I had won over the Populazzi, I had no doubt that my membership in their club would be immediately revoked if Eddie lost interest in me.

He draped an arm around my shoulders. "You know me, though. I like 'em dangerous."

Everyone laughed as the bell rang. I'd spent the whole period entertaining the Populazzi . . . and it had been easy!

"So my house after school, right?" Trista asked as we left the cafeteria. The whole group murmured in the affirmative.

"Cara?" Trista asked.

Me? She was asking me to go to her house after school?

"Yeah! I'd love it!" I said. Then I remembered my reality and winced.

"Oooh, shoot. I'm sorry, I can't."

"Why not?" Trista asked.

I so didn't want tell her. I was sure it would sound lame. Still, I couldn't think of anything better, so . . .

"I'm kind of grounded."

"For what?" Trista asked.

Gee, um, because my parents found out I was sneaking around dressing emo, which I only did to get Nate, which I only did to get higher on the Popularity Tower, which is why I'm so totally jazzed to be friends with all of you now!

Ah, no.

"Because my parents caught me . . ." I'd started the sentence without knowing how I'd finish, but the answer was suddenly obvious . . . "stoned. They smelled the pot on me; that's how they knew."

"Did you ask Mommy and Daddy how they knew the smell?" Gemma asked. "That would have been my first question."

"You smoked pot with Nate?" Kristie sounded disappointed.

"We'll figure something out," Trista said. "We'll call your cell tonight."

I shook my head. "No calls."

"What are your parents, psycho? You're on your computer, right? We'll get your e-mail from Eddie," Trista said.

That settled, we all took off for class, and I rode through the rest of the day in a haze of my own Populazzi-ness. The second school let out I raced to my car and called Claudia to tell her everything.

Well, almost everything. I kind of left out the most important part. I meant to start with it, I really did . . . I just couldn't.

"Did Marsh mention me at all?" she finally asked.

Claudia tried to sound casual, but I could hear the hope in her voice, which sucked. I needed her to know Marsh was *not* a good guy, but the truth would really hurt her. What kind of friend would I be if I did that?

"He didn't," I said, "but I have to tell you, Claude, I hung out with him a lot today, and the guy's kind of a jerk."

"Maybe he doesn't want you to know he's interested, because he knows you'll tell me and he doesn't want *me* to know. Maybe he wants to be a challenge."

"Maybe . . ."

This would be the time to tell her Marsh had a girlfriend. She'd be furious, but we'd rake him over the coals until she couldn't even imagine feeling anything but venom toward him. It would be the best thing in the world for her.

But even if she was good and angry when we were talking together, what if she got sad once we hung up? And what if she called Marsh to talk to him about it? He hadn't given her his number, but how hard was it to call 411? And if she spoke to him, how long would it be before he said something about being her very first kiss? She'd know I'd spilled it, and . . . then what?

I didn't want to know what happened then. No way.

Besides, this would sort itself out. Marsh was never going to call Claudia. And as long as she thought she had a chance with him, Claude would never call Marsh. Eventually, she'd lose interest. It would be fine.

In the meantime, I needed to change the subject, so I told her about lunch at the Populazzi table. I didn't go into my Nate stories. They suddenly felt a little . . . wrong. I just said it had gone really well—so well that Trista had invited me to her house.

"And so spread wide the Golden Doors of the Populazzi Palace for one Cara Leonard!" Claudia announced.

"I couldn't have done it without you."

"Oh, your mission is nowhere near complete, my friend," Claudia corrected me. "Right now you're a Penultimate. By the end of the year, you will be the *Supreme* Populazzi."

I wanted to tell Claudia that only a bloody coup would tear that title away from Trista Camello, but I knew she wouldn't believe me. She had faith in the Ladder, and everything that had happened to me so far seemed to prove her right.

Chapter *twenty-six*

The truth was that I had no desire to depose Trista. I didn't want to be her. I was happy just being part of her circle. Hanging with the Populazzi made me memorable, even to people who didn't know me. I wasn't invisible anymore, and that felt amazing. Even more amazing was having a solid group of friends. I missed that a lot, especially since Archer and I hadn't been hanging out. If I really cemented my place among the Populazzi, I'd never be lonely at Chrysella again.

By the time I got home that afternoon, Kristie had already e-mailed me. She was stunned that I didn't seem to be on Facebook. She assumed it was some kind of glitch, like I'd used a weird nickname on my account. She told me to sign on and friend her and the rest of the group right away.

I actually didn't have a Facebook account. Mom and Karl had been against it until I was sixteen. By that time, I didn't see the point. Who was I going to find on it, Claudia? We already e-mailed all the time. It seemed redundant. Neither of us had bothered.

Now I couldn't join fast enough. I signed up and sent friend requests to all the Populazzi. I wondered if they'd think it was lame that I didn't have any other friends on my account. Then I remembered they already thought my parents were crazy, so maybe it wouldn't seem weird if I said Mom and Karl hated Facebook and I'd had to beg them to let me sign up.

Trista accepted my friend offer immediately. The whole group was at her house, and they'd sat down at the computer to find me and chat.

"Grounding sux!" she wrote. *"Got 2 get you out of it—big plans for us this year!"*

This *year*. She was already assuming I'd be with them through the year. She could only have been getting that from Eddie. It was so strange to think he was that into me. Really, we'd only spoken for a couple hours, that was it.

Not that I was complaining. It was just strange.

Once Trista logged off, I called Claudia with the latest. I used my cell, but spoke softly since technically it was still for emergency use only. Claudia signed up for Facebook, too, disguised as "Rosalind Arden," an apparent homage to *As You Like It*. She didn't post a picture or profile; she only wanted to be a fly on my wall and see the Populazzi's posts.

"If anyone asks, tell them I'm your cousin from Kansas. No, Missouri."

"Why would anyone ask?"

"Just if they do. I don't want anyone to go poking into your old life through Facebook. Rosalind Arden is a cipher. She is invisible."

"She is insane," I said before we clicked off. Moments later a chat box appeared on the screen from Rosalind: *"Minnesota!"* I laughed as I clicked it away, then tooled around looking for other people I knew. I found Archer, which was weird, because he'd never mentioned he was on Facebook. He must have signed up recently. Would Trista think it was weird if she saw him on my friend list? I remembered her clapping for his poem on the first day of school and figured she'd be fine with it.

I sent Archer a friend request, then Mom called me down for dinner. By the time I got back up to my prison cell—er, room—he'd confirmed me as a friend, but he wasn't online. Bummer. I'd thought it would be fun to chat, especially since I was sure he had all kinds of questions about my new Populazzi status.

The next two weeks were like Populazzi boot camp. Trista even spelled it out that way: I had a lot to learn if I was going to be one of them. Some of the lessons were obvious, like Thou Shalt Not Fraternize with the Happy Hopeless. That came up when Robert Schwarner, of course clad in his *BeastSlayer* cape, decided to come into The Heap and say hello. Or more precisely, to come in, stride right up to me, and say, "'Why, you slimy, double-crossing, no-good swindler.'"

"What?" Brett sneered like he smelled feet.

"Is he talking to you?" Ree-Ree asked.

Actually, he was talking to Han Solo, and he was being Lando Calrissian, but that explanation could only make things worse.

The horrible part was I had seen it coming. My eyes had drifted to the doorway of The Heap just as Robert walked by, and the second he saw me, I *knew* he was going to come in, no matter how hard I screamed inside my head for him to *stopstopStopSTOPSTOOOOOOP!!!!!*

Now Robert plopped down on a chair next to me. He put

his feet up on a game table, making himself at home. I shot a frantic look to Eddie, but he was engrossed in picking at a small hole near the bottom of his SIX-PAC T-shirt, featuring Pac-Man, Ms. Pac-Man, and four Pac-babies. No help at all. And despite what Robert had said about him and Eddie once being friends, Robert didn't even glance in Eddie's direction.

Nope, he made it good and clear to all the Populazzi that I was the lucky one he'd come to see.

"What's up?" Robert asked, as if we were all alone and no one were watching, when in fact everyone but Eddie was glaring death at me for pulling such an obvious contaminant into their midst.

I was sweating. I didn't want to be mean to Robert, but I had to get him out of the room. Quickly. And without the Populazzi thinking I was friends with him and accepting me meant accepting him, too. If that was the case, I was sure they'd have no problem excommunicating me, even if Eddie wanted to stay a couple.

I smiled at Robert through clenched teeth. "Hi," I began. "You don't usually hang out here."

"Nope."

Kristie was now chewing her perfectly manicured nails, a sure sign she was wildly uncomfortable.

Gemma crunched up pieces of notebook paper and lobbed them at Robert's feet.

Then one landed at mine.

"Robert," I asked quickly, "are you really sure you want to be here?" I smiled, but I knew it didn't hide my panic, which was fine. Maybe he'd feel for me and get out of the room faster.

Brett cut to the chase. "Schwarner, get your fat ass out of here."

Robert tilted up on one hip to glance appraisingly at his backside. "Hmm. Actually, I think it's looking rather trim these days, but I'll keep your concern in mind. Thank you."

Brett jumped up. Marsh did the same but hung back, letting Brett take the lead. "You trying to mess with me?" Brett asked. "'Cause if you are, I'm right here."

"Oh, I wasn't doubting your presence in the room," Robert replied. Then he turned to me. "So . . . how are things?"

I was going to kill him. I could see it in his eyes. He knew *exactly* what he was doing, and he was doing it just to make my life difficult.

"Brett, sit down," Trista said. "I'm sure Cara can handle this herself."

It was a challenge, and everyone in the room knew it.

"Robert, can I talk to you outside a second?" I asked.

"We can talk right here," he said. "We're all friends, right?"

Well, there it was. I'd given Robert an out—a perfectly good out—and he'd chosen not to take it. He in fact did the opposite: he *set me up* for what I had to do next, like he was daring me to do it! So fine, I would, but I wouldn't like it, and it wouldn't be my fault at all. It would all be on him.

"No, Robert," I said, "we're *not* friends. These are my friends, and we'd appreciate it if you'd leave us alone."

He leaned forward, pinning me with his stare. "'If you strike me down, I will become more powerful than you can possibly imagine.'"

I leaned forward, too. "The Star Wars movies are ridiculously overrated. Goodbye, Robert."

That was it. Robert rose and strode out of the room, his cloak billowing around him as he left.

"Fuh-*reeeeek!*" Ree-Ree said.

"Does it make you want to bed him?" Gemma asked.

Ree-Ree took a moment to think about it. "Do I get to wear the cloak?"

"Hey, I'm right here!" Marsh complained.

My attention, however, was on Trista. She didn't say anything, but she wore a pleased smile and I knew she approved. If I hadn't known better, I'd almost have thought she and Robert had worked together to test my loyalties. I briefly considered writing Robert a thank-you note.

While the Shun Happy Hopeless thing was no surprise, there were all kinds of other rules I discovered as I found my place in the Populazzi. An early lesson was Thou Shalt Not Eat Weird Food, which I learned when they served sundaes in the cafeteria and I mixed a bowl of peanut butter and chocolate syrup. The sneer from Trista got me out of my seat within seconds to throw it away. I inwardly vowed she would never see me dip a french fry in a shake.

There were other lessons, too, like Thou Shalt Never Make a Joke (Even a Playful One) at Trista's Expense. Thou Shalt Always Participate in Trista's Social Plans was another, but it was waived for Gemma and me: for Gemma when she was out of town and for me while I was grounded. But I still knew it was a biggie.

The list went on and on. And then there were the zillions of acronyms I had to learn. If something was bad, it was "LA," for Lame Ass, or "Super LA," for Super Lame Ass. Something wonderful was "CHIW," for Chills-Worthy. People to be avoided were "NOKs": Not Our Kinds. Then there were the acronyms that had evolved since I'd arrived in their midst, like "TA" for Robert Schwarner ("Trim Ass") and "BL" for Nate Wetherill ("Bong Lover").

I told Claudia everything I learned, except for Marsh's dating status, and she sucked in every detail. She saw us as two halves of a single social scientist. I was on the ground doing fieldwork; she was back in the lab compiling the data. She imagined publishing a book one day, a treatise on what makes the Populazzi tick, which high school students could buy and use as a blueprint for how to skyrocket to the top of their own school's Popularity Tower.

Claudia imagined the book would be huge. I had to agree. Who wouldn't want this life? Sure, there were rules, but in return I got a group of girls who treated me like a sister. We ate lunch together, we hung in The Heap every morning before the bell rang and after lunch, and one of them was always around to fall into step with me between classes and chat.

There were *endless* things to chat about. Like Marsh and Ree-Ree's dramas. I'd thought Ree-Ree was crazy at first, like everybody said. But she wasn't, not really. Even the eye-scratching thing was exaggerated. It had happened, but Ree-Ree was provoked. This girl Bridget had found out her married dad was sleeping with Ree-Ree's single mom, and Bridget had called Ree-Ree out on it at the bus stop, saying all kinds of horrible things.

"Which is stupid," Ree-Ree said as we walked the halls. "My mom didn't do anything wrong. She wasn't the married one."

I saw on Facebook that Ree-Ree's mom listed "Men" among her favorite activities, and Ree-Ree seemed to feel the same way. She craved excitement, especially in relationships.

"It's the conquest, Cara. It's a rush," she said one day as we walked to class. "If Marsh and I were always together, we'd get bored."

"But you said you love him."

"I do. But never as much as when one of us is trying to win the other one back. It's very sexy."

It didn't make a lot of sense to me, but that was something I'd come to appreciate in Ree-Ree. She had a unique take on things.

Kristie was far more traditional and innocent.

"Do you think Eric is husband material?" she asked me.

I had no idea. The word "husband" wasn't even on my radar. "You mean, like, will he be in ten years?"

"Ten years? I want to be on my third baby in ten years. Kerry—she'll be the youngest. Karly and Kyler will be her older brother and sister."

"You've actually thought this all out?"

"That's what high school is for: finding the right boy to take care of you forever. And for learning enough that I can help my kids with their homework."

"What about college?"

"Of course! If I don't find my husband here, I'll have to find him in college, right? And don't worry," she added, linking her arm through mine, "no matter when I meet him, you'll still be at the wedding."

Gemma, meanwhile, had already been given an open invitation to pretty much every college in the country. It wasn't just because she was on the pro tennis tour. She was also brilliant. To us, she was like a worldly-wise big sister who showered our group with her knowledge.

"Life outside is no different," she said. "It's just like high school. If you're hot and you're smart and you take no crap, you'll get everything you want."

While Gemma had the scoop on the real world, no one knew how to navigate Chrysella better than Trista. And following her lead was easy. Being a Penultimate wasn't like being a DangerZone. There was no specific uniform. Trista was all about individual style—as long as whatever we wore looked good enough to be "aspirational."

She thought my basic jeans and tops were a fine place to start but I needed some additional pieces and accessories to make my wardrobe work. She e-mailed me lists of links to items I should buy. I thought it was cool that she didn't make assumptions about what I could afford. If she liked something for me, she always sent at least two different versions: one higher end and one budget-friendly equivalent.

When I told her my credit card had been confiscated as part of my grounding, she told me to save the links until she "took care of things." In the meantime, she brought in items of her own or had the other girls bring in things to supplement my wardrobe. I never minded taking Trista's suggestions. She brought out a personal style I didn't even know I had.

Turned out "casual chic" was my thing: skinny blue jeans, tunics, heels, and limited but very specific accessories, like just the right textured shoulder bag, long necklace, or earrings. Trista also tweaked my makeup routine. She showed me how to blend different blushers, bronzers, lip glosses, and eye shadows to create the perfect look for my face: one that seemed totally natural but made my eyes and smile pop. My hair was still a mess of straight layers that looked best tied back, but I told Trista how curly it would get and she was thrilled. With the right highlights and product, she said it would be my crowning glory.

Even my mom noticed the change in me once I started taking advice from Trista. "You look so sophisticated lately, Cara," she said during dinner one night. "Like you're really taking care of yourself."

I ignored the implication that I had looked like a slob before and simply took the compliment. "Thanks. It's my friend Trista. She gives amazing fashion advice."

"I like the makeup, too. You look very collegiate. Doesn't she look collegiate, Karl?"

Karl lowered his paper for all of a second to look at me, then he disappeared behind it again. "Very collegiate," he muttered.

It was only two words, but Mom nearly jumped out of her seat with delight. Not only had Karl spoken to me, he'd admitted I looked "collegiate," which was the highest praise imaginable.

Much as I didn't want to get caught up in Mom's and Karl's head games, I felt pretty warm and fuzzy about it, too.

The next day, Karl showed up at Chrysella.

Trista, Ree-Ree, and Kristie were walking me out after school when I saw him. He was standing by my car, his long, lanky body practically bent double as he tried to shield his cell phone call from the wail of the wind.

No good could come of Karl being here. Sure, he'd acknowledged and half complimented me the night before, but he could still say anything now, and the Populazzi were right here to witness it.

"Cara!" Karl called, then he quickly got off the phone and walked toward us. He had a huge grin on his face, as if his appearance in the Chrysella parking lot was a special treat I could only be thrilled to receive.

"Aren't you going to introduce me?" he chirped.

"Um . . . sure. You guys, this is Karl, my stepdad. Karl, this is—"

"Trista Camello," Trista interrupted. She had a huge, confident smile on her face, and she strode toward Karl with her hand outstretched. "It is *such* a pleasure finally meeting you, Mr. Ralston. I can't even tell you what a joy it's been getting to know Cara. You and Mrs. Ralston have clearly done an incredible job raising her."

Wow . . . gush much? If I tried pulling off something like that it would sound completely fake, but Trista made it work. Karl lit up. I think he even blushed as he shook her hand. "Thank you, Trista," he said. "It's a pleasure meeting you, too. Cara's told me a lot about you."

I briefly considered asking *when* I'd told him a lot about her, seeing as we hadn't had a single conversation since I'd entered Trista's orbit, but Trista was already introducing Karl to Kristie and *Renee,* which apparently was Ree-Ree's real name. Trista then complimented Karl on his coat and cajoled him into giving her the name of the store where he'd bought it, since it was *exactly* the kind of gift she'd been seeking out for her own father. Like everyone else, Karl glowed under Trista's attention, and I could tell he was disappointed when she finally excused herself and the other girls so they could catch some of the guys' basketball practice.

"Oh!" Trista called back after they'd turned to go. "I'd love to pick your brain about Northwestern sometime. Cara's been *raving* about it. It sounds like an exceptional school."

That did it. Karl went supernova. "Anytime, Trista. Anytime." Then, as he turned to smile down at me, Trista shot me a knowing smirk and wink . . . and I finally got it. She'd said she'd help with my home situation, and charming Karl to within an inch of his life was her way of doing it. I didn't know if it would work, but I loved that she'd made the effort. It proved she really did think of me as one of them.

"So . . . our new friends seem very nice," Karl said. He did that when he was being playful: made everything plural like it belonged to us both. I was supposed to balk and call him on it, but after spending several weeks disowned, I didn't have the energy.

"I have a surprise for you." He gestured to his car. "Come on."

"What about my car?"

"We'll get it later."

Karl stared straight ahead as he drove, but his voice was cheerful. "Guess where we're going?"

"I don't know. Where?"

"Pat's . . . Steaks," he said.

Pat's totally lived up to its hype as the best cheesesteak place in Philly, but it was all the way in the city, so we almost never went. Something was seriously up, but after several minutes of silence, I knew Karl wouldn't tell me unless I pried it out of him.

"Why?" I asked.

"We received your report card," Karl said. "It was exactly as you and your mother had said: straight As. Clearly you did not go quite as astray as I'd first believed. I have already apologized to your mother for not taking her at her word when she told me she spoke to your teachers. I should have. I also should have been more careful in choosing my words to you when I was upset. You are not a stranger, you are not dangerous, and you will always be my daughter. I love you."

Karl was sweating and he had the steering wheel in a death grip. I stared at him, my heart beating a little faster in anticipation. Was this it? Was he going to lift the grounding?

"Cara?"

"Oh." I realized he was waiting for absolution. That had never been a problem for me, telling Karl what he needed to make him feel better. But this time . . . I couldn't. The words wouldn't come. Still, he seemed like he was about to lift my punishment and I had no desire to stop him, so . . .

"It's okay," I managed.

That probably wasn't the ideal response to "I love you." Karl squeezed the wheel tighter. I tried again.

"I mean . . . I know. You know . . . I know."

Oh, that was eloquent. I'd get a Pulitzer one day for sure.

The white faded from Karl's knuckles as he relaxed and nodded. "I *do* know. Thanks, Cara."

Wow. Maybe I *would* get that Pulitzer. I almost giggled, which would have been disastrous because I'd have stopped Karl from saying what came next.

"I hereby lift your punishment and return all privileges. Which leaves only one important item to discuss: American or provolone?"

The answer was obviously provolone. As we huddled over the steaks and cheese fries, Karl told me he had already faxed my report card to Dean Jaffe at Northwestern, who was *very* impressed. The dean had cemented his plans to come to Philly, and we were officially on his books for lunch April twenty-fifth. I did my best to give lip service to what I knew should be some of the greatest news ever.

Truthfully, though, I had no room in my head for anything but visions of my new life as a fully functioning member of the Populazzi.

Chapter *twenty-seven*

"Oh my God, you could not possibly be any cuter!" I squealed. Yes, squealed. I defy any human being not to squeal when faced with a twenty-pound love-pig of a black fuzzy mutt with little white paws, a little white bib and chin, and wide pointy ears that moved completely independently of each other, and either flopped down or perked straight up depending on his mood. This was Riley, Trista's dog, and at the moment he was lying on his back, begging with his front paws for me to go back to scratching his belly. Of course I obliged.

My grounding had been lifted yesterday, and today was our day of celebration. I had already done a little celebrating last night: I'd used my freshly returned credit card to buy the laundry list of clothing and accessories Trista had been e-mailing me. I was smart about it, though. I had my mom come check out all the links first. Given Trista's impeccable taste, Mom loved everything. She was especially impressed by Trista's responsibility in suggesting lower-cost alternatives to each item.

She gave her explicit approval of every purchase and had even been inspired to do some shopping for herself.

Today the guys had an away game, and Gemma had gone off for several weeks to play in some tournaments. That left Trista, Ree-Ree, Kristie, and me. We caravanned to Trista's house, but I *had* to call Claudia, so I put her on speakerphone and kept the cell in my lap so Kristie wouldn't look through her rearview mirror and wonder if I was hiding a secret cache of other friends.

I was especially thrilled to have Claudia on the line when we passed through an automatic gate and pulled into Trista's driveway—or more accurately, Private Road.

"Uh, Claude? The street is named Trista Way."

"Of *course* it is!" Claudia gushed. "Is it a shallow road? Is it beautifully paved in gold but rotting away underneath? Is it lined with street signs telling you what to do?"

"Okay . . . I see goats."

"Goats?"

"Goats. There is a pen of actual goats to my right."

"Do you think they eat the goats?"

"I do *not* see Trista eating goat."

"What would you do if she served you goat? She's Supreme Populazzi. You'd have to eat it."

"*Ugh!*" I made a formal declaration that when and if the time ever came that I was Supreme Populazzi, I would never make anyone eat goat.

"Hey, Claudia," I said as I neared the end of Trista Way, "remember how I told you Nate's was pretty much the biggest house I'd ever seen?"

"You take it back?"

"I take it back."

It honestly seemed silly to refer to Trista's house as a "house." It was more like three or four houses pushed together, all united by a network of columns and massive turrets. Seriously, turrets. If we were living in another century, I'm fairly certain the place would have qualified as a castle.

Of course it had its own parking lot. As I pulled in behind the other girls, I hung up, swearing to call Claudia back the second I left. I walked toward the three-story archway hooding the entrance and wondered if Trista's room was in a turret. Had it been me, I totally would have chosen a turret room.

"Cara!" Trista called. "This way! My house is over here."

"Your . . ." I jogged to catch up with her, Ree-Ree, and Kristie as they walked down a cobbled path. "I'm sorry, did you say your *house?*"

"Present for my sixteenth birthday. I got to move into the guesthouse."

The guesthouse was down a long hill from the main house, and the pool sat between the two buildings. Trista's place was a perfect miniature of the main house, complete with mini columns and an arched entranceway. No turrets, though. The grand tour took all of five seconds and included two rooms: The Hang and The Hole.

The Hang was Trista's bedroom/hangout room. It was carpeted in plush blue shag and housed her queen-size bed, covered with layers of brown and blue patterned comforters and pillows, one small worktable and a chair, plus several brown and blue beanbags and oversize pillows. The wall opposite the bed held a wide shelving unit filled with books and keepsakes, all surrounding a large wall-mounted flat-screen TV. A small but beautiful bathroom with a toilet, sink, and shower/tub branched off The Hang. When I fantasized about my ideal dorm room at Northwestern, I dreamed it would be exactly like The Hang.

The Hole was technically a kitchen, but as Trista explained, her parents hadn't bothered renovating it for her, since they knew she couldn't cook. They also hoped she'd go to the main house and sit with them for meals. Everything in The Hole was stark white, which showed off every smear and stain, both new and ancient. You had to enter The Hole single file; it couldn't hold more than one person across. Still, it had a working sink, fridge, oven, a fully stocked pantry, and two stools that put you at the perfect height to munch on a bowl of cereal at the end of the counter.

There was more. A full wall of sliding glass doors along the far side of The Hang opened to a tented cencrete patio filled with electric tiki torch heaters and padded double chaises. It was like an additional room. There was a small doggie door built into the sliders, which is how I first met Riley. The pooch bounded in the second we arrived, ready to leap all over us and lick us to pieces.

That cemented it for me. Trista's place was perfection. I never wanted to leave.

"And now," Trista said, "the Liberation Celebration Libations!"

Trista ducked into The Hole and emerged with a stack of red plastic cups and a bottle of champagne. She handed the bottle to me. "Pop the cork?"

I had never popped the cork on a bottle of champagne, but it wasn't a problem. The girls cheered and Trista poured . . . and I started to panic inside.

I couldn't drink champagne. I'd be driving home in a couple

hours. If champagne made me feel anything like the beer I'd had with Nate did, I'd be a swimmy mess in about two minutes. Still, I'd look like a complete loser if I was the only one saying no to the champagne, especially since it was in my honor.

Kristie must have seen the look on my face. She leaned in close and said, "We're all driving, so we're just taking the tiniest sip to celebrate."

"Yeah." Ree-Ree lounged back in her beanbag and gazed wistfully at her red plastic cup. "We don't really raid The Hole unless we're staying over."

"Which they do every Saturday," Trista said. She plopped down in a beanbag next to me and clinked my plastic cup. She drained her drink—she was already home. "Saturday's club night. Friday sometimes, but Saturday for sure. Always okay to crash here Saturday night, so it's cool to GYBO."

"Get Your Buzz On." Kristie giggled.

"Grab her cup, Cara!" Ree-Ree said. "KBG!"

"KBG?" I asked.

"Kristie Buzz Giggle," Kristie said, shoving her cup in my hands. "Don't let me drink any more."

"I'll take it." Trista downed the little bit of champagne left in Kristie's, Ree-Ree's, and my cups.

"Shall we bring out . . . the List?" Ree-Ree asked. Without waiting for an answer, she walked to The Hole and came back with a creased piece of yellow legal-pad paper. The front was split into four columns with the scrawled headers "Trista," "Ree-Ree," "Kristie," and "Gemma." Under each was a list of names, and next to each name was a small *H* or *S*.

"The List of Conquests," Ree-Ree said. "All the guys we've ever fooled around with. 'H' means hookup; 'S' means sex."

I ran my eyes over the sheet of paper again. Gemma's and Ree-Ree's lists were far longer than the others' and peppered with far more *S*s. Kristie's was next longest, and every name was followed by an *H*. Trista's had only four names, ending with Brett's, the only name to be awarded an *S*.

"Gemma's pulling way ahead of me." Ree-Ree tsked. "Marsh and I might need to take another break. Or who knows?" she said to me. "Maybe you'll beat us both out."

She flipped over the paper, and for a second I felt like Ebenezer Scrooge looking at his own tombstone. Next to the fresh column Ree-Ree created for me were three other columns, all scratched to oblivion with ballpoint ink. I wondered what my predecessors had done to earn their excommunication.

"All right," Ree-Ree said. "Shoot."

I was grateful I'd seen the other side first. I wouldn't lose face by having a short, virginal list. Still, I couldn't name *only* Nate and Eddie. And even if I thought Archer might be an acceptable hookup for someone in the Populazzi—which I didn't think he was—his wild freak-out at the touch of my lips was hardly something I wanted to publicize.

Yet that, as Claudia had told me, was the beauty of being new to Chrysella. I could say anything, and no one would know. I gave a list of six names "from my old school," mostly guys I'd had crushes on at one time or another. I also included Fred Crumston, Claudia's and my least favorite teacher, who always had at least one string of spittle connecting his upper and lower lips. They vibrated when he spoke. Just picturing it made me nauseous, but I knew how much Claudia would laugh when I told her about it later. I ended with Nate and Eddie.

Ree-Ree sighed. "You are so offering no competition."

"Because we're not competing; we're immortalizing," Trista said. "So what's the craziest place you've ever fooled around with a guy?" she asked me.

I had no story of my own, so I adopted an entertaining rumor I'd heard about a Pennsbrook couple after hours at Sesame Place theme park near Yardley. It involved a Big Bird costume and Ernie's Bed Bounce. The girls loved it and jumped in with their own favorite stories.

The afternoon whizzed by, but Trista wouldn't let me leave until she'd fully briefed me on the parameters of my new life as a nongrounded member of the Populazzi. The Hang was *the* after-school spot, and if I could convince my parents to let me stay for dinner, that would be ideal. Trista always preferred to have food delivered and eat in The Hang with her friends rather than in the big house with her family. I promised to try, but since "Family Dinner Every Night" was a major tenet of Mom and Karl's parenting credo, I doubted it would happen.

"We can help with that," Trista said. "Tell your parents we're coming for dinner tomorrow night." She turned to Kristie and Ree-Ree. "Got that? Tomorrow after school, Cara's house."

My brain ran over every inadequacy of our new house. But Trista hadn't asked if she could come over; she'd declared it. End of story.

"The under-twenty-one clubs in the city are Super-LA," Trista continued, "so you'll need a fake ID. You'll probably never use it. A lot of the bouncers know us and are cool. It's just in case. I'll shoot you a link. Send a hundred dollars cash, upload a picture, and it's done. You can even overnight the money and have them overnight the ID. Whole thing takes less than a week. We've all used it; it's great."

It was dusk by the time I had to leave for dinner. Kristie and Ree-Ree were staying and had no desire to brave the cold, but Trista offered to walk me to my car. "I'm glad you were sprung," she said before I got in.

"Me, too. Thanks for helping."

Trista shrugged off the compliment, then reached out her arms. I thought she was going to hug me goodbye, but instead she placed her hands on my shoulders and fixed me with a stare. She was smiling, but her fingers dug into me a little, the pressure just this side of painful.

"The most important thing, Cara? No secrets. Ever." She squeezed her fingers a bit harder, as if pushing the message into my body. Then she released me with a cheery "See you tomorrow!"

Chapter *twenty-eight*

"Oh my God, it's *Titus Andronicus*. Don't eat anything she cooks in The Hole; it'll be made from the bodies of the scratched-out List girls."

I was on my way home from Trista's, and I'd just told Claudia about the shoulder-digging moment.

"I know!" I said. "But she was only like that for the one second. The rest of the time was amazing. And I'm kind of okay with the threatdown thing. It's like the Mafia: I'm family now, so I need to remember who's Boss. It's weirdly cool."

"How are you getting the ID money?"

Claudia so knew my life. I've never had a job. Karl believed the school year was better spent studying. During summer vacations, he felt volunteering at the animal shelter, taking creative writing courses, and traveling with the family would look better on my Northwestern application and give me more personal essay material than slinging popcorn at the movies or waiting tables.

The only downside to this was that I never had more than

about twenty dollars in cash. It hadn't been a problem before: Mom and Karl always gave me what I needed; I just had to ask for it first. Call me crazy, but I had a feeling that asking for fake ID money wouldn't go over well. I could lie, but it had to be a lie where the only answer was a hundred dollars in cash. If they told me to put whatever it was on my credit card, I was sunk.

Luckily, I had thought this through before Claudia asked.

"Only answer: Mom's stash."

"My thoughts exactly."

Mom had no idea I even knew about her stash. She kept it balled up in an old lopsided ceramic cookie jar I'd made for her in third grade and which now sat on a high shelf in the back of her closet. The stash was a huge wad of hundred-dollar bills, which she'd secretly peeled off Karl's casino winnings. Mom didn't need the money; she and Karl had a joint account. Claudia and I figured she tucked it away so she could feel a little bit independent.

We'd raided the stash before. Never more than one bill, and only for really important things, like the matching birthstone necklaces we once got for each other at the exact midpoint between our two summer birthdays. Mom never noticed. The wad was big enough that a single hundred here or there made no difference. She wouldn't miss the one I'd use for the fake ID.

The next day at school I was a wreck. Not about the money and the ID—I was petrified about the Populazzi girls coming over. I'd asked Mom and Karl about it at dinner the night before, and they'd agreed immediately. The mere mention of Trista appearing on our doorstep was enough to get Karl to toss aside his newspaper for the rest of the meal. Mom was just as excited and grilled me about delicacies Trista, Kristie, and *Renee* would most enjoy.

I suppose I should have been happy about their enthusiasm, but it only made me more nervous. Honestly, I didn't know what worried me more: super-rich Trista's horror at our average-size lifestyle or Karl finding some fatal flaw in one of the girls that would make him ban them from my presence.

I should have had more confidence in Trista. She spent all our free time that day pumping me for added information about Mom and Karl. Thus armed, Trista, Kristie, and Ree-Ree made it impossible for my parents not to fall even more in love with them. First they hung out with Mom in the kitchen. Mom was making her signature turkey chili, and Kristie dove in to help, chatting about her own favorite "cold-weather recipes" while gushing over the genius of Mom's.

"This recipe actually reminds me of one of my favorite chefs," Kristie said. "Have you ever heard of Cat Cora?"

"Are you kidding?" my mom asked. "Here, I want to show you something."

Mom flung open the cabinet in which she kept all her cookbooks and pulled out everything Cat Cora had ever written. Of course, I'd already told Kristie Mom had those books, just like I'd told her Cat Cora was mom's culinary role model and the main reason she never missed an episode of *Iron Chef America*. Yet Kristie's interest had sounded so genuine, Mom didn't question it.

"I've been to her restaurant at Disney World," Ree-Ree said as she and Trista bustled to set the perfect table, which was arranged around a beautiful floral centerpiece they'd brought along themselves.

Ree-Ree had never been to Disney World. With the exception of a few vacations with Trista's family, Ree-Ree had never left the tri-state area.

"Oh, Kouzzina! I've been dying to go there!" Mom said. "How did you like the food?"

Ree-Ree wasn't much of a student, but she'd clearly studied the restaurant review Trista had e-mailed her. She didn't miss a beat discussing its ins and outs.

Mom could have spoken to the Populazzi all night, but the moment Karl came downstairs for dinner, my brilliant friends turned all their attention to him. Kristie asked a million questions about Northwestern, which she and Trista both said they'd decided was their first-choice college. Ree-Ree told story after story about her grandfather, whose high-roller exploits at the Atlantic City blackjack tables were legendary. Trista commiserated about the Philadelphia Eagles' devastating Super Bowl loss and discussed exactly what "their" team needed to do to get back on its feet.

I was in awe. By the time they left and Trista gave me a final wink, Karl would have been more than happy to let me move in with any of them.

"I am very impressed, Cara," he said. "I like your new friends quite a bit. You're an excellent judge of character."

Actually, Trista was the excellent judge of Mom's and Karl's characters, but it netted out to the same thing: total freedom. I went right to Trista's every day after school. On Friday, I brought an overnight bag—I'd be staying for the whole weekend. Kristie and Ree-Ree were, too. They almost always did on weekends. Now I'd have the same regular routine.

We didn't do anything special on Friday. Since we didn't have to drive, Trista made all kinds of concoctions in The Hole and we drank them up. They tasted much better than either the beer or the champagne I'd tried. Trista used so much juice that everything was fruity and delicious. I wouldn't have even known I was drinking alcohol until everything got *so* swimmy that I had to lie on a beanbag and wait for the room to stop spinning. It wasn't a horrible feeling, though—as long as I didn't try to stand up, I could still laugh and have fun.

Saturday we didn't wake up until the middle of the afternoon. I'd never slept in like that unless I'd had a high fever. I did have a little headache but nothing too terrible. Trista hadn't let me go to bed before I'd had a full bottle of water and a couple Tylenol: hangover protection, she'd said.

We were all starving, so Trista called over to the main house and begged the housekeeper to make and bring over mass quantities of pancakes, bacon, and coffee. At three in the afternoon, the four of us were sprawled out all over The Hang, still in our pajamas and stuffing ourselves with piles of greasy, salty, syrupy deliciousness as we laughed and watched lame shows on TV. It was the first time I felt completely relaxed and at home with the Populazzi. As if they really were my sisters.

We got dressed and lazed around for several more hours, until it was time to get ready to go out. Saturday night was club night. Trista had been right: my fake ID had taken no time at all to arrive. I'd had it sent to Trista's house. Just before I'd ordered it, I realized my parents would attack any nondescript envelope addressed to me. Even though we were on good terms now, they'd still either open it or assume it was junk mail and shred it. When I explained the situation to Trista, she said her parents wouldn't even see the envelope. The housekeepers sorted anything addressed to Trista out of the family mail right away and delivered it to her little house.

The first time I saw the ID, I was shocked by how perfect it looked. I held it up next to my real license, searching for inconsistencies. If anything, my fake ID looked better, since I'd uploaded a slightly nicer picture. Not too nice, though, since Trista had said that could make bouncers suspicious.

The guys were supposed to meet us before we all went out, but Trista wouldn't even let them on the property until we were all ready and looked good enough to pass her inspection.

Per her request, I'd brought several options so she could choose my outfit for the night. I laid them all out on her bed: the best of my new casual chic options plus a few cute dresses that I loved.

Trista looked concerned. "Hmm."

"What? You liked those, remember? You picked them out."

"I like them for *school.* We're going *clubbing.*"

"How about this?" I asked, fingering my favorite dress. "It looks really cute on."

"Try it."

I changed into the dress and spun around for Trista, Ree-Ree, and Kristie.

"It's okay," Ree-Ree said.

"It's cute!" That was from Kristie.

"It *is* cute," Trista said. "But you want to look hot. Let me see what I've got."

She rummaged through her closet and came out with a handful of options. As I took off my dress to change into the first one, Trista stopped me.

"Whoa, whoa, wait a minute: bra check."

"Bra check?" I asked. I was wearing my best white silky bra, the same one I'd worn for my ill-fated attempted makeout session with Archer. I'd put it on specifically for the occasion.

"You *definitely* need a better bra."

I looked at myself in the mirror. "What's wrong with my bra?"

"It's just sitting there. It's not *doing* anything."

I had no idea my bra was supposed to have skills. "What exactly is it supposed to *do?*"

"Check it out." Trista peeled off her shirt to reveal a skin-tone lacy bra. "See what this is doing? It has structure. It's pushing me up and in and giving me shape. Free-floating boobs are great when you're naked, but under clothes you need structure. What are you, B-cup?"

"Yeah."

"Thought so. Rees and I are Cs. Kristie, do you have another bra here?"

"Sure." Kristie pulled one out of her overnight bag and handed it to Trista. It was pretty, but at the same time it was far thicker and more substantial than any bra I owned. It almost looked like it could stand up by itself.

"Perfect," Trista said. She held it up to show me. "See this? Pushup and padded. *This* will do something for you. Put it on."

I did, then Trista had me reach into each cup and scoop the boob so it sat the right way on the padding. She tightened the straps a little, then broke into a huge smile.

"See? Two-second boob job—you look amazing!"

She spun me back to the mirror.

"Oh my God . . ." Trista was right. Just like that, my boobs were a cup size bigger, or at least they looked it. I even had cleavage. I turned side to side, catching the look from every angle. "This is . . . wow!"

"Exactly. Now wait till you see how good they look under the right dress."

Trista had me go through several options from her closet. Finally I tried on a flirty blue babydoll with matching heels, and Ree-Ree and Kristie burst into applause. I spun in front of the mirror. I couldn't stop staring: I looked curvy and sexy and fabulous. Trista's one remaining concern was my undies—they showed panty lines. Luckily she had several brand-new, tag-still-on thongs, so I changed into one of those.

Perfect.

"Now, ready for hair and makeup?" Trista asked.

I'd assumed I'd do my hair and makeup the Trista-influenced way I'd been doing for school, but apparently not. Trista worked on both for me, talking me through every step so I could do it next time on my own. By the time she was done I looked amazing—and about five years older than I actually was.

The guys must have called three times while she was getting me ready, and three more while she did up herself. I apologized for slowing everyone down, but Trista wouldn't hear it.

"You have to stop thinking that way, Cara," she said. "You're worth the time. We all are."

She said it as though it were obvious, but the words startled me. I had always been taught that making someone wait—especially making Karl wait—was the ultimate sign of disrespect. But maybe that wasn't always true. Maybe I *was* worth the time.

I took a deep breath and stopped stressing about the clock. I felt incredibly grateful to be under Trista's wing.

When we were all ready, I kept staring at the four of us in the mirror. I remembered seeing these girls hanging out in their tree, as the Pussy Posse at Halloween, and on the dance floor at Eddie's party. They had seemed like another species then, beautiful creatures far outside my reality. But if anyone looked at us now, they'd have no idea I was new to the group. I fit in perfectly.

I couldn't wait for Eddie to see me. It was funny: we'd been a couple for a while now, but we really hadn't been that involved in each other's lives. We hung out at lunch and in The Heap, but after school he had practice, and weekends had been out since I'd been grounded, so we didn't see each other that much.

And he wasn't big on e-mail and Facebook like the girls, so we didn't talk a lot either.

That was okay—it had given me time to cement my place in the group. Now Eddie and I could start having a normal relationship, and it would begin the minute he saw me in my perfect outfit.

I was sure it would be like in a cartoon, where his tongue would pop out of his mouth and roll onto the floor. These were pretty much Brett's, Marsh's, and Eric's reactions when they saw their girlfriends. They all immediately took the girls into their arms, kissing and ogling them as if they couldn't get enough.

Eddie was the last one to get to Trista's. "He has to get all dolled up," Marsh explained, which I didn't realize was a joke until Eddie came in wearing the same thing he always wore: jeans and a T-shirt. Today's tee was black and white, which I supposed made it formal. It featured two braces-wearing penguins who had kissed and stuck together, and the caption read COLD FUSION. In deference to going out, he'd tossed a casual blazer over the ensemble.

I didn't care. Guys could get away with that kind of thing. Besides, the more dressed down he was, the more I'd stand out next to him.

"Save the *beer*st for last," he said, mitigating his late arrival with a six-pack he'd pulled from his fridge at home. The guys pounced on it.

I'd been standing back in the shadows. I wanted to make a moment out of Eddie seeing me. My heart was pounding. It felt like stage fright. For the first time ever, I was playing the role of hot girl, and I was about to step out of the wings.

I walked toward Eddie, a shy smile on my face. "Hey."

Eddie looked me up and down. I waited for his reaction. I could barely stand it. Finally he smiled. "You fit right in."

I practically jumped up and down. He'd hit it exactly. It was just what I'd been thinking myself. I thought he'd kiss me, but instead he gave a roar and darted behind me, grabbed my waist, and plopped us both down into a beanbag chair. I squealed happily. It wasn't exactly the reaction I'd expected, but maybe Eddie wasn't as comfortable as the other guys with a lot of kissing in public. Besides, I was still in his arms, so I was good.

The limo came about a half hour later. The guys grabbed their beers, we girls each grabbed a freshly Trista-made cocktail, and we piled in. Trista wasn't trying to be ostentatious with the limo. Her parents required it. They knew we'd drink, and they didn't want any of us even to think about driving.

During the ride, Trista told me the key to getting into clubs without getting carded was confidence. "That, and looking CHIW, which we do."

I believed her, but when we actually got out of the car, I was glad we'd been drinking. The now-familiar fuzziness would make it easier to act confident and unafraid as I actively tried to break the law and walk into a twenty-one-and-over dance club.

There was a huge line to get inside, but Trista strode right to the front, Kristie, Ree-Ree, and I at her heels. The guys hung behind. Trista called the bouncer by name and gave him a close hug and major eyeful of her cleavage. Then she and the girls chatted with him like old friends.

"And this"—Trista put her hands on my shoulders and pushed me forward—"is Cara."

The bouncer slowly ran his eyes over my body. If I hadn't been tipsy it might have made me uncomfortable, but instead I stared right back at him. He was mountainously tall and muscular, but he was cute. And young. Could he have been in college? From movies and things, I imagined bouncers to be older, unsmiling, and intimidating, but he wasn't that at all.

"Cara, huh," he said. "Do you care-a if I stare-a?"

I burst out laughing. Had he really just said that? I imagined telling Claudia about it and laughed even harder. But then I heard Trista clear her throat and realized I wasn't exactly being alluring and flirtatious. I pulled it together as best I could and looked up at the bouncer with what I hoped seemed like genuine admiration. "You are *so funny!*"

As I said it, I placed my hand on his chest. It was a lot like leaning against a wall. A really fuzzy wall. What was his blazer made of? I started rubbing it. "You guys, you have to touch his jacket—it's so soft."

Trista, Ree-Ree, and Kristie joined me in petting the bouncer's chest. We all agreed the material felt insanely good.

"I love it," I said. "I just want to cuddle up with it."

I blushed when I realized how that sounded, but the bouncer only smiled. "I like your new friend," he told Trista. "You guys can go inside."

He gave me a wink, and I wondered if Eddie would get jealous.

Trista linked her arm through mine. "Impressive," she said as we made our way to the door. "You had me worried for a minute, but you pulled it off. You're a natural."

Nothing felt better than a Trista compliment. I practically floated into the club.

Clubbing with the Populazzi was a million times different from going to the Works with Nate. Trista, Ree-Ree, Kristie, and I all danced together, losing ourselves in the beat and the flashing lights. Marsh loved to dance and was almost always out there with us. The other guys floated in and out, sometimes dancing, other times watching from the bar.

We kept ordering drinks, but I was sure I was sweating out the alcohol as fast as I was drinking it. My fuzziness never grew. I felt just soft enough at the edges not to worry about how I looked and let my body move any way the music pushed it.

We stayed until the club closed. We were all starving afterward, so we had the limo stop at Denny's for a late-night breakfast. It was almost five in the morning when we got back to Trista's, so of course we were all staying over.

The Hang was too small to offer any real privacy, but we did the best we could. Trista and Brett got the bed and buried themselves in a sea of covers. Kristie and Eric pulled several oversize pillows and their sleeping bags into the closet and blocked the entrance with beanbag chairs. Ree-Ree and Marsh ducked under a heap of blankets in the middle of the floor.

I gave Eddie a nervous smile. I was suddenly very aware that even though we were surrounded by people, this was really the first time we'd been alone since that night at his party.

"I have an idea," he said. He opened the narrow linen closet by the bathroom and pulled down the last of Trista's blankets, then took them out to the patio, where he piled them onto a double chaise. It was freezing, but Eddie turned on the outdoor heaters and crawled under the blankets. I was so cold, I didn't even feel self-conscious about cuddling tightly against Eddie. He put his arms around me and I rested my head on his chest, my leg thrown over his. We were a little island of warmth in the middle of the tundra.

I enjoyed the coziness for a minute, then picked up my head and scooted higher on the chaise to look Eddie in the eye. "I had a great time tonight," I said.

"I'm glad."

He kissed me then—a long, sweet kiss that warmed me even more. I leaned in for another . . . but Eddie's mouth opened in a huge yawn.

"Sorry," he said. "I'm what they call a sleepy drunk. Promise you won't hate me if I crash out?"

"I promise." I even crossed my heart. I guessed I was what they call a dorky drunk.

"Great." Eddie kissed my nose, and then he lay back and guided me into cuddle position.

"Mmm, my spot," I said, claiming his chest as my pillow. I could feel him laugh for a second, and then his breath came long and slow.

He was asleep.

I looked out over Trista's yard. Beyond the strings of white lights, everything was cloaked in blackness. I couldn't believe my life. I had spent the whole night dancing with my friends, and I was about to go to sleep cuddled up with my boyfriend. Just before I closed my eyes I saw little flakes dancing in the glow of the Christmas lights. I almost giggled. It was too perfect—I was living in a snow globe.

I snuggled even closer to Eddie and fell asleep.

I woke up to the sun blasting through my eyelids. Eddie was still out, so I gently untangled myself from him. My hot-girl dress felt weird and sticky on my body after sleeping in it, and while Kristie's brilliant bra had been my best friend the night before, it now felt stiff and confining.

I slipped inside The Hang, which was all but silent. Trista

and Brett were asleep on the bed, and I felt weirdly like a kid sneaking through her parents' bedroom. There was no way I could stay here without waking everyone, and I didn't feel comfortable roaming around Trista's property by myself. I figured I'd go home. I ducked into the bathroom to quietly wash up and change. I tiptoed around the blanket pile that was Marsh and Ree-Ree as I gathered the rest of my things, and then I wrote Trista a note to thank her and took off out the door. I shot Eddie a quick text as I waited for my car to warm up, so he didn't think I left because anything was wrong.

Over the next week, Trista helped make sure I wouldn't ever get caught again without the proper clubbing attire. We hit Forever 21 and Victoria's Secret to get me a few choice dresses, bras, and thongs. And though Trista was insane-o rich, she was all about a bargain. I spent barely any money, so there wouldn't be any credit card issues.

Two Saturdays later I experienced my first Populazzi holiday: Valentine's Day. I'd never had a boyfriend for Valentine's Day, and I was racking my brain about what to get him, but Trista said there was only one acceptable V-Day gift: lingerie.

"You really think Eddie would look good in lingerie?" I asked.

I was joking, but Trista didn't get it. She looked at me as if I was hopeless. "The lingerie is for *you*. We'll all go shopping together this week to get it."

She didn't mention *where* we'd go, a fact Claudia seized on. She was convinced Trista would take us to some crazy-exotic sex shop filled with weird paraphernalia. Every time we spoke, Claude tortured me with more bizarre details of the imagined den of iniquity, and there was no way I was going to be able to handle the outing without turning bright red and hyperventilating over the idea that someone might see me. I didn't even want to think about what I'd do if I had to use my credit card.

"What," Claudia said, "you don't think Karl would be cool with a charge from Priscilla's Passion Pit?"

"Stop."

"How about Lolita's Love Loft?"

"That's it. I'm not going."

"Sexistentialism?"

"No. There's no . . . Okay, if it was actually called Sexistentialism I might have to go inside."

As it turned out, I didn't have to worry. Trista took us back to Victoria's Secret, a place I could enter without a qualm and which would look totally acceptable on a credit card statement. I did feel weird going to the "sexy" section of the store, flipping through filmy, lacy things that required far more confidence and cup size than I actually had.

I couldn't even begin to choose anything to try on, but luckily I didn't have to—what Trista pulled for me was perfect. It was more like a slip than anything hard-core, with thin shoulder straps, a lacy top, and a mesh skirt that came down to the tops of my thighs. It was red, so the mesh was a little see-through, but not so much that it would be embarrassing. It was tasteful and cute—I actually thought I looked pretty in it. Trista and Kristie picked out beautiful and tasteful things as well. Ree-Ree's . . . I saw it on the hanger and wondered if they were selling it to wear or to use for cat's cradle. For Ree-Ree it was perfect.

On Valentine's night, we made the guys wait outside until we were ready to reveal our presents. We actually made them wait an extra ten minutes after that. I thought that was a little mean given the freezing weather, but Trista said it built "delicious anticipation."

Finally, Trista had me unlock the door, but I didn't open it. I ducked into the bathroom with the other girls, and then Trista yelled for the guys to come in. Only when they'd shut the door and taken seats did Trista hit the remote to turn on music so we could strut our lingerie-clad selves into the room.

The guys loved it. They hooted and catcalled like wild, Eddie as loud as any of them. The whole night, it seemed as if Eddie couldn't take his eyes or hands off me. He stared at me, whatever I did. When I sat in his lap while we all played drinking games, he kept running his hands up and down my little slip.

The attention made me feel beautiful and sexy . . . but also a little scared. Eddie and I had been pretty tame in our make-out sessions so far. I knew even Kristie was doing a lot more. I wondered if he'd take the lingerie fashion show as an invitation to go a little further. Not that a little further was a problem, but a lot further might be. Eddie and I hadn't talked about whether or not he was a virgin. Things might be on the table for him that weren't at all for me.

When we eventually made it out to our chaise and started kissing, it kept nagging at me. Part of me wanted to say something, but stopping a perfectly wonderful makeout session to define things that might not even need defining seemed like the worst turnoff in the world. I did *not* want to turn Eddie off. But wouldn't stopping things when we were actually getting close to doing something I didn't want to do be even more of a turnoff?

"Eddie," I finally said between kisses.

"What's up?"

"I just want to make sure . . . I mean, I don't know how . . . how far you wanted to go, but . . ."

Ugh. I looked away. Was it possible to be any lamer? I didn't think so. I was sure I'd turned as red as my slip.

Yet as my mind raced through ways to convince Eddie not to break up with me, he put his fingers under my chin and tilted my face to his. "Hey . . . it's okay. I like you. For real. That's why I want to go nice and slow, okay?"

Relief flooded through me. "Perfect," I said. And I was so happy that I practically tackled him to get back to the kissing, which we did for most of the night before we fell asleep in each other's arms. After the sexual hyperspeed of Nate, it was wonderful to be with a guy who wanted to take things slowly. It meant things with Eddie could stay more innocent and romantic, which I loved.

Back when I was grounded, I'd felt as though I was living only during the week, when I escaped to school. Now that I was a full-time member of the Populazzi, it was the opposite—I lived weekend to weekend. That was when everything important happened. The weekdays were all about planning to make those weekends great. I knew my schoolwork was suffering—I didn't have as much time to study. I supposed there'd be consequences when Mom and Karl got my next report card, but that was ages away.

In the meantime, I had something more pressing to think about: next weekend's winter formal. It would be the first school dance I'd ever attend with a date on my arm. Gemma would still be out of town, but Trista, Ree-Ree, Kristie, and I had an endless list of things to do to prepare: hair appointments, mani-pedis, dress hunting . . . Trista even wanted to decorate The Hang with a wintery theme, just to keep the mood going when we all went back to her place after the dance. I was in fact brainstorming ideas to enhance that very project . . . when out of nowhere, in the middle of English class, I was brutally ambushed and put on trial.

Chapter *twenty-nine*

$\mathcal{I}$ didn't even realize it at first; I wasn't paying attention. It was Friday, the formal was the next day, and the only thing on my mind was the splash Trista, Ree-Ree, Kristie, and I would make in our spectacular new ensembles. It wasn't until Mr. Woodward cleared his throat that I noticed he was standing over me, and every pair of eyes in the room was boring into my face.

"So?" Mr. Woodward asked.

Uh-oh. Clearly I had been asked something, but I had no idea what it was.

"Um . . . I'm sorry, can you please repeat the question?"

"It would be my absolute pleasure," Mr. Woodward said. "In fact, let's go ahead and do a little reenactment of everything that just happened. Like we're TiVo."

I took a deep breath. Mr. Woodward seemed giddy. That did not bode well for me.

"The class was discussing *The Crucible*," he said. "You remember we're doing our unit on *The Crucible*, yes?"

"Yes."

"Wonderful. You've been so silent lately, I sometimes fear you believe your top-of-the-table perch is more a tanning bed than a vantage point for learning. Well, then. The question arose, 'How exactly do people get caught up in the kind of groupthink we find in Miller's play?' And Mr. Jain said . . ."

Mr. Woodward turned to Archer. He blushed but didn't ignore the tacit request.

"I said, 'Maybe you should ask Cara.'"

"Oh, you said it far more pointedly than that, Mr. Jain. Let's not back away from our stance now. And I believe you even added the phrase '*she*'—referring to Miss Leonard, of course— 'seems to be an *expert* in groupthink.'"

Mr. Woodward turned back to me. "So I ask you, Miss Leonard: how *do* people get caught up in Arthur Miller's level of groupthink?"

Groupthink? Why would I be an expert in groupthink?

I looked at Archer and was about to ask him the question— when suddenly I got it.

At least I thought I got it. But that couldn't really be it, could it? Was Archer . . . were *Mr. Woodward* and Archer really accusing me of groupthink because I was part of the Populazzi?

They couldn't be. This was the middle of English class. They couldn't gang up on me and pass judgment on my social life in the middle of English class.

And yet . . . what else could they be talking about? And why else would everyone in the room be leaning in and sucking up the drama? It was because I was a Populazzi now. What happened to me was interesting. *Especially* if it was embarrassing.

Anger shot through me, and it was all I could do to stop myself from leaping off the table and screaming. In that moment, I hated all of them, but I reserved a special ring of fire for

Mr. Woodward and Archer. Especially Archer. He was supposed to be my friend.

With effort, I calmly addressed Mr. Woodward. "I'm sure Archer's trying to compliment me on my *expert* ability to analyze *The Crucible*, which I appreciate. The answer is that people get caught up in groupthink out of fear, because they're afraid to be different and out of step with the majority."

"Well done," Mr. Woodward said. I was quite sure he wasn't referring only to my answer about Miller's play. He went back to lecturing, though the bulk of the class was nowhere near as interested as they'd been two minutes ago. I kept my eyes only on Mr. Woodward, and though I raged inside my head, I let my face show nothing but keen intellectual interest.

I confronted Archer in the hall after class.

"What the hell was that?"

"My compliment to your literary genius?"

"Stop it. We both know what you were talking about. What are you, jealous that I have other friends?"

"Yes, that's exactly it. I'm jealous. I'm jealous because I want to have as much fun laughing at people and excluding them as you do."

"I don't do that. *We* don't do that."

"Do you even talk to anyone who's not in your über-popular little clique?"

"You're mad at me because you think I'm in a clique? Are you ever *not* hanging out with the Theater Geeks?"

"'The Theater Geeks'?" he balked. "Are you perchance referring to the group of close friends I've had for most of my life because we share a wealth of similar interests?"

"What makes you think I don't 'share a wealth of similar interests' with my friends, too?"

"Cara, I've gone to school with them forever, remember?"

"Which doesn't mean you know them! You don't hang out with them. You wouldn't, because then you'd have to step out of your own exclusive little clique."

"And why are you dating Eddie?" Archer asked. "How did you even get to know him? You never said two words to him, then all of a sudden you're tucked under his arm all the time and prancing around in step with all the other trophy girls. It's gross. It makes *you* seem gross."

"Oh, that's really nice," I said. "Why do you even care who I date? What does it matter to you?"

Archer lunged forward a little. "It—"

But whatever had tried to explode from his mouth didn't come out. He closed his eyes and took a deep breath, pinching his mouth into a small, tight dot.

"It doesn't," he finally said. "It doesn't matter to me at all. We're late for class."

He walked away. I wanted to throw something and smack him in the back of the head, but I was pretty sure it would be a suspendable offense, and I didn't want to get grounded all over again. Stifling a scream, I turned the other way and stormed off toward precalc.

Yes, Eddie and I had started going out quickly. Yes, I'd barely known him when we'd started dating. And yes, lots of times it felt like I was more involved with Trista, Ree-Ree, Gemma, and Kristie than with Eddie, but so what? I was happy! Eddie was happy! Who cared about anything else?

I thought sitting in precalc behind Trista would make me feel more centered and together, but it didn't. Super LA Archer's voice kept bouncing around in my head and I couldn't stop questioning everything about my relationship with Eddie.

Was I with him *only* to be part of the Populazzi? I knew Claudia would say it didn't matter, but it did to me. Sure, I was climbing the Ladder, but I liked to think I was doing it with some integrity. I went after Archer because I *wanted* to go after Archer. And even though I turned myself inside out for Nate, I did it because I was crazily attracted to him. Plus I genuinely liked Nate . . . at least for a while.

So what about Eddie? Well, I liked Eddie. He was a nice guy. No, we didn't have a major physical relationship, but that was on purpose. I *preferred* it.

But was that because I was being smart and cautious or because I didn't really feel strongly enough about Eddie that way? And if that was the case, was it fair to stay his girlfriend just to keep my place in the Populazzi?

"YES!" Claudia's voice shouted in my head . . . but I wasn't entirely sure.

This was crazy. Of course I liked Eddie. I was letting stupid Archer worm his way into my head. Eddie was my boyfriend. We were great together, and tomorrow we'd prove it to the whole school at the winter formal. No one who saw us together would doubt for a second that we were among the most CHIW couples in the school.

I of course spent that night at Trista's, and she, Ree-Ree, Kristie, and I used all Saturday to get ready for the formal. Gemma called in on speakerphone just before the guys were due to pick us up. Trista had e-mailed her pictures of us in our dresses, and Gemma gave her full approval. She was in Barcelona and said the party scene was not to be believed.

"You girls have to travel with me sometime," she said. "It'll blow your mind."

I wondered if she was thinking of me as part of that traveling group. I hoped so.

"So, Cara," Gemma said, "give it up. What's Eddie like in bed?"

"You'll be disappointed, Gems," Ree-Ree said. "Our Cara's going the Kristie route: she's the Big V."

"You say that like it's a bad thing," Kristie said.

"Yes, Kristie, I do."

"Innnnteresting," Gemma said. "'Cause you know I tried to hook with him, right?"

"With Eddie?" I asked. I was stunned. I'd heard Gemma *never* hooked up with Chrysella guys.

"You didn't tell her?" Gemma sounded surprised. "No secrets, right?"

"Yours to tell, Gems," Trista said.

"What happened?" I asked.

"Don't stress, chica; I don't want your boy. It was a humanitarian mission. Eddie hadn't had a girlfriend since sixth grade. Four years of tension—I thought the boy needed relief."

"So you and Eddie . . ."

"Nope," Gemma said. "That's why I'm curious—what's he like? 'Cause I have to tell you, I don't get turned down a lot. My theory was he had a TWP and didn't want me to know."

"TWP?" I asked.

"Teeny-Weeny Peenie," Ree-Ree noted.

"Oh," I said.

"So does he?" Gemma asked.

Honestly, I knew nothing about Eddie's peenie, teeny-weeny or otherwise. But I couldn't say that in front of the other girls, not after the amount of time Eddie and I had been together. Even my fellow V-girl, Kristie, would be appalled by my lack of progress.

A horn beeped.

"That's the guys, Gems!" Trista said. "Call soon and we'll give you the recap!"

Trista hung up and we poured out to the driveway. As we'd planned, we'd decorated The Hang just for this evening. We didn't want the guys to see it until the formal was over, so Trista had arranged for tonight's limo to pick them up first, then come get us.

Snippets of my fight with Archer kept echoing through my head, but I forced them away. This was my winter formal, and I wouldn't ruin it by getting all neurotic about my feelings for Eddie. I climbed into the limo and immediately curled into "my spot" under his arm.

Kristie climbed in right behind me. "Awwww," she said when she saw Eric. "You wore a tux!"

"Someone's getting blown tonight," Ree-Ree said.

"You told them?" Eric cried.

"Eric . . ." Kristie glared at Ree-Ree.

The tux had been a major point of contention between Kristie and Eric all week. She'd *really* wanted him to rent one, but he believed tuxes were only for proms. She had indeed promised him a big reward if he wore one, but she clearly thought it was the height of impropriety for Ree-Ree to discuss this particular brass ring.

"What, no love for the man with his *own* tuxedo?" This was from Marsh. He knew exactly how good he looked in a tux and jumped at any and every chance to put one on.

"You don't have to wear a tux for me to think you're hot,"

Ree-Ree said, crawling onto his lap. "I think you're hot in nothing at all. *Especially* in nothing at all."

"What about me?" Eddie said. "You guys don't like my tux?"

Eddie was—shockingly—wearing a blazer over jeans and a T-shirt. This particular T-shirt was all black, emblazoned only with a box of hemorrhoid pads bearing the brand name TUCKS.

Everyone groaned, and Trista turned to Brett, who of course was in a tuxedo. "Really? You let him get in the limo like that?"

Brett raised his hands in defense. "I tried to talk him out of it. Didn't work. What did you want me to do, pull off his clothes and change them? I don't roll that way."

"I think you look great," I told Eddie, then kissed him to prove it.

On the ride to school we each downed a single drink, just enough to get a little buzz on, which was perfect since there'd be hell to pay if we were obviously drunk at a school dance. Per Trista's mandate, we arrived an hour after the party started so we could make the grand entrance she'd choreographed. The guys went in first. Their arrival would get everyone's attention and make sure all eyes were on the door for us.

Once we knew everyone was looking, we breezed in like a bridal procession. Going along with the wintery theme, Trista had helped Kristie, Ree-Ree, and me pick out gowns in shades of ice blue, while Trista herself wore shimmering silver. We floated to our respective boyfriends and hit the dance floor, swaying to the slow song the DJ had started to play as if on cue. Knowing Trista, it probably was.

I rested my head on Eddie's chest and closed my eyes. I enjoyed the feeling of his arms around me, his body pressed close to mine. I looked up at him, but he was gazing around the room.

"Eddie," I whisper-spoke.

"Hey."

"I'm really happy to be here with you."

"Me, too. I'm really happy to be here with you, too."

I kept smiling up at him, and after a moment he leaned down and pressed his lips to mine. It wasn't a long kiss, but it was sweet, and I stood on tiptoe to reach up for another when the first one was over.

Then the song ended, and Eddie excused himself to go raid the food table, which was fine. I knew he wasn't much of a dancer. I stayed out on the floor and danced every fast song with the girls and Marsh; then Trista, Kristie, and I dragged out our boyfriends for the ballads, which the DJ was smart enough to keep few and far between.

Two hours whirled by like nothing, and all too soon the DJ was announcing the last songs of the night, all of them slow. I looked for Eddie at the snack table, but he wasn't there. I thought maybe he'd slipped out to the bathroom; I headed for the door so I could nab him the second he came back.

I only made it a few feet before I stopped in my tracks.

Walking across the room toward me was Archer Jain.

He wore a tuxedo, and the smile he gave me made my stomach flutter.

My body was such a traitor. After yesterday's inquisition, I had been sure I was over Archer forever. But now . . . I couldn't imagine what caused his change of heart. I also didn't care. In my mind I could already feel his arms around me; I could hear the soft rumble of his voice in my ear as he admitted what he'd felt for me all along.

He held his hand out and I took a deep, shaky breath as I reached to take it . . .

. . . then watched as he walked right past me. I spun around and saw Sue beaming with happiness as Archer pulled her close. She rested her head on his chest, and they swayed together to the music.

I had to move. I was way too close, and I was staring. I *tried* to move, but my body wouldn't listen. It was frozen. Even though I knew any second one of them could look over at me and—

Sue looked. Her blue eyes narrowed, and I knew she could tell exactly what I was thinking. She turned her face up to Archer's, and he looked down at her adoringly. With the sweetest of gestures, he brushed a stray wisp of blond hair from her face, then bent to share a long, gentle kiss that pulled every inch of my intestines slowly out of my body and onto the floor.

I couldn't breathe. I couldn't watch this anymore. I felt the tears building behind my eyes, but I couldn't get my feet to move—my God, why wouldn't they *MOVE!*

"Cara?"

I wheeled to see Eddie in his ridiculous Tucks T-shirt. "Want to dance?"

"I've got to go. I'll be back."

I *walked*—I wouldn't run. Running in heels would make noise, and noise might get Archer's attention, and I could not could not could *not* let him see me running out of the room.

I locked myself in a bathroom stall and plopped onto a toilet seat mere seconds before I would have passed out. I didn't even care that the toilet had no lid and I hadn't put down a cover and who knew what my dress was soaking in. I had to sit, and I had to be alone. I thought I should put my head between my knees, but even in my current barely human state I couldn't get my face that close to an uncovered public toilet bowl, so I just rested my elbows on my knees and buried my face in my hands.

Of course Archer had a girlfriend. That was part of the Ladder, right? Claudia had said it from the beginning. That's why it wasn't bad if I didn't always have strong feelings for the guys on the rungs, because I was doing them a favor. My attention made them more desirable, so when I moved on, they'd get a new girlfriend right away. It was *supposed* to work this way.

But not with Archer. Not with Archer.

The way he looked at Sue . . . the way he kissed her . . . he *kissed* her . . .

It was official, then. It wasn't that he didn't want a girlfriend; it wasn't that he was overly shy, or nervous, or gay. It was that he wasn't attracted to me.

Not that this was new news; I'd known it for months. And it wasn't like I'd been sitting at home doing nothing since he and I had imploded: I was on my second boyfriend. But still . . . actually seeing him *kiss* a girl . . . kissing *Sue* . . .

Over and over again I replayed it in my head. I imagined their very first kiss. No running away in horror from that one. Had he made the first move? Had they been in Archer's basement? Maybe watching a movie together, his arm around her, Archer completely unable to concentrate because he was too transfixed by her dimpled cheek, the hair tucked behind her ear. Archer leaning in closer . . . closer . . .

I had to stop. This was not helping my ability to breathe, and I was about a minute away from throwing up, which would be even worse on the dress than sitting on this hideous toilet seat.

I got up and left the stall. I checked the back of my dress in the mirror as best I could. It didn't look like I'd gotten anything horrible on it. I leaned on the sink and stared at my face, willing myself to stop freaking out and think rationally.

So Archer had a girlfriend. So what? How did that make

anything any different than it was an hour ago? It didn't. If anything, it just made Archer a complete jerk. What was our fight yesterday about if he had a girlfriend? What was he doing getting all up in my relationship with Eddie? Now that Archer had a girlfriend, he was the arbiter of love for everyone?

I stood up straight and gave myself a steely look, fortifying myself to make a decision.

Archer had a girlfriend. Good for him. I had a boyfriend. And from now on, I wasn't holding anything back from my boyfriend. Archer could do whatever he wanted with Sue. More power to him. I had Eddie—and tonight I was going to show him exactly how much I wanted to be with him.

Chapter *thirty*

Once I'd made the decision, I wanted to act on it, so I felt nothing but impatience as I danced the last song with Eddie, making sure to keep my eyes far, far away from Archer and Sue. In the limo on the ride home I downed a few drinks, to make sure my resolve didn't falter.

Trista, Ree-Ree, Kristie, and I had been excited about the postformal reveal of The Hang's new look, but now it was one more obstacle I had to get through before I could do what I wanted. Still, it was pretty; we'd done a great job. The Hang was strung with white Christmas lights, like the kind on the outdoor patio, and we'd re-covered all the pillows, beanbags, and bedding with fluffy white fabric that approximated a recent snowfall.

No matter how motivated I was, I couldn't just lead Eddie away and jump him. Trista controlled when we broke up into twosomes, and at the moment she and Kristie were popping into The Hole to get us all snacks and drinks.

I decided to make the most of the time while I waited. I'd never successfully seduced anyone, but I'd seen enough of the other girls at work that I figured I could do a decent job of it, especially when I was feeling good and fuzzy. I kept my hands on Eddie, running them along his arm, his back, and his thigh. He said that tickled, so I repositioned myself and massaged his shoulders for a while—until he said my nails were digging into him. No problem. I settled in front of him and sprawled back in his arms, hiking up my skirt and adjusting myself so he'd have an easy view of my padded and pushed-up cleavage.

When Trista gave the signal, I was sure Eddie had to be all kinds of turned on and ready to go. We grabbed blankets and pillows and headed out to our regular place on the chaise.

I liked that my first time would be outdoors; it would make a good story later.

Eddie and I curled up under the covers and he tried to pull me into "my spot" under his arm, but I wasn't having it. Not tonight. Instead I climbed on top of him and plopped myself down in a commanding straddle—

"*Ow!*" Eddie cried. "Geez, watch where you're sitting."

"Sorry," I said. I lifted up a little so I wasn't hurting him, then leaned down and kissed him, thrusting my tongue into his mouth—

Eddie recoiled and turned his face away. "Cara, what are you doing?"

He was confused. Of course. I had never come on this strong before. But tonight it was only the beginning.

"Don't you like it?" I leaned down and nuzzled his neck. I kissed it, then kissed his ear, nibbling the lobe ever so gently . . .

"Hey!"

Okay, I'd meant it to be gently. I was drunk. My spatial relationships were a little off.

"Sorry," I said. "Let me try again."

I dove back down for his ear, but he wrapped his arms around me and rolled us over so we were lying side by side.

"You know what? I'm reeeeeeeally drunk and sleepy. How about we just rest." He pulled me back into that spot under his arm and guided my head onto his chest.

I stayed this time, but I didn't rest. I slowly moved my hand down his chest and stomach, then paused at the waistband of his jeans to expertly undo the button . . .

At least I tried to expertly undo the button. I didn't have a lot of leverage lying on my side and using one hand. How did people do this so easily in movies? I yanked hard on the fabric, trying to get a better grip—

Eddie grabbed my hand. "Cara, what's up? I thought we were taking things slow."

"We were. But I don't want to take things slow anymore."

I clambered on top of him again, then reached back and unzipped my dress. I pulled it over my head. All I had on now was a padded pushup bra and matching thong. At any other time I might have felt shy, or at least a little cold, but now I only felt driven. I rolled back my shoulders.

"Like it?" I purred.

"Cara . . ."

"Here—gimme a second."

I leaned forward to work on his jeans again. I had a much better angle and the use of both hands, so I got the button open easily. I pulled down the zipper and tugged at the waistband . . .

"Um . . . this would be easier if you'd lift your butt a little—"

"Cara, don't—"

"It's okay. I want to," I whispered.

I kissed his stomach, then slid down to the top of his boxers—

"Cara, *stop!*"

He rolled away, whacking me in the face with his hips.

"Ow!"

"I'm sorry."

"What is wrong with you? Are you the only guy in the universe who doesn't like a blow job?"

"Will you keep your voice down?"

"NO!" I shouted, then lowered my voice to an urgent whisper. "I want to have sex with you, Eddie. Tonight. Now."

I tried to push him back down onto the chaise, but he wouldn't move. Fine. I dove toward his lap, but he grabbed my shoulders and roughly pushed me away.

"Jesus, Cara, stop! I don't want to have sex with you! I'm gay!"

He turned bright red after he said it and wheeled toward The Hang.

"But you're my boyfriend. You can't be gay."

"Shut up!" Eddie hissed, checking The Hang again. "Look, you can't tell anyone, okay?"

"But it doesn't make any sense. If you're gay—"

"Stop! Stop saying it out loud!" Eddie's eyes were pure panic.

"Oh my God . . ." I finally realized, "I'm your beard!"

"Again, voice down."

"Stop telling me to be quiet!"

"Then stop saying things so loud!"

"I have no desire to out you, okay?" I whispered.

I suddenly felt very naked in my bra and thong. I pulled the blanket around me.

"You're mad," Eddie said.

"Not that you're gay. I don't care if you're gay. I'm mad that you lied to me! I'm mad that I made an idiot out of myself trying to seduce you when it must have made you completely nauseous!"

"You're not an idiot and it didn't make me nauseous. If I were straight, I'd have been very turned on."

"Now you're condescending."

"I'm trying to make you feel better. Is it working?"

"Eddie, you can't be gay. You kissed me. A lot. How could you do that if you didn't like it at least a little bit?"

"I don't like broccoli either, but I can force it down when I need to."

"Oh, that's really nice."

"I'm just saying, it's the truth."

"But why? Why did you ever go out with me?"

"Gemma," Eddie said. "A week before my party she came on to me and I blew her off. If I hadn't come up with a girlfriend, she'd have told everyone I was gay just to save face."

"So what? Tons of people are gay. Nobody cares about gay anymore."

"Are you kidding? Was your old school in Yardley or the Castro?"

"Where?"

"People say they're cool with gay, but a lot of them really aren't. Especially high school guys. Especially high school athletes. *Most* especially high school athletes whose dad left their family to marry another guy."

"*What?* Who—"

"Brett. He's the worst, but it's not only him. Believe me, it's easier if I'm quiet about it."

"Okay . . . so why me?"

"Because I didn't need to be straight to give you what you wanted in a boyfriend."

"What do you mean?"

"Come on, Cara. Maybe a lot of people at Chrysella don't, but I pay attention. I saw the way you looked when you got here, I saw you hanging out with Archer Jain, I saw you go all emo-girl to get Nate Wetherill, and I saw how excited you got when I invited Nate to my party. You're a climber."

"I am not!" I cried.

Eddie just looked at me.

"I'm not," I insisted. "I may have done some climbing, but I am not a climber. That's not who I am."

"Whatever. I never even asked you out, Cara. You know why? I knew I didn't have to. I knew I could get you in with my friends and you'd go right along with it."

I was so beyond offended that I wanted to scream at him—except he was right. Then I remembered something.

"Okay, fine—then you're a climber, too. Robert Schwarner said you used to be friends. What did you do, dump him to be more popular?"

"You really want to know? Robert dumped *me*. I tried to kiss him in fourth grade and he freaked out."

"Oh."

"Don't get me wrong, Cara. I don't care that you're a climber. I like it. It works for me. It means we can help each other. I am totally happy to keep things the way they are. You keep me looking hetero, and I'll keep you in with Trista and the girls."

"I don't like that you think I'm that shallow," I said.

"You don't like that I think it or that I *see* it?"

"God, you don't even like me, do you?"

"Of course I like you. I wouldn't want to hang out with you this much if I didn't like you. I might not respect you, but I like you just fine."

That was it. I needed to get away immediately. Not that I had a lot of options. I was too drunk to drive home, and The Hang was occupied. I slid off the chaise, keeping the blanket wrapped around me.

"What are you doing?" Eddie asked.

"I'm going for a walk."

"Cara, it's freezing. You're only warm because we have heaters."

I needed shoes, but I couldn't bear to stuff my feet back into heels. "I'm taking your sneakers," I told Eddie as I shoved them on.

"You'll swim in them."

"I'll deal."

Eddie was right, of course. His sneakers were several sizes larger than my feet. Walking in them was like strolling in flippers. I basically had to shuffle and covered all of an inch at a time.

"You still haven't told me," Eddie said as I attempted to move. "Are we still together? 'Cause believe me, you might think the girls are your best friends, but if we break up, you're history to them."

I didn't want to believe him. I wanted to scream at him that he was wrong, that the girls weren't just my friends, they were my sisters. I was one of them, and I would be whether or not Eddie Riegert deigned to call me his girlfriend.

But then I remembered the List and the other columns with owners scratched out of existence. Maybe the Populazzi girls would keep me in their circle . . . but maybe they wouldn't.

Did I really want to risk it? Trista, Ree-Ree, Kristie, and Gemma were now my only friends at Chrysella. If they dumped me, where would I be?

"Cara?" Eddie prodded.

"Yes," I said softly, hating myself for being just what he said I was. "We're still together."

"So you'll keep my secret?"

I glared at him. I'd hoped it went without saying that if I was going to keep acting like his girlfriend, I wouldn't advertise that he was gay.

"I need you to say it, Cara."

I hated him.

"I'll keep your secret."

"Good."

That was the extent of Eddie's concern. He lay back on the chaise and curled under the blankets as I trudged over the snow-covered ground. It *was* freezing, and I had no clue where I actually intended to go . . . until I looked up to the main house. Someone had left the lights on in the large basement room that led out to the pool, and through a glass sliding door I could see Riley, my favorite dog, curled up on a couch. *That's* what I needed. I turned and started the long, slow trek to the house. I had no clue if the slider was even unlocked, but I didn't care; I'd crawl through the dog door if I had to.

Clutching the blanket tightly around me, I slogged up one hill, around the pool, and up another hill. With each step, snow tumbled into my giant clown sneakers and froze my feet. They were soon numb, and I slipped, lost hold of the blanket, and slid down several snowy feet on my bare butt. Could the night get any better? I didn't think so. Finally I neared the main house, and Riley's right ear pricked up.

"Hey, boy," I cooed. He must have heard me through the glass because he lifted his head and gave me a tongue-out doggie smile that for one moment made everything in the world all right.

The sliding door opened when I tugged on the handle. Leaving it unlocked seemed like the height of irresponsibility, until I remembered the whole property was gated, so a few open doors probably weren't a big deal.

The warmth of the room melted me, and I closed my eyes a moment to let it seep into my frozen pores before I kicked off Eddie's shoes and staggered to the couch.

Thump-thump-thump-thump. Riley's tail beat happily against the cushions as he waited for me to get comfortable.

"Okay, boy, come here."

Riley obeyed, bounding onto my lap so he could lick my face while I scratched his fuzzy black body. I gently grabbed his little head and kissed him right on his snout. Riley took this as a sign that we were now on intimate enough terms that he could roll over and present his belly for some serious rubbing.

As I scratched, I looked around the room, which seemed like a giant finished basement made for casual entertaining. On the vast brown-shag-covered floor sat not just the couch on which Riley and I cuddled but also two love seats and a couple recliners—all of which gathered around a large plasma TV with the works. Across the room to my right was a bumper pool table. Off to the left was a 1950s-diner-style kitchenette with lots of steel, Formica, and red leatherette. The lights in that area were all off, but someone had been there earlier. I saw a huge pile of Tastykakes wrappers, empty soda cans, and an empty pint of ice cream. They were strewn on the carpet, as if a bunch of people had feasted on the floor. I knew Trista had a twelve-year-old little sister. Maybe she'd had a slumber party with her friends and they hadn't bothered to clean up.

I felt the couch shake. While I scanned the room, I'd stopped scratching Riley, and he pumped his front paws up and down, begging for more. I laughed and went back to work.

Huuuuuuulllllllll!

I froze. It sounded like someone was gagging. Riley didn't seem to notice. It was odd, since his little radar ears usually perked up at anything unusual.

Huuuuuuaaaaaaaaaaaaaa!

That time the noise ended in a painfully scratchy croak. More silence, then the punched-in-the-stomach sound came again, this time followed by a splash.

Now I got it. I winced and hoped that someone was actually sick, since the alternative was that Trista's sister or one of her friends was already making herself throw up at age twelve. I probably would have to tell Trista tomorrow. She should know.

I heard the sink running and several moments later heard the knob turn. I considered hiding just to save the kid some embarrassment, but that didn't seem right. She should be aware someone knew, especially if I planned to say something to Trista. I pulled the blanket tighter around myself and watched as the door opened and a figure dressed in a bulky, knee-length sweatshirt padded out. She was hunched over and looking down. A curtain of lank chestnut hair obscured her face.

Then she lifted her head.

I gasped. I couldn't help it.

"Trista?"

At the sound of my voice, Trista snapped up to her full height and her red, watery eyes and nose flared as they focused in on me. It was like I'd unleashed a demon from hell.

"Are you *spying* on me?"

"No, I—"

"You've been plotting, haven't you? You've been *looking* for something to use against me. You came here on purpose because you *knew!*"

"No!"

"I swear, if you say one word about this to anyone—*anyone*—Ree-Ree, Brett, *a-ny-one,* I will destroy you. Remember how quickly I made you one of us? That's how fast I can make you the biggest pariah Chrysella has ever known. You're nothing without me, Cara Leonard. You're no one. You're dirt. You *need* me."

Wow. Here I'd been about to tell Trista I would never dream of using this against her because she was my friend, and her first instinct was to destroy me. And I'd thought Eddie and I were friends, too, but he was only using me. I'd even thought Nate and I had had a real connection, but that turned out to be a complete disaster.

And Archer? My supposed best-friend-outside-of-Claudia? What was that he'd called me? Oh, yes. Gross. He'd said I was gross. Even my parents were a misstep away from turning their backs and disowning me. And what had I done that was so horrible? I'd climbed the Ladder, yes, but I hadn't done it callously. I had done it by finding friends, real friends, people I cared about and who I thought cared about me.

Except they didn't. None of them.

And in that moment, with Trista's fiery vomit-breath burning my face, I realized that my motives didn't matter. If trying to be genuine and make real friends got me to the same place as being a soulless social climber, why open myself up for heartbreak? I had only one step left if I wanted to reach Claudia's goal of Supreme Populazzi and Brett Seward's date for the prom. Twenty-four hours ago—twenty-four *minutes* ago—I wouldn't have dreamed of deposing my friend and stealing her boyfriend, a guy in whom I had no romantic interest whatsoever.

But now? Now I *wanted* to do it, just to prove that the girl they all shoved aside and didn't care about could rise up and be queen of the school.

This was the new me, and I'd start living her life right now by grabbing the golden opportunity Trista was presenting me.

"Actually, Trista," I said, "*you* need *me*. You can destroy me if you want, but then I'll tell everyone your secret, and it sounds like you don't want that."

Her eyes lost focus for a moment. I was sure she'd expected me to cower and grovel, but I wasn't playing that anymore.

"So what are you saying?" she asked. "What do you want?"

"I want to be you."

"You can't be me; *I'm* me."

"Not anymore. We're going to switch places."

"Oh, really? How do you think that'll happen?" she asked.

"Basic transition of power. First you'll teach me everything I need to know to be like you. Then I step forward, while you fall back into the shadows."

"I don't do the shadows. No one would believe it if I tried. They also wouldn't believe *you* as me."

"That's not true. People can change their opinions of people pretty easily. I've seen it happen. If you and I both act like we've switched places, everyone else will follow."

Trista shook her head. "I can't *teach* you to be me."

"Really? You taught me to be me. You had all kinds of rules for how to be part of your group: what I could say, what I could do, what I could wear . . . It makes me think you'd have a set of rules for yourself, too. Things you do that keep you in charge."

Trista fixed me with a flat-eyed glare, but I didn't care. I stared right back. I gave her nothing.

She sat on the couch and I knew I had her.

"So either I go with this . . . or you tell everyone what you saw."

"Exactly."

She called Riley onto her lap and thought about it as she scratched his chest.

"Fine," she said. "It's a deal."

Chapter *thirty-one*

It's amazing how time flies when you turn off your heart. The whole month of March seemed to zip by in a blur. *Little Shop of Horrors* went up that first week, but I played sick when the rest of the Populazzi went to see it. It was bad enough that Archer and Sue kissed and held hands in the halls all the time; watching them fall in love onstage would have made me ill.

March brought spring weather, which was unusual. I still needed a jacket to be comfortable outside, and with every breeze came a whiff of arctic chill, but it was nice enough for the Populazzi hangout to shift from The Heap back outside to the Oak. The first time I climbed into its branches, I couldn't help but peek at the windows of the main building and remember my first day, when I could only stare out, awed and intimidated.

I thought about my time with Nate, too—how I could always see the Oak from his rock. I'd never figured out exactly why he'd gone so crazy after we broke up. The madness hadn't lasted after I'd gotten together with Eddie. For all of Nate's outsider mystique, I guess not even he messed with the Populazzi.

But I was curious, so one day when we were all at the Oak after lunch, I climbed to a high branch and looked down at the rock. I could see Nate there, sitting and playing guitar like always, but now some other girl was perched by his side. It took me a minute to recognize her as Dinah, one of the Theater Geeks. It wasn't the distance that made her so hard to pick out, it was her look. I couldn't believe it—she had dyed her dirty-blond hair bright red and wore buckets of eyeliner and an outfit she could easily have retrieved from Mom and Karl's haul to Goodwill.

I wondered if Archer had told her *she* was gross. I doubted it.

I shook out my head of finally-returned-to-normal curls and shrugged. If Nate and Dinah made each other happy, more power to them.

As for myself, I wasn't looking for happiness. I was looking for results. To the casual observer, nothing in my life had changed after the winter formal. I was still Eddie's girlfriend; I still spent all my time with the Populazzi; I still went to The Hang after school and on weekends; Saturday night was still club night. It all looked exactly the same.

Only now I was Trista's protégée. Whenever we could, usually late at night, we slipped away from the other girls and the guys and into the basement of the main house so she could feed me her pearls of Supreme Populazzi wisdom.

"Become Supreme Populazzi with help *from* the Supreme Populazzi," Claudia had marveled when I'd told her the whole story. "It's Machiavellian. It's brilliant."

I said I'd wait to accept that label until the technique had actually worked, but I did feel good about the plan.

"No secrets," Trista reminded me during one of our sessions. "I always say that, and it's the most important thing you need to know."

"But *you* have secrets."

"Because I'm at the top . . . for now. If you want to be at the top, you'll keep your secrets to yourself but know everyone else's," she said. "Gemma, Ree-Ree, and Kristie wouldn't dream of going against me because I have too much dirt on them."

"And because they're your friends."

Trista looked at me blankly. "What do you mean?"

"They wouldn't do anything against you because they're your friends."

"Whatever. People are selfish. Give them the chance and they'll take what they can get. Look at you." Trista didn't say it accusingly, just as a fact of life that confirmed her philosophy. "Always assume you're on your own and everyone else wants to bring you down. It's the only way to stay the best."

Another night, Trista and I were playing Wii Fit while we talked. I was working on the tree pose, but I kept losing my balance. "Look away or something," I told her. "I can't do it when I know you're staring at me."

"That's a problem. If you want to be really popular, you have to assume you're being scrutinized every second, because you probably are. You have to *thrive* under that pressure."

She executed a perfect tree pose.

During another session, Trista made us ice cream sundaes in the basement kitchenette.

"You know one word that'll help you be like me?" she asked.

In my head I started running down the alphabet: *Artificial, Bogus, Conniving, Devious* . . .

"No idea," I said. "What word?"

"Magnet." She dropped a cherry on each of our dishes, then set them on the counter so we could dig in. "Everything about me is a magnet. Like the way I look. I look good, right?"

"Well, yeah. You're really pretty."

"I'm *beautiful.* I work at it. Beauty is a magnet. Not just to get guys either. Women are more impressed by beautiful women. It's a fact. Know how my mom got my dad?"

"She was beautiful?"

"She was beautiful. And she's going to lose him unless she gets beautiful again. He warns her about it every day."

"He does?"

Trista nodded. "She gained weight. She was a size two when they met. Now she's a ten. Know what he gave her for her birthday?"

I had no idea.

"Box of sexy lingerie," she said. "All size twos."

"Subtle message." I wasn't sure what had the bigger yuck factor: the message or the fact that Trista knew all about it.

"I thought it was pretty straightforward," she said, completely missing my sarcasm. "He's not attracted to her at this weight. She has fewer friends, too. I've seen their high school yearbook—she was *it.* Now she has maybe two good friends, tops."

She took a big bite of the sundae, and a question started nagging at me. "Trista," I asked, "are you going to throw up when we're done?"

Trista thought about it. "Probably not," she said. "Real bulimics are like that: they disappear after every meal and get rid of it. That's not me. I only do it once or twice a week. Three times at the most. And it's only after a *binge,* not just a meal or a dessert."

"What's the difference?"

"Are you kidding? Okay, once when I was really stressed out, I took the car and hit McDonald's for a Big Mac, large fries, and shake, DQ for a dipped cone, and Dunkin's for a half-dozen donuts. Downed the cone and the fries in the car, the rest back here."

"Ew."

"Exactly. Who wants all that in their body? I had to get rid of it. That one sucked, though—too much doughy stuff— almost impossible to get up. I didn't think I'd be able to do it, which was a complete nightmare. Can you imagine?"

"No," I replied honestly.

"Now I'm smarter. I choose things that come up easier. Soft-serve ice cream, giant bowls of cereal with milk, that kind of thing. And lots of fluid."

It was weird. She was talking about the intricacies of her bulimia like it was a hobby, not a disease.

"But . . . it's really bad for you, isn't it? I mean, does it hurt?"

"Sometimes, but if you do it enough, it's harder to trip your gag reflex, which comes in *very* handy, if you know what I mean."

I did know what she meant, but somehow juxtaposing it with vomiting made the whole thing highly unappealing.

"Maybe you should talk about this with your parents or something," I said. "Maybe they could help."

"Oh, yeah, that'd be great. I went crying to Mom after my first time. It was, like, ninth grade and I'd eaten a whole box of Frosted Flakes—no milk, I didn't know—and scratched the hell out of my throat to get it up. I was totally freaked and I told Mom, but she didn't say a word, just kept filing her nails.

I finally begged her to say something, and she goes, 'What am I supposed to say? What kind of mother do you think it makes me if my daughter's a bulimic!'"

"Wow," I said. "Okay, so maybe not her, but—"

"People don't want to see your weaknesses, Cara. And you can't let them. Not if you want to be a magnet."

She looked at me as if to make sure I'd gotten the message, then went back to her sundae. "I like talking to you about this stuff, though. It's nice."

It *was* nice . . . which was weird. Trista and I had been having so many late-night conversations and she'd opened up so much to me, I felt closer to her than I ever had before. Claudia was my reality check. She reminded me that the only reason Trista was being so honest and genuine was that I had dirt on her. If she could have, she'd have thrown me to the wolves in a heartbeat.

The magnet thing became Trista's favorite metaphor for popularity. She brought it up again toward the end of March, right before spring break.

"So I've been thinking about our transition of power," Trista said, lining up a tricky shot on the bumper pool table.

"What about it?"

She sank the shot and lined up another. "It won't be easy for people to buy it. I'm *so* magnetic that, no matter how magnetic we make you and no matter how much I try to sell it for you, I'm not sure it'll work."

"Are you going back on our deal?"

"Will you forget what you saw?"

I just looked at her.

"Exactly," she said, sinking another shot. "So I can't. But I had an idea: a big public way we could officially set you up as the new me."

"What's that?"

"The spring party." Trista put down the pool cue and plopped onto the couch. "Every year I throw a party after spring break. Everyone knows about it, but the actual invitation list is very selective. Big but selective. The party is epically CHIW—the kind of thing people talk about for months. If you really want to be me, this year *you* throw that party. I'll help, but we'll make sure everyone knows it's *yours*. Your magnet-tude will skyrocket."

I liked the idea a lot. I'd been wondering how we'd get everyone to see me as the new Supreme Populazzi, and this seemed like the perfect plan.

But the strategy had come from Trista, so I was suspicious.

"You really want to do this for me?" I asked.

"Of course not. But you know my secrets, so I need to keep you happy."

She was right. "Okay," I said. "Let's do it."

"Great. Where? Not your house. I've been to your house."

"What's wrong with my house?"

"It's fine . . . for a house. But not for an epic party. And even if it were, would your parents get out of the way?"

No. My parents would never get out of the way for a party. They would in fact very much want to be *in* the way and policing every moment. Plus Trista was right: the house was nowhere near epic. I needed a spot like Trista's. Or Nate's.

Or my dad's.

I smiled. "I just might know the perfect place."

Chapter *thirty-two*

$\mathcal{M}$y dad and I had an interesting relationship. I had last seen him a year ago, and I had made him cry. We'd met on neutral territory: a Wendy's. He'd asked me to meet him at his house, but ever since I'd turned thirteen and he boycotted my bat mitzvah because I wouldn't let the Bar Wench get called up for an Aliyah, I had refused to set foot on his property.

I didn't hug my dad when I saw him last. I didn't even smile, which in my pre-Nate-training days was an effort for me. I simply sat across from him, perfectly straight-faced, dipping my fries in my Frosty and regaling him with every story I remembered from my childhood in which he'd let me down. All those times when I was three, four, five years old, totally in love with my daddy and waiting for him to pick me up for a scheduled visit. And waiting. And waiting. And waiting. Until he'd finally cancel.

I reminded him of my school plays in fourth and fifth grade. He'd come—but he'd been on the phone the whole time, bouncing in and out of the theater.

I reminded him of the times he *had* picked me up for our

father-daughter visits only to run up to his computer the minute we got to his house, leaving me with the Bar Wench, who expected me to help her take care of her whiny sons.

I showed absolutely no emotion as I dragged him through the muck of Memory Lane, and I made him cry. I loved that I made him cry. It made me feel accomplished, powerful, and strong. It made me feel *right*.

Given that our last *two* annual visits had played out that way and given my vow never to set foot in his house, it was more than a touch hypocritical of me to try to have a party there. Then again, it fit perfectly with my new philosophy to keep my emotions at bay and do whatever was necessary to get what I wanted.

I described Dad's house to Trista. She thought it sounded perfect, but of course she knew I had to lay some groundwork before I asked to throw a party there. She suggested I use the two-week spring break to reconnect with him, then pop the party thing on him afterward. She also recommended I show her Dad's house so she could see if it was "magnetic" enough. I was pretty sure it was, but Trista's taste was dead-on, so I agreed. I called him at his office to make an appointment.

"Leonard Engineering," his secretary answered.

"Um, hi. Is Lenny there?" I asked.

Yes, my dad's name really is Leonard Leonard. I long suspected that this was the actual source of all his problems, and he might have been a far better husband, father, and person if his parents hadn't been so cruel.

"May I ask who's calling?" the secretary asked.

"Sure. It's his daughter, Cara."

"His . . . daughter?" She was clearly unaware that Leonard Leonard even *had* a daughter. Nice.

"Just a minute," she said. "I'll see what I can do."

To his credit, my dad picked up the phone right away and managed to sound like he was happy to hear from me.

"Cara! Hey! To what do I owe the pleasure?"

I sifted through his tone for snarkiness but found none, so I gave him the story Trista had worked out for me. It sounded disingenuous to me, but she knew what people needed to hear, so I went with it. I said now that I was almost a senior, I'd been thinking a lot about what came next—college, probably moving away—and before it happened I wanted to try to make things better between us.

Dad got weepy. I didn't feel any sense of accomplishment about it this time, just awe that Trista's skills were so well honed. Dad assumed I'd want to meet on neutral ground, but I said no, the house was fine.

"Even if Lisa and the boys will be there?" he asked.

I choked back gagging noises and painted a smile on my face, even though I was on the phone. "Sure! I'd love to see them."

A couple days later, on the first day of spring break, Trista and I drove to my dad's house. She seemed pleased when we pulled into his driveway. "Very nice. This could work for you."

The house was nowhere near as vast as Trista's, but it was big and it was impressive. Dad and Lisa had worked with an architect to design it from the ground up, so it was a modern marvel of skylights, angles, and gables. Trista led the way to the front door and rang the bell.

I knew I was doing this for a greater purpose, but I still felt very weird being there. I was glad Trista was with me—she'd make it easier. I had a feeling I could hang back and let her do all the talking and everything would be perfect.

Dad opened the door and seemed shocked to find a supermodel on his doorstep when he'd been expecting his daughter.

"Hi," Trista said.

"Well, hello," Dad replied, and I saw a flirtatious twinkle in his eye that made me nauseous. I leaned in close to Trista.

"Hey, Dad! Sorry, I should have told you I was bringing my friend."

"Oh!" He quickly rearranged his body language from provocative to paternal, then gave me a hug. He turned to Trista. "You must be Claudia, right?"

I doubled over laughing. Both Dad and Trista looked at me like I was a mental patient, but I couldn't help it. Eventually I pulled myself together.

"Sorry. No. This is Trista Camello. From my new school, Chrysella. Trista, this is my dad."

"A pleasure to meet you, Mr. Leonard," she said.

"Call me Lenny."

I waited for it.

Nothing. Trista didn't even flinch. Was she just being polite, or had she really not caught the Leonard Leonard thing?

"Can I get you girls something?" my dad asked. "A soda maybe? A snack?"

"A little water would be great, thanks," Trista said, and as we followed Dad into the kitchen, she leaned close to my ear. "Your dad's cute," she whispered.

"Ew. Stop. He is not."

Though I guess he was, in a gross-even-if-I-never-see-him-he's-still-my-dad-so-shut-up kind of way. I mean, he was forty-two, which wasn't *that* old, and he was in good shape. I got my curls from him, though he wore them close-cropped and darker. And I supposed it was attractive that he usually had a big smile on his face. You know, when I wasn't making him cry.

But still . . . his name was Leonard Leonard. And he was my dad.

"Where are Lisa and the boys?" I asked as if I cared.

"They went out. Spring break—Lisa took them to the park."

That's what he said, but the obvious truth was that the Bar Wench had jumped ship so she wouldn't have to face me. Given that I had zero desire to see her, it made no sense that I'd feel hurt by this—but I kind of did.

Trista had finished her water now and looked around the kitchen. "Your house is beautiful," she told my dad. "Is it true you and Lisa designed it yourselves?"

Dad looked surprised—and a little proud?—that I had clearly shared this information with Trista. "Yeah, we did. A long time ago, but . . . hey, would you like a tour?"

"I'd *love* one," Trista said.

Dad's tour didn't hold any surprises for me, but for Trista I could see it was a revelation. She especially loved the basement. It was fully finished and carpeted, and the bulk of it was split into two large rooms. The first held a pool table, large-screen TV, and giant sectional couch. From there you could traipse down two steps to the other room: a fully functioning pub, complete with bar, jukebox, fireplace, dance floor, wine cellar, and several small tables. The rest of the basement held two bathrooms, plus several little nooks outfitted with couches and other intimate seating arrangements.

"Magnetic?" I asked her.

"*Very* magnetic. This is *exactly* what you need."

So now I had my mission. I had to spend enough quality time with Dad that I could ask to host a party at his house—*without* the presence of him, the Bar Wench, or their kids.

And without telling Karl or Mom what I was doing. They would freak out.

I ended up making three lunch dates with Dad during spring break. Lunches were the best times to catch him. He was a workaholic, but he always needed to eat.

Lunches were best for me, too, since I was half-grounded. Mom and Karl had received my latest report card, and the news was not good: Bs and Cs. They immediately cut off my weekends at The Hang and demanded I be home for dinner each night. I tried to make a case that the punishment should start *after* spring break since it's not as if I had any schoolwork to do, but they warned me I was treading on thin ice. Unless I wanted my sentence to grow exponentially worse, I'd stop fighting them about it. Hence, lunches with Dad.

I worried at first that I wouldn't have anything to say to him. It's not like we had a ton in common. He didn't read, we didn't know the same people, and we didn't hang out at the same places. But Dad loved being social, and he adored being the life of the party. So as long as I made every one of our lunches a party, it was a huge success. I always brought along at least three of the Populazzi, and for the last lunch of the break, I brought the whole gang.

Dad was thrilled to fete us with a hugely decadent lunch at his favorite steak place. He even ordered drinks for all of us, promising to pay for cabs both to take us home and to help us fetch our cars when we sobered up. He talked baseball with the guys, he laughed with the girls . . . The only bad part of the whole meal was when Ree-Ree got up to go to the ladies' room. She stopped at my chair to whisper in my ear, "Gemma and I made a bet to see which of us can bed your dad."

"Ew! No!" I shouted. Everyone looked at me as Ree-Ree

waved and took off, leaving me to try to explain my outburst, which of course I couldn't do. Though the more I thought about it, the more I figured I'd have a better relationship with my dad if either Gemma or Ree-Ree were my stepmother instead of the Bar Wench.

But then I'd have to see my dad's name on the List. And whichever one got him would spill about everything they were doing in bed.

Ew. So ew.

As lunch came to an end, Dad looked at me from across the table. His eyes were a little misty, and I couldn't tell if that was from emotion or the two Crown Royals on the rocks he'd had with his steak and potato.

"Cair, baby," he said, "I don't know what triggered it, but I'm glad you came back to me."

Suddenly my head got very crowded. The daddy-adoring four-year-old me melted and wanted to race into his arms for a huge hug and a cathartic cry. The angry me wanted to spit in his face for having the gall to think a few laughs and expensive meals made up for an entire childhood of disappointments. Mom and Karl were in my head, too, warning me not to believe a word Dad said. "I'm the one who was there for you!" in-my-head-Karl screamed. "Sperm Donor! Sperm Donor!" screeched in-my-head-Mom. "Ask him about the party!" hissed in-my-head-Trista.

"Ow!" I winced. Someone had kicked me in the shin. It was Trista, and her hiss hadn't been in my head at all. She nodded toward Dad—now was the time.

"So, Dad," I began, diving into yet another script Trista had written for me, "I wonder if I could ask you a favor . . ."

"Anything, baby. Anything."

"Wow, okay, um . . . we were all talking," I said, "and we really wanted to have a spring party, but we couldn't figure out a good location . . ."

I was already off-script. I was hemming and hawing and hedging and trying to get back to that No Emotion place in my head, but it was hard. I was *riddled* with emotion. Guilt that I was being nice to Dad behind Karl's and Mom's backs. Guilt that I was using Dad for his house. Anger that I was feeling guilty when Dad *deserved* for me to use him. I could barely get my tongue around it all to speak.

"What, you want to use the house?" Dad asked.

I scanned his voice for indignation. There didn't seem to be any. In fact, he seemed to be more *offering* than asking.

"Um . . . yeah. I mean, if we can . . ."

"We'd *love* to!" Trista said. "Thanks so much, Lenny!"

"No problem," he said. "Just let me know when so I can make sure Lise and I don't already have it booked."

"We'll work around you, of course!" Trista said. "A Saturday night would be best. Whatever one's good for you."

Dad pulled out his phone and tapped a quick note. "Done. Just e-mailed Lisa." He looked at me. "I'll call and let you know what she says."

Dad wasn't the one who called me. *Lisa* called me.

"This is not your house," she said. "Do *not* think this is ever going to happen again."

That's what she said. What I heard was that I was having a party at the house!

"Got it. So what day would be best for you?"

"April twenty-fourth."

I had already hung up and was about to call Trista when I realized the horror of that date. It was the day before my lunch with Dean Jaffe of Northwestern. The interview had always been a huge deal, but ever since my less-than-stellar report card, Karl had been drilling into my head that it now meant *everything*. Only the strongest recommendation from the dean, plus an immediate upswing in my GPA, could secure my place at the one college that held the key to my future. There was no possible way Karl was going to let me out of the house the night before. I wouldn't be surprised if he had that whole Saturday mapped out with a full slate of prep sessions followed by an early bedtime.

I briefly considered asking Lisa for an alternate party date, but there was no way. She'd see a request like that as the perfect out. I had to just go with it and trust that I'd find a way around the Karl issue when the time came.

Meanwhile, Trista and I had planning to do. We'd agreed that making the party a successful transition of power required finesse. Everyone, including the Populazzi, had to know that *I* was the one putting it together. Yet to make it magnetic enough, Trista had to secretly call the shots.

Her first priority was my guest list. It was a work in progress. She e-mailed me the first draft while we talked on the phone and played with it over the next couple days until she was satisfied.

There were lots of people on the list I didn't know, but I wasn't surprised by most of her picks. Naturally, I'd invite the Populazzi from every class, including the seniors. All the upper-level Cubby Crews who had made the cut for Eddie's party were invited, though Kristie's now-ex-boyfriend Eric was *not*. The DangerZones were in, with the notable exceptions of Nate Wetherill and his now-DangerZone girlfriend, Dinah.

Even some college kids were on Trista's list, mostly recent Chrysella alums who'd been Populazzi. Some Populazzi from nearby schools made the cut, too. The Pennsbrook Populazzi, thankfully, were too far away to be on Trista's radar.

Everyone on the list would jump at a chance to come to a Trista Camello spring party, but we needed them just as eager to come to *mine*, even though some key people on the list barely knew me or didn't know me at all. We decided to do a Facebook event invitation that included a totally hot picture of Trista and me together and said flat-out that Trista was canceling her spring party this year because mine would be so much better.

Aside from the Facebook invitation, Trista wanted to invite two people via a separate e-mail: Seth Minkoff and Jordan Ross. They were weird picks. I knew Seth—or at least I knew *of* him. He was in my physics class. I had always thought of him and Jordan as hard-core Computer Dorks, barely a Tower tier above Robert Schwarner and Gabe Friedman. I had even seen the two of them barreling down the hall singing Monty Python's "The Lumberjack Song."

Dressed in red flannel lumberjack shirts.

On several occasions.

I couldn't fathom why Trista wanted them, but she said she always included a couple of charity cases on her guest lists. It was her way of giving back. I sent them an e-mail and invited them.

The person I *didn't* invite was Claudia. It felt horribly wrong to leave her out, but I knew from the moment Trista had come up with the plan that I'd have to. I couldn't risk having Claudia in the same place as Marsh and Ree-Ree. She knew the two of them were together now—I'd told her they'd "started" dating about a month after Eddie's party. But Claudia still wasn't over

Marsh, so I worried about what she might say to them—and I worried more about what they might say to her in return.

Better to keep her in the dark. I hadn't told her anything about the party—not the idea of it, not the lunches with my dad leading up to it, nothing. It was hard censoring myself that way, but I'd done a good job. She had no idea, and she never would.

My biggest hurdle was still Karl, but I had come up with what I thought was a brilliant excuse. I said Saturday was Trista's birthday; she was having a full-weekend slumber party at her house to celebrate, and she'd be devastated if I weren't there. Karl liked Trista enough to be sympathetic, but he was adamant: any other weekend but *not* when I was meeting Dean Jaffe at the end of it. No amount of begging or cajoling changed his mind, so eventually I had to bring out the big guns: Trista herself came over for dinner.

As always, she was brilliant. She kissed up to Karl like crazy and assured him over and over that she would personally guarantee I got enough sleep and made it home bright and early Sunday to get ready for the lunch. She even used the NFL to help make her case. Most teams rarely practiced hard the day before a big game, she said. They busted their butts all week but pared it back the day before, to make sure all the players were healthy and rested when they needed it most. If I stayed home and stressed both nights before my interview, I might psych myself out and freeze up in front of Dean Jaffe. But if I spent those days relaxing at Trista's, I'd be fresh, calm, and ready for anything. This was my Super Bowl, and if Karl let me prep for it with a weekend at Trista's, I'd not only win it, I'd even beat the spread.

Bringing in both football *and* gambling was pure genius. Karl couldn't resist. He gave his permission, but I considered it tenuous at best. It was vital that I give him no reason whatsoever to reconsider, so I didn't complain even as my semigrounding started to make me crazy.

My cell rang and I checked the caller ID: Claudia. It was a week before my party, and I was trying to slog my way through a novel. Once upon a time, huddling in my room with a book would have been a near-perfect Saturday night, but now I couldn't even concentrate—I was too tortured imagining Trista and the gang out dancing without me. Talking to Claudia would be the perfect distraction.

"Know what the problem is with finally getting a life?" I asked as I answered the phone. "You totally miss it when it's gone."

Silence. Then, "You're having a party?"

My brain whirled. How did she know?

I raced to my computer, surfed to Facebook, and scanned my wall. Trista must have had everyone post before they went out tonight. It started with Trista's *"Miz Hostess—Countdown 1 week 2 MEGA-CHIW par-tay! Super LA need not apply!"* Then Kristie weighed in: *"Hey C—LMK if U need help setting up. So X-ited!"* Ree-Ree and Gemma came next, and all their postings inspired others to write about their own excitement, most likely to prove to the Facebook-sphere how cool they were to merit an invitation.

This was not supposed to happen. The party had its own event page. *That's* where everyone had been commenting, not on my wall where Claudia could see it!

"Cara?"

She sounded so small and uncertain. It was completely unlike her. I felt horrible.

"Yeah . . . I'm having a party."

"And you weren't going to invite me?"

"I wanted to invite you. It's just . . . Marsh and Ree-Ree . . ."

"You told me about Marsh and Ree-Ree. I know they're to-gether now. You know I know that."

I felt my rib cage squeezing in on my heart and lungs. I had no idea how to explain this without telling Claudia what I'd revealed about her and how I'd lied about Marsh and Ree-Ree getting together *after* Eddie's party. I felt sick to my stomach imagining how she'd react, and even though I knew I deserved her anger, it didn't make me any more eager for it.

Then suddenly I realized I had a way out. I could tell Claudia a *half* truth, one that wouldn't hurt her feelings as much . . . and maybe wouldn't make me quite so despicable.

"It's not you, Claude. It's Ree-Ree. She's crazy jealous. If she saw you and Marsh and got even the vaguest idea that you were ever together, she'd go nuclear. Party-destroying nuclear. And the party is supposed to take me from Penultimate to Supreme Populazzi, so if the party's destroyed—"

"Wait—you're saying you were keeping the party from me for the sake of the Ladder?"

"Yes."

My ribs were closing in tighter. Would she believe me?

"Well, that's madness," she said. "After all the work we've done, do you seriously think I'd *ever* get in the way of the Ladder? Don't you know me better than that?"

"I do! But I also know you'd love to come to the party, so I figured if you didn't know about it, you wouldn't have to feel bad about not going."

"Why wouldn't I go?" Claudia asked.

Um—wasn't that what we were just talking about?

"Because . . ." I floundered, "you just said you wouldn't want to get in the way of the Ladder . . . and Ree-Ree seeing you *would* get in the way . . . or it *could* . . ."

"Only if Ree-Ree suspected Marsh and I had a thing," Claudia said, "which she won't."

"She won't?"

"No. Not if I pretend Marsh and I have never met."

"But . . ." My brain spun with a million contradictions before I truly took in what she meant. "You really . . . you would do that?"

"Of course! If I act like I don't know him, Ree-Ree can't get jealous. She never saw me at the other party, she has no idea who I am . . . she'd never even suspect. I don't have to say a word to Marsh. Or her. I won't even *look* at either one of them. No interaction, no jealousy, no danger to the Ladder."

And no chance Marsh or Ree-Ree would say something to Claudia that I didn't want her to hear. I was still running her solution around my brain at hyperspeed to look for holes, but I found only one. "You're sure you'll be able to stay away from him?" I asked.

"Cara . . . a little credit. It's not like I was in love with Marsh—we hung out one night, and that was months ago. I'm pretty sure I can find other things to do than moon over him and bother his jealous girlfriend. I don't know if you're aware, but I have a history of great success at Populazzi parties."

My rib cage finally unclenched as I laughed out loud. "Yeah, you do."

"So how did you get Karl to let you have the party at the house? Aren't you practically grounded?"

"Um . . . the party's not here. It's at my dad's house."

"What? The Sperm Donor? And the Bar Wench? How have

you not been telling me about this! I'm shutting up now. You're spilling. I want to know everything!"

Claudia and I talked for hours, and I filled her in on the whole story of the party, beginning to end. I even sent her the Facebook event page link so she could check out the invitation and guest list. Though Claudia still thought it was crazy that I hadn't told her everything immediately, she understood my motivation. She agreed that the party was the perfect way for Trista and me to publicly switch places, but it had to go off without a hitch. If all went well, I'd be seen as Supreme Populazzi by the time it was over, with Trista simply my highest-ranking Penultimate.

I felt great about the plan. To be honest, it was already working. The party was all anyone was talking about at school. And whenever someone would ask Trista about it, she'd say something like "I really don't know. You'd have to talk to Cara—this one's all her. It's going to be epic, though. I wouldn't miss it for anything." Ree-Ree, Kristie, and Gemma, who was back from her latest tournament, said similar things.

It's not that they knew about the master plan—they didn't—but they did know I was planning a party that would put every other event of the year to shame. Everyone knew it, and people looked at me with newfound respect and admiration. My guest list determined who was *someone.* Everyone wanted to be my friend. Even senior class Populazzi went out of their way to talk to me.

And for the first time in my life, I wasn't worried about what to say. The party was on my mind 24/7. I was constantly talking to Trista to compile lists of everything I needed: all the right music, food, and decorations. I spent every day between the end of school and dinnertime racing around to buy supplies. I paid for it all with my credit card—I'd find an explanation for Karl later. I stayed up late every night burning CDs and making iPod playlists. In my head I staged every square inch of Dad's house and choreographed every second of the party the way I wanted it to unfold. I could make scintillating conversation about this party to *anyone,* and people always lit up at the sight of me, like they always had for Trista.

The party hadn't even happened yet, and already I felt like *that girl:* that beautiful, confident, charming girl I'd always admired but never dreamed I could be.

I was so close. I just needed to seal the deal.

Chapter *thirty-three*

$\mathcal{F}$riday, the day before the party, I was so excited I could barely breathe. Not that there was time to be nervous: I had a zillion things to do and just over twenty-four hours to get it all done.

Thankfully, I had Claudia. She was as excited about the party as I was. She said in some ways, it felt like her ascension to Supreme Populazzi, too, and she wanted to be as involved as possible. This was a huge break for me, since Trista had recommended the Populazzi *not* be involved. That way, according to Trista, they'd be as surprised by the finished place as anyone, and it would be clearer even to them that the party was mine alone. I saw her point, but without Claudia's help, there's no way I could have managed it all.

I raced home after school and got my stuff together. The trunk of my car was already packed with decorations I'd amassed over the past couple weeks, but I had several more bags of stuff, all of which I'd tucked inside suitcases stored in the garage so Karl and Mom wouldn't see. I loaded the bags into my back seat, then took a trip inside to grab my clothes, makeup, and all the other personal things I'd need. Once I'd checked and rechecked to make sure I hadn't left anything out, I ducked back in to say goodbye.

"Tell Trista happy birthday for us," Mom said.

"I will."

"Get a good night's sleep tomorrow," Karl added. "And make sure you're home by eleven Sunday morning. Dean Jaffe's coming at noon and I want you here and ready."

"Got it. That'll be great."

"It better be," Karl said. "You need to put on the show of your life to make up for your grades last semester."

"I will. I totally will."

I could tell by Karl's face that I could've been more enthusiastic, but my mind was halfway out the door, and I was dying to follow it. I called out a last goodbye, then raced to the car and drove to Wegmans, where I was meeting Claudia.

The plan was to get all the food and drinks for the party, load them into Claudia's car, then caravan to Dad's. He had arranged for his whole family to be away for the weekend, so Claudia and I would have all night and all day tomorrow to prepare.

Claudia couldn't get over the fact that she was going to see my dad. She vaguely remembered meeting him at my sixth birthday party, but that was it. And she had *never* seen the Bar Wench. We couldn't stop talking about it at Wegmans, and we were still at it as we walked up to his front door with our first armfuls of party food.

"What if I think your dad's cute, too?" Claudia asked after we rang the bell. "Wouldn't it be wrong?"

"And weirdly incestuous."

"Very Greek drama. Somebody'd have to poke their eyes out for sure. But who?"

That's when the Bar Wench opened the door. Awesome.

"Hello, ladies," she said. The Bar Wench was the same age as my dad, but her skin looked more sun-dried and weathered. She tried to hide that with thick foundation, but it pooled in the tiny cracks around her eyes, making the fissures more pronounced than they would have been otherwise. She wore her dyed black hair in a pixie cut that had probably been very sexy when she was in her early twenties, but now it just seemed mannish. She wasn't dressed yet—she wore slippers and a royal blue silk bathrobe.

With no small amount of bitterness, she told us she had arranged full-weekend sleepovers for both her boys, and she and Dad would be heading down the shore. They'd all be back late Sunday afternoon, and she expected to find the house in the same condition it was in right now. That said, she retreated upstairs. She never once attempted to make any kind of physical contact with me, and she never introduced herself to Claudia.

"She must know she's world-renowned as the Bar Wench," Claudia explained. "It's like being Mick Jagger; it's superfluous to introduce yourself."

An hour later, we'd unloaded both our cars and managed to get everything we needed into the fridge, when we heard my dad jogging down the stairs.

"Cair, baby? That you down there?"

"'Cair, baby'?" Claudia whispered. "What is he, a lounge act?"

Pretty close. At least he looked the part in his white suit with the black silk shirt.

"Aha!" He pointed at Claudia. "The braids! You had those ten years ago. *You* are *Claudia!*"

"Did you really recognize the braids," Claudia asked, "or is it that you knew I was coming?"

"Little of each," Dad said. Then he beckoned for us to lean

in close. "I left a surprise for you in the hall closet. Lise doesn't have to know." He put his fingers to his lips as the Bar Wench clip-clopped downstairs, wearing a pantsuit that clung a little too tightly to her middle.

"Have fun tomorrow," Dad said. "Make sure you tell people they can crash here if they're too drunk to drive."

"But *downstairs.* Everything needs to stay *downstairs,*" the Bar Wench added. Dad laughed as he led her out of the house, urging her not to worry. The last thing we heard her mutter before the door closed was ". . . hate the thought of those kids getting into my underwear drawer . . ."

"I'm getting into her underwear drawer right now," I said.

"Totally. What do you think the surprise is?"

We ran to the closet. All the way in the back was a full keg on a small rolling dolly, and it had a note taped to it that said, "Have fun! Love, Dad."

"Oh my God, I kind of love Leonard Leonard," Claudia said.

"It's pretty cool," I agreed, even as I heard Mom's voice in my head railing over what kind of parent would possibly think it was okay to provide a keg of beer for an underage party.

Claudia and I stayed up until the wee hours of the morning prepping the house per Trista's guidelines. We put out tea candles; we strung miles of white twinkle lights; we put colored gels over bulbs. We made sure every room would have music, either a stereo playing CDs or a speaker dock hooked to an iPod. We tested every connection to make sure everything worked. We rolled the keg from the closet to the kitchen. We put tiki torches out on the massive back porch and made sure they were filled with fluid. We put out lighters so we wouldn't have to look for them when it was time to light the torches and candles. We put out extra chairs so people could hang outside and look at the lake beyond Dad's backyard. We pushed back furniture in the living room to create a dance area. We checked all the supplies in the bathrooms. We made a timeline and a checklist for everything we needed to do the next day: set out snacks, drinks, ice, cups, utensils, napkins; order pizzas; and of course get gorgeous.

By the time we were done, we were exhausted and starving. We didn't want to bust into the party food or get anything dirty by attempting to cook, so we took great pleasure in raiding the Bar Wench's pantry, and even greater pleasure in crashing on her bed.

We didn't wake up until early afternoon. Claudia and I both felt the same frizzle of nerves. We couldn't wait for the remaining hours to zoom by so we could finally get to the party, but we also wanted them to drag so we'd have time to get everything done.

We worked through our checklist until 6:30, when I went upstairs to start getting myself ready. The plan was for me to beautify while Claude stayed on party prep. Trista, Ree-Ree, Kristie, and Gemma were coming over around 8:00, at which point Claudia planned to disappear upstairs both to get herself ready and to stay far away from Ree-Ree. Once the party was rolling, Claudia would slip downstairs, blend into the crowd, and enjoy.

"Oh my God, Cara," Claudia gaped when I joined her back in the kitchen. "You *are* Supreme Populazzi."

"You think?"

She pulled me into the dining room, with its floor-to-ceiling mirrors, and we both stared at my reflection. My dress had a close-fitted, gold-brocade tank top belted with a sleek, sparkly black miniskirt. I wore chunky black heels, but my hair was the ultimate accessory, hanging wild and free over my shoulders. My makeup was subtle but perfect.

Honestly? I looked hot.

"This is it, Cara . . ." Claudia said, and I finished her thought before she could say it: "The night everything changes." I led her back into the kitchen and poured us drinks so we could toast our success: Malibu rum and pineapple juice for me, club soda for her.

"Last time, we *attended* a Populazzi party; today you're *throwing* a Populazzi party," Claudia said.

"To the Ladder?" I offered.

"To the Ladder."

We clinked glasses as the doorbell rang. Claudia raced upstairs. The junior class Populazzi had arrived.

Once Claudia was out of sight, I let the girls in. They of course looked incredible. We all hugged and kissed like it had been ages, which it felt like it had.

"So, so CHIW, Cara," Trista said, taking in the scene from the foyer. "Show us everything."

I led them from room to room, basking in their awe. Gemma, Ree-Ree, and Kristie were especially impressed. They hadn't seen the house before, and I could tell they were doubly blown away by its decorated glory.

The first guests rang the bell at 8:15, fifteen minutes before the party was scheduled to start. Trista stopped me from letting them in.

"So uncool to show up early for a party. No one gets in until a half hour after it starts."

"But people are standing there," I said, peering through the peephole.

"Good. Then they'll be all primed and ready when we finally open the doors."

Trista had me turn up the music so people would hear it

thrumming outside the house. She poured us all drinks, then had us enjoy them by the door, so all the guests outside would hear us talking and laughing and know they were in for a good time.

I felt bad leaving people out there, especially once eight thirty came and they were actually on time, but I trusted Trista. The four of us each had another drink, and at a quarter of nine, she had me turn the music even louder.

"Preshow time!" she screamed.

She pulled the drapes across the two living room windows, which faced out to the front yard. She pushed a floor lamp a couple feet behind each. "Who's doing the silhouette dance?"

Gemma and Ree-Ree jumped for it. They each stood between a lamp and a window and gyrated to the music. The crowd outside hooted and hollered, and Trista and I joined in the cheers. At one point I looked over my shoulder and saw Claudia peeking out from upstairs. She caught my eye and made a face at the grinding girls. I shrugged and laughed.

"Tagging out!" Gemma called.

"Really?" I asked as Ree-Ree dragged me to her old spot.

"It's your party, Cara!" Trista said. "You've got to work it!"

Trista herself was already working it, to what sounded like the delight of the crowd outside. I downed the rest of my drink in a single gulp of courage, so everything faded away except the music. I danced. I didn't even sense time passing, but suddenly Trista grabbed my hand, pulled me to the door, and shouted that it was "time to get this party started!"

At her nod, I threw open the front door, and people flooded in.

The biggest night of my high school career had officially begun.

Chapter *thirty-four*

$\mathcal{I}$ was still so dizzy and fuzzy from the dancing and the drinks that the stream of people blurred together. Trista greeted each one with a smile, sometimes a hug, a secret joke, a compliment, a quick anecdote, or an observation that let the person know he or she mattered, because Trista noticed something special about them. Once she was done, she sent each guest to me: "our hostess for the night."

While I'd been a master conversationalist leading up to the party, now that it was here, my go-to topic was moot. What was I supposed to say to a sea of people I barely knew? I ended up following Trista's mastery with "hello," "hi," or, if I was feeling particularly silver-tongued, "thanks for coming."

The line of partiers seemed endless. Once everyone was inside, the whole house vibrated with a million different voices.

"Congratulations." Trista smiled. "Your party's a success."

She wanted us to go down to the bar and meet our friends, but I said I'd catch up later. I wanted to walk through the whole party and see it in action for myself.

Every room was crammed with people. In the kitchen they chatted in clusters around trays of snacks. Out on the porch, they sat or leaned against the rail and talked as they took in the view of the lake, the flickering tiki lights dancing on their faces. Back inside, people sprawled in the family room, and in the living room they took a cue from our preshow and danced.

In the basement the noise roared even louder. This was the true crux of the party. Someone had turned on the Wii, and people gathered around to play or watch. The pool table was surrounded as well, but when I saw Eddie, I pushed through the crowd to wrap my arms around him.

"Hey," I said.

"Hey, Cara. Great party."

"Thanks. I worked really hard on it."

"Yeah, you did."

There was something in his voice I didn't like. I decided to ignore it. "Where are the girls?"

"Down there." He nodded to the pub. "While you're there, can you get me another bottle of beer?"

"Sure."

"Thanks." He gave me a quick kiss on the lips, then leaned over to line up his next shot.

The pub room was jammed. People sat two to a seat at the tables, and a knot of others agonized over the jukebox buttons. The dance floor was packed.

"Cara!" Trista squealed, and I turned to see her and Gemma dancing on the bar. Brett was playing bartender, and while I had always thought he seemed cool and distant, this was apparently his element. He took requests, but what he seemed to enjoy most was scrutinizing people, then offering them the perfect drink for their personalities. "You're a supercharged dude who's always amped, but when you kick it, you kick it hard-core. You need Hpnotiq and Red Bull."

Amazing—he was the Alcohol Psychic.

"Brett, hook this girl up!" Trista cried as I got to the bar. Brett covered his eyes with one hand, pointed around with the other, then stopped and opened his eyes. He grabbed the bottle he was pointing to, poured a shot, and slid it down the bar. It stopped right in front of me.

"What is it?" I asked him.

"Don't ask. It's perfect for you. Just drink it down."

Those were more words than he had said directly to me in my whole time as a Populazzi. I took them seriously and drank. The taste was hideous.

"It gets better later." Brett winked. "Trust me."

"Girlfriend, get your butt up on this bar and start dancing!" said Gemma. "This is your party. Grab the spotlight!"

With Brett's tonic working its way through me, I was ready. Trista and Gemma both reached out to help me up; but before I could make it, Trista let her arm go limp.

"Oh no, look!" She pointed at the pub tables. "No more pretzels!"

"I'll get more later," I said. But Trista said empty snack bowls were poor party protocol. And since I'm a sucker for both alliteration and Trista's hosting skills, I gathered the bowls to go refill them. Trista had Brett give me one more shot for the road. I grabbed a beer for Eddie and headed up to the pool table.

I was just wondering if Claudia had joined the party yet when I saw her. She was playing Dance Dance Revolution on the Wii with Ree-Ree while Marsh cheered them on.

My rib cage squeezed my lungs to nothing. I staggered closer. I hoped Brett's drinks were so strong I was hallucinating.

I wasn't.

"Claude?" I croaked. "Can I talk to you a second?"

"Now?" she asked, clearly unhappy about the idea.

I nodded.

"Okay. Marsh, wanna step in?"

"Sure!" He stood by Claudia's pad until they could time it perfectly: she jumped off, he jumped on, and they made the wand hand-off without Claudia's Mii missing a beat.

"What are you doing?" I hissed when I'd pulled her aside.

"Ree-Ree came up to *me!* She said she liked my dress, and we started talking. She's really nice."

"She's really nice" wasn't a common first response to Ree-Ree. This was weird.

"What about Marsh?" I asked. "I thought you weren't going to speak to him."

"Right, 'cause that wouldn't have been weird at all when Ree-Ree introduced us," Claudia said. "Fear not for the Ladder, Cara. Marsh and I both acted like we'd never met before. Ree-Ree has no idea. It's fine. We're having fun!"

Eddie wrapped me in a bear hug from behind and plucked his beer from my hand. "You are the *best girlfriend ever,* Cara!"

Claudia ran back to her game. "Outta the way, Marsh; I'm back in!"

"Ooh, are you filling those?" Eddie nodded to the pretzel bowls in my hand. " 'Cause we're almost out of chips and guac here, too."

Chips and guac. Poor party protocol. I grabbed the additional bowls and took everything upstairs. I stumbled on the way up and laughed so hard that I had to sit a minute on the steps. Brett's shots were working full force now, and I liked it. It helped me ignore the nagging sense of Very Not Good I'd had back with Claudia, Marsh, and Ree-Ree.

I got the snack bowls refilled, but it seemed like suddenly everyone needed something: more ice, more mixers, more candy, more nuts, more cheese, more dip . . .

"How are you not up here dancing yet?" Trista called down from the bar on one of my many trips to the pub room.

"I know! There's so much stuff to do; I feel like I haven't had a break!"

"Totally get it. That's hosting. But look at the result: the most CHIW-lacious party of the year! Brett, hook her up. Poor girl needs it bad."

Brett hooked me up with a shot of something colorful and fruity this time, and its fuzzy haze helped a lot. Running around filling and delivering is much more fun when you're buzzed enough to make it feel like you're dancing as you go.

Hours whizzed by like this, until suddenly it was very late and several guests—several Super LA guests—started leaving. That's when I realized I hadn't documented a single moment of the party! I grabbed my phone and put it in video mode, but I was way too wasted to shoot anything coherent. I just kept the camera on and cruised all around the house and out on the deck. I was a one-person reality TV crew, catching the action as it unfolded. Maybe someday I'd edit the footage and send it to MTV. It could start a hot new series: *High School House Party!* or maybe *House Party High!*

As I stumbled/giggled/tripped down the stairs, I turned the camera on myself. "Testing, one-two-three-four-five-six-seven . . ."

I forgot what comes after seven.

I tripped and fell on the last step.

"Public service announcement," I said into the camera. "Don't drink and walk. Very dangerous."

I roamed through the pool room and the pub with the video running, zooming in for extreme close-ups of random people's anatomy.

"Ear cam!" Zoom to an ear.

"Nose cam!" Zoom to a nose.

"Drool cam!" Zoom in on someone fast asleep in a chair.

The close-ups were fun. I did a bunch more.

I turned the camera back on myself. "Super-spy video!" I whispered.

I wandered the rest of the basement, down the hall that branched into all the little nook areas. I softly hummed what sounded to me like spy music and stretched the camera into each nook. I didn't know if anyone was in them or not—it was mystery footage. That was how I finished each time. I'd pull my arm back and do an extreme close-up of my face as I whispered dramatically, *"Mystery footage!"*

I had my outstretched arm and camera in one of the nooks and was about to pull it back out when I heard weird noises.

Not weird. I recognized those noises! People making out! Reality show gold! I let the camera keep rolling awhile and worked hard to stifle my giggles. Then I got a great idea. I leaped into the room and flipped on the lights.

"*Boo!* Say cheese!"

"OFF! TURN THAT CAMERA OFF!"

It was Trista's voice, so I automatically obeyed as she half scrambled/half fell off the lap of—whoa!—Seth Minkoff. *WHOA!* A strategically *undressed* Seth Minkoff!

"Oh my God!" I screamed.

"Shhhhh!" Trista hissed. "Turn out the lights!"

I did. "Trista, were you having sex with Seth Minkoff?"

"Um, I can answer that," Seth said. "Yes. Yes, she was."

"Shut up!" Trista snapped.

"What? I'm proud."

"Trista!" I wailed. "Brett's right in the next room!"

"And I'd like him to *stay* there, so get the hell out and shut the hell up!"

I staggered out, dazed, but then I heard loud clapping from the pub room. I realized that was a smart place to be. Another one of Brett's psychic cocktails would be really good right now.

Brett was there, but he had new dancers keeping him company. Ree-Ree was on the bar, and the applause was from the crowd encouraging Claudia to climb up as well. I couldn't believe Claudia was going to dance on a bar, but she looked elated as Ree-Ree helped her up.

I threaded my way through the crowd. "Hook me up, barkeep," I said to Brett. He slid me a shot glass of something purple. Grape juice? I drank it. *Not* grape juice. Yow. I nodded for another.

"Ladies and gentlemen," Ree-Ree called out once Claudia was steadied. "I want you to meet my good friend and fellow bar dancer, The Amazing Miss Claudia!"

Applause from the room. I hooted.

"I have a special song picked out for Claudia, in honor of her beauty and her innocence. I say 'beauty,' even though most people would agree that her deathly pale skin and big spooky eyes are totally vomitous!"

My stomach dropped completely out of my body.

Ree-Ree had been *planning* this. She'd been building to it all night. She'd acted like Claudia's friend just so she could humiliate her in front of everyone. Claudia realized it, too, but she was too stunned and horrified to escape.

"Some might say that making out with her would be like making out with a corpse!" Ree-Ree said. "My own *boyfriend* said that! Can you believe it?"

The crowd roared, eating it up. Then Ree-Ree spoke gently to Claudia. "Did Cara tell you that, Claudia? Did she tell you Marsh said it was like making out with a dead person? Not that it's your fault." Ree-Ree turned again to the crowd. "It is *not* her fault, everyone, because our little corpse here had *never been kissed* until Marsh did her the favor a couple months ago. A couple *months* ago! Virgin lips before that! A toast to virgin lips!"

"To virgin lips!" a huge chunk of the room called out.

It was enough to unfreeze Claudia. "Excuse me," she whispered, then quickly climbed down behind the bar. She pushed her way out of the room with her head down.

"Come on! Stay! Dance!" Ree-Ree called as Claudia left. "I have a special song for you! Hit it, Gems!"

Gemma hit a button on the jukebox, and Madonna's "Like a Virgin" blared. What seemed like hundreds of voices laughed and cheered. Many of them sang along.

I ran out of the room. Claudia had a head start, and I had to push through a lot of people, but I finally saw her on the stairs, heading to the top floor.

"Claudia . . ." I wanted her to wheel around and scream at me, some Shakespearean invective in iambic pentameter that would damn my soul to eternal torment.

She didn't say anything. She didn't even stop. She walked into the guest room where she'd left her stuff, then started carefully returning everything to her bag.

"Claudia, let me explain—"

"It's obvious. You chose them."

I wanted to object, but all I could say was, "You weren't supposed to ever know."

It was hollow even to me. Claudia didn't bother to respond. She pulled her bag over her shoulder and walked back downstairs. I followed, but I didn't say anything until we were out of the house. The last thing I wanted was to call more attention to her.

"I'm coming with you," I said once we were outside.

"Don't. Your friends are waiting."

She got into her car and I watched her drive off. It was a beautiful spring night, but I wished it were freezing cold. I wished I were shivering in my little tank dress, maybe catching hypothermia. Some kind of real, physical torture so I would feel as horrible as I deserved.

Instead I took my still–pleasantly swimmy head and went back inside to my party, the greatest social event Chrysella Prep had seen all year.

The moment I walked in, Eddie pulled me into his arms. He and a knot of jocks were on their way to the kitchen, and he swept me along.

"Hey, Cara!" He gave my neck a nuzzle for the crowd.

"Hi."

Eddie saw my frown and laughed. "No way can you be upset about anything tonight. Look at all this! This is your big moment, right?"

I managed a small smile. "Right."

"Okay, someone needs a drink."

Yes. Eddie was right. I needed a drink. I would feel far, far less awful if I had another drink. I saw champagne in the kitchen. Had Claudia and I bought champagne? Didn't matter. I let Eddie pour me a glass and I drank it down like water. I tried to walk to the couch after that, but my knees buckled. I laughed and tried again . . . but I fell to the floor.

Now *that* was funny.

"See? You're having a good time," Eddie said. He put an arm around me and half led/half carried me to the couch, where he deposited me among a sea of throw pillows. I closed my eyes.

"Thanks, Eddie. I love you."

"You're funny. Here."

He tucked a blanket over me and I snuggled into it, letting the party fade into a mottled wail of white noise.

I must have fallen asleep, because when I opened my eyes, everything was quiet. Quiet—and disgusting. I was lying on a couch in the family room, which was littered with half-eaten food, passed-out bodies, empty cups, and—oh God, vomit? Really?

My whole body felt heavy and cloudy, but I rose and staggered into the kitchen. Through the open sliding door that led to the deck, I could see it was still dark outside. Several flies danced around the boxes of unfinished pizzas. People had been smoking—even with the door open, the room reeked. A tower of cupcakes was decorated with snuffed cigarette butts. Someone had left the refrigerator door open.

I heard giggling upstairs and followed the sound to the master bedroom. An alarm rose in the part of me that was still functioning rationally. I opened the door and saw Brett Seward, fast asleep. He wore only his boxers and was sprawled out on the bed. Trista was the giggler. She stood in the doorway to the master bathroom.

"Trista?"

She waved me over. I followed and saw Ree-Ree and Marsh in their underwear, passed out asleep in my dad's Jacuzzi tub. It was filled with water.

"Trista! That isn't funny! They could have drowned!" I walked into the bathroom and reached between them to push open the drain.

"They didn't."

"Wait—what are you wearing?"

She had on a bright red teddy that was way too conservative to be one of her own. She couldn't have . . .

"Just a little something I found over there," she said, pointing to the dresser.

"You went into her underwear drawer?"

"She has some cute stuff. You know, for someone her age."

"I'm glad you're up," I said, letting it go. "You've got to help me clean. The place is a disaster."

"I'm not helping you clean."

"You have to!"

"No, I don't. I didn't even clean when the parties were at my own house. Why do you think my parents banned me from throwing them?"

This took a second to settle in. "Wait," I said. "You told me you weren't throwing the party so *I* could do it and build my reputation."

"And you were dumb enough to believe me. You threw me the greatest party I've ever had. Thank you."

"What? No. This was *my* party. We put it together for *me*. Everyone knew it was mine. They all talked to me about it. People I didn't even know talked to me about it."

"Cara, people don't even know who you are except in relation to me. Do you really think they would have shown up for a Cara Leonard party? I was the one who met them at the door; I had the crowd of people around me all night long; I was at the center of this whole night. Ask anyone where they were tonight, and every single one of them will say they were at Trista Camello's party."

I shook my head and glared at her. "You are going to help me clean this house, or I'm going to tell everything I know about you."

Trista met my glare. "No one will believe you. Not after this party. It was exactly what I needed. Anything you say now, I can bat away: jealous rumors from an ex-friend."

"An ex-friend?" I loathed myself for the way my voice broke over the words and for the tears starting to well behind my eyes. Hadn't I already known that Trista and I weren't really friends?

"It's over, Cara. I have to cut you loose. It was good talking to you about things, though. I really did like it."

"What if I promise not to say anything bad about you?"

Trista shook her head. "You could change your mind. And later there might be people who'd believe you. Good luck with the cleaning."

She had backed me out as she spoke and now shut the door in my face.

Had I just begged her to stay my friend?

I walked to the staircase landing and looked down over the horror of a house. I could see the very beginnings of sunrise through the window. Dad and the Bar Wench were coming back "in the late afternoon," which meant I had to start cleaning now, but even then it was doubtful I'd make enough progress. I collapsed into a chair to think about where to begin . . .

. . . and woke up with the sun glaring in on me. What time

was it? I picked my way downstairs and into the family room, stepping lightly over strewn bodies that made the house look like the Normandy shore at D-day. I peered at the clock on the mantel: twelve thirty.

Twelve thirty.

No. Nononononononono.

A million sirens screamed in my head. I was still wearing my dress. Could I get away with it? No. I had lain in God knows what when I fell asleep, and brown goo smeared down one side. I raced to the guest room, yanked off the dress, and pulled on a cute skirt and top from my duffle bag.

I peeked in the bathroom mirror. My curls were matted down on one side from sleeping on them. Luckily I had an elastic, and I pulled together a ponytail. Makeup had smeared my face into a preschool finger painting. I sopped up the worst with a wet washcloth. No time to shower, but I reeked of alcohol. I scoured the vanity for perfume but found only air freshener. It would have to do. I sprayed it all over my body, then raced downstairs.

My phone. Where was my phone? I ran back up, but I couldn't find it with my stuff. I grabbed one of Dad's cordless phones and called my number, running from room to room and listening for the ring.

When I got to the pub room, I saw my cell sitting on the bar. It wasn't ringing. I hadn't charged it and it was dead. It was amazing I'd even found it. I hoped that was a good omen.

I ran back upstairs. If I murdered the speed limit, there was a chance I'd still make it for Dean Jaffe. Yes, it meant leaving Dad with a filthy house full of sleeping strangers—which was incomprehensible—but at that moment the alternative seemed even worse.

I drove no less than eighty miles an hour the whole way and walked into my house at exactly one o'clock. I wasn't early like Karl had wanted, but I was right on time.

"Hi!" I called.

Karl and Mom were sitting in the family room, all dressed up. Mom looked like she had been crying, which made no sense at all. Maybe her allergies were acting up. Dean Jaffe wasn't there yet. I walked in and stood between them. "Are you guys as excited as I am?"

"Hey, Cara," Karl said cheerily, "how come you smell like boozy air freshener and look like a two-bit prostitute after a rough night?"

"What?"

"Dean Jaffe left a half hour ago," Mom said. "Lunch was at noon. We asked you to be home at eleven."

"No! Lunch was one o'clock! I know it was one o'clock!"

"Noon," Karl said. "But of course being a Northwestern man, Dean Jaffe was here early, at eleven forty-five. By noon he was concerned that you hadn't arrived. By twelve fifteen he suspected this was your way of showing your uncertainty about Northwestern. By twelve thirty he decided that you weren't mature enough to attend his school. Congratulations, Cara. You've officially ruined your life."

The phone rang. Neither Mom nor Karl showed any interest in answering it, until Mom noticed the caller ID. She looked at the phone like it was an alien, then reached over and picked it up.

"Lenny?"

Chapter *thirty-five*

In one of the Elizabeth George mysteries I'd been reading, a vicar dies by hemlock poisoning. The vicar knew he was dying but was powerless to do anything about it as he suffered forceful seizure after seizure. His tongue swelled to several times its size, filling his mouth and cutting off his air. It succeeded in doing this despite the fact that the vicar had nearly managed to chew it off. He had clawed his face in agony, one of his eyeballs had burst from the pressure of his asphyxiation, and he was tortured to the point where it must have been sheer, blissful pleasure to surrender to death.

My next several hours were a lot like that.

Not surprisingly, Dad had called because he had come back early from the shore to find Hiroshima in his house. Even across our living room, I could hear the Bar Wench screeching, "My underwear drawer!" in the background.

From the second-hand description I got through my mom, it sounded like the remaining party guests were in no hurry to leave, so the Bar Wench had Dad call the police. That got rid of everyone, though there was still a mess of epic proportions. I of course volunteered to clean it up, but Mom said they were getting a professional cleaning crew. I was no longer welcome anywhere near Dad's house. If I showed up there, the Bar Wench swore she'd get a restraining order. Dad himself wasn't talking about legal action, but he did have Mom tell me that right now, he had no desire to see me ever again.

This was bad enough, but of course the phone call led Mom and Karl to ask a rash of obvious questions. What the hell was I doing at my dad's house when I was supposed to be at a party at Trista's, for example. And since when the hell was I even talking to my dad at all?

Much as I begged the ground to open up and swallow me whole, it somehow failed to do so, which meant I actually had to stand there and explain everything to them. Every lie, every deception, every intricate, layered ruse.

Mom sobbed. Karl seethed.

And when it was over, they kept sobbing and seething. They didn't scream. They didn't shout. Karl didn't calmly hand down one of his baroque punishments. They just sat there. For ages. Finally Karl turned to Mom and quietly asked, "How come Lenny's the lucky one who doesn't have to see her again?"

"I wish I knew," Mom said.

I stood there, waiting for my punishment, my lecture, *something*—but nothing ever came.

I went up to my room, but I didn't know what to do with myself. There was no one I could call. I couldn't sleep. I couldn't concentrate on anything. I felt too much. I felt guilty and heartbroken. I felt furious at Trista, at Ree-Ree, at Eddie . . .

but mostly at myself. I hated myself. I *loathed* myself. I desperately wanted to get away from myself, to disconnect, to shut myself off and escape my own brain.

I grabbed the car keys.

I knew Mom and Karl wouldn't stop me. It seemed I was as dead to them as I wanted to be to myself. Remembering Trista's advice, I eschewed Dunkin' Donuts and went straight for the McDonald's drive-through. I didn't get a burger. I got four thirty-two-ounce Chocolate Triple Thick Shakes and five large orders of french fries. I popped the top on one of the shakes immediately and started dipping and munching as I drove home. It felt good. I didn't have to think. I could concentrate on my favorite mix of flavors: the crispy saltiness of the fries and the sweet, smooth richness of the shake.

When I got home, I noticed Karl's car wasn't there. He and mom must have gone out. Good. Better.

I put the top back on the shake, grabbed my tray of drinks and bag of fries, ran up to my room, and shut the door. I tried to eat slowly so I could savor the taste, but that left too much time to think. It was better, far better, if I just stuffed—dipped and ate, dipped and ate, dipped and ate, breaking it up every now and then with a huge swig of shake.

By the time I was halfway through the feast my stomach felt painfully distended, and I didn't even like the taste of fries and shake anymore, but if I stopped, I'd have to go back to feeling, and that wasn't an option. So I kept going. I wanted the dipping, eating, and swigging to go on forever.

Too soon it was over. I'd finished everything, and I was left with nothing but the feeling of all that food—a thick poison sloshing in my belly. I thought I might throw up without even trying.

I crawled into the bathroom and shut the door. I had never

asked Trista *how* she made herself throw up. I just assumed she stuck her finger down her throat. I lifted the lid of the toilet. The faint scent of disinfectant filled my nose and made me even more nauseous.

Good. Maybe that would help.

I leaned forward, resting my forearm on the edge of the toilet seat and reaching a finger down my throat as far as it could go.

I gagged. I coughed.

I didn't throw up.

I tried it again and again. My fingernails rasped the back of my throat.

Nothing. Coughing and gagging, that was it.

I began to panic. What if I couldn't do it? What if I was stuck with everything I'd eaten? I could feel the mass of it in my stomach, large and bulbous and festering. I couldn't keep it inside me. I'd lose my mind if I had to.

I leaned further over the bowl, thrusting my finger deeper and deeper, swirling and scratching and searching for the trigger that would finally end the—

Bliss! A waterfall of half-digested shake and French fries poured out of me. Immediately, I dove back in, ignoring my watering eyes and running nose. My body knew what I wanted now, and soon another lava flow erupted. I was purging; purging my sins, triumphantly scraping them out of my body over and over until there was nothing left.

I was empty.

I was also dizzy.

My heart raced and pounded like I was being chased, but I had no energy to run.

I curled up on the oval bath rug and went to sleep.

When I woke up, I couldn't swallow. For just a second, I didn't know why.

Then the rancid sweet smell hit me and I remembered.

I reached up and flushed it away without even looking,

My teeth felt mossy. My jaw ached and the glands beneath were swollen like golf balls. I could smell the sick on my hand. I had to wash it away. I tried to stand, but I was too woozy. I rested on the rug a bit then used the sink to pull myself up. I saw myself in the mirror: Red, watery, and blotchy. I ran the tap and splashed cold water on my face.

I had no idea how this worked for Trista two or three times a week. If she thought she wasn't a "real" bulimic, she was crazy. I felt completely wrecked . . . but the worst part was I could already sense every hideous feeling I thought I'd flushed away still lurking, just waiting to pounce on me again.

I tried to put myself back together. I brushed my teeth, sipped a big glass of water, and popped a throat lozenge. I went back to my room, opened my window, and took another nap to try to clear my head.

When I woke up, I still felt completely lost. I went to my computer and checked my mail.

Trista Camello had invited me to join a new group on Facebook: Cara Leonard Is a Great Big Whore.

So it begins.

I clicked on the link and joined so I could read all the posts. Trista had been busy. She'd already put together a pretty large group. So far seventy-five people believed I was a Great Big Whore.

All the Populazzi were members of the group. Even Eddie, who I thought needed me to be his beard. I guess he now agreed with Trista that my word would be easily discredited. Nate Wetherill was a member. That was quite a coup, since I thought he never used his computer for anything but psyche-delic screen savers. He was kind enough to post an MP3 of his "Succubus" song for the group. There were lots of other mem-bers, many of whom I didn't know by name, but their profile pictures looked familiar: I'd seen them at my party less than twelve hours ago.

Sorry—I meant *Trista's* party.

The posts themselves were pretty fascinating. Some were even laughable, like the one from the Jock who said I'd man-aged to "cheer on" the entire basketball team during a five-minute time-out. Some were practically investigative reporting, like the Scenester who posted, *"The Many Faces of Cara Leonard,"* along with a frumpy picture of me from the start of the year, a picture of me as emo-girl, and a picture of me looking fabulous at the start of last night's party. Some posts took a grain of truth and ran with it, like one that started with my penchant for odd foods and extrapolated to me being part vampire. That, she explained, was why I did emo so well. Every post ended with *"Cara Leonard is a great big whore."*

The most recent post was from Trista. It reached out to any-one who might know people at Pennsbrook, so everyone could find out what I'd really been like before I came to Chrysella.

Time to leave my bedroom. Mom and Karl were back home, I realized. Their door was closed, but I could hear their TV. I went downstairs and heated some chicken noodle soup, which I ate in front of the TV until I was ready for bed. I figured I'd check the Facebook page again in the morning. No sense killing the suspense before then.

Sure enough, by the time I got up on Monday, the legions of people who thought I was a Great Big Whore had grown to one hundred fifty. Some of these were from different states. One was from Germany. Weird. Several new members were from Pennsbrook. None of them were people I knew well, but I recognized the names and faces. Not surprisingly, they dished all they knew about me, which was basically that I was a misfit who had only one friend and peed herself in class. Even that story got twisted over the course of several posts, until it seemed like Claudia and I were actually lesbian lovers who had made some kind of weird cultish pact to pee only in our pants and continued doing so right up until the day I left for Chrysella.

I probably should have been upset, maybe screaming for justice. I wasn't. I was numb.

When I walked into school, once again I felt every pair of eyes on me, but it was very different now. I didn't meet anyone's stare. I walked right to my locker. Hanging from its handle was a large diaper, heavy with something yellow I hoped was apple juice.

It didn't smell like apple juice.

The halls were not my friends. It seemed like everyone on every tier of the Tower had nothing more interesting to do than stare at me and laugh or make jokes. Gabe Friedman started singing Nate's "Succubus" song as I walked by, but he added his own touch: a beatbox. Robert was right next to Gabe and didn't join in. He looked at me sadly, then pointedly turned his back. A couple of Genius guys squatted and made *sssss* sounds as I walked past. A Cubby Crew of lesbians handed me a petition they'd signed begging me to renounce my own lesbianism, since I was giving the group a bad name.

I was thrilled when the bell rang, but class wasn't much better. The second I sat, everyone in a five-seat radius shifted away, leaving me a lonely island. I purposely hadn't sat near Archer, so he wasn't one of the people who moved, but I was sure he would have. He'd established long ago that he wasn't a fan of mine. Compared to him, the rest of the school was late to the party.

As for Mr. Woodward, it seemed like for once in his career, he wasn't sure how to handle the situation. I got the sense he didn't want to make things worse for me but didn't know how to make them better. He chose to basically ignore me, but I caught him tossing sympathetic glances my way. It was unbearable.

I didn't even dream of trying the cafeteria for lunch. I hit the vending machine for a Zone bar and Diet Coke and locked myself into my car. I tried calling Claudia, but of course she didn't answer. I'd been calling her since the party—calling, texting, e-mailing, Facebooking . . . she wasn't responding.

I wished everyone else was as disinterested in me as Claudia, but by Monday night Cara Leonard Is a Great Big Whore was up to two hundred members. By Tuesday morning it had climbed to 225, and among the newest members were all the Theater Geeks—including Archer Jain.

Every day held another surprise, and every day I'd find more strange things stuck to my locker. Every day people would feel a little braver and jeer a little louder in the halls. And every day I'd at some point catch Trista's eye, and she'd give me a smug smile that left no doubt as to who was in control.

I spent two weeks like this. It helped that the school year was almost over, and I could throw myself into studying. We had SATs, and I also had AP tests in English Language, English Literature, French, Physics, and U.S. History. My great scores on these were originally supposed to help me get into Northwestern. I understood that wasn't an option anymore, but other colleges were, so I wanted to do the best I could.

I tried contacting Claudia every day. Nothing.

I tried talking to Mom and Karl, but Karl wouldn't meet my eyes. Mom just sniffed and said she wasn't ready.

I saw Eddie walking through the halls with a new girlfriend. I hadn't even known we'd officially broken up. The girl was in a Cubby Crew called the Chasti-Tease. They took abstinence vows. Perfect.

Trista had said she'd destroy me, and she had. I suppose it served me right. Fly too close to the sun and you're asking to get burned.

One Monday I saw a small group of people bunched around a sign in the hall. I was curious, so I waited for them to clear away, then checked it out. It was another poster from the junior prom committee. A bunch of signs had been going up lately: information about tickets, corsage sales, tuxedo rentals . . . It seemed like there was a new set of flyers every day. Today's was asking for video footage. The committee wanted to edit together a junior year retrospective.

I had some video footage. I remembered stumbling through the party, shooting it with my iPhone. I thought I'd been capturing the greatest night of my life. Had you asked me then, I'd have imagined myself watching the footage constantly, editing it down to maybe five perfect minutes that I'd post on Facebook so everyone could revel in its fabulousness and comment again and again about how amazing the party had been and how amazing *I* was for throwing it.

As it turned out, I hadn't even looked at what I'd shot. I hadn't exactly been interested in reliving the night.

Yet the more I thought about the footage, the more I wanted to see it. I *needed* to see it. I'd been a walking callus for so long that I craved *feeling,* even if it meant slicing myself open and bleeding.

I waited until after school. The minute I got home, I hooked my phone into the computer. Better to watch it on the bigger screen. More potent. I plugged in my noise-canceling headphones to really immerse myself in the experience.

It was even harder to watch than I'd expected but not because of the content. I'd been so drunk when I'd shot it that the picture kept moving and swaying. I thought I might get seasick. The actual stuff I'd shot was pretty innocuous: people hanging out and having a great time at a party. Knowing what happened after made my stomach ache, but the footage itself was honestly pretty boring. At least it would be to anyone not featured in the shot.

I made myself watch anyway and take every bit of it in. It hurt and I deserved to hurt.

The image now was the deck. I'd taken the camera out there and filmed each little cluster of people. I remembered I'd wanted to capture the feel of the night as it was, so I hadn't tried to get people's attention or let them know I was shooting them. It was dark enough that it had worked easily—no one looked at the camera or acknowledged it in any way.

I saw group after group of people I couldn't name if I tried. Then I saw Eddie. He was standing with a Genius. Their heads were bent close, and they spoke in low voices.

"Have you come out to anyone at school?" the Genius asked.

"No, dude, no," Eddie said. *"You?"*

"Nah. So . . . um . . . you want to—"

That's when my camera swung over to a very drunk Cosmopolitan girl trying to use a funnel to pee off the deck like a guy.

I rewound to the Eddie conversation and watched it again. Wow.

He was on tape admitting he was gay. He didn't flat-out say it, but anyone who saw this would know. Eddie would freak if this got out.

I wondered if I'd caught more.

I kept watching, but I wasn't dragging myself through the mud now. I was fascinated.

I didn't see anything else between Eddie and the Genius, but a while later I'd caught part of a conversation between Kristie and her new boyfriend, Tyler.

"Why can't we leave?" Tyler asked.

"Trista wouldn't like it," Kristie said.

"So what? She's your friend. She'll get over it."

"She's not my friend! She's the social police—I hate it!"

Oh my God—this was amazing! I was dying to hear more, but the camera lurched to four guys stuffing peanuts up their noses, then seeing how far they could snort them across the room.

What had I been thinking? The Kristie conversation was gold!

I turned the sound all the way up to see if I could hear more in the background, but I couldn't.

The tape continued to roll. Soon I saw myself in a super-unflattering mega-close-up whispering, *Mystery footage!* A little bit later, the screen went dark and I heard weird noises that I knew now were Trista and Seth Minkoff.

The footage was going to end too soon, and it killed me. If I'd had any clue about what would happen later that night, I never would have listened to Trista and turned off my phone. Footage of Trista Camello with Seth Minkoff would be priceless.

"Boo! Say cheese!" I said on the computer. I had flicked on the lights, but the camera was unfocused.

Now it zoomed in on Trista's angry face. I hadn't gotten Seth in the shot. I could've kicked myself.

"OFF! TURN THAT CAMERA OFF!" Trista raged.

The image went wild as I lowered the phone. Was it showing the carpet? My leg? I couldn't tell. It kept moving around.

Wait a minute—why was it still moving around? It should have been off. When Trista had told me to turn it off, I had turned it off.

Hadn't I?

"Oh my God!" I screamed on the screen.

"Shhhhh! Turn out the lights!"

The image went dark, but the sound didn't stop.

It didn't stop!

I hadn't turned off the phone at all. I thought I had, but I was still taping! My heart raced as I kept listening.

"Trista, were you having sex with Seth Minkoff?"

"Um, I can answer that. Yes. Yes, she was."

"Shut up!"

"What? I'm proud."

"Trista! Brett's right in the next room!"

"And I'd like him to stay there, so get the hell out and shut the hell up!"

A minute later, the screen wasn't dark anymore. I couldn't make out what I was seeing, but I heard clapping. Then the image went dark and still. I heard my own voice say, *"Hook me up, barkeep,"* then Ree-Ree saying, *"Ladies and gentlemen . . ."* and I hit stop. I remembered finding my phone on the bar the next day and realized I must have put it down then and it had kept recording until the charge ran out.

I knew what came next, and I didn't want to hear it—especially not when I was on a giddy high from what I'd discovered.

I had proof that Trista was cheating on Brett. With Seth Minkoff.

I could ruin her. Just like she ruined me.

And why stop there? I could bring down Eddie, too. And there would definitely be drama in Populazzi-land if everyone saw Kristie's conversation about Trista.

This was awesome. I had everything I needed to get the ultimate revenge—but what was the best way to use it? I could post it on Facebook, maybe under a new group named Real Stories of the Populazzi. Or even under Cara Leonard Is a Great Big Whore, since the group was already so big.

The only problem with posting the clips was that they'd have to stand alone, and there was so much more I wanted to share. If I could somehow show the video myself at school, I'd have an audience. I could spill everything: Trista's rules, the fake IDs, Eddie's sexuality, Trista's eating disorder, everything.

It didn't matter how many people heard me. Even if there were just a few, word would spread. Within a day, everyone would know.

What would happen then? The junior class Populazzi would implode. As a group, they would cease to exist. And then what? What happened when the entire top of the Tower ceased to exist? Would another tier move up, or would the mantel of ultimate popularity pass to someone else? Someone who had done something bold and dramatic enough to change the social fabric of the entire school?

Someone like me.

It wasn't impossible. And if it happened, I would be Supreme Populazzi. A very different Supreme Populazzi than I'd imagined before the party, but Supreme Populazzi nonetheless. And for the final nail in Trista's coffin, I could ask Brett Seward to take me to the prom. It would be a dark, twisted version of what Claudia had dreamed for me when she'd first told me about the Ladder.

I liked it.

I surfed to Facebook, to the page for Cara Leonard Is a Great Big Whore. I posted, *"Trista, let's talk face-to-face. Friday at The Heap, 8 a.m. Everyone is invited."* In the spirit of the group, I ended with *"Cara Leonard is a great big whore."*

Now everything would change.

Chapter *thirty-six*

The next day was Tuesday, and the whole school was buzzing about my post and what it might mean. I heard it all: some hoped for a catfight, some thought I'd break down sobbing, some worried I might go Columbine. A few people came right out and asked me what I planned to do, but I wouldn't answer.

Only the Populazzi seemed completely disinterested. I wondered if they'd even show up Friday morning. Not that it mattered: the result would be the same either way.

I spent the week preparing. I'd have loved a lecture hall with an IMAX screen, but The Heap and my laptop would have to do. Edited together, my three favorite clips were barely two minutes long, so I'd have plenty of time to talk before the bell rang, even if I showed the video more than once. After I'd had my say, I'd post the footage online, so everyone could enjoy.

Thursday night I ran through my spiel one last time. It was solid and it was devastating. I felt strong, powerful, and righteous. I couldn't wait until morning. Just before bed, I hopped on to Cara Leonard Is a Great Big Whore to see what people were saying. Most sounded as excited about tomorrow as I was. I bet I'd have a great turnout.

As I was about to log off, a new post appeared. It was from Robert Schwarner. *"Anger, fear, aggression. The dark side are they. Once you start down the dark path, forever will it dominate your destiny.'"*

It was a Yoda quote.

Robert, with whom I hadn't spoken since I'd sent him away from The Heap, was sending me a Yoda quote through a site called Cara Leonard Is a Great Big Whore.

He could have been sending it to the group, of course—there was certainly a lot of anger and aggression there—but I got the feeling he'd meant it for me.

So why post to the group?

I looked to see if he was online so we could chat. He wasn't.

I read the quote again. What was his problem? Was he seriously telling me not to be angry? I *deserved* to be angry! As for fear, I thought I was showing a pretty spectacular *lack* of fear by standing up for myself in front of the entire school. Aggression? The Populazzi had been *plenty* aggressive. Wasn't it about time someone gave it right back to them?

Stupid green Muppet.

I turned off my computer and went to bed.

I kept thinking about the quote.

Worse, I *saw* it: Robert Schwarner, sitting in a swamp on a log, his face green, saying the quote in his squeaky Yoda voice.

The quote was crap. That's all it was. Happy Hopeless fanboy crap.

I tossed and turned all night.

Eventually it was morning. I sighed. It was time.

I put on a very special outfit, grabbed everything I needed, and drove to school, making a quick stop on the way. By the time I got to Chrysella, the hall outside The Heap was crammed with people, but the crowd parted to let me inside.

This could have been because of my date with Trista.

Or it could have been because I was dressed like Princess Leia.

Not *exactly* like her. I hadn't had time this morning to go to an actual costume store. I wore my puffy white robe, with my curls pinned up in makeshift buns on the sides of my head. Instead of a blaster, I held a Ping-Pong paddle.

Trista was waiting in The Heap, along with the rest of the Populazzi. Once I entered, it was like I'd broken the seal keeping non-Populazzi out. Spectators started to creep inside to get a better view.

Trista rose to meet me in the middle of the room. It was a standoff at high noon—or eight a.m. She looked me up and down.

"What are you wearing?"

I pulled a thumb drive out of my bathrobe pocket.

"Trista, on this drive, I have a very interesting video. One I guarantee you don't want people to see. It's from a party. Stuff that happened after the word 'boo.'"

Everyone started to murmur. Trista's smug smile faded a moment, but she forced it back into place. "You don't have *anything*," she spat. "You're lying just to get attention. That's all you want. You'll make up anything for it."

She sounded strong, but her eyes were frightened, and in

them I could see her mind searching for a solution that would help her save face.

"The video is real," I said, "but you're right—I do want attention. At least I did. School sucks when you're invisible. You feel like you don't even exist. I always thought if someone like you noticed me, everything would change. And it did. When I started hanging out with you, the whole school knew who I was. It was amazing. It made me feel like I mattered. I loved it so much, I didn't even care that the person everyone knew wasn't me at all."

More people had pushed into the room, and the crowd was getting antsy.

"Hey," called a guy I'd last seen passed out on my father's floor. "When are you showing us the video?"

"I'm not," I said.

No one seemed to believe me. Some people laughed; others shouted, "Shut up!" "Come on!" "Just do it!" One of the Computer Dorks pushed to the front to offer his laptop, as if that's what was stopping me.

"No, I'm serious. I'm not."

"So why the hell are we all here?" another guy shouted.

"I don't know. *I'm* here to try to be me again. That's why I'm dressed this way. It's for the two people at this school who liked me for me. They saw a girl I can't even find anymore, but I know she's someone who won't hurt another person just because she can."

Silence. Then Ree-Ree called out, *"Looo-serrr!"*

The crowd seemed to agree with her. They groaned and groused and even cursed as they filed away. Several started singing Nate's "Succubus" song. Others made peeing noises.

Trista moved closer to me. She kept her voice low.

"No one believes you really have anything on that drive . . . but you do."

I nodded.

"Why wouldn't you use it? I would."

"I know."

Trista looked at me like I was speaking another language she was struggling to understand. She gave up. "Suit yourself."

She walked to the other side of the room, where Brett was waiting. She folded herself into his arms for a long kiss, then the two walked out, arm-in-arm. The still-thick crowd streaming out parted to let them pass.

"You do know Princess Leia wore a white dress and not a furry white robe, right?"

I turned. Robert Schwarner was behind me.

"I didn't have a white dress. And I only changed my plan this morning, so I didn't have time to get one."

"Hmm."

"Come on, can't you be a little impressed? Do you have any idea how hard it is to get corkscrew curls into buns?"

"They're really supposed to be more braids."

"You know, you're awfully judgmental for a guy who runs around in a *BeastSlayer* cloak all the time."

"'I cannot teach him,'" Robert/Yoda said to no one in particular. "'The boy has no patience.'"

"That one doesn't work. I'm not a boy. And Yoda *does* teach Luke after he says that."

Robert sighed, shaking his head with the resignation of an old Jedi master who'd seen it all.

"Robert, I'm really sorry. I hate myself for the way I treated you . . . enough to impale my skull with the better part of fifty bobby pins and a full can of hairspray to look as much like

Princess Leia as possible—if Princess Leia had a penchant for fuzzy bathrobes."

"You know, there are places where you can get real Princess Leia costumes. I could take you."

"You sure you'd want to? It's not easy to be my friend right now. I'm a bit of a social liability."

"'Stay and help you I will,'" Robert Yoda'd.

The crowd had now cleared enough that we could leave The Heap. We walked the hall together in an easy silence.

"Hey, Robert," I said before I ducked into English class. "They're great movies. Not overrated at all."

"Apology accepted."

I walked to my island of a seat. For a second I thought I'd mess with people and sit someplace new, then watch everyone scatter. If I really didn't care what anyone thought, it would have been funny.

The minute class ended, I beelined for the door, pausing only slightly to set my Ping-Pong paddle in front of Archer. I didn't want to embarrass him by having an actual conversation with him, but it was a gift and I wanted him to have it. The paddle was brand-new, and on its handle I had written a short message in permanent ink: *I hate horror movies.*

I saw him frown as he read it, but I didn't let myself linger. I wanted to get through this day as soon as possible. The less time I spent at Chrysella the better . . . plus I had plans.

It took a while after school to get everything ready, but I finally made it to Yardley. I rang the doorbell, then ducked behind the bushes. If Claudia was home, I knew she'd be the one to answer. Lenore had a phobia about people coming to the house unexpectedly.

Claude came out and saw my two baskets right away. The

first held an assortment of fifteen adorable stuffed deer, all smiling up at her. The second basket held a colander with a big red bow on one of its handles. Inside it, I'd placed a huge pile of snickerdoodles. The top five cookies were each frosted with a single letter and together spelled the word "MERCY."

Claudia looked over the whole spread.

"First of all," she said as if I were right there in front of her, "it is patently unfair to engage the aid of the deer friends, who—judging by their happy little smiles—do not know all the details. Second, these do not look like Harriet Ralston snickerdoodles. Finally, the quotation is 'the quality of mercy is *not* strain'd.' So if you're looking for forgiveness, it would make far more sense to put a bow and cookies on the *absence* of a colander."

"Points duly noted," I said, still crouched in the bushes. "May I have a rebuttal?"

Claudia nodded.

"The deer friends wanted to come," I said, emerging from the bushes and joining her on the porch. "I told them it was a bad idea and might seem manipulative, but they didn't care. As for the snickerdoodles, they're store-bought, though I added the frosting letters myself. Mom and Karl aren't speaking to me, so I didn't think asking for cookies would go over well. As for the last one, I have no rebuttal . . . except I'm not sure where on the absence of a colander the bow would stick."

"Points taken."

We just stood there a second. It was terrible. In nearly twelve years, Claudia and I had never had a major fight. Now I felt like there was this giant balloon of awfulness between us, and I had no idea how to pop it and go back to how things had been.

"I did choose them," I said. "It's the worst thing I've ever done in my life. I swear, I would do anything to take it back."

"You can't."

I didn't want to believe it, but I knew she was right.

Claudia sat on the step. "I wish I could take it back, too."

"You?"

"The Ladder was all my idea. I pushed you into it, even when you didn't want to. I felt like as long as we were working on it together, we'd stay connected and I wouldn't lose you."

"Claudia . . ."

I wanted to tell her she could never lose me, but I'd already proven that wasn't true. I shut my mouth.

"Then when the thing happened with Marsh, I got this idea that both our lives would be magically transformed," she said. "I wanted it so badly. I don't know . . . maybe if I were you, I'd have done the same thing."

"You wouldn't have."

"Maybe not . . . I don't know. But you wouldn't have done any of it without me. I've been your Lady Macbeth. You were fine with Thane of Glamis, but I pushed you to be king. It's only right I'd get a little blood on my hands."

"Settle for pink frosting?" I asked. I reached into the basket of snickerdoodles and handed her one. The balloon of awfulness was still there, but it was a tiny bit smaller. I didn't know if it would ever go away entirely.

As we sat and ate, I told Claudia everything that had happened since the party: the Facebook group, the video clips, and what I'd done that morning.

"Three hundred people think Cara Leonard is a Great Big Whore?" she asked.

"And growing. I'm quite the cultural phenomenon."

Claudia picked up a second cookie and scraped off the icing with her teeth. "So you had the chance to become Supreme Populazzi, and you let it go."

"Yeah. You're not disappointed, are you?"

"No."

"Swear on the Bell?"

"I do. I've actually been thinking about it a lot, and I realized something."

"What's that?"

"Thane of Glamis is a wicked awesome position."

"It is," I said, biting into another cookie. "Wicked awesome."

Chapter *thirty-seven*

I couldn't believe my first year at Chrysella was almost over. The next week was finals, and I again studied like crazy to try to make up for the damage I'd done to my GPA. I only had to go in for the actual tests, so there wasn't a lot of time for me to be harassed. My locker still seemed to be a diaper magnet, but I hoped summer vacation might change that.

When I was at school, I hung out with Robert Schwarner and Gabe Friedman. Gabe hadn't been keen on the idea at first, but he'd relented when I asked him to teach me his broadsword moves. I hadn't asked him just to be nice. I actually thought they were cool and I wanted to learn. Claudia was amused that I seemed to have found the Happy in the Happy Hopeless.

"Happy" was kind of a stretch for me. Claudia and I were talking constantly the way we used to, but it was different. Karl still wasn't acknowledging me, and I didn't know how long it would last. Mom was speaking to me again, but something fundamental had changed.

Life was supposed to change, I knew that. But this felt off. Like I'd gotten lost somewhere and was still navigating through weird back roads to try to get to the main drag. It had been a long time since I'd made decisions based on instinct, without any angle or strategy, but I was trying to do that now. I tried to really pay attention and be honest with myself. It seemed like it should be simple . . . but it was incredibly hard.

The week of the junior prom, I almost expected Robert or Gabe to ask me. Not as a romantic thing. I imagined they'd want to go as a three-person unit: the Fellowship of the Prom. I probably would have said yes. It would have been fun with them . . . maybe. Even though I'd feel like I was swallowing glass every time I saw Archer and Sue together.

Turned out Robert and Gabe had long-standing plans for prom night: all six Star Wars movies, in order, back to back. I was invited to join, but they weren't starting the movies until six p.m. That meant they wouldn't get to the three I liked until after midnight, and I had an eleven o'clock curfew. A self-imposed curfew, actually. It felt important to show Mom and Karl I could be disciplined and responsible on my own.

I thought about Archer a lot that week. I only saw him briefly, at the English exam, but that was on purpose. I came in at the last second and left with time to spare, so there was no chance to talk. Not that I imagined he wanted to talk, but I didn't want to take the chance.

Of everything I lost, Archer hurt the most. At least Claudia, Karl, and my mom were still in my life. But with Archer . . . now that I was being honest with myself, I wasn't sure I could ever be friends with him. It just hurt too much.

Still, I couldn't help checking up on him. I'd go to his Facebook page and read his posts. They were all about prom. He was taking Sue, of course, and kept trolling for advice. Should the corsage match or complement the girl's dress? Should a good boyfriend open the limo door or let the driver do it? Was it okay to keep his date to himself all night, or was it good manners to let other guys dance with her? He was clearly nervous. It was sweet. My heart broke that he wasn't asking all those questions about me, but I was happy for him.

The Saturday morning of prom, I still hadn't decided what I was going to do. I felt like I had to do *something*. For a while I'd had sleepover plans with Claudia, but she'd canceled. Pennsbrook's junior prom was the same night, and she'd been shocked when a very cute and very shy Cubby Crew guy asked her to be his date. His name was Henry—like King Henry, which only seemed right. Claudia had never noticed Henry before, but now he was all she thought about. She was smitten in a huge way.

"Is it horrible that I'm bailing on our sleepover to go out with Henry?" she asked me.

"You're not just going out with him; you're going to *prom* with him. It would be horrible if you *didn't* bail."

I spent Saturday morning on my bike. I hadn't gone for a ride in my new neighborhood since we'd moved from Yardley, and it felt great to stretch and move my body. I rode past my whole year: past Chrysella, past Archer's house, Wegmans, Nate's house, Eddie's and Robert's houses . . . I even rode past the turnoff to Trista Way.

I let the year sift through my head as I pedaled. I'd made so many mistakes. I'd hurt so many people, including myself. And yet . . . there were good things that had come out of the Ladder, too. I would never have gotten close to Archer without it. Much as losing him hurt, I wouldn't trade the time we'd had for anything. I loved most of the songs I'd studied to attract Nate and still listened to them all the time. I'd started a new relationship with my dad because of the Ladder, and even though it was demolished right now, he was my dad: one day we'd pick it back up. Probably he'd be the one to make me cry about what I'd done, then maybe we'd be okay. I'd even learned things from Trista that I still used. When it came to clothes and makeup, and caring about myself enough to look my best, she'd been like a big sister to me.

If I really could go back and undo all that, would I?

Maybe I would—probably I would. The bad stuff was still pretty awful. But if I did, I'd lose a lot of things that were now part of who I was.

The year had happened. I couldn't erase it, so I had to embrace it. Celebrate it, even.

And all of a sudden I knew exactly how I wanted to do that. I pedaled hard to get home as quickly as possible. I showered, put on makeup, grabbed my purse, gave a little pat to the mini Liberty Bell on my night table, and started out the door . . . but something didn't feel right. I felt like I should share the moment with the world, or at least whatever part of the world happened to be paying attention.

I went to my Facebook page. Mine, not Cara Leonard Is a Great Big Whore, which had grown a life of its own and expanded to comment on other "whores" at schools around the country and the world. Quite a legacy I was leaving.

I filled out my status: *"Seeking the symbol of my independence. Happy prom night, everyone."*

I hit Update and watched the message appear on my wall. Much better. Now I could leave.

By the time I drove downtown and parked my car, it was

almost four p.m. I got lucky: there was one available ticket for the next tour of Independence Hall. I grabbed it. It hadn't changed in the four years since I'd been there last. That shouldn't have been surprising: it had barely changed in the two hundred fifty years before that. I guess since I felt so different from the person I'd been back then, part of me assumed everything else in the universe would have changed, too.

After the tour, I went to the Liberty Bell Center and stared at the enormous version of the bell I looked at every day. It was stunning in person: strong, beautiful, and powerful . . . but scarred. Yet without its crack, it would only be a bell. My own scars might not be as visible, but they were just as integral to the person I'd become. The only big difference between us was that even cracked, I still felt like I could ring.

That, and it was a centuries-old piece of molded metal, while I was a human being. But I was waxing philosophical. I let it go.

I stayed with the Liberty Bell until closing time, then walked to my next stop: the Bourse for a nutritious dinner of a soft pretzel and soft-serve chocolate ice cream, excellent for dipping. I also grabbed a pack of Peanut Butter Kandy Kakes for later, then went searching for the perfect table.

That's when I saw him. His back was to me. Black hair cut bluntly at the nape of his neck, the polo shirt, the Gatsby hat.

I briefly wondered if Archer had a twin who'd been given up for adoption, only to be discovered by me right here and now.

No, it was Archer—which seemed even more impossible. I moved closer to his table and saw him dip a french fry into a chocolate milk shake, then plop it into his mouth.

Now *that* was impossible.

I set my tray next to him at the table. He didn't look at me, just sat there dipping fries.

"You're committing a crime against food," I said, taking a seat. "You're lucky I don't report you to the Hague."

"You wouldn't get out the first word. You're Public Enemy Number One in the Food Crimes division. They'd give you thirty lashes with a licorice whip before you even opened your mouth." Archer nodded to his shake and fries. "This is really very good. You should try it sometime." Then he frowned at my tray. "You're not going to defile that soft pretzel, are you?"

I broke off a piece of pretzel and dipped it. Delicious.

"No," Archer said. "That's not just a crime against food; that's a specific crime against Philadelphia. You can be deported to Jersey for that."

I was dreaming. I had to be dreaming. I must have fallen asleep after the bike ride and only imagined my whole trip to Philly, because there was no way Archer and I would be here together, talking and laughing like the past six months had never happened. I didn't know if that could *ever* happen, but it certainly wouldn't be happening tonight.

"How are you even here?" I asked him.

"Let's see . . . my mom and dad met in New York, many years ago—"

"Archer . . . it's prom night. You're going to the prom. It starts in an hour."

"It does start in an hour, but I can't go without a date. I mean, I *could* go, but it's not generally done."

"You have a date. You're going with Sue. You got her a corsage that complements her dress, you're letting the limo driver open the door for you, and you're letting her dance up to half the dances with guys you know are just friends."

"You've been reading my Facebook page."

I blushed. "Maybe."

Archer dipped another french fry. "Sue broke up with me. She saw me carrying around this Ping-Pong paddle and got upset because she thought it meant I'd rather be with somebody else."

My heart started thumping wildly, but I somehow managed to sound calm. "A Ping-Pong paddle? That *is* a strange thing to carry around."

"Not when you're as good a Ping-Pong player as I am."

"Of course."

"So this Ping-Pong paddle," Archer continued, "it was pretty unique. It had a message written on it. It said, 'I hate horror movies.'"

"Curiouser and curiouser."

"Exactly. But the person who gave it to me had asked me to watch a horror movie with her."

"Weird. Was the movie any good?"

"I wouldn't know," Archer said, meeting my eyes for just a moment. "I wasn't really able to concentrate on the movie."

"Archer . . ."

"I want to talk about it, Cara. What happened?"

Hadn't he been there? Was he really going to make me relive it? I took a deep breath and concentrated on pulling my pretzel into bite-size bits.

"I liked you," I said. "A lot. And I thought maybe you liked me, too . . . but then I tried to kiss you and you ran away screaming . . . so I knew you actually didn't."

"Oh," Archer said to his fries. "Because I actually *did* like you . . . a lot . . . but I don't exactly have a lot of . . . experience. I panicked a little and felt like the biggest loser in the universe . . . and everything got very horrible very fast."

"You . . . *did* like me?"

"I *do* like you, Cara," he said. "I wanted to tell you, but you said never talk about it again, and I figured you were so completely turned off and disgusted by my freak-out that you weren't interested anymore. I thought that's what you liked about Nate and Eddie. They knew what they were doing."

"No! Archer, Nate and Eddie were . . . they were different. I never liked them the way I liked you. I only went out with them because . . . It's stupid and ridiculous, but I swear I never would have gone out with either of them if I thought you were even remotely interested in me."

"So . . . if things had been different that night . . ."

"Everything would have changed."

Archer looked up and met my eyes when I said this, and my insides started shaking. I wanted so badly to believe what it seemed like we were both saying. I couldn't take it if I was wrong, but if there was even a chance . . .

"Did you come here to find me?" I asked.

"I saw your Facebook update. I remembered."

I pulled my chair closer to his. Our knees touched, and we both leaned forward ever so slightly. Only inches separated us.

"Archer . . . I want to kiss you now, but I need to know you're not going to run away."

"I promise."

I took a deep breath and saw that he did, too. Then we both leaned forward—and bumped foreheads.

"Ow," he said.

"We are so not good at this," I said. "I hope it's not some kind of a—"

He took my face in his hands and pressed his lips to mine.

I was wrong: we were soooo good at this. Kissing Archer was nothing like kissing Nate or Eddie. Kissing Archer was exactly what I'd always dreamed it would be. It was as if everything inside me had been clenched since that one night, and now I was bursting, so filled with happiness that I couldn't even contain it all. Tears welled in my eyes, and when we eventually pulled away, I let out a sound that could have been a sob or a laugh.

"Let's go to the prom," Archer said.

Now I laughed. "Next year? Sure. It's a date."

"No, tonight. I want you to come to the prom with me. I have tickets. We can leave now and be right on time."

"We're not dressed for the prom."

"I think you look beautiful. Do I look okay?"

I smiled. "You're perfect."

"Great. Let's go."

"Archer . . . I don't know if you've noticed, but it's not easy to be around me these days. People don't like me."

"*I* like you. I don't care about anyone else. Do you?"

That was easy. "No. I don't. Let's do it."

Archer was right—even with a quick stop to drop my car at his house, we got to the prom just in time. Everyone stared when we walked in. In a sea of gowns and tuxes, we were dressed for a day at the park. It only made it more fun. We giggled like little kids as we got our official photos taken, making goofy faces and posing as if we were playing football instead of standing for a formal portrait. When the Cara Leonard Is a Great Big Whore contingent tried to shun us from their tables, we grabbed napkins and made a picnic area on a corner of the floor. We danced all night long, and when Trista and Brett were voted prom queen and king, we jumped up and down, hooting and cheering louder than anyone.

By the time the last song played, Archer and I were both covered in a light sheen of sweat, exhausted and revved up at the same time, and I for one was happy. Truly happy. The only thing that could stop me from grinning like crazy was to leap up on tiptoe and melt into his kiss.

"Cara?"

"Yes?"

"I'm going to slaughter you at Ping-Pong when we get back to my house."

"No way. Kissing does not preclude degradation, my friend. You are going *down,* and you are going down *hard!*"

A couple dancing next to us glared, and I realized I'd once again managed to make something innocent sound dirty.

"Just . . . stop me from talking, okay?"

"My pleasure," said Archer. He leaned in to kiss me, and as we swayed together to the last notes of the song, I felt myself turn back onto that main drag. It wasn't the same spot where I'd first veered off, but I felt like from here, I'd finally be able to find my way.

Acknowledgments

First and foremost, the hugest thank-you imaginable goes to Samantha McFerrin, editor extraordinaire. Sam, you are a true genius for looking at what I had when we began this process and seeing what it could one day become. Your wisdom and insight have been invaluable to me, and this book would not be what it is without you.

An equally huge thank-you goes out to Fonda Snyder of Alchemy Ink, without whom this book never would have happened. Fonda, you have always believed so strongly in me and my work, and you've always steered me in the right direction. You are a true friend, mentor, and champion, and I'm so thrilled to be working with you.

Thanks to everyone at Houghton Mifflin Harcourt who helped bring this book to life, including managing editor Amy Carlisle, associate art director Carol Chu, publicity manager Jennifer Groves, senior marketing manager Jennifer LaBracio, and legal counsel David Eber.

To Annette Van Duren, my wonderful agent, thank you for always being in my corner. You are the best.

Big thanks to Crystal Patriarche, PR wonder, and to Betsy Cohen, whose Web design and teaching skills are beyond compare.

Thanks to all of my earliest readers, including (but not limited to—I can all but guarantee I'll mess up and forget someone) Jen Klein, Jule Selbo, Myra Zerr, Jennifer Nellis, Elizabeth Towns, and Marisa Cody. Your input and support helped me tremendously.

Thank you, Mom-Mom Eva and Mom-Mom Sylvia, for your unconditional love; and thanks to Pop-Pop Irv and Pop-Pop Nate, who are gone but always remembered.

Thanks to Deborah Kaminsky for keeping me (reasonably) sane, and to Helen Vitaris for loving my daughter almost as much as Randy and I do.

To the past and present members of the Debutante Ball, and the amazing bloggers and writers I've met through the site: I can't thank you enough for your wisdom and support. There were mountains of things that as a first-time novelist I didn't know. Thank you for helping me navigate.

To Randy and Maddie: Maddie, I am blessed to be your mommy. I'm so proud of you, and I love you with all my heart. Randy, I would not be who I am, or do what I do, without you (I mean that as a good thing). You love me through sleeplessness, stressiness, and mind-like-a-sieve-iness. I love you beyond any words . . . and you know how much I love words. Love to Riley too. And give that dog a treat—he's starving!

Finally, thank you to everyone reading this book. It's a privilege to share it with you, and I so appreciate your willingness to pick it up and dive in.